Praise for the Suspense Novels of Daryl Wood Gerber

"This was a fast-paced action-packed drama that immediately grabbed my attention, quickly becoming a page-turner as I could not put this book down."
—*Dru's Book Musings*

"The frantic plot will keep readers on edge."
—*Kirkus Reviews*

"The novel's plot is thick and the prose is more than rich enough to sustain it. Its shifting perspectives will give readers an even greater sense of excitement as the many pieces of the puzzle fall into place. Readers will be shocked by this exciting, fast-paced thriller's twists and turns."
—*Kirkus Reviews*

"Daryl Wood Gerber has proven again to be a gifted storyteller and one to watch in this genre. An absolute must-read!"
—*Escape with Dollycas*

"This is an edge-of-your-seat, can't-put-it-down thriller. If you like Dan Brown's thrillers you will want to read this!"
—Goodreads

"*Day of Secrets* is an action-packed, suspense-filled, riveting book. I was glued to this story, could not put it down, and didn't want it to end."
—Goodreads

Books by Daryl Wood Gerber

The Cookbook Nook Mysteries

Final Sentence
Inherit the Word
Stirring the Plot
Fudging the Books
Grilling the Subject
Pressing the Issue
Wreath Between the Lines
Sifting Through Clues

The French Bistro Mysteries

A Deadly Éclair
A Soufflé of Suspicion

Writing as Avery Aames

The Long Quiche Goodbye
Lost and Fondue
Clobbered by Camembert
To Brie or Not to Brie
Days of Wine and Roquefort
As Gouda as Dead
For Cheddar or Worse

Suspense

Girl on the Run
Day of Secrets
Desolate Shores
Fan Mail

FAN MAIL

DARYL WOOD GERBER

Fan Mail
Daryl Wood Gerber
Copyright © 2019 by Daryl Wood Gerber
Cover design and illustration by Dar Albert, Wicked Smart Designs

Beyond the Page Books
are published by
Beyond the Page Publishing
www.beyondthepagepub.com

ISBN: 978-1-950461-29-5

All rights reserved under International and Pan-American Copyright Conventions. By payment of required fees, you have been granted the non-exclusive, non-transferable right to access and read the text of this book. No part of this text may be reproduced, transmitted, downloaded, decompiled, reverse engineered, or stored in or introduced into any information storage and retrieval system, in any form or by any means, whether electronic or mechanical, now known or hereinafter invented without the express written permission of both the copyright holder and the publisher.

This is a work of fiction. Names, characters, places, and incidents either are the product of the author's imagination or are used fictitiously, and any resemblance to actual persons, living or dead, business establishments, events or locales is entirely coincidental. The publisher does not have any control over and does not assume any responsibility for author or third-party websites or their content.

The scanning, uploading, and distribution of this book via the Internet or via any other means without the permission of the publisher is illegal and punishable by law. Your support of the author's rights is appreciated.

FAN MAIL

Chapter 1

Midafternoon traffic was creeping along. Everyone on the road was edgy, thanks to the blistering heat. As I turned up the air-conditioning, I noticed two voice messages on my cell phone. Both were from my gynecologist, recorded earlier this morning before the office opened. Dr. Fisher always went to work by sunup, but she said she would give me my test results *after* the weekend. Why call me on Friday? Why hadn't either rung through? My insides snagged. It had to be bad news. On the other hand, it was only a small lump. Probably nothing.

Too impatient to wait, I pulled to a stop on the side of the road and played the first message. No one spoke; the message stopped abruptly. How I hated spotty reception in Lake Tahoe. I selected the second message. The doctor said, "Aspen," and the call cut off again. She'd sounded out of breath. In a hurry.

I phoned her back, but after twenty rings and no answer, I ended the call. "Dang it!" I slapped the steering wheel on my Jeep and resumed driving, ticked off at my doctor, my body, and the world.

At the junction near Tahoe City, dozens of cars were parked along the side of the road. Tourists in swimsuits and sandals, plenty of them with sunburns, stood bent over the rail at Fanny Bridge, named for the road crew foreman's maiden aunt Fanny McGillicuddy Wilkerson, not for the countless people exposing their rear ends to passersby as they viewed the trout below.

As I made a right turn toward town, out of nowhere a sedan whizzed past me and then abruptly screeched to a halt. I honked the horn. The driver flipped me off and opened the passenger door for a pedestrian, the jerk.

While I waited, I drummed the center console concerned about Dr. Fisher's call. Why had she sounded so breathy? Why had she hung up after saying my name?

Chill, Aspen. She could have done so because she realized she had her days wrong. She was busy. Heck, there were times I couldn't figure out what day of the week it was until I consulted a calendar.

Forcing worrisome thoughts from my mind, I drove through town and made a left on Polaris Road toward North Tahoe School.

Minutes later, I waited in the carpool lane like all the other mothers, although I wasn't a mother. A half year ago, my niece Candace moved in with me. When she first showed up, she was timid and confused and battling bulimia. Now, she was fourteen and fairly confident and could cook circles around me.

Candace loped to the curb and posed next to the passenger door, hand on one hip and fifteen-pound book bag balanced on the other. She swiped perspiration off her forehead and threw a nasty look over her shoulder.

I rolled down the window. "What's going on?"

"I'm hot and cranky. Everyone is."

"Well, lose the 'tude before you climb into the car."

"Can I drive?"

"Not a chance."

"Aw." She pouted then cracked a smile, making my breath catch in my chest. Sometimes she looked so much like me—dark hair, green eyes, the Adams's turned-up nose—even I had trouble remembering she wasn't mine. Except for a few minor details like DNA, she could have been. That and the fact that I'd never had children. My ex-husband hadn't wanted them. My boyfriend, Nick Shaper, did, but I refused to have a child without being married, and we weren't there yet. I was thirty. Plenty of time.

"In the next couple of weeks, I'll let you behind the wheel," I promised. Occasionally on a Saturday, I took Candace to an empty parking lot and allowed her to drive. I wanted her to be ready and fearless when she got her permit. "But not today. Not with everyone behaving like a maniac."

"It's the heat. It's almost a hundred degrees." Candace slipped into the car and fastened her seat belt.

"How was your day?"

"So-so."

"Was today's final hard?"

"Not too bad." Candace was ready to be finished with homework and dive into summer. She had plenty of things planned. Waterskiing and hiking with her best friend, Waverly, and to my dismay, movies and beach trips with the new boy in her life, Rory. His name made me think of Irish brawls and free-for-alls. Danger signs flashed in my mind. I nudged them aside. Parenting was proving to be one of the greatest challenges of my life.

"Which final did you have?" I asked.

"English. I think I aced the essays."

"Great."

Since obtaining official custody of Candace, I'd moved her education to the top of my priority list. For months, I'd tutored her so she would be ready to enter high school. When living with her mother—my sister, Rosie—she'd missed the first two months of eighth grade because she'd stayed home to take care of Rosie, who had suffered from a severe infection. Luckily, Rosie had shared her love of books with Candace, so the girl was a good reader, but her math and language skills needed help.

"What's Monday's test?" I asked as I made a right on North Lake Boulevard.

"Napoleon to the present."

I moaned.

She giggled. "Luckily, I like history."

"Glad to hear it." History had never been my strong suit. My cell phone rang. I pressed the speaker button on the steering wheel.

"Aspen, it's me." Nick usually sounded upbeat and energetic. Not this time. He sounded tired. A detective for the Placer County Sheriff's Office, his work ran the gamut from breaking up bar fights to high-end crime. We'd been dating ever since he—*we*—solved the murder of my friend Vikki. "I can't make dinner."

"Okay." I hadn't told him about the lump. I'd planned to tonight. The conversation would have to wait. I was okay with that because, before we spoke, I wanted to get confirmation from Dr. Fisher that cancer had not infiltrated my body. "What's up?"

"There's been a murder."

"Oh, no. Who?"

"Dr. Kristin Fisher."

"Oh, no." A flurry of emotions stuck in my throat as the doctor's face flashed before me. Not forty-eight hours before, I'd sat white-knuckled on her examination table as she'd explained in measured, reassuring tones that I was going to be fine. In the two years since I'd moved to Lake Tahoe, we'd had many conversations . . . about teenagers and family skeletons and women's rights. "She was my gynecologist," I said.

"Mine, too," Candace's eyes filled with tears. I'd set up all sorts of doctor appointments for my niece after she'd moved in. Dr. Fisher had been one of them.

"You and three hundred others," Nick said. "She must have had the largest practice this side of Sacramento."

"When did she die?" I asked. "How?"

"No, Aspen. You don't need to—"

"Nick, I can handle anything since Vikki's murder." I'd been the one to discover my friend bludgeoned to death, and though I was only a process server working for my aunt's detective agency, I'd delved into Vikki's murder with a vengeance.

Nick cleared his throat. "Dr. Fisher was killed early this morning. Her office assistant found her."

"Nick, she called me this morning. Early. The first call ended abruptly."

"The first?"

"She called back. I thought she was going to give me the results of a test. I—" Guilt roiled inside me. *Had the killer attacked her as she was reaching out to me? If only I'd answered.* "Tell me what happened."

"I don't want you to investigate," Nick said. "I don't want you to relive . . . you know."

I liked that he worried about me. Other than my father, no man ever had. "I understand, but at least tell me how she died."

"Are you on speakerphone?"

"Yes."

Nick sighed, his reluctance obvious.

I grabbed my cell phone from the cup holder and switched to telephone mode. I knew it was illegal to drive with it in my hand, but for Candace's sake, I had to do it. "It's just me now," I assured him. "Go on."

"There was quite a struggle. She was stabbed in the abdomen. It was gruesome. A scalpel was used."

My stomach lurched. I forced the bile down.

"We found the weapon. Wiped clean. No fingerprints on it."

"Any suspects?"

Candace cut me a sharp look.

"Her nurse is in New York on vacation. Her office assistant was having breakfast with her boyfriend."

"Who else is on your list?"

"Besides the multitude of patients," Nick continued, "we'll be questioning her ex-husband. He's a pediatric surgeon in Reno. We'll be looking at the money angle, of course, because of the size of the practice."

"Considering the weapon, it sounds like a crime of passion. Spur of the moment."

"What was the weapon?" Candace asked.

I silenced her with a look. "Did you review patient files, Nick?"

"A few."

"Mine?"

"Why? Do you have secrets? Perhaps another lover?"

I welcomed his teasing during such a grim conversation. "As if. You're all the man I can handle." After the debacle of my marriage, I hadn't believed I could love anyone again. But Nick was different. Special. A man filled with integrity and courage. He had been by my side as I took on the responsibility of raising Candace. He'd helped me deal with her illness. How many men would have done that?

"Most of the files were strewn on the floor," he said. "A real mess. Detective King is going through all of them." Kendra King was Nick's number two in command. "As one of the doctor's patients," he went on, "you'll be contacted at some point. I've got to go. Sorry to be the bearer of bad news."

"We're going to the Tavern for dinner," I said. "If you can swing by on your way home, please do. You've got to eat."

"Man, I hate this part of my job."

"I know." I blew him a kiss and received one from him in return.

Candace swiveled in her seat. "Dr. Fisher was so nice. Who would kill her?"

"I don't know."

I rolled down my window to let the scent of pine inside, but the aroma didn't calm me as it normally would. Sorrow gripped my heart and my mind was a jumble of thoughts. Who had killed Kristin Fisher and why?

Chapter 2

"Did Nick tell you who the suspects are?" Candace asked as I maneuvered the Jeep around curves toward the Homewood Tavern, my go-to restaurant for more than a year. Over the past hour, she'd asked me numerous questions. I hadn't provided any responses. She deserved my attention.

"The doctor's ex-husband is one."

"No way. I met him. At the office."

"I didn't." And I was always with her for appointments.

"You'd gone to get a coffee. He was nice." Though still timid in some ways, Candace had strong opinions about murder and didn't hesitate to voice them. Crime investigation shows on television had become her passion. "He was gentle."

"Gentle people commit crimes."

"How did it happen?"

Up until now, she hadn't asked that question. I was hoping she would skip it. I shuddered as the few details Nick had revealed cycled through my mind. I chose the one that I could share. "There was a struggle. The office was a mess. Files were strewn everywhere."

"Maybe it was a robbery." Candace tugged the hem of her white cable-knit sweater. When we'd met in the foyer to leave for dinner, we'd laughed. We had dressed the same—sweater over jeans.

"I'm starved," I said, eager to change the subject. "Are you hungry?"

"Sort of."

I pulled into a spot in the Tavern parking lot. As I set the handbrake, I gazed past the rustic building and caught a glimpse of the lake and surrounding mountains, which were a majestic purple in the waning light. The image helped me draw a deep calming breath. Lake Tahoe was magnificent. As long as the English Channel and half again as wide as San Francisco Bay, it shimmered with blues and greens that artists loved to recreate.

We took the front steps two at a time and pushed our way through the restaurant's saloon-style doors. Inside, laughter and the strains of the Beatles' "Hard Day's Night" greeted us. A few regulars standing by the colorful jukebox recognized me and waved. I waved back. The bar area was filled with sunburned patrons. People often forgot about how intense the sun's rays could be in Tahoe's altitude. The city was a mile above sea level.

"Follow me," I said to my niece.

As was typical in summer, even after a hotter than hot day, the night was chilly. A fire crackled in the stone fireplace. The piquant aroma of burning wood was delicious. I steered her into the bar toward one of the many oak tables for two, each set with a hurricane candle.

Gwen Barrows, the owner of the restaurant and a good friend, was nowhere in sight. The newest addition to the staff, Peggy, a bony-shouldered bartender, was flipping channels on the television hanging above the bar. She stopped on ESPN, which was broadcasting the latest skateboard competition.

"Hey, Peggy," a red-faced man at the bar yelled. "When did you install the squawk box?"

"Last week. Nowadays, people want to keep in touch with news and sports."

"Not me."

"This place doesn't cater only to you," she quipped.

I tossed my leather tote on the chair and said to Candace, "Pepsi or Seven-Up?"

"Pepsi with a cherry?" Despite her newfound confidence, she hadn't quite learned how to give an order without a question mark.

"Peggy—"

"On it," she replied.

"Pour me a glass of the house chardonnay."

Gwen diligently watched her expenses and income, but she never cut corners on liquor. There were more than ten quality beers on tap at all times, as well.

In less than a minute, Peggy filled the order.

"Aspen, can I pick some songs on the jukebox?" Candace asked.

"Sure." I handed her a couple of quarters.

She grabbed her drink from the counter, sauntered toward the machine, and dropped in a coin. She depressed a button and seconds later her narrow hips began swaying in rhythm to the Eagles' "Take It Easy." A girl after my own heart. I adored classics by the Eagles and Elvis and Sinatra, but I also enjoyed the latest from Beyoncé and Lady Gaga.

"Hey, darlin'." Gwen sashayed through the kitchen doors, an apron around her waist, white V-neck T-shirt revealing her curves, her red hair carelessly curly. "How's my daredevil PI? Any Friday specials? Discounts on subpoenas or for tailing cheating husbands?" Not that she would need my services. Gwen wasn't married. She had dumped her last philandering husband years ago.

"I actually delivered a restraining order this morning," I said. "On a runner."

"What's a runner?"

"A guy who has been on the move, changing address after address so he won't get caught."

"Aha. Inside lingo. I like that. Makes me feel like one of the team." Gwen wanted me to quit my job and return to being a therapist, but I wouldn't. Couldn't. Dealing with emotionally troubled teens at the Bay Area Rehabilitation Clinic, also known as BARC, was not how I wanted to spend the rest of my years. The suicide of my last patient had nearly sent me over the edge. My current employment was stimulating and basically safe, seeing as most of my duties involved serving papers or following errant spouses from a distance.

Gwen wiped perspiration off her upper lip. "Peggy, pour me a water please."

Peggy moved away to handle the order.

Gwen motioned in her direction. "That Peggy is as edgy as a hen in a rooster's bedroom." My friend's southernisms tickled me. She'd moved to Tahoe from North Carolina years ago, but the accent and jargon had remained. "I don't think that girl will last a month, you ask me."

"She seems good with the customers," I said. "In nothing flat, she put that sunburned guy at the end of the bar in his place."

"Good. That dude drives me to drink."

Gwen lifted the hatch and moved behind the bar. As the plank slammed into place, the television volume grew in pitch.

"Turn it down, bozo." Gwen glared at a stocky man who had taken it upon himself to tweak the sound.

He pointed to his ears. "I can't hear."

"Get a hearing aid."

I took a sip of my wine.

Gwen jabbed her thumb in the direction of the TV. "Well, look who's gone prime time."

I peered at the television screen. *KINC Evening News* was on. Gloria Morning, the reporter who had covered Vikki's murder for the *Tahoe Daily Tribune*, had switched careers. She was now a co-anchor on the year-old news station.

"Do you think KINC will make a go of it?" Gwen said.

"Who knows?"

Reno was the strongest market in the surrounding area, boasting affiliates for NBC, ABC, and CBS. KINC, which was located in the town of Incline Village at the north end of the lake, had been making a play to become the main news source in the Lake Tahoe area. Its popularity had risen twenty percent since hiring Gloria. With a pixie face, Cupid's bow mouth, and big doe eyes, Gloria was charming but not in the least intimidating. A winning combination.

"She reminds me of a young Katie Couric," Gwen said.

"Funny you'd say that. In time, she hopes to move to a major network."

After Vikki's murder was solved, Gloria had begged me for an exclusive interview. I'd agreed. To my surprise, she had shown great sensitivity with her questions. Since then, we had become friends and met for coffee the first Friday of every month. Due to her busy schedule, I had yet to introduce Gloria to the Tavern, and more importantly, to Gwen.

"Did you hear about this, Aspen?" Gwen pointed at the television. A picture of Dr. Fisher had come into view.

"Nick informed me. I'm so upset. She was my doctor."

"It's harrowing. And here I thought Tahoe was once again serenity personified."

On the television, Gloria said, "Many of you know I had the opportunity to interview this popular doctor. The interview aired last night. Here's a snippet of what she shared with me."

Dr. Fisher's cream-colored office appeared on the screen with Gloria perched on the patient's table in a dressing gown. Dr. Fisher, who had turned fifty in February, though she barely looked forty, held a file in her hand. Her white jacket looked crisp and fresh. Her understated diamond necklace sparkled. "The most important thing when conferring with your gynecologist is to ask as many questions as you can."

Seeing her alive made every ounce of me ache. I swallowed hard.

"Remember, you are responsible for your body." She smiled warmly into the camera. "I have an exhaustive checklist that I go over every time I meet with a patient."

She wasn't kidding. I had answered the questions more than once.

Like a blip on a radar screen, the interview vanished and Gloria, looking appropriately somber, reappeared on the KINC newsroom set. "Sources from the Placer County Sheriff's Office reveal that the doctor's ex-husband, Dr. Edward Bogart, a pediatric surgeon in Reno, is a person of interest."

I said, "Who leaked that?"

"Dr. Fisher's office assistant, I'll bet." Candace drew next to me and sipped her soda.

Shoot. She had been listening to the news report. The music on the jukebox hadn't distracted her. How I wanted to protect her from the real world. She'd experienced enough suffering in her young lifetime.

"Sweetie, this isn't something you should be concerned about."

Candace gave me a look that only teenagers could manufacture, head cocked, mouth twisted with mock contempt. "Dr. Fisher was really cool."

"Yes, she was."

"You know, murder is always about money or revenge."

"Okay, that's it," I said. "No more crime shows for you. I don't care how attractive the leading actor is."

"C'mon."

I sliced the air with my hand, ending the argument.

"What does Nick think?" Gwen asked.

I kept mum.

"Don't try to pry anything out of her. She won't say a word," Candace said to Gwen. "Hey, what if one of the patients got a bad prognosis and lashed out?"

"Or didn't like the doctor's bedside manner?" Gwen said, leaning forward on her elbows, caught up in Candace's ardor for villainy.

"Or the killer was Gloria Morning?" Candace chimed.

"Gloria wasn't a real patient," I said.

"You don't know that," Gwen countered. "And are you excluding her because she's a friend, because—ahem—you've thought friends were guilty before."

I moaned. Gwen was referring to when I'd suspected her of killing Vikki. Long story, another lifetime. Luckily, she had forgiven me my idiocy. I downed a swallow of wine. "No way would Gloria, or anybody I know for that matter, do something as horrible as—" I stopped short. Tears surfaced. I willed them to stay put.

"As horrible as what?" Candace reminded me of an alert kit fox with its ears perked up.

"Do me a favor." I aimed a finger. "Go see if there are any French fries available in the kitchen."

Candace hated being dismissed, but she went anyway.

"What else is bothering you?" Gwen laid her hand over mine. "You're as tight as—"

"A snare drum?" I asked.

"I was going to say a top."

I shrugged. My ex was a conductor. Out of habit, I'd learned to compare things to musical instruments. "I was waiting for some news from Dr. Fisher."

"About?"

"I have a lump."

Gwen signaled Peggy to tend the bar and left her post. She perched on the stool next to mine. "You never noticed it before?"

"Nope."

"Did your mother have any lumps, benign or otherwise?"

"No." My mother had been fifty-five and in good health when she and my father were killed. I'd never know the odds of whether she would have contracted breast cancer.

"And Rosie?"

"Not to my knowledge," I said.

My older sister was a mess. Using heroine and more had ravaged her body. Detecting breast cancer, I imagined, was low on her list. Seeing as I had no desire to call and ask, the secrets of her medical history would go with her to her grave.

"Hey, Gwen, refills," yelled a guy at the end of the bar.

Gwen scanned the area. "Where did Peggy go?" She huffed. "Darlin', I'll be right back." She went about her business with the elegance of a dancer, arms moving rhythmically as she emptied old drinks and poured new ones.

Left alone, I mulled over my last conversation with Dr. Fisher. She'd told me that knowing one's genetic history was not as reliable as it used to be. Now, one in eight women would develop breast cancer. Even women without a family history of the disease could get it. I could be a statistic.

When Gwen returned, she covered my hand with hers, the warmth reassuring. "The results were due when?"

"Monday, but with the murder . . ." I hung my head in shame because I was thinking of my own problem and not Dr. Fisher's death.

Gwen squeezed my hand. "Ask Nick to let you peek in your file. He can do that. After all, somebody will take over the doctor's practice. They'll be reviewing everything. For all you know, they may already have an interim physician seeing to emergencies."

With three hundred patients' files needing to be sorted out, mine, in the big scheme of things, was insignificant. Other patients had to come first. I sat straighter. *Other patients . . .*

"Gwen," I said, "Candace may be right."

"About what?"

I pulled my cell phone from my tote and dialed Nick. When he answered, I said, "I think your killer may be a patient or someone related to a patient. Not Dr. Fisher's ex-husband."

"Why?" he asked.

"Call it professional courtesy, but another doctor knows how long it would take to rearrange all of those files on the floor. A patient with something to hide is who I'd suspect."

"Aspen . . ." I pictured Nick scratching the stubble on his chin, trying to maintain his composure.

"I think it's one of the patients, too," Candace said over my shoulder. She set a plate of fries on the bar along with a bottle of catsup. "Because there was no reason to throw around the files unless he was covering up something. He was angry."

I said, "He could be a she."

"Freshen your soda?" Gwen said to Candace.

"Yes, please." Candace leaned in to me. "Tell Nick that when I get angry, I break something. Like when I broke that perfume bottle after Mom called."

I winced, recalling the incident all too vividly. A gallon of Clorox had been required to remove the stench from the bathroom. I told Nick Candace's theory.

"I'm *theoried* out," he said. One of the reasons he had left the San Jose Police Department and found a position with the Placer County Sheriff's Office was because there had been too much murder, too much blood. Dealing with repeated savage acts had damaged his soul. The homicides cropping up in Lake Tahoe had to be magnifying the pain. "Good night. I'll call you tomorrow."

"I miss you," I said, knowing I wasn't overstepping. He needed to be wanted as much as I did. Our respective divorces had pared a pound of trust from our hearts.

Nick said to a woman who'd yelled his name in the background, "I'll be right there." To me, he said, "I miss you, too."

As I pocketed my cell phone, worry cut through me. The sheriff's department was understaffed and overburdened. What if Nick and his crew couldn't solve Dr. Fisher's murder? She deserved justice.

No, no, no, Aspen. Stand down. If I interfered, I could lose Nick. We had boundaries. He did his job; I did mine. Plus, the memory of a gun aimed at my head last January still made me shudder. And what would Max say? Maxine Adams, my aunt and the owner of the private investigation agency where I worked, had opinions on everything from the daily forecast to the balloting process. When it came to taking risks for no reason, she was more of a mother hen than Nick. No, I would keep my nose out of it.

If only I could shake the memory of Dr. Fisher calling me and uttering my name.

Chapter 3

Over the weekend, Candace and I carried out our normal routine. I gardened and cooked and ran with our retriever, Cinder, a rescue that had survived a fire. Candace studied and slept. Neither of us said much. Our mutual sorrow of knowing another person who had been murdered saturated the air.

Sunday night I slept fitfully. Just after three a.m., I awoke drenched in sweat. I remembered bits and pieces of the nightmare. My test results. Papers and files strewn everywhere. Scalpels and pools of blood.

Too revved up to sleep, I knew that I had to do something about Dr. Fisher's murder, with or without Nick's approval. At my core, I was a problem solver. I wanted to help people find clarity. To find peace. That was why I'd become a therapist. That was also the reason why I'd changed paths and become a private investigator. Finding solutions for everyone, not just emotionally charged teens, fulfilled me.

I sat up in bed, opened my laptop computer, and for the next three hours researched Dr. Fisher's ex, Edward Bogart. There were dozens of articles about him. As I read through them, I made notes on legal pads. Bogart was respected in his field and donated a lot of time to fund-raising for the Children's Heart Association, Reaching for the Cure, and other pediatric organizations. As far as I could tell, no one had anything bad to say about him. Was he truly a saint? Why had he and Dr. Fisher divorced?

When my eyes were too tired to continue, I created a file—my aunt demanded a written file for every case—stuffed my notes into it, and tossed it on my bureau.

At sunrise on Monday, I dressed in jogging shorts, cropped T-shirt, and running shoes, and opened Candace's door. Out bounded Cinder.

"Let's go." I attached his leash to his collar.

Together we headed toward Meeks Bay, drinking in the morning air. Exercise always cleared my mind and rid it of cobwebs. However, it didn't necessarily fill it with solutions.

When we returned, I showered and donned jeans and a red plaid shirt. On my way to the kitchen, the doting dog at my heels, I caught a glimpse of myself in the mirror. Major yuk, as Candace would say: dull eyes, limp hair. Applying blush and lip gloss hadn't helped.

"Are you okay?" Candace asked as she opened the refrigerator. She was dressed for school, a backpack slung over one shoulder.

"I'm out of sorts."

"Did you eat?"

"No."

"You need to eat." She swiped a yogurt and banana from the top shelf and grinned as she offered them to me. "Aha. Who's the adult in the room now?" She was teasing me because, ever since she'd moved in, I'd made sure she ate right. No more anorexia or bulimia. No more attempts at starving herself or purging. My hounding had paid off. She was a healthy, exuberant teenager. Her face sobered. "Oh, right. You're off-kilter because of Dr. Fisher's murder."

I nodded and rubbed Cinder's ears. "I'm certainly not out of sorts because of my run. No, sir. We had a good run, didn't we, boy? Yes, we did."

Candace grabbed a power bar from a container on the counter and juggled it and the yogurt and banana in front of me. "Choose one."

I snatched the power bar and said, "Let's go."

After checking the dog's water, filling his bowl with kibble, and making sure his doggie door was open—he would have free rein of the fenced-in yard—I drove Candace to school and then continued on to Incline Village.

I parked my Jeep in front of a ranch-style house on the highway and traipsed to the bungalow at the rear. Max's husband, my uncle, now deceased, had bought the property over thirty years ago. With age, the ferns and evergreens in the front had grown into a virtual forest. A drift of orange alpine lilies led the way to an arbor overrun by clematis vines.

The moment I stepped into the small house, I drank in the sweet aroma of coffee. At first glance, the main room resembled a den, with couches and love seats and antique lamps in clusters. Beneath its homey veneer, the Maxine Adams Detective Agency was a state-of-the-art operation, equipped with up-to-date computers, fire alarms, and security devices.

"I'm here!" I called.

Three enormous calicos that were nestled on satin pillows in the nook by the bay window raised their heads in greeting and went back to sleep. They weren't unfriendly; I simply didn't rock their world. I think they could smell Cinder on me.

Mornings were traditionally slow at the agency. Our two veteran investigators, Yaz and Darcy, liked to sleep in and work late. Rowena, our chatty receptionist, was missing in action, too. I swear that woman had my aunt wrapped around her little finger. She wouldn't file; she wouldn't type. She was one-third the size of my aunt, but apparently power came in a variety of sizes. I was dying to know what hold the woman had over Max. It had to be juicy. She'd known my aunt since college.

My aunt, on the other hand, regularly showed up at dawn, made a pot of coffee, and reviewed every newspaper she could get her hands on.

"Good morning, sugar. About time you arrived." Max lumbered from the kitchenette toward me, draped in yet another muumuu—this one black with yellow hibiscus flowers. "I'm famished and wasting away to nothing." At six feet and three hundred pounds, she towered over me. Ever since she nearly starved on an anthropology research expedition in the Andes, food had taken on another level of importance for her. "Blueberry muffin? I made them fresh."

"Sure." I had eaten my power bar on the drive, but I would never turn down one of my aunt's baked goods.

"Let's go over today's goals. Oh, wait, coffee." Max shambled across the hardwood floor, always swept clean of cat hair. She was finicky about that. "Here we go."

She brought mugs of coffee to the table along with two of the biggest muffins I'd ever laid eyes on. I peeled off the wrapper and took a bite. Whole berries exploded in my mouth.

"Delicious. Um, Max, I'm going to take on a new case. It's—"

"First things first. Great job getting the runner on Thursday."

"Caught him at a gas station. He was driving on fumes."

"Funny how cars don't run forever. Patience is a virtue, I always say." Max pushed a sheet of paper in my direction. "So today, we have a garbological investigation."

"Not again," I moaned. "You know that's my least favorite thing."

"It's a nasty business, but someone has to do it. Yaz has a bum knee." Yaz Yazdani, a former marine, had seen action overseas. "And Darcy refuses. You know I can't force her." Darcy Doherty, the more senior of our two investigators, was an expert at tracking down money trails. When not working, she was skydiving. "Use gloves and a clothespin."

I scanned the page in front of me, noting directions to a target's house not far from the office as well as arrival times of housekeepers and a cadre of delivery people. "Who are we raiding?"

"A woman whose ex-husband thinks she's pocketing some of the profits from their mutually owned company."

"How are we supposed to find that in her garbage?"

In the past few months, my duties had expanded from being a process server to tailing people and Dumpster diving; however, there were some aspects of my job I didn't understand. Going through someone's discards was one of them. On my first garbological adventure, I'd climbed into a Dumpster outside an apartment building to search for evidence of an extramarital affair and realized too late that, even though there was a ladder on the outside of the container, an exit ladder was not attached to the inside. After a moment of panic, my brain kicked into gear, and I realized I could pile garbage bags on top of each other and scale my way out. Because of that fateful foray, I always carried an extra set of clothing and shoes in my car.

"Look for receipts for expensive items," Max said. "Things a woman on a moderate budget can't afford. Perfume or jewelry. Vacation memos. They should be cash receipts. She hasn't charged a cent in months." My aunt rose and fetched a tin of brownies from the kitchen counter. "Almost forgot to offer you one of these. Just in case you're in the mood. Double-double chocolate. Sinful." She placed the tin on the table and moved to another desk to review a stack of mail. "FYI, it's possible our client might be imagining things."

"Got it." It wasn't my job to diagnose the client.

Max tossed a few envelopes in front of me along with a letter opener. "Before you head out, let's get some of this miserable paperwork out of the way."

"First, I need to discuss the case I want to take on."

"Don't keep me hanging. Speak."

I twisted in my chair to meet her gaze. "Did you hear about the doctor who was killed?"

"Kristin Fisher. It's all over the news."

"She was my doctor."

"Dang." Max dumped the rest of the mail on the table. "I'll admit I'm not psychic and I don't have your family's Washoe blood"—Max had married my uncle following her anthropology excursion to South America—"but when I saw Gloria Morning report on the murder, somehow I knew you'd be involved."

I wasn't psychic, either, but Washoe Indians, a peaceful tribe that had inhabited the Lake Tahoe area before settlers moved in, were known to be quite sentient, and I was one-eighth Washoe. My great-grandmother Blue Sky had been one hundred percent Washoe. My great-grandfather, an Irishman, had fallen hard for her the moment he'd set eyes on her.

"How did Dr. Fisher die?" Max asked. "Gloria didn't go into details about the murder."

"I doubt the sheriff has told her or anyone in the media anything."

"I assume you've spoken with Nick, though."

"The murderer stabbed her with a scalpel."

My aunt moaned. "How is Nick going to feel about you poking around?" The moment the two of them had met, they had hit it off. Nick appreciated smart, savvy women.

"He's not going to like it one bit."

"That's what I thought." She aimed a finger at me. "Think long and hard about that, sugar."

"It will be difficult but I've got to do this."

"Because of your folks. Because of Vikki."

How well she knew me. My parents' murders had gone unsolved. Group therapy had been a way to heal myself after their deaths.

Luckily, my friend Vikki's murder had been solved. That had helped me find a modicum of peace.

"What else did Nick allow you to know?" my aunt asked.

I told her about the mess of files and the chaos. "Other than that, he was pretty tight-lipped."

"I'm surprised he shared as much as he did." Max sat in her chair and folded her arms on the tabletop. "Did he mention that there were additional murders with the same MO?"

"Using a scalpel?"

"Using a sharp implement."

"No. Why?"

Max thumped her chest. "I feel it. In here. There will be."

"But the murderer used an instrument found in the office, which means it wasn't premeditated. It was a crime of passion."

"Oh?" Max smirked. "Now you're an expert?"

My cheeks warmed.

She patted my shoulder. "Listen, if you're going to investigate, you have to promise something. No gathering evidence without permission. No visiting the crime scene unaccompanied. You want to ask questions? Fine. You want to delve into the doctor's personal life, go ahead. That's open territory. But—"

I raised a hand. "I know the parameters."

"What do you think you can add to the investigation?"

"I knew Dr. Fisher."

Max clucked her tongue. "Did you eat with her? Talk dirt with her? Were you best friends with her like you were with Vikki? No." She tapped the table with her fingertip. "You want to help because you hate that murderers exist and many get away with it. I understand that. I feel the same, but—"

"It's more than that. I admired Dr. Fisher. She was kind, intelligent, and caring. She truly wanted to help her patients. We weren't cogs in the machinery to her. She asked about our lives. She . . ." Emotions caromed inside me. "She didn't deserve this."

"Nobody does."

Chapter 4

Around noon, I carried out my garbological exploration but didn't come up with any tangible documentation corroborating our client's theory. I did find a bunch of machine-shredded receipts, so I collected what I could and brought it to the office. Max would have to determine whether we were getting paid enough to reassemble the documents. It could take days or weeks.

Later, as I was finishing my report, my stomach grumbled. A power bar and a muffin—even one as large as I'd downed—were hardly enough to keep a grasshopper alive. I slapped the folder closed and went to the refrigerator, where Max kept plenty of fruit and yogurt in stock.

As I was reaching for a peach, the telephone rang. I turned to answer it.

"I'll get it," Max shouted. She recited the name of the agency and then listened. "Well, hello, lover." She tucked the phone between chin and shoulder and giggled like a schoolgirl. "You are so slick." Knowing Max didn't have a boyfriend, I could only guess who was on the other end. "I would be the luckiest woman alive if you did." She let out another string of giggles, followed by a smooch into the receiver. "Yes, I'll see you soon." She turned to me. "Lover boy is asking for you." She thrust the receiver in my direction.

I grabbed it from her, mock scorn in my glare.

Reeling with laughter, she slipped outside for a vape cigarette break.

"Hi, Nick," I said. "You just made my aunt's day."

"She made mine. Listen"—he sounded as tired as he had last night—"my car broke down. The radiator blew." His aging Wrangler had been running on borrowed time. "Can you give me a lift after I get off work? The service station won't be done fixing the hunk of junk until tomorrow morning, and everybody else is out on assignment."

"Will you stay for dinner?"

"Of course." We spoke for a few minutes. He avoided discussing the murder and I, chicken that I was, didn't mention my plan to investigate. Certain conversations were better had in person.

When I replaced the receiver, Max returned. "Is everything okay?"

I filled her in.

"Did you tell him about, you know . . ."

"No. I will. Promise."

Max stored her vape cigarette in a drawer and popped a Tic Tac in her mouth. "Do you plan to cook him dinner so you can soften him up before you break the news?"

"Exactly."

"Then if I were you, I'd barbecue. Men love a good barbecue." Max bustled across the room and reached into a cupboard. She pulled down a packet of three-by-five cards, withdrew a couple, and placed them under the Xerox machine cover. When the copying was done, she shoved the printed sheet into my hand. "Here's a couple of recipes. My favorite sauce. Finger-licking good. The other one . . . beans to die for."

I received the recipes gratefully and packed up my things. It was nearly two p.m. "Right now, I need to get to the middle school in record time."

"When is graduation for Candace?" she asked. "I forgot to mark it on my calendar."

"Thursday, next week. I'll send you a text."

"About investigating the Fisher murder," she said. "Any sign of danger, you back off."

"Yes, ma'am."

• • •

When I picked up Candace, she begged to go to Waverly's house to hang out. Waverly's mother would bring her home. I could tell the summer itch was near, so I agreed, but only with the proviso that she come home in time for dinner and studying.

As I drove off, I dialed Dr. Fisher's office, hoping Detective King hadn't concluded her investigation and closed the place down. I wanted a referral to another doctor. On the third ring, the office assistant, Heather, picked up. Quickly, I offered my apologies for her loss, and then I asked to whom she was referring Dr. Fisher's three hundred-plus patients. She recited a name and a number. I thanked her and was about to hang up when I heard her stifle tears.

Knowing the sorrow she must be suffering, I asked if she would like to meet for coffee. Though we hadn't spoken more than a few words over the course of the last year, she jumped at the chance. She was getting off work in a half hour. We agreed on meeting at View by the Lake, a charming café located in a mall in the center of Tahoe City. I'd become a regular at the place because my book club meetings were held at the adjoining bookstore.

On the way, I phoned the doctor that Heather had referred and made an appointment for tomorrow morning. Having the appointment didn't put me at ease about my situation, but at least it was a step forward to getting answers.

When I arrived at the café, the heavenly aroma of coffee wafted to me. I spotted Heather sitting at the corner table, her bony shoulders jutting from a snug tank top, her eyes red-rimmed and hair tousled. She caught sight of me and waved.

I weaved between gingham-covered tables. "Hi, Heather," I said as I sat in the chair opposite hers.

She seemed fragile and ready to crumble, like many of my previous therapy patients at our first meeting. Numerous used tissues lay wadded on the table. She gestured to the half-empty mug of black coffee resting on a napkin. "Can I get you a cup? The waitress said to serve ourselves."

"Sure. Black." I could've fetched it for myself, but making the offer had appeared to relax her.

She shuffled across the floor, her feet barely leaving the wood, and poured a mug of steaming coffee from a large silver thermos. When she set the cup on the table, it nearly toppled over. I righted it and mopped up the splash.

"Sorry," she said.

"It's okay. Sit. Tell me how you're doing." I kept my voice gentle and warm. Coaxing a grief-stricken person to talk required sensitivity.

"Did you know Dr. Fisher was my mother?" Heather asked.

"I had no idea." I couldn't see the resemblance. Heather had a thin, straight nose; her mother's nose had been broader and turned up. Heather's eyes were blue; the doctor's had been a dark hazel. "I guess I don't know your last name."

"It's Bogart."

"Does the sheriff know about your relationship to—" I hesitated.

"To my mother? I think so. I can't remember if I told them. I can't remember everything I've said." Heather grabbed a used tissue and mopped her cheeks. "I'm sorry. I can't seem to stop . . ." She rotated a finger in front of her eyes.

I reached for her hand, but she recoiled. "Have you spoken with anyone, perhaps a therapist, about what happened?" I asked. "I know what you're going through. My parents were murdered."

"Both of them?"

"Mm-hmm. Almost thirteen years ago." The memory still cut me to the core.

Heather rolled her lower lip between her teeth. "No therapist. Not yet."

"I've got the name of a good one."

"No. Thanks."

I took a sip of coffee. "Have you spoken with your father?"

"Edward Bogart will never be my father."

I was bewildered by the animosity in her tone.

"I'm a sperm bank baby. After my mother had me, she met Edward."

"How old were you when they married?"

"One. He adopted me, but they divorced eight years later and he renounced the adoption."

Ouch. That had to hurt. What kind of man was he? I'd assumed Kristin Fisher and her ex had been married a long time because, as Candace had said, she'd met him at the office. Possibly it was one of those marriages where after the couple divorced they became better friends, the trials and tribulations of married life no longer an issue.

Heather coughed out a sad laugh. "Talk about irony. She gave me his name and then changed her own back."

"You could change yours legally."

"I suppose I could. I'll think about it."

"Why did they divorce?"

"Edward treasured his career and wanted to devote all his time to it," Heather explained. "Also, he decided he didn't want the burden of children."

"I see," I murmured, though I didn't, really. He was a pediatric doctor. He ought to enjoy children. Maybe he was like the grandparent who loved being with the grandchildren but couldn't wait to hand them back to the parents.

"Let me rephrase that. He didn't want the burden of *me*. He expected perfection. I couldn't rise to the occasion."

By the age of nine? What a jerk.

Heather ripped open a packet of sugar, dumped the whole thing into her coffee, and licked her finger in order to mop up sprinkles that had fallen on the table.

After a long silence, I said, "So after they divorced, your mother raised you as a single parent?"

"Uh-huh."

Another thought occurred to me. Was it possible Heather killed her mother? No, my gut told me she was innocent. I doubted she could have overpowered her mother. She was at least twenty pounds lighter and she was a bundle of frayed nerves. Also, Nick said she had an alibi; she had been with her boyfriend. Granted, her boyfriend might lie on her behalf, but I didn't get that vibe.

"Heather, your mother rang me that morning. I know she had a habit of coming in early."

"Everyone knew she came in early. She was the most dedicated doctor anywhere."

"She'd sounded out of breath on the phone. Do you know why?"

Suddenly, it dawned on me that she might not have called me to share test results. Maybe she had reached out because I was a private investigator and she'd wanted me to help her with an issue. But then the killer showed up and ended the call.

Everyone knew she came in early.

"Finding your mother must have been a terrible shock," I said. "You were too shaken to notice much else, but can you remember whether anything other than the mess of files was different from normal? Was one particular file separate from the rest? Were cabinets unlocked or hanging open?"

She shuddered; her teeth began to chatter. "I told the police—"

"The sheriff," I corrected.

"Right, them. All of the drawers were locked when I got there. Mother secured everything at night. It was just the files on the floor and the scalpel. It didn't belong."

"What do you mean?"

"It wasn't ours."

So I was wrong and my aunt was right. The killer had brought the weapon along, meaning the murder was premeditated.

"Where did the sheriff find the scalpel?" I asked.

"Under the examination table. It took three of the sheriff's men to move it."

Aha. That was why the killer had left it behind.

Heather picked up a tissue and shredded it in a matter of seconds. "The blood—" She drew in a sharp breath. "There was so much of it."

I reached for her hand again. This time she allowed me to take hold. "Heather, this is very important. Are you sure the scalpel wasn't from your office?"

"Yes. It had a white handle. All of ours are silver. We get them from a supply company." The shivering ceased and tears resumed.

"I really think you should consider seeing a therapist. You'd like the one my niece goes to." It was the doctor Candace had been seeing to discuss her fight with bulimia. "She can help you through this."

"I don't know."

"I'll give you her number and you decide, but it would be good for you to talk to someone. You've suffered a severe shock." I wrote the psychiatrist's number on my business card and handed it to her. "Is anybody helping you with funeral arrangements?"

"Edward said he'd do it." So at least she had spoken to the guy. "He's in my mother's will."

"She didn't exclude him after the divorce?"

Heather shook her head.

"You'll need to consult a lawyer, too."

"I didn't kill her."

I smiled gently. "You'll need a lawyer to help with your mother's estate."

"Oh, right." She dabbed her nose with a shredded tissue and gazed at me with wide eyes. "Would you—" She paused.

"Would I what?"

"Would you mind staying a while longer?" Heather drew into herself. I could identify. After my parents were murdered, it had taken every ounce of energy for me to breathe.

"Of course."

For a long time, we talked about Dr. Fisher's patients. Without divulging histories, Heather shared that some might have felt animosity toward her mother. Not every pregnancy or treatment went according to plan, although a natural casualty would not have been her mother's fault, Heather added quickly. Life wasn't fair. She said that most of what she told me she'd already shared with the sheriff's department. I let her ramble.

An hour later, as we waited for the waitress to return with the bill, Heather talked of her dream of attending design school. "I was never much of a student. That's why I didn't go to college and started working for my mother."

"You've got a quick mind. What about trying junior college? You could get your basic requirements out of the way and then aim higher."

She took a sip of her coffee.

"Don't give up," I said, channeling her mother. "Even though life is throwing you a curveball, you've got to keep trying. You've got potential."

As I climbed into my Jeep, I thought again about the scalpel the killer had brought to the doctor's office. Where had it come from?

Chapter 5

At dusk, as I walked to the back porch with a Heineken for Nick and a glass of wine for me, I nearly stumbled over Cinder, who was darting back and forth trying to catch a pair of rascally Douglas squirrels. The rodents chased each other around the base and up the trunk of the large white fir that jutted through a hole in the wood-slatted patio. A seed cone fell from the tree and whacked Cinder on the head. He barked and whimpered in an effort to communicate that the sky was falling.

Nick chuckled.

I set our drinks on the patio table and nursed my dog. "It's okay, boy." I scratched him behind the ears. "You're a dope, but it's okay."

"Food smells good," Nick said, lifting his beer and taking a swig.

I could hear the ribs sizzling on the barbecue. The spicy aroma of the sauce made my taste buds go wild. "It's Max's recipe."

"That means it's a winner."

I nabbed my wineglass and sat on a cushioned bench, an adjunct to the railing. Luckily, the evening had cooled to a comfortable sixty degrees. I'd donned a light sweatshirt over my jeans.

Though my cabin was in the hills nestled among hundreds of pines, I had a modest view of the lake. Tiny whitecaps drifted across the deep blue expanse. Seagulls plunged headlong into the chilly water, returning to the surface seconds later with their meals. I drank in deep gulps of peace and tried not to think about my meeting with Heather or her mother's murder or my test results.

"What's ticking inside that overly active brain of yours?" Nick chilled his neck and temples with the bottle of beer. At thirty-nine he was as handsome as a leading man. I couldn't resist the long dimple down his right cheek. His standard black T-shirt clung to his muscular chest. A hank of blue-black hair flecked with gray dangled mischievously down his forehead. When I'd first met him during the investigation of Vikki's murder, sparks had flown. Not the good kind. He'd considered me a suspect; I'd thought he was missing cues. When I finally realized he was good at his job and measured everyone without bias, I gave in to the feelings I had for him. After he finalized his divorce, he gave in to the feelings he had for me. We started dating once the case concluded.

"C'mon," Nick said. "Your face is scrunched up. Fess up."

I swallowed hard, wanting to kick myself for being such a coward. *Tell him. Blurt it out. Suffer the consequences.*

"Are you thinking about the murder?" he asked.

"Yes. And no."

"Does it have to do with this?" He reached beneath the lightweight jacket he'd placed on the patio table and withdrew a manila envelope. "Your medical file."

"How did you—"

"You said the doctor called you regarding test results." He offered it to me.

I opened it and scanned the first page. A notation said the radiology lab had requested that the doctor touch base. "Did you read through this?"

"No. It's private. But you seemed concerned about the mess of files at the doctor's office, and seeing as I was there today, I *borrowed* it."

"I had some tests. At the imaging center."

Tension crept around his eyes. "For . . ."

"I had a mammogram."

"Routine?"

"Yes. Well, it was until they found a lump, but they couldn't tell me whether it was benign. Diagnosis is up to the imaging tech and Dr. Fisher. They sent results to her. Like I told you, she called me on the morning she was killed, but the call ended abruptly. I figured she hung up because she realized she'd meant to call me Monday. After the weekend." I squelched the tears pressing at the corners of my eyes. "But seeing this"—I tapped the notation—"it doesn't look good. If all was fine, the radiologist would have left her a complete message."

"That's not necessarily so." Nick sat beside me and took my hands in his. Gently he rubbed my fingers. "We'll get the results and you'll see that you're fine, okay?"

"I've been referred to another doctor. He squeezed me in for an appointment tomorrow morning."

"Good."

"If the lump is malignant—" The word caught in my throat. I couldn't tell by his gaze how he felt. He was a master at hiding feelings. Was he worried? Would he pull back? If we'd been together for years, we could weather the outcome, but some men fled when they heard the word *cancer*.

"I'm not going anywhere."

"I didn't—"

He pressed a fingertip to my lips. "I can read your mind."

"No, you can't."

"I love you. I'll help you get through this. Whatever *this* is."

For the first time since I'd discovered the lump, I relaxed. I tapped the file. "Thank you for *borrowing* this." I set it down and took a sip of wine. "So what is going on with the murder investigation? Can you fill me in?"

"Detective King is organizing the files. Detective Hernandez is helping her."

"Anyone coming up from Auburn?"

"We'll see."

The main office for the sheriff was located in Auburn, the nearest large city southwest of Tahoe, about an hour and a half away. The coroner was located in Auburn as well.

Nick placed my feet in his lap. "King thinks your take on this is on the mark, by the way."

"How so?"

"She thinks the murder was a crime of passion."

"What about the weapon?" I asked. "I spoke with Dr. Fisher's daughter, Heather, the office assistant."

"Heather was Dr. Fisher's daughter?"

"Yes. Dr. Fisher had her as a single mother, but a year later married Dr. Bogart, and he adopted her. Heather thought she'd told you, but it might have slipped her mind."

He motioned for me to continue. "Why were you talking to her?"

"I asked for a referral. Heather was crying. Thinking I could help, I invited her to coffee. My forte is dealing with young people."

"Go on. What did she say?"

"The scalpel used in the murder wasn't from the office. It had a white handle. Theirs are silver."

"I'll look into it."

I sipped my wine. "What evidence do you have?" I asked, happy to get my mind off *me* for the moment and on to a more pressing subject. "Any fingerprints?"

"None other than those of the office staff. The scalpel was wiped clean. The killer must have worn gloves."

"Heather said you found the scalpel under the examination table, which was too heavy for the killer to move on his own."

"Heather is a blabbermouth."

"Do you have any other evidence?"

"There were a number of hairs, both animal and human," Nick said. "The doctor owned a dog."

Cinder sidled to Nick and shoved his head under his hand for attention. The word *dog* got Cinder every time.

"Oh, my. Will Heather take it?" I asked.

"That's the least of my worries."

"I'm home!" Candace cried as she opened the screen door and stepped outside.

Nick swung away from me. I dropped my feet to the porch.

Candace raised an eyebrow. "What's going on?"

Nick avoided the question and said, "How's school?"

"One more day. Yay! Summer, here I come." She did a jig and sat on a chair facing us, her expression serious. "I've been thinking about the murder. Why was Dr. Fisher in the office so early?"

"Candace," Nick warned.

Candace shot a finger at him.

Over the past few months, Nick and Candace had become buddies. Though she'd liked him from the start, when she had first moved in, she hadn't wanted to share me with anybody, not even Nick. The fear that he would take me away from her was at the core of her anxiety. Throughout Candace's young life, her mother had dumped Candace with neighbors so she could spend time with her various boyfriends.

Nick had done his best to win Candace over by showing interest in her studies and in the rest of her life. He'd even taken her snow skiing in a whiteout and waterskiing in the rain, wetsuit and all. Over the course of a few months, she began to trust that she wouldn't be relegated to her room every time he stopped by. Now, she inserted herself into the conversation with ease.

Nick said, "We're checking phone records. She might have had an appointment, but there wasn't one recorded on the calendar."

"She was an early bird," I said.

"That early?"

"I think"—Candace leaned forward, ready to discuss the case, colleague to colleague—"she had a lover."

"Candace." My sharp tone made her flinch.

"For criminey sakes, Aunt Aspen." *Criminey* was a semi-curse word that I used; so had my mother. Archaic and almost pristine, it sounded funny coming from a teenager. That and the fact that she had called me *Aunt* Aspen. She used the word only when she was royally ticked off and attempting to exert her teenage power. "I'm fourteen."

"Yes, you are. Almost a grown woman."

"So did she, Nick?" Candace pressed. "Meeting a lover first thing in the morning might mean he was married and couldn't slip out at night."

Nick cut me a look.

I fanned the air. "Answer her. You know she won't be satisfied with a shrug."

"We're considering the possibility."

"Bet she did." She bounded to her feet. "How long before dinner?"

"Three minutes," I said.

"Can I make a phone call?"

"A quick one."

The girl dashed inside.

"What's going on with her?" Nick asked.

"She's got a boyfriend. Rory."

"How old is he?"

"Sixteen. Supposedly, I get to meet him soon."

"Want me to run a background check on this guy?"

"Could you?"

Recently, Candace and I had discussed her blossoming sexuality. She assured me that the last thing she wanted was a baby or a disease and that sex education classes had completely informed her about how to avoid both—bless the school system. During our chat I didn't raise the issue of my sister's promiscuous tendencies. There was no need to bring something up about her when she wasn't there to give her side of the story.

Nick kissed me tenderly and moved to the barbecue. He raised the lid and checked the ribs. "Ready."

"Great. I'm starved." When we sat down to dinner, I'd tell him about the rest of my talk with Heather.

As I opened the kitchen door, the landline phone rang, disturbing the serenity. After a couple of rings, Candace yelled through her bedroom window, "Phone call for Nick."

He stepped inside while checking his cell phone, probably wondering why whoever was on the line hadn't called him on it. I followed him. "Cell's out of juice," he muttered and picked up the landline's receiver. "Shaper." As he listened, his face turned grim. "Uh-huh. Got it. On my way." He ended the call and met my gaze. "I need to borrow your car."

"Why?"

"There's been a second murder."

"Another doctor?"

"A high-end restaurant owner. Stabbed with a butcher's knife."

Chapter 6

No way was I letting Nick go by himself. Driving around the lake at dusk could be hazardous. Before we left, I set out a dinner plate for Candace, ordered her to lock the doors and windows, and made her promise not to let anybody in, no matter what. She didn't put up a fuss. A history of caution had been born in my niece the night she had been taken hostage by Vikki's murderer. I called my neighbor and asked her to be on the lookout for suspicious characters. She said she'd do me one better. She would send Opal, her eighteen-year-old daughter, to hang out with Candace. I thanked her, to which she replied: *Anytime, anywhere.*

By the time Nick and I arrived at the crime scene, it was nearly seven. The sun had set. The mountains were a deep purple. A bank of clouds rising over the Nevada side of the lake looked as if they had been dusted with saffron powder. Cars, campers, SUVs, and a few television news vans lined the road. The crowd of onlookers was thick.

Yellow crime scene tape already secured the location. An officer lifted the tape and allowed me to drive into the parking lot. There was only one car parked there—a Mercedes coupe. Naturally vigilant, Nick paused to take in the area before striding across the lot to the restaurant. I kept pace.

Vittorio's Ristorante boasted no flashing neon lights, no heavy-duty advertising. The only indication that the building was a place of business was the tiny brass sign to the right of the carved double doors: *Vittorio's.* Located on a ritzy strip of property between Kings Beach and Carnelian Bay, the restaurant drew the type of clientele willing to pay top dollar. The scampi and fresh lobster dishes had earned rave reviews.

Detective Kendra King crossed the pavement to greet Nick. King, in her late thirties like Nick, was beautiful in a sporty way. An avid rock climber, she had scaled nearly all the formations in the Tahoe area. "The victim was found at around five p.m.," she said.

"Why'd it take you so long to reach me?" Nick asked.

"We tried your cell phone."

"Right. The battery's dead. Sorry." He motioned for her to continue. "What've we got?"

"A tech is documenting interior and exterior. Two others are gathering evidence." King gestured toward a stocky guy who was focusing his camera on the entrance to the restaurant's kitchen. "The victim is inside."

"Show me the way," he said, accepting a pair of sterile booties from King and slipping them on over his Timberlands.

Neither King nor Nick paid attention to me as I followed in their wake. The other officers standing outside didn't object to my presence, most likely accepting that Nick had granted me access.

At the entrance to the kitchen, Nick stopped. I bumped into him and apologized and then covered my nose with my hand. "Man!" The stench of death hovered in the opened doorway.

"Go back to the car," he ordered. "You're not part of this." There was an edge to his voice. "In fact, go home. I'll catch a ride. I'll call soon as I can." He proceeded inside as if my departure was guaranteed.

Aberrant interest wasn't what made me stick around. I wanted to be supportive of Nick and, in order to do so, I needed to see what he saw. Not through his eyes, through my own. Plus, observing the crime scene might help me in my efforts to solve Dr. Fisher's murder. What were the odds of two people dying at the hand of a different perpetrator in Lake Tahoe in the space of four days?

"There wasn't a fight, Nick," King said while donning her booties. "This was swift."

A few feet inside the modest kitchen, Nick stooped beside the body of a dark-haired man. He was facedown, his head toward the door, feet in the direction of the main restaurant. A butcher knife jutted from his back, near his kidneys. Blood had congealed on the man's expensive pinstriped suit.

Without entering, I scanned the room for clues. Blood splatter on the tile floor and metal-lined walls reminded me of a Rorschach test, with most of the blood remaining on the body and a minimal spray at the outer edges. The kitchen utensils hung in an orderly fashion on hooks jutting from the ceiling. Pots and pans were arranged on shelves. Blue licks of gas flickered just below the burners on the state-of-the-art Vulcan stove. A-frame evidence tents stood in various places near the body and on the kitchen counters.

Where were the employees? I'd worked in a restaurant during college. The sous chef and manager should have arrived hours ago. Salad preparations should have been lying on the cutting board and frozen foods should have been thawing. And then it occurred to me that the restaurant might be closed on Mondays.

"It's nothing like the Fisher murder," King said, breaking the silence.

She was right. Although a scalpel and a carving knife were sharp, they were completely different weapons. Perhaps the heat of summer was stirring up bad vibrations.

As if Nick heard my unspoken thoughts, he glanced over his shoulder. His forehead tightened and his eyes grew steely. He crossed to me, braced my shoulders with his hands, and kissed me on the cheek. "I told you I'd catch a ride. Get out of here." Not expecting disagreement, he returned his focus to the murder scene and ran his hands through his hair.

A kiss wasn't enough to shoo me away, and something in my gut urged me to remain, so I opted for a lower profile. I edged to the side of the door but remained within visual range of everything that was going on. By the lack of attention from everyone else on the scene, I assumed nobody had heard Nick give me an order to disappear. If he spotted me again, I'd deal with his anger at that time.

"Kendra, do we have a name?" Nick asked.

"Tony Vittorio, the owner. I'm going back outside. I'll handle the press."

Nick crossed the narrow room and joined two of his people, Detective Felipe "Phil" Hernandez, a fit Latino in his early thirties with thick black hair and prominent eyebrows, and Detective De Silva, a fresh-faced female, new to the team, who was jotting notes on a steno pad. They discussed various possibilities of how the crime went down, pointing toward the swinging doors leading to the dining room and back to the body.

A technician with rust-red hair was crouched near the doors, working her magic with tweezers. I watched with fascination as she lifted and deposited each piece of evidence she found into separate bags: hair and fibers into paper bags; leaves and food particles into plastic bags. What a tedious chore. She initialed everything.

"Hey, Nick," she said. "Welcome."

"Red," he said. "Bring me up to speed."

"In a sec."

Hernandez said, "Tahoe used to be considered a safe place to vacation."

"This guy isn't killing tourists," Nick replied.

"Do you think it's the same perp?" De Silva asked. "It's sure not the same MO. The scene at Fisher's office was chaotic. This one is fairly neat."

If this was neat, I'd hate to see messy.

"I suppose the killer could be a transient," Hernandez said.

"Let's not theorize," Nick snapped.

"Wait until this story hits the news," De Silva said. "Lake Tahoe will turn into a ghost town."

I disagreed. Gore seekers would show up in droves.

Nick glowered at her. She flinched. His glare could wither the bravest soul. He eyed Hernandez. "Any witnesses?" he asked.

Hernandez shook his head. "Enzo Vittorio, the executive chef and brother of the victim, found him."

"Where is he?"

"In the dining room. Detective King told him not to move. All reservations for tomorrow have been canceled. The waiters and busboys have been alerted to stay home. We'll interview each of them."

I shifted closer to the door.

Nick must have sensed movement. He spotted me. So much for my low-profile routine. I splayed my hands, begging for mercy. He knew my nature. A therapist didn't get to the root of a client's problem without being curious. A PI didn't either. He frowned and refocused on Hernandez. I could tell by the way Nick's shoulders rose and fell that I'd be taking heat later.

"Go on, Phil," Nick said.

"We think a lefty did it." Hernandez pointed at the victim. "Upward thrust from left to right."

De Silva agreed and flipped to a previous page on her notepad. Reading from it, she recited the length of the knife's handle and approximate length of its blade, given its use in the kitchen.

I wondered whether Dr. Fisher's killer had been left-handed. Would that connect the two crimes?

"How many on the kitchen staff?" Nick asked. "Sous chefs, et cetera?"

De Silva rattled off a list. "We have each of their addresses."

"Why are you hanging around here then? Go. Get answers."

"Sir." The woman nearly curtsied as she made her exit.

Nick rotated his neck to free the tension and shifted his gaze to the crime scene. "I'm assuming the weapon is from this kitchen?"

"Straight out of the block to your right," Hernandez said.

"Red, can you talk to me now? Do we have trace evidence?"

"Hundreds of prints on the door." She aimed a finger. "No prints on the weapon, wiped clean. We also have a couple dozen hairs or so. Human and animal." She returned to her work.

Detective King stepped through the door. "Nick, reporters want answers." She hooked a thumb toward the outside.

Nick squared his shoulders. As he passed me, he said, "Stubbornness runs in your blood, doesn't it?"

I offered a supportive smile. "Remember I'm on your side."

He mumbled something, his sarcastic undertone unmistakable, and continued marching toward a reporter from KINC.

Seeing as he didn't remind me to leave, I took his silence as approval to stick around. Yes, I was pushing the envelope, but even when I'd worked at BARC, I'd bucked the system. To help my patients.

Quietly, I skirted to the front of the building. The main dining room wasn't designated part of the crime scene. It wasn't roped off. I slipped inside and tried to become one with the stained oak walls and fake ficus tree as Detective Hernandez approached a square-jawed, middle-aged man who was sitting in one of the brown leather booths.

The man's white jacket was unbuttoned. He held a toque in his hands. The executive chef, I assumed. Why had he suited up on a day when the restaurant was closed?

Behind the man on a ledge to his right sat a celadon vase filled with sunflowers and ferns. There were a dozen more like it in the bistro. A variety of mirrors on the walls reflected the light of the chandeliers and cast a surreal glow around the room.

"Mr. Vittorio, I'm Detective Hernandez."

"Call me Enzo."

"Let's go through your story, sir."

"I told the other detective—the woman—everything."

"Humor me. Take me through it, too." Hernandez poised a foot on the seat of the booth and crossed his arms on his thigh, giving the impression that he was relaxed and easy to talk to. "You told Detective King that you came in around five and found your brother."

"I told her quarter to five." The man had an Italian accent. "I phoned 911 right away. No time delay."

"Thank you, sir. And you said there was no one else around?"

"Nobody."

"You told my associate that you came in earlier, around ten in the morning."

"To cook a turkey. Slow roast. I always make broth on Mondays. It takes a long time. You smell it?"

Now I did. In the kitchen, the odor of death had prevailed.

"I went home. I ate lunch. I returned at a quarter to five."

"And the rest of the staff?"

"We are closed on Mondays."

Hernandez nodded. He already knew that.

"Who did this to my brother?" Enzo Vittorio asked. His voice crackled with emotion.

"That's what we hope to find out. Tell me about your staff."

Vittorio ticked off the names on his fingertips as if he were reciting a recipe—a teaspoon of this, half cup of that. The *saucier*, better known as the person who made the sauces. The *poisonnier*, aka the woman who prepared the fish. The *chef de partie*, or line chef. The pantry chef. The pastry chef. The sous chef.

Hernandez continued to ask questions, often repeating one or two to see if Enzo Vittorio's story changed. About a half hour later, Nick strolled in. He didn't glance in my direction, which meant my ploy of blending in like a potted plant was working. He, too, pressed the chef. As he got to the part where Enzo Vittorio was naming the kitchen staff, De Silva raced in, out of breath.

"Detective Sergeant Shaper, sir, I met up with the sous chef. He's dead in the water." She covered her mouth then dropped her arm. "Not *dead* dead but he's sicker than a dog. It smelled like a hospital at his house. He's got some kind of bacterial infection. I didn't ask for doctor reports, but he looked paler than a—" She stopped short of saying *corpse*.

I felt sorry for her. She was so green she hadn't learned crime scene etiquette.

"Meet with all the others before reporting back, De Silva," Nick ordered.

"Sir. Yes, sir." She lingered for a moment until she realized Nick wanted her to go *stat*. Turning crimson, she shot out of the room.

At nine p.m., when I was certain a few more hours might elapse before Nick was ready to call it a night, I stepped outside and rang Candace. True to character, she chastised me for being overly protective.

"Sue me," was my adult comeback.

"I'll get an attorney tomorrow," she teased. "C'mon, don't worry about me. Opal and I are watching *C.S.I.* reruns. By the way, make sure you tell Nick to ask whether the victim had a will or something, because you know—"

"Whoever inherits has something to gain. Got it, you crime show nut."

After a long pause, Candace said, "Is it really gross?"

"Grosser than gross."

When I returned to the dining room, Enzo Vittorio was slumped in the booth, an unlit cigarette shoved between his lips, gray bags beneath his bloodshot eyes. Nick didn't look much better. His skin was slack.

"Mr. Vittorio, one more time," Nick said. "How long have you worked for your brother?"

"Seven years. I already told you this. I come from Italy to help out. Please, I need a break."

"Sure. Go ahead."

Vittorio thanked him and weaved through the tables toward the restroom.

As he slipped by me, a prickly sensation ran up my neck. I watched him pad along the narrow hallway. Before he entered the restroom, he glanced over his shoulder at the detectives, neither of whom was looking in his direction, and a slow, evil grin spread across his face.

Chapter 7

Nick released Enzo Vittorio around ten p.m. and ordered his team to start cleaning up. It never ceased to amaze me how much work was involved in securing a murder scene: taking photographs, collecting evidence, and removing the body. Nick supervised the activity with the command of a general. Throughout it all, he didn't make eye contact with me, which made me wary.

An hour later, as I drove him home, his anger surfaced. "How could you take advantage like that?"

My fingers clenched the steering wheel. I'd never been a good combatant. Not with my parents. Not with my ex-husband. I didn't want to fight with Nick. I had defied his orders. But I'd learned a lot. I was ready to admit that two different people had carried out the Fisher and Vittorio murders, and Enzo Vittorio was high on my list for the second.

"Why didn't you go home when I told you to?" he asked.

"I thought you could use moral support. A fresh set of eyes. I observed."

"Uh-uh. I'm not buying it." He swiveled in his seat. "Be honest. You thought you could learn something that might help you solve Dr. Fisher's murder. *You.* Let me remind you that my people are handling that case. Not you."

"I have every right—"

"No, you don't. You have no rights at a crime scene."

I stopped at a red light. "Why are you attacking me? All I did—"

"I'm not attacking you. I'm setting things straight." His eyes blazed with fury.

I focused on the road, trying to form a justifiable argument. I couldn't. I'd been in the wrong. I hadn't tampered with evidence, but I should have left. As a therapist, I'd been just as dogged, which was why I'd become mired in my patients' lives—at a risk to my own health.

"Tony Vittorio's brother is hiding something," I said. "I saw him on the way to the restroom. He—"

"Aspen, c'mon. Just say it. By sticking around, you could've mucked things up."

"I was careful to stay out of the way. I never once entered the crime scene."

"All it takes is one of your hairs to float inside. Now I have to rule you out as a suspect"—he slapped his thigh—"again."

"Again?" I inhaled sharply. "I was never on your radar regarding Vikki and you know it. I—"

His cheek twitched. Then his mouth. He was messing with me.

I let out the breath I'd been holding. "I'm sorry."

"I worry about you," he said. "I don't want this dark reality to enter your world."

"But it has, don't you see?" I sighed. "With my parents' murders, my sister's drug abuse, my ugly divorce, Vikki's death, and now the murder of my doctor, I'm numb beyond belief when it comes to dark reality."

"Life hasn't been easy for you."

"Or for you. You've got to stop trying to protect me."

"It's my nature." He brushed his knuckles along my jawbone. "I love you more than you know."

"I love you, too."

"Seeing as you did stick around to *observe*—"

"Was Dr. Fisher's killer left-handed?"

"Most likely."

"So the killer could have done both crimes."

He pursed his lips, weighing the theory. "Tell me about Enzo Vittorio. What do you think he's hiding?"

I replayed the executive chef's jaunt to the restroom and how he'd turned and smirked at Nick and Hernandez. I asked why his chef's uniform was pristine. Wouldn't cooking the turkey have soiled it? Had he changed? And why was he an employee instead of a full-fledged partner with his brother? Perhaps professional jealousy was a motive for murder. In addition, I mentioned what Candace had suggested, that possibly Tony Vittorio had written his brother into or out of his will and, therefore, money was the motive, adding that maybe, to keep his hands clean, he'd hired a hit man to off his brother.

Nick listened and didn't discount anything. He said he'd have his staff hunt for a second uniform. In addition, he would look into Enzo's communiqués and see if he had an associate. And he would question Tony Vittorio's widow to see whether there might be some other reason for bad blood between the brothers.

"On the other hand," Nick said as I veered onto his street, "this could have been a random attack."

"Why, because the killer used a knife instead of a gun?"

"Because the weapon wasn't brought to the scene."

"What if this began when a fight turned nasty, like a fight over the direction the restaurant was headed?"

"Good point."

"Do you think the same killer murdered Dr. Fisher?"

"It seems unlikely. Speaking of Dr. Fisher, tell me what else you wanted to say earlier about her daughter, Heather?"

Quickly, I recapped what Heather had told me about Edward Bogart not wanting her and about the doctor including him in her will. "Have you met him?"

"I did. He's an upstanding guy."

"He donates to a lot of charities."

Nick raised an eyebrow. I explained that I hadn't been able to sleep so I'd researched the man.

"He has a solid alibi," Nick said. "He was doing a heart replacement in Reno. The surgery began at seven that morning. He was in prep at six. The kid lived."

"Glad to hear it." I mentally checked Edward Bogart off my suspect list. "Then you only have three hundred patients to interrogate."

"Plus vendors and personal friends, though the doctor was quite solitary, it turns out."

"No lovers?"

"She hadn't dated in years." Nick rubbed his neck and yawned. "I'll put Hernandez on scalpel detail."

He laced his fingers in my hair and kissed me. Delicious warmth coursed through me, but the thought of Candace waiting for me at home doused my passion like a cold shower.

I pulled away and whispered, "I promise I'll find a night soon when we can, you know . . ."

"Make love for hours?"

"Mm-hm."

Nick kissed me one last time and slipped out the passenger door.

As I drove, I made a mental note to set up a sleepover for Candace at Waverly's.

• • •

When I arrived at the cabin, every light was on, which made my heart skip a beat. What was wrong? Had Opal left? Had Candace experienced a scare? Flashbacks of her being held hostage careened through my mind. I dashed inside and found Opal slouched in one of the leather chairs in the living room, reading a book.

"Hi, Opal."

Cinder was nestled on the horsehair rug that my father's older brother had handed down, his eyes closed. He stirred but didn't rise to greet me.

Opal, a studious girl with narrow features and lank hair, gave me the same indifferent response. "Hey, Miss Adams."

"Where's Candace?" I moved to the wall behind Opal's chair and righted one of the snowshoes used by my great-grandmother Blue Sky to hike into the Tahoe Basin area. Sometimes I wondered if her spirit entered the house and toyed with the snowshoe to let me know she was watching over me.

"I'm here." Candace shuffled into the foyer clad in pajamas and looking as innocent as a six-year-old. She was holding a written message in her hand. "Gloria Morning called an hour ago. She said she tried your cell phone but it went straight to voice mail."

I glanced at my cell phone. *Missed call.*

"She said it doesn't matter what time you contact her"—Candace stifled a yawn—"she needs to talk to you. Tonight. It's about the restaurant guy that was murdered." Her voice didn't falter at the word *murder*, which made me worry about her jaded reaction. "She sounded sort of panicked, but not *in danger* panicked. You know?"

"Thanks."

"I'm going to bed. Night, Opal." She trudged to her room, her slippers never leaving the floor.

Eager to know why Gloria needed to talk to me, I thanked Opal and offered to pay her.

She declined and said, "It's what neighbors do."

When the front door closed, I went to the kitchen and dialed Gloria. She picked up after the first ring.

"Oh, thank heaven, Aspen, it's you. Saturday . . ." Gloria sounded out of breath. "Saturday I received a note about Dr. Fisher. Some delivery person brought it to the studio. I thought it was bogus and dismissed it."

"*Bogus* how? What did it say?"

"It said, 'Dr. Fisher will never hurt you again.' Aspen, she never hurt me, so, like I said, I dismissed it. I mean, I know she was killed, but I didn't have anything to do with her other than the interview. I thought to myself, I'm a celebrity. I should expect to get off-the-wall mail. People want a brush with fame."

"Go on."

"Then I got another letter. Tonight. Delivered to my doorstep. About the restaurateur who was murdered."

My shoulders tensed. Were the two deaths related after all? "What did it say?"

"'Tony Vittorio will never hurt you again.' And now he's dead!" Gloria faltered. "Stabbed. It's horrible. Disgusting. The person who signed the letters—both of them—wrote 'I did it for your glory.'"

"Do you know who sent it?"

"I don't have any idea." She sounded shaky. On the edge. "Aspen, he knows where I *live*."

"Okay, take a deep breath. Calm down. You have to contact the sheriff."

"At this time of night? Are you nuts?"

"They answer twenty-four-seven."

Gloria mewled. "Why would someone kill Dr. Fisher or Tony Vittorio for me? I barely knew them."

"You interviewed Dr. Fisher. Did you interview Mr. Vittorio?"

"Yes. In April. It was very professional. Lots of people were on the set. He didn't hurt me. He didn't even raise his voice. Why is this happening to me?"

I let her self-centeredness slide and didn't point out that what was happening to her—if anything was really happening—was far less important than what had happened to Kristin Fisher and Tony Vittorio. Each person viewed her drama as primary. I had with my mammogram test results.

"Have you dined at Vittorio's?" I asked.

"Yes."

"Did you go with anyone?"

"My fiancé, Beau."

"Is it possible Beau thought Mr. Vittorio was flirting with you or coming on to you?"

"No way." Gloria blew her nose. "And Beau doesn't . . . *didn't* . . . know Dr. Fisher." Gloria sucked back a sob. "Aspen, this is awful. Somebody wrote that he was killing for my glory. *Killing.*" Her voice skated upward.

"I can hear you. You don't need to shout."

"I've locked all my doors and set the alarm. I'm scared."

"I don't think you need to be. If the notes are sincere, whoever wrote the notes wants to protect you. Not hurt you."

She let out a jagged sigh and murmured her agreement.

"Tell me more about your visit to the restaurant," I said.

"I told Tony . . . Mr. Vittorio . . . that I intended to review the restaurant, so he wined and dined me . . . *us*. Beau and me."

She sounded on surer footing now. Was her weeping an act or was I becoming the suspicious type? When I'd begun working at BARC, I'd given everyone the benefit of the doubt. After a year or so, distrust had invaded my soul. How I wished I could do something about that.

"Why would a killer send me these notes?" Gloria rasped.

"I'll bet the killer didn't send them. As you said, you're a celebrity. What if a fan heard about the murders and is trying to get your attention?"

"He got it all right."

Again, I said, "You need to call the sheriff. Ask for Nick. He's handling both cases."

"I can't, Aspen. Can you imagine the field day the press will have if this gets out?"

How the tables had turned. Gloria was the one who had broken the news about Vikki's murder. I appreciated freedom of the press, but not when that freedom turned into rumors and innuendo.

"I've got a career to protect," Gloria went on. "Camille already thinks I'm attracting bad publicity."

"Who's Camille?"

"Camille St. John. My producer." Gloria drew in a breath. "I want to hire you to find out who this creep is."

"I can't—"

"You have to. It's what you do."

"Finding creeps is not what I do." No, my job was much nobler. I scrambled through garbage for a living and served restraining orders. What would my colleagues from BARC think? Did I care? I'd given up my career as a therapist and become a private investigator so I could help clients solve tangible problems. Gloria had one.

"Please, Aspen, I need you. I know you'll keep it hush-hush."

Fatigue weakened my defenses. I agreed to come to the television station in the morning after my doctor's appointment and discuss the situation. Before ending the call, Gloria blessed me with a dozen *thank-yous*.

I dialed Nick. He didn't answer. Knowing he could sleep through a train wreck, I gave up and crawled into bed, but I couldn't sleep because a disturbing thought was running roughshod through my mind. My aunt had sensed more murders with the same MO would occur. Was she right? Would the murderer kill more people for Gloria's sake?

Chapter 8

At six a.m. Tuesday morning, the alarm clock blared. I awoke with a jolt and realized I'd set the wake-up call early because I had the doctor's appointment and then the meeting with Gloria. In less than an hour, I jogged with Cinder, showered, and threw on a white blouse and jeans tucked into ankle boots. I even donned a pair of gold earrings and a tad of makeup.

When I ventured into the kitchen to fix breakfast, Candace was sitting at the table in her nightgown, the dog nestled by her feet.

"What are you doing up, you goon?" I asked.

"I couldn't sleep. I'm too excited about the beginning of vacation."

"Waverly and her mom aren't coming for two more hours." Candace and her friend were going hiking. "Go back to bed. Get your beauty rest."

"Yeah, okay, you're right." She kissed me on the cheek and skipped to the bedroom with a promise to call me when she re-awoke. Cinder trailed at her heels, her devoted companion.

The doctor's office was located in an unpretentious gray office building across the main highway from Boatworks, a shopping mall in Tahoe City. Other tenants included a realtor and a tax accountant. I parked in the back and returned to the front along a rocky path overrun by alpine dandelions. Temperatures were already soaring. Brisk air-conditioning, unusual for Lake Tahoe and a shock to my system—we prided ourselves on not needing to use the AC—slapped me in the face the moment I stepped inside the doctor's office.

A while later, a starched nurse showed me to a room that reeked of sterile alcohol. I dressed in the two-piece paper gown and waited fifteen minutes until the doctor, whose hair was as white as his attire, walked in. He shook my hand feebly and said in a monotone, "I'm Dr. Coke."

He wished he had that much fizz.

"Aspen Adams."

"Yes, I know."

If I didn't watch out, I was going to fall asleep on the spot.

Coke opened the manila file that he was carrying. "I communicated with the lab, as requested. You do indeed have a lump. It's dense."

I didn't need to pay another doctor to figure that out. The mass felt like a frozen pea whenever I probed it. The paper that covered the examination table crackled beneath my tapping fingers. "Did the lab say whether the lump was benign?"

"I recommend that you have an ultrasound." The doctor turned a page. "We'll get a better idea of what's going on after that."

"Can't you tell me anything now?" Patience was not my virtue.

"It's a small dense mass."

"You already said that." Tension gripped my shoulders. The man hadn't looked up from my file. I bent at the waist and peered at him. "Hello, I'm over here."

His eyes narrowed and the skin on his neck turned splotchy. "I see you, ma'am."

"Please, it's been a trying week."

"Ma'am," he repeated, his indifference palpable, "we have a date open a week from tomorrow to do the ultrasound."

"Nothing sooner?" I couldn't disguise my exasperation.

"If you want answers, you'll have to work within our time frame."

My Irish blood surged to boiling point. How could Dr. Fisher's office have referred this insensitive man? Maybe he was the reason her practice had grown to three hundred patients.

Clambering off the table, I said, "You know what? I'm going to find a doctor with more warmth. Thank you for your time." I tossed off the paper bodice.

Dr. Coke froze, mouth agape. Was he shocked that a patient had the gall to dismiss him or surprised to see me half naked?

"You can leave, sir," I said.

The moment the doctor fled from the room, I slumped into a chair. I wasn't cruel. The man hadn't deserved my wrath. I drew in a long calming breath, dressed, and retreated to the front desk to apologize. The office assistant said nothing and asked for my credit card to cover the insurance copayment.

Head hanging in frustration, I strode to my Jeep. As I was opening the driver's door, my cell phone rang. I whipped it out of my tote and answered.

Candace said rapid-fire, "Aunt Aspen? Waverly's sick. Can I go with you to work? Spending my vacation alone is a bore." I explained that I was on my way to meet Gloria Morning, to which she said, "Please, please, take me with you. You know I watch her show. She's so cool."

I didn't want Candace to stay home alone, so I agreed. Minutes later, I picked her up. She was wearing a black floral V-neck over jeans and carrying a pink zipper hoodie, in case she got cold in the car.

"You look cute," I said.

"Thanks." She hitched her raggedy denim purse higher on her shoulder. "I wanted to dress up a little bit for meeting Miss Morning."

On the beginning of the drive north around the lake, Candace gushed about Rory. He loved to ski. He was super smart. And he was handsome. She particularly liked the way he combed his hair. Sort of like a surfer. I'd heard it all before but I didn't mind. The fact that she was outgoing and not as retiring as she'd been when she'd first come to live with me was a blessing. Halfway to Incline, she drifted to sleep, her head resting against the passenger door.

The silence provided me a moment to consider Gloria's situation. Was the killer reaching out to her? Why? Did she personally know the killer? Was it someone close to her?

KINC, located on the California side of the Cal-Neva border, was the bright spot between two drab buildings. Its dramatic aqua-and-green theme reminded me of the décor in the classic television show *Miami Vice*. Further down the street hung a sign welcoming motorists to Nevada as well as neon beacons encouraging gamblers to visit various establishments. Nothing about the border area captured the beauty of Tahoe or the natural pleasures one could experience while hiking through the woods or spending time on the lake. The district had been designed to grab the attention of risk takers. But the rent was cheap on the California side, where gambling was prohibited, and for a fledgling company like KINC, saving money was a necessity.

I parked on a side street, and Candace and I strolled to the entrance. As was *au courant* these days, a gigantic picture window allowed the passing public to view the news anchors at work on their morning set. KINC's current catchphrase was: *Dare to get up close and personal.* A group of people, some with their noses pressed to the glass, were doing just that, even though no anchors were present.

We entered the lobby. Acting as if she owned the place, Candace crossed to a partition to examine the series of photographs depicting the history of Lake Tahoe hanging on a wall.

To the right behind a blue lacquer desk sat the receptionist, a lithe young woman with a curtain of orange hair and a nose ring. A multiple-line telephone rested inches from the woman's porcelain fingertips. On the turquoise wall behind her hung a three-foot chrome logo for KINC. On either side of that were poster-sized photos of Gloria and her co-anchor, Vaughn Jamison, a chiseled blond in his late thirties who, in my opinion, didn't possess all the mental keys to the kingdom. Could he have sent Gloria the notes? Perhaps he was feeling insecure about his senior position at KINC. Did he hope a scare might unnerve her and make her quit?

I stepped up to the receptionist. "Hi."

"Hey. What's up?" The young woman smiled, exposing orange plastic braces attached to her almost straight teeth. "I mean, what can I do for you?"

"I'm here to see Gloria Morning. My name is—"

The door leading to the studio burst open and Vaughn Jamison stormed past me, his face blazing red, his fists balled. Perspiration marred the front of his cream-and-blue Hawaiian shirt. "Marie, I'm taking the rest of the day off."

"What's wrong?" the receptionist—Marie—cried.

"Everything." Vaughn shot through the exit and veered right.

Marie said, "Sorry about that. Vaughn can be . . ." She mimed locking her lips. "You were saying?"

"I'm Aspen Adams."

"Oh, yeah. Gloria said to keep an eye open for you." She pushed an intercom button on the telephone. "Gloria. Miss Adams is here."

Seconds later, Gloria stepped through the door by which Vaughn had come. She looked sassy in a hot-pink silk dress, her makeup perfect and her hair glistening with a dose of spray. Heart-shaped earrings dangled from her ears. A matching silver necklace glimmered around her neck. "Aspen, I'm so glad you came." She clasped my hands and kissed me on both cheeks.

The receptionist said, "Gloria, Vaughn said he's taking the rest of the day."

"Yeah, yeah. He's in a mood. I'll let him cool down and call him later."

"What happened?"

"He's not happy with me. He . . . Oh, never mind." Gloria turned her attention to me. "Thank you for coming."

I studied her face. A wary strain was evident around her eyes. I said, "I'm sorry to see you under these circumstances."

"Life can't always be chatty lunches." She was referring to our last get-together. She spotted Candace. "Your niece?"

I nodded.

"I see the resemblance. She's very pretty."

"Thanks."

Gloria glided across the green carpet and thrust out her hand. "Candace, I'm Gloria Morning."

Candace beamed as she pumped Gloria's hand. "I know who you are. I like to watch current events."

"Nice to hear." Gloria gestured to a chair near the receptionist's desk. "Why don't you stay out here and chat with Marie."

"I'd rather go with you," Candace said like a conspirator.

"Fine." Gloria gripped Candace's and my elbows. "Marie, hold all calls."

We traipsed down a brightly lit hall until we reached a dressing room with a sign on the door that read *Miss Morning*. Gloria prodded us inside and locked the door with a bolt. Instantly I felt claustrophobic. The room was small and the temperature intense.

"I'm a wreck." Gloria caught a glimpse of her face in the beveled mirror attached to the white dressing table. "And I look it." Frowning, she removed half a dozen dresses from a canvas director's chair and tossed them over the top of a clothing rack filled with suits and silk blouses. "Have a seat."

Neither of us did.

"What am I going to do?" Gloria asked, her voice cracking. She leaned on the edge of the dressing table, palms grasping the rim. "Please tell me you've come up with an idea."

Candace was old enough to hear the full story, so I didn't hold back. "Tell me everything again. From the beginning."

"I don't know any more than I told you last night." With jittery hands Gloria pulled two nondescript envelopes from a white Dolce & Gabbana clutch that was lying on the dressing table. She thrust them at me. "Here."

I donned a pair of latex gloves that I kept in my tote, opened the first envelope, and pulled out the letter, which was typed on a piece of generic white computer paper. A hint of roses clung to the message, suggesting a woman, not a man, might have written it.

> *Dr. Fisher will never hurt you again. I did it for your glory. Keep your heart open for my love.*

"Did Dr. Fisher hurt you?" I asked.

"Of course not." Gloria attempted a smile, but the corners of her mouth twitched with tension. "She was totally professional. After we completed the interview, we shook hands."

"She wasn't your doctor?"

"No."

"Why did you choose to interview her?"

"Camille suggested it. She said the woman had a huge practice, and our viewers deserved to know the latest in women's health."

I reviewed the second note, written on the same nondescript paper—no hint of roses.

> *Tony Vittorio will no longer hurt you. I did it for your glory. Keep your heart open for my love.*

Gloria sniffed. "Like I said last night, Tony Vittorio never did anything to hurt me. What is this about? Why target me?" She nibbled the cuticle on her right thumb, which resembled raw hamburger. Was chewing it a regular thing or had the habit just started?

I shook the paper. "This one was delivered to your house?"

"Yes. The envelope was lying on my doorstep. On the mat."

"How did you spot it?"

"I'd gone out to dinner with a girlfriend. I saw it when I got home at a quarter to eleven. The general public didn't learn about Tony Vittorio's murder until the eleven o'clock news. That's why I know it's from the killer."

Candace said, "Because he had insider knowledge."

Gloria nodded.

"A few others might have known," I said. "Those who stopped to watch what the sheriff's staff were doing. Someone could have tweeted it. Where did you eat?"

"At Sunset. It's near Garwood's. Do you know it?"

I did. It was known for its Pacific Rim cuisine and great view.

"How did the author of the note know where you lived?" Candace asked.

Gloria mewled. "I've been wondering the same thing. I suppose he could have followed me home from work." She wrapped her arms around her torso. "Ever since I've hosted the 'This Is Your Tahoe' segments—"

"I love it when you do those," Candace cut in.

"Thank you." Gloria giggled spastically, like a boat whose engine wouldn't turn over. Jangled nerves were to be expected with a scare. "Ever since then, I've been getting a lot of fan mail. Until now, I'd appreciated the adulation."

The segments highlighted patrons of the arts, restaurants, special interest projects, and interviews similar to the one with Dr. Fisher. I'd seen a number of them. Gloria was incisive, but from what I'd gleaned in reviews of the show, some of her guests had been less than thrilled with the pieces that had aired. That could be why her producer wasn't happy with her.

"Go on," I said.

"Also, a few weeks ago, I wondered whether someone was following me."

"You didn't mention it when we met for lunch the other day."

"And sound like a nutcase? As if."

Candace peeked over my shoulder, trying to read the note. "Miss Morning, I think the word *glory* is a play on your name."

"I thought the same thing." Gloria began her thumb chewing routine again.

I felt for her. Being the target of this kind of campaign could be unsettling. "The sheriff's team is interrogating anyone related to Tony Vittorio as well as Dr. Fisher. Relatives, employees, you name it. I'll tell Nick about the letters you've received." Before leaving the house this morning, I'd phoned him but hadn't reached him, so I'd left a brief message, sans details. "In the meantime, I'd like to meet your coworkers."

"Why?"

"If the author of the note has a crush on you, it could be someone you know. I'll also need to meet your fiancé and your neighbors."

"Beau works here. He's the director of the show."

How did I not know that?

Gloria took the letter from me. "Tell me honestly. Do you think this guy, this *fan*, killed Tony Vittorio and Kristin Fisher?"

"A woman could have written them," I stated.

"A woman? No. Uh-uh." Gloria began to gnaw her lower lip. "You don't think I faked these, do you? Please tell me you don't." There was no guile in her doe-shaped eyes. Only fear. And exhaustion.

"I was thinking your producer might have."

"Ha! Camille wouldn't take the time."

"Who is on-site right now?" I asked.

"Everybody from this morning's taping is around, except Vaughn."

"What happened between you two?"

"I stepped on one of his lines on the morning segment. He said I did it on purpose. He's such a Neanderthal." She glanced at her watch. "FYI, I've got a 'This Is Your Tahoe' segment scheduled at two. I'm interviewing a casino owner."

"Then let's get cracking."

Gloria set the envelopes aside, grabbed a tissue, and wiped mascara from under her eyes. "Follow me."

Chapter 9

The soundstage was huge. It not only housed office cubicles, but it boasted three distinctly different sets. One, a living room–type set, was fitted with a royal blue couch, floral winged-back armchairs, and potted silk plants. A mural of a sunny day at Lake Tahoe adorned the set's wall. On the center set stood a blue lacquer news desk and a pair of hard-backed chairs. The logo for KINC was written in white across a blue tweed wall. Multiple mini-televisions were latched to a metal rod on the left. Beyond the array of TVs, a gigantic white screen hung from the rafters. The rightmost set was decorated like a library, with bookcases and rattan furniture and beautiful pictures of Emerald Bay, the jewel of the lake.

"Wish I had a sweater," I said as we moved deeper into the area. Gel-covered lights glowed overhead, but none offered warmth.

"The temperature in here can freeze an Eskimo," Gloria said. "Want me to send someone to fetch one from my dressing room?"

"No, I'll survive."

Candace threw on her zippered hoodie and wrapped her arms around her torso. She peered overhead and gasped. I followed her gaze. Teetering on one of the catwalks was an older man with winter-white hair. He was adjusting a pair of spotlights.

"That looks dangerous," Candace whispered to me.

"Don't worry. I'm sure he's done it for years."

A woman in overalls with a tool belt slung around her hips passed by us whistling the show's theme music. I admired her dedication.

"Gloria, you're on in thirty," a voice announced through a speaker.

Gloria said, "Aspen, Candace, follow me. I've got to review the questions for my guest, but I can introduce you to a few people before I do." She climbed onto the living room set.

Candace followed her. "What kind of questions?"

"Good ones." Gloria grabbed a notepad that was sitting on one of the wing-backed chairs. Already she seemed more relaxed, as if telling me about her fear had eased the strain. She made a beeline toward a glass-enclosed booth that held bays of audio equipment.

Outside the booth sat two men on director chairs. The one with salt-and-pepper hair reminded me of a scruffy middle-aged pirate, home after a four-month journey; the younger man resembled a choirboy dressed in his Sunday best.

"Hello, Rick," Gloria said.

The choirboy stood, nodded politely to us, and quickly retreated to the other side of the room.

"Rick Tamblyn is shy," Gloria said. "He's our new broadcast technician and audio engineer. Signed on in May." She addressed the pirate. "And this is Tom Regent. Tom, this is Aspen Adams and her niece, Candace."

Tom stood. His chair was marked with his name. "Pleased to meet you." His jeans were tattered and his T-shirt stained. He sported a pack of cigarettes in the rolled-up cuff of his sleeve. His powerful arm muscles flexed as he extended a hand toward me. We shook. He didn't back off on his grip.

"Aspen is an old friend." Gloria smiled warmly. "She's a journalist, and she's doing a piece on, um, television stations."

Candace said, "No, she's—"

Gloria bumped Candace's arm to silence her.

I shot Gloria a look. I knew she was worried about her job and concerned that news about the notes she'd received might jeopardize it, but lying about my profession was unnecessary. On the other hand, who was I to judge? I'd made up plenty of alternative biographies in order to serve subpoenas.

"Get you ladies a drink?" Tom asked.

I eyed the coffee mug in his left hand. He hadn't disguised the vodka very well. During my teen years, without realizing it at the time, I'd lived the life of a detective out of self-preservation because I'd needed to stay aware of when my older sister was high so I could avoid her frightening mood swings.

"No, thanks," I said.

"What do you do here, Tom?" Candace asked.

"I'm a cameraman."

"I love photography."

"Tom is the best in the biz," Gloria said. "He makes me look good."

"Doesn't take much." He winked and elbowed my friend, his devotion to Gloria as obvious as his alcohol-laced breath. How long had he been in love with her? More importantly, would he kill somebody to protect her, even if there were no threat?

"How long have you worked at KINC?" I asked.

"Since the beginning. Me and Camille go way back."

"How far is way back?"

Tom chuckled low and slow. "Camille and me, we gave massages at a ritzy place in Reno, and then the Hyatt in Incline, and then we bought our own spa, and then"—he let the word hang—"about seven years ago, she invested heavily in the stock market and made a killing. That's when we talked about putting this setup together. We both love the news. I'm the brawn. She's the brains and the money."

Gloria said, "Camille lives on Lakeshore Boulevard."

I whistled. Lakeshore Boulevard in Incline Village was expensive real estate.

To Tom, I said, "How long ago did you and Camille break up, if you don't mind my being nosy?"

Tom pursed his lips. "How did you know we were an item?"

"I'm paid to be on the ball."

Gloria regarded me with respect. Obviously, she had been in the dark about Tom and Camille's former relationship.

"We broke up a few years ago. Amicably."

"Of course amicably," Gloria said. "Otherwise, you wouldn't be working here."

"The boss and me, we never lived together. She said she liked separate places. Said we had a sort of Tracy/Hepburn kind of relationship. Truth? We fought like cats and dogs. If we'd have lived together, we would've killed each other."

I winced at his choice of words. Gloria did, too.

"Now that we're working here, with no, *you know*"—he glanced at Candace; I got his drift, no hanky-panky—"things are good between us."

Who had ended the affair? Tom or Camille? Could Camille be carrying a torch for the guy? Did their previous relationship influence Gloria's current situation? Perhaps Tom was trying to make Camille jealous by flirting with Gloria. Even so, I didn't see how killing Tony Vittorio or Kristin Fisher fit the scenario.

Tom said, "Gloria, Finn Ambrose will be here in a few minutes. You ready?"

"Sure am."

"I've got to prepare." Tom grabbed his cup of coffee. "Nice meeting you, Aspen. Candace." He strolled away.

Gloria said, "Mr. Ambrose just opened a casino in South Lake Tahoe. Ambrose Alley. It's ritzy and top-notch with twice as many gaming tables as all the other casinos. We tried to tape the interview in May, but all our equipment blitzed in an electrical storm."

Because of the surrounding ring of mountains and intense heat, huge tempests could crop up around the lake. Hair-raising cracks of lightning, rumbles of thunder, and phenomenal white-capped waves were part and parcel of a spectacular storm.

Gloria turned to Candace. "Hon, you want something to eat? There's a table over there packed with food."

I put my hand at the small of my niece's back and nudged her.

Candace didn't budge. "No, thanks, I'm not hungry."

"Are you sure?"

"C'mon, Aspen, I ate breakfast," she said tartly.

Her teenage patience only had so much elastic. She wanted autonomy. Her therapist had warned her that I might hover for years. I did my best not to crowd her, but no matter how much she blossomed and no matter how much her skin tone improved and the luster of her hair returned, I worried that her battle with food would recur.

"Can I see what Tom's doing?" Candace asked.

Tom was supervising the angling of lights across the room.

"Sure," I said, "but don't get in his way."

Candace hurried off.

"Does Tom often drink during the day?" I asked Gloria.

"Always, but he's never missed work. Actually, he's the most reliable guy here. What I call a functioning alcoholic."

"He's got a major crush on you."

"So do some of the other guys. You'd think they'd never seen a pretty woman." Gloria brushed a stray hair off her face. "Tom's a rare bird. Keeps super busy so he won't drink more than he can handle. He's a dedicated reader, too. He peruses magazines all the time. There are a dozen in that book bag hanging on his chair."

And probably a flask of vodka, I mused.

I watched as Tom showed Candace how to set up the camera. She climbed onto the stage and held his light meter, acting like a carefree kid on a field trip.

"On weekends, he's a spelunker," Gloria continued. "He never drinks when he's exploring caves. Caving, he says, helps sweat out the poisons."

"I visited a few caves near Squaw Valley when I was a teenager. There were old Indian etchings in some of them. Most had bats."

"Yeah, Tom told me there's some rare varieties of bats in the caves near Mt. Rose. Bloodsucking kinds." Gloria shuddered. "You won't convince me to go spelunking. We had bats in my grandma's attic. One time they nested in my hair. I'll never forget—" She shuddered and then waved to someone behind me. "Hey, Beau, come here." To me, she said, "That's my fiancé."

Standing in the opened doorway leading to the lobby was a striking man, the glow from the lobby's bright lights outlining his stalwart form. A hank of straw-colored hair hung into energized eyes. With determined strides he made his way toward Gloria. From the way he strutted, it was obvious he considered himself more man than any woman could hope for.

He grabbed Gloria in a bear hug and kissed her firmly on the cheek. "Hiya, babe."

"Ouch, you jerk, get away." Gloria pushed him back. "What in the heck are you wearing?"

"Jeans."

Almost painted on.

"Very funny. I mean this." Gloria tugged a silver tooled button on his brown-and-white horsehair vest.

"It's a gift from my sis."

"She has no taste."

Beau kissed her again. "That's what she says about you. Who's your friend?" The guy's teeth were as white as Bermuda sand.

Gloria radiated devotion. "Beau, I'd like you to meet Aspen Adams. Aspen, Beau Flacks."

How apropos. His name sounded like a weightlifting machine.

"Pleasure," Beau said, a twinkle in his gaze.

Out of the corner of my eye, I noticed Tom glaring in our direction. Jealousy knew no bounds.

"Aspen is, um, a journalist," Gloria said. "She's doing a piece on television stations, so she's going to be asking some questions around the place."

Beau regarded her warily. "Uh-uh, you're lying." He slung an arm around her shoulders. "What's really going on?"

"Whatever do you mean?" Gloria batted her eyelashes, but she couldn't keep up the ruse under his steady gaze. "Okay," she said, "I'll tell you, but you've got to keep this between us. Aspen is a private investigator. I hired her because I received a couple of nasty fan letters. She's here to do some digging." She pecked his cheek. "Don't let on to Camille, okay? I don't need to deal with her grief."

"Aspen, excuse Gloria and me for a minute, will you?" Beau led her away.

When they were about ten paces from me, Beau said something and motioned in Tom's direction. He wasn't happy. Reading lips, I could see Gloria say *I'm sorry* and *Relax*, and then she kissed him passionately. Appeased for the moment, Beau rolled his neck to loosen the knots and shook out his shoulders. He ushered Gloria back to me.

"Gloria!" a sharp-edged woman shouted. She clip-clopped across the floor in four-inch high heels, her chic pencil skirt squeezing the spa-honed flesh above her knees.

"That's my producer," Gloria said.

Camille St. John possessed the kind of cheekbones a jeweler could cut diamonds on. Her eyes, heavy on ice-blue makeup, were probing. In a sinewy hand that had massaged who knew how many bodies, Camille was carrying an envelope. She thrust it at Gloria. "More fan mail for you."

Gloria's body tensed. She didn't take the envelope. "Who's it from?"

"Does it appear to be opened? No, it does not. The girl with the spiky purple hair delivered it." Camille forced it into Gloria's hands and crossed her arms, which were a perfect bronze without a blotch of imperfection. Hard to maintain in middle age. "Is the script for the interview ready on the teleprompter?" Camille asked Beau.

"Yes, ma'am."

"Don't ma'am me, bozo." Camille turned to me. "Who are you?"

"Aspen Adams." I offered a warm smile. "I'm a friend of Gloria's. I'm a journalist doing a piece on television stations."

Camille cut a look at Gloria. "Did I know about this?"

"I cleared it with you weeks ago," Gloria stated. Man, she was quick on her feet.

"Fine." Camille fingered her short white-blonde hair. A barbed wire tattoo encircled her left wrist. Interesting. My sister had the same, inked on after serving six months in jail. "Finn Ambrose is in the green room," Camille went on. "He's been to makeup already, not that he required any. He's such a handsome man. Go. Now."

"On it." Gloria kissed Beau on the cheek and scurried away. "Aspen, follow me."

As we passed her dressing room, she stepped inside and tossed the letter onto her dressing table.

"Aren't you going to open it?" I asked.

Chapter 10

"I'm scared. If it's bad . . ." Gloria flapped a hand. "I don't want to mess up this interview. Afterward, okay?" Before I could argue with her, she said, "Follow me," and hurried from the room. She stopped in front of a door marked *Green Room* and knocked. "Mr. Ambrose, we're ready for you."

A man in his fifties with steel gray hair opened the door. He wore a gray linen suit and a plum silk shirt, unbuttoned two buttons, no tie. His skin was a warm brown. Tanning booth or natural, I couldn't quite tell. He clenched a toothpick between his teeth. "Miss Morning, what a pleasure to see you." He tossed the toothpick into a nearby garbage can, licked his dentist-bleached teeth, and clasped Gloria's hand.

Gloria blushed, a coquettish reaction I hadn't expected from someone who had earned a bachelor's degree in sociology and a master's in political science at Stanford University. "I'm so sorry we had to cancel our first session. The darned storm—"

"No problem." Ambrose straightened the three strands of gold chains around his neck with manicured fingers.

"Are you ready?"

"Let me get my son." He yelled into the green room, "Tripp, let's go."

A brown-haired, feebler version of Finn Ambrose exited the room. Like his father, he wore a linen suit, but he was underweight and his freckled skin was pasty. Had he been confined indoors for a long stint?

"Tripp, this is Gloria Morning. Miss Morning, my son, Tripp."

Gloria said, "We've met. So nice to see you again. If I recall, you're into American history."

"Ye-es." The young man stuttered ever so slightly. "And art. I make lamps." He seemed transfixed by Gloria. I wasn't surprised. The effect she had on men, both young and old, was astonishing.

"Follow me," she said, neglecting to introduce me. I understood the oversight. She was engrossed in her role as hostess.

I trailed them across the soundstage to the library set. Camille asked Finn Ambrose to take a seat in one of the wing-backed chairs so she and Gloria could go over the schedule with him for the interview. Finn Ambrose asked her to give him a moment. His cell phone was buzzing. He had to take the call. She directed him to her office cubicle and suggested Tripp get something to eat.

Tripp ambled to the food table and grabbed a bagel. As he was slicing it, Candace sidled up on his left. Tripp accidentally poked her in the ribs with his elbow. She *eek*ed and he immediately apologized.

"My fault," she said, laughing. She picked up a bagel and introduced herself.

Instantly, the younger Ambrose's tentative manner changed. Female attention, even teenaged attention, seemed to put him at ease. His words came freely. Living in his imposing father's shadow had to be a chore.

Knowing I had a few minutes before Gloria's interview began, I wandered around the soundstage, taking note of the various racks of film equipment and storage rooms while trying to ascertain where the various coworkers were situated. The white-haired man on the catwalk had disappeared. So had the woman in overalls. Tom was brushing dust off a camera lens with a chamois cloth. Rick Tamblyn had joined Gloria on set and was fitting her with a microphone pack.

Inside the booth, Beau was fiddling with audio equipment. Rick left the set, entered the booth, and nudged Beau, who nodded good-naturedly and ceded his spot.

Camille paced the newsroom set, her forehead pinched. Since the "This Is Your Tahoe" segment wasn't live, I didn't understand her anxiety. Mistakes could be fixed and another electrical storm wasn't in the forecast.

"Tripp," Camille barked and beckoned him with a finger.

Tripp had moved away from Candace and was standing near the office cubicles. Was he trying to listen in on his father's conversation? He hurried to Camille. "Yes, ma'am?"

"Fetch my stopwatch. It's on my desk." She gave him directions.

Like a happy puppy, he trotted off, passing the senior Ambrose as he exited Camille's cubicle.

Finn Ambrose joined Gloria on set and sat in the designated chair.

Mouth moving, Gloria gazed at the twelve-inch screen perched atop Tom's camera. I'd worked on the live news in high school and recognized that she was reading her script as it scrolled beneath the monitor.

Over a loudspeaker, Beau said, "Ready, babe?"

"Just a sec," Camille said. "Tripp!" The young man hustled to her and handed her the stopwatch. "Ready, Beau," she yelled. "Tom, don't mess up. Gloria, if you're done with your princess routine . . ."

Finn Ambrose frowned.

Gloria cut Camille a withering look. "Ready," she said, sitting tall.

"Let's put one down." Camille twirled a hand at Beau.

Gloria said, "Aspen, you and Candace take a seat over there. Tripp, you can join them if you like." She pointed to a trio of director's chairs, each marked with the word *Guest*. "Tom, do your magic." With the calm of a seasoned pro, she patted Finn Ambrose's knee. "If you don't like what I ask or you don't like how you answered, let me know and we'll reshoot."

He smoothed the front of his silk shirt. "Ready."

Gloria spoke into the microphone that Rick had fastened to her lapel, "We've got clips of Mr. Ambrose's casino, don't we, Rick?"

Over a speaker, he said, "Yep, we've got great footage." I'd expected his voice to be squeaky. Surprisingly, it was a vibrant, confident baritone. Maybe he really was a choirboy. Out of nowhere, I recalled an adage my childhood pastor had often invoked: *Busy hands keep a man from doing the devil's work.* Was Rick Gloria's protector? Had he authored the note?

"And we're on in five, four, three . . ." Beau's voice trailed off.

"Welcome to 'This Is Your Tahoe.'" Gloria smiled into the camera like it was her best friend.

A live display of the interview appeared on the screen to the set's right.

"Today, my guest is Finn Ambrose, proprietor of the fabulous new casino, Ambrose Alley, located in South Lake Tahoe. Mr. Ambrose—"

"Finn, please." The man grinned magnanimously.

"Finn, you've never owned a casino before. Why start now?"

He opened his hands and refolded them. "Well, I've had multiple successes in the restaurant and hotel business. I decided doing both on a grand scale was the way for me to go at this time in my life."

"Why Lake Tahoe?"

"Can you imagine a more beautiful place to set my new venture?"

As Gloria skillfully led Finn Ambrose through a dialogue about his career and the travails of casino ownership, Tripp slid his chair closer to Candace.

I said to Tripp, "Your dad is coming across great."

"He always does. He's very aware of his image," he added, a trace of bitterness in his tone.

"How old are you?" Candace asked.

"Eighteen."

"Are you getting ready to go off to college?" I asked.

"No. I've been sick. I'm taking classes at Lake Tahoe Community, until, you know, I get caught up."

A prolonged illness would explain his pallor.

"What were you sick with?" Candace asked.

"It doesn't matter. It's over. I'm healthy now. I won't look like an albino bat for much longer." He chuckled.

I said, "Gloria mentioned you're studying American history."

"Yeah . . . well, no. I was thinking about history as a major, but now I'm thinking I'll build hotels, so I'm taking some art and architecture classes. I work at the casino, too. Dealing cards."

I balked. "Aren't you a little young to—"

"Are you good at cards?" Candace cut in.

"I've got good hands." Tripp lowered his gaze and studied his fingers. "Plus I can remember four decks of cards without breaking a sweat, and I always know who's got what. My mother could do the same."

Gloria raised her voice, drawing my attention back to the set. She splayed a hand. "Here's a preview of the glamour and pampering you can expect at Ambrose Alley."

As a prerecorded reel began, Gloria leaned toward Finn Ambrose. "We'll be cutting in a preview of the inside of the restaurant at this point, too."

"Hope you got a shot of my new executive chef. What a find he is.

With a terrific track record." He winked slyly. "Between us, I stole him from Vittorio's Ristorante."

My ears perked up.

Gloria blanched. "Tony didn't mention that to me."

"Tony didn't know. His brother can keep a secret."

Had Finn Ambrose hired Enzo Vittorio? If so, how come Enzo didn't mention his new job to Detective Hernandez or to Nick at the crime scene? Was that what he'd been grinning about?

"Finn, I . . ." Gloria swallowed hard. "I guess you didn't hear."

"Hear what?"

"About Tony Vittorio."

Tripp leaned toward Candace and whispered, "Dad hates Tony Vittorio. They've owned rival restaurants for years."

"What about him?" Finn asked Gloria.

"Tape's rolling," Beau announced.

"I'll tell you after," Gloria said, bad news to be delivered at another time.

"And back in three, two . . ." Beau's voice trailed off.

With gusto, Gloria dug into the next segment. She teased Finn about his choice of décor, which she explained were antiques from a French bordello mixed with Native American artifacts.

Tripp said, "My mother despised my father's taste in furniture. She didn't like anything cheap. Her side of the family, the Virginia City Vogels, came from money."

Why was he referring to his mother in the past tense? I wondered if she had divorced his father, abandoned the family or, worse, died. Perhaps grief had made him ill.

"What do you think of the décor, Tripp?" Candace asked.

"It's red." Tripp shrugged. "My father loves red stuff. I'm partial to the Native American artifacts. I'm part Paiute Indian."

Candace studied his face. "You don't look it."

"Only half. On my dad's side."

"Tell me about them."

"They were bloodthirsty," Tripp replied.

"Bloodthirsty?" Candace shuddered.

"Yep. They attacked white settlers as they moved into the Tahoe area during the 1800s. They were always at odds with the Washoe Indians over territorial rights, and when the settlers came, they were tenacious. But they lost, and by 1860 the Paiute lineage pretty much dried up. The Battle at Pyramid Lake, which is northeast of here, was the final blow."

The young man knew his history.

"A few gentler souls left the tribe and blended with the newcomers. They're my ancestors."

"Wow," Candace said. It was one of her favorite words.

"Dad inherited all sorts of arrowheads and hides from one of our relatives."

I studied Finn Ambrose and wondered about his Paiute heritage. Had poaching a chef from Vittorio's Ristorante not been enough for him? Did he kill Tony Vittorio to eliminate the competition? If so, what might link him to Kristin Fisher?

Chapter 11

My cell phone vibrated in my jeans pocket. Nick was calling. I moved away from the set to answer.

"Hi," he said. "Got a minute?"

"Are you returning my call?"

"What call?"

"I left you a message." Occasionally, spotty reception made it impossible for a cell phone to record or retain messages. "What's up? Did you get your Wrangler back this morning?"

"I did and it's purring. Listen, I'm at the Truckee Hospital."

Memories of Candace struggling for survival six months ago flashed through my mind. The image invariably made me tense up. "And?"

"Heather Bogart was right. The scalpel that the murderer used was stolen. It turns out the hospital is the source. An employee does daily inventory and one is missing. Detective King is cross-referencing a list of staff and patients at the hospital with the list we compiled for the doctor."

"And if the murderer wasn't an employee or patient?" From where I stood, I could see Candace and Tripp whispering and giggling as if they were old friends. "What if the killer was a visitor or a supplier?"

"Good thought. I'll check those names out, as well." Nick sounded exhausted. "Where are you?"

"At KINC watching Gloria Morning conduct an interview."

"Why?" Nick asked, an edge to his voice. He didn't like Gloria. Not only because she'd covered Vikki's murder as a newspaper reporter. He also didn't appreciate her on-screen manner. Her delivery was too perky for his taste.

"Gloria is why I left you the message." Briefly, I told him about the two notes she'd received and the fact that she'd hired me to delve into it. "Nick, the letters suggest that the Fisher and Vittorio murders are related. Gloria interviewed both people in recent weeks."

"Are you sure the letters are legit and Gloria didn't write them to herself?"

I exhaled. I supposed I ought to consider that angle even though she swore she didn't. "They seem real."

"Okay."

I hated how tentative he sounded, as if discounting my instincts. I pressed on. "Have you heard of Finn Ambrose?"

"The restaurateur and hotel chain owner."

"Yes. He has opened a new casino in South Lake Tahoe." I told him how Finn Ambrose and Tony Vittorio were rivals and that Ambrose had poached the executive chef from Vittorio's Ristorante. "He didn't outright say Enzo Vittorio's name, but there's only one executive chef. Remember how Enzo smirked at you and Detective Hernandez, like he had a secret?"

"You saw him smirk. I didn't."

"He did. Maybe Enzo and Finn Ambrose conspired together to kill Tony Vittorio."

"Interesting theory."

When I returned to my chair, Gloria was concluding the interview. Candace and Tripp, suffering a lapse in their conversation, were watching quietly. As I sat there, I considered the recent letter Gloria had received. Even though Nick hadn't mentioned a third murder, I itched to read it.

"Thank you, Finn Ambrose." Gloria turned toward the camera and offered a brilliant smile. "And thank you Lake Tahoe for watching 'This Is Your Tahoe.'"

"That's a wrap," Beau announced from the recording booth.

Camille clapped. "Good show, everyone." She approached the set, hand extended. "Thank you, Mr. Ambrose."

He rose and took her hand in both of his. "The pleasure was mine."

Camille's cheeks reddened.

Rick tended to Ambrose's microphone and Gloria removed hers.

"Finn." Before he could retreat to the green room, Gloria caught up to him and put a hand on his arm. "Earlier, when you mentioned Tony Vittorio—"

"Tony, Tony, Tony," Finn said. "The restaurant business is a tough one. If he knows what's good for him, he should expect me to poach his chef. If he paid him better—"

"Tony Vittorio was murdered last night," Gloria blurted and glanced at me and back to Finn.

"What?" Finn clapped a hand to his chest. "Murdered? How?"

"Stabbed."

"This is terrible news. Horrible."

Gloria's lower lip quivered. "I didn't want to tell you during the interview."

"Do the authorities know who did it?"

"Not yet."

"I can't believe it." Finn shook his head. "Tony was a dear man with a great wit. He will be sorely missed."

Tripp joined his father. "You okay, Dad?"

"I just received tragic news, son. A friend of mine died." Finn took Gloria's hands in his. "I'm glad you didn't tell me earlier. I wouldn't have been able to finish the interview. You were wonderful, by the way. Keeping that tragic information to yourself and pressing on. Amazing. What do they say in show business?"

"The show must go on," she chimed.

"That's it. You were a consummate professional." Finn started for the exit but turned back. "Please come by the casino anytime. I'll comp you and a guest for dinner."

"Goodbye, Miss Morning," Tripp said.

"Goodbye, Tripp." Gloria pecked his cheek.

I spotted Beau in the booth. He wasn't happy with Gloria's exchange with the Ambroses. Just outside the booth, Tom was ogling Gloria, too, while twisting his camera cord into a knot. Working on a set with adoring men had to be a challenge. I didn't know how Gloria managed it. But then she hadn't, had she? One of her ardent fans might be a murderer.

I rushed up to Finn Ambrose. "Sir, before you go, could you spare a minute? I'd like to ask you a few questions."

"About . . ."

Gloria blanched. "Oh, Finn, I forgot to introduce you. This is Aspen Adams. She's a journalist, and she's—"

"She's not a journalist," Tripp cut in. "She's a private detective. Candace told me. She used to be a therapist, but she gave that up and moved here. She lives in the Homewood area, and she went to Stanford University. And she's part Washoe."

I glared at my niece. She shifted feet. We'd have to discuss what information was and was not privileged.

"Is that true? You're a PI?" Finn Ambrose asked me.

"Yes." I raised my chin, proud of my profession.

"If you want to question me, shall I presume it's about my relationship with Tony Vittorio? I didn't kill him, if that's what you want to know. And I'd love to tell you more about our prickly history"—he offered a winsome smile—"however, right now isn't a good time. I have an appointment at my casino in a half hour. I'm already running late. Perhaps you could come to my office and we could converse there." He patted my shoulder as if I were a good puppy and strode toward the exit. "Tripp!"

An uneasy feeling crawled up my spine as I watched Finn Ambrose and his son move toward the exit. If he thought exonerating himself of murder before I could even ask a question was a wise choice, then he didn't know me very well.

Without so much as a *pardon me*, Camille butted past me and took hold of Finn's arm. She escorted him and his son to the lobby while gushing about the wonderful interview he'd given.

Gloria raced to me and guided me toward her dressing room. Over her shoulder, she said, "Candace, honey, we'll be back in a sec." Once we were inside the cramped quarters, Gloria said, "So what did you think?"

"Of?"

"Finn Ambrose. Isn't he chic? And so successful."

How could I tell her that I was contemplating whether the guy was a murderer?

Dodge and deflect, I decided. "Let me see the letter Camille gave you." I donned my latex gloves and held out my hand.

"It's probably harmless." She grabbed it off the dressing table and thrust it at me.

It was a plain white envelope with Gloria's name typed to the front and a piece of hair stuck under the flap. "You said you've received lots of fan mail."

"They're all under here. In a bin. You know"—she rummaged beneath the dressing table—"I think you're right. The other notes might have nothing to do with the murders. Some kook sent them to me looking for prime-time coverage." Gloria spoke as fast as her tongue would allow. The stress she was trying to mask was evident around her eyes. "Fifteen minutes of fame and all, right?" She rose. In her hands were at least fifty envelopes, each slit neatly across the top. "None of these are offensive." She dumped them on the top of the dressing table, found a fresh mini-garbage bag, and loaded them into it. "You can take your time reading them." She handed me the bag. "But don't lose them."

"Gloria, we'll figure this out. If I have to call in the sheriff, I will. And I'll be back to ask questions of everybody who works here. I'd like to spend some time with each employee. Alone. That includes your co-anchor, Vaughn Jamison."

"Are you kidding? He's passive-aggressive. Milquetoast."

"He didn't look very passive-aggressive when he marched past me earlier, although a passive-aggressive person might write letters like the ones you received."

"But Vaughn wouldn't kill."

"I'm not certain the author of the notes is a murderer," I said, reiterating Nick's reservations.

Gloria flicked a finger. "Read the one you're holding."

Using a nail file sitting on the dressing table, I opened the envelope and pulled out a sheet of standard bond paper. As I unfolded the sheet, Mylar stars fell out. The note was typed but a young hand had written the signature.

> *Dear Miss Morning, I love your show. You are the greatest. I love to see you smile and laugh. Don't ever change.*
>
> *Sincerely,*
> *Brittney, age eight*

"What does it say?" Gloria asked.

I read it aloud.

"That's so sweet." There were tears in Gloria's eyes as she chewed on her already ragged thumb. "See? So many are like that. Why did that horrible person send the others?"

Why, indeed?

I stowed the two letters from the anonymous admirer as well as the newest letter into the garbage bag with the others and laid my hand on my friend's shoulder. "Put some vitamin E on your thumb. It'll heal in a week."

"Will do."

I gave her a hug and asked if she was going to be okay.

She nodded and sank into her makeup chair. "Beau will make sure I get home safely."

Beau. God's gift to women. Was he to be trusted?

When I went to retrieve Candace, she was chatting animatedly with Tom Regent. The rest of the crew had vanished. As I drew near, I heard Candace asking Tom about camera angles, lenses, and the best equipment. In her arms, she held a number of DVDs in jewel cases.

"Where'd you get those?" I asked.

"Camille let me borrow them. They're last month's shows. I missed a lot of them because of school." Candace's gaze grew tentative. "It's okay, isn't it? I mean, we can return them any time, Camille said."

"Sure. It's fine." I turned to Tom and thrust out my hand. "It's been a pleasure."

He shook with me and patted Candace on the back. "Great daughter you have. She's just like you. Pretty and inquisitive."

"I'm her aunt."

"My apology. You look so much alike."

"I'll take that as a compliment."

"Yes, ma'am, and hey, if you want to ask me more questions, you go right ahead." Tom cocked his hip to one side, striking a casual pose.

"Okay, where were you yesterday around three or four in the afternoon?" Might as well address his alibi for the Vittorio murder first.

His gaze cut up to the right. "Let's see. I was getting exterior shots of Ambrose Alley around that time."

"By yourself?"

"Yes, ma'am."

"You and Gloria are on good terms?"

"The best."

"How do you feel about Beau?"

"An adequate director. Bit of a blowhard."

"Did you know Dr. Kristin Fisher?"

"Only via the interview." His forehead creased. "Anything else?"

"No, not for now," I said, because honestly I couldn't figure out his motive. Yet.

I wrapped my arm around my niece's shoulders and led her out of the studio. The glare of sunlight hurt my eyes. I started to perspire. The heat index must have risen ten degrees since we'd gone into the studio. "Boy, it's hot."

"No kidding." Candace shrugged out of her hoodie, climbed into the Jeep, and flung the DVDs on the rear seat. "Air-conditioning. Please."

I tossed the bag of fan mail into the backseat and skimmed the DVD titles. Most were marked with dates in April and May and a few from June. Could Gloria's interviews of Tony Vittorio or Kristin Fisher be among them? If so, would I find something that suggested either of them had harmed Gloria? What if their interviews were so awful that the ratings had fallen? I stifled a bitter laugh. Lousy ratings would not have been the reason Gloria's admirer would have killed two people. If the notes were to be believed, the killer had assumed the role of protector, intent on excising a malicious person from Gloria's life.

My goal was to identify the culprit and stop the madness.

Chapter 12

Candace twisted in the passenger seat, her face flushed and eyes pinched. "Are you mad at me, Aspen?"

"What? No, of course I'm not. Buckle your seat belt."

"As we were leaving, you glowered at me. You reminded me of Mom for a second."

I winced. The last thing I wanted to do was to come across like Rosie. How I wished I could clock my sister for how she'd treated her daughter.

"I'm not mad. I'm concerned. We have boundaries about what we're allowed to tell people. You didn't know Tripp longer than ten minutes, and yet you gave out all sorts of personal information."

"I'm sorry." She worried her hands in her lap.

As we drove past Vittorio's Ristorante, a number of people were standing on the shoulder of the road taking photographs. My stomach knotted. Would curiosity for the macabre always lure onlookers? How I hoped his murder would be the last for a long time, and my aunt's premonition about more murders was wrong.

My cell phone jangled. I pressed the button on the steering wheel to answer. "Hello?"

"Aspen! You. Won't. Believe. It." Gloria's voice spiraled upward. "You just won't!"

I peeked at Candace. Her eyes were as wide as an owl's. I said, "What happened? Are you okay?"

"I'm fine. But a whole string of lights and gels fell. Like a hailstorm. There I was sitting on the set, reviewing my notes for tomorrow's schedule, and suddenly lights were crashing. Everywhere. And electricity was sparking."

"Are you hurt?"

"No, I jumped off the set so they missed me, but they were heading straight for me." Gloria gulped in a series of quick short breaths. "Aspen, the murderer is after me. I'm sure of it."

"Calm down. Did anyone see what happened?"

"Camille. And Beau. And Tom. Beau railed at Camille for skimping on chintzy equipment. Tom, too. Camille shouted that it was an accident and stormed out. Then Beau and Tom left."

"I thought Beau was going to see you home."

"Turns out he had a doctor's appointment. I'm not sure where Tom went."

So much for the men in her life standing by her side.

"Are you alone at the studio?" I asked, wondering if I should make a U-turn.

"Yes, well, no, that's not true. I'm not *alone* alone. Marie is at reception. And Rick is cleaning up some technical stuff. But I'm alone in my dressing room. Aspen, you've got to help me." Her voice quavered with anxiety.

"Attacking you doesn't make sense, Miss Morning," Candace said, raising her voice to be heard. "The person who wrote the notes doesn't want to hurt you."

Gloria said, "Do you think he wanted to kill someone else? Camille was on the set right before me. What if he wanted to kill her for my glory?"

I shivered.

"Aspen, please find out who's doing this. Please. I'm going to leave here and see my therapist. And I think I'll hire a bodyguard for tonight. Bye." Gloria ended the call.

"She can be quite dramatic," Candace said.

True, but was she overreacting now? I didn't think so. I'd seen the notes. And how in the heck had equipment fallen on the set? Had the white-haired man rigged it? What about Rick or Tom? One of them must have overseen the placement of the gels and such.

"You've got to tell Nick what's going on," Candace said. "He should—"

"I know what he needs to do," I snapped and instantly regretted my tone. "I'm sorry. I shouldn't have brought you to the studio today. You don't need to worry yourself with Gloria's problem or with murder."

"I'm a big girl. I can handle it."

She was a big girl. Just not big enough.

"Sweetheart, I want to find more things for you to do this summer in case your friends cancel. How about camp? There's a wonderful sleep-away camp called Walton's not far from here. It has horseback riding and hiking and lots of girls your age go to it. I went there as a girl. I'm sure I could—"

"I'm too old for camp."

She was right. The kids her age would already be counselors-in-training. "Okay, in the meantime—"

"If I go on an appointment with you, I have to act as professionally as you do. Got it." She smacked her thigh. "And a PI never reveals anything to anybody except to the authorities or to her client. Ever."

I chuckled. "You've read Aunt Max's handbook."

"I blew it today, but I'll learn. Promise. If Gloria wanted us to pretend that you were a reporter, we needed to do what she wanted. I said *we* because you and I"—she motioned between us—"we were a team the moment we entered the . . . Aspen, watch out!"

I swerved out of the way of a bare-chested man in a swimsuit trying to run across Highway 28 as we neared Magic Carpet Miniature Golf. "Jerk," I muttered.

Candace twisted in her seat. "Hey, since we're a team, I've got some opinions about the people who work with Gloria if you want to hear."

"No, thanks." I didn't want Candace dwelling on the case. To be honest, I didn't want to brood over it myself.

Candace crossed her arms and pouted. The teenager sulk, I'd dubbed it when working at BARC.

Reluctantly, I said, "Okay, talk. I'll bet you have good instincts."

Candace faced me again, her eyes gleaming with pride. "Tripp's nice."

"He doesn't work with Gloria."

"He's sweet," Candace went on, "but he's pretty immature for eighteen. Tom's cool. I mean, Mr. Regent."

"Why do you think he's cool?"

"He didn't treat me like a kid. He took time to explain."

Tom seemed nice enough, but I was pretty sure an angry sea raged inside him. Plus, he had a serious crush on Gloria. Did he kill two people for her *glory*? Why? What was his motive?

"I don't like Miss St. John," Candace said.

"She loaned you the DVDs."

"She did it to make me think she's nice, but she's a phony." Candace pulled a lip gloss from her purse and dabbed her lips. "And she's too buff."

I cut Candace an amused look. "You have no idea how much work it takes for a woman in her forties to keep fit. I'll bet she devotes hours at the gym to look that good."

"Hah! You mean to look that hard."

Was Camille strong enough to wrestle Dr. Fisher into submission or overpower Tony Vittorio? She couldn't be taller than five-foot-five, but she had been a masseuse, which meant she was strong.

"What did you think of the director?" I asked.

"Beau? He's full of himself, and it was super obvious that he didn't like Tripp's dad one iota. He's like an open book."

I felt the same. Beau had won Gloria's heart. Was he afraid of losing it? Did he question her loyalty because she flirted unabashedly with other men? Had he killed to regain her undivided attention? The notion made me shudder.

As we neared the Placer County Sheriff's Office, North Lake Tahoe, a gray building that housed not only the sheriff but also the superior court, jail, and district attorney's office, I thought of Nick. He was skeptical that the notes were truly linked to the murders. We needed to talk.

I pulled into the station's parking lot. It was empty except for a sedan and a couple of SUVs, none of which were Nick's Wrangler. On the off chance the Wrangler was back at the body shop and Nick was in, I suggested Candace stay in the Jeep and I traipsed inside.

A narrow hall faced reception, which also doubled as the records office. A bulletproof window, inset with two metal speak-thru grills and two slots beneath the window for depositing things like IDs or payments, divided the foyer and the office. To the left, through a glass door, was an L-shaped foyer that served as the waiting area for superior court.

The reception/records office was arranged with large horizontal case file drawers, a set of floor-to-ceiling wooden cubbies, and a cubicle fitted with oak desks and more filing cabinets. In addition, there was a gigantic bin for documents due to be shredded and corkboards with announcements posted to them. My favorite thing in the office was the note affixed to the inbox: *This is the* only *inbox*.

To the left, out of view, was the jailer's office. Straight ahead was the door leading to the jail and other rooms on the lower floor, including a large kitchen and the evidence room. Unseen stairs led to the second floor, where the captain, lieutenant, detectives, and deputies had their offices and held their briefings.

A freckle-faced clerk who preferred to go by her last name, Zook, approached the bulletproof window. "Hi, Aspen. Help you?"

"Is Nick in?"

"Sorry, no."

"I have something pertaining to the recent murders that I'd like him to see."

"You can leave whatever it is with me."

I didn't feel comfortable releasing Gloria's notes. I worried they might get lost in bureaucratic paperwork. "I'll hold on to them for now. Thanks. Please tell Nick that I stopped by."

"Well?" Candace said when I climbed into the driver's seat. She was keeping rhythm on the dashboard with rock music so loud that even the avid fan would go crazy. "Was Nick there? Is he putting our tax dollars to work?"

I turned down the music. "I hope so."

Chapter 13

When we arrived home, Candace retreated to her room to play a video game. I fed Cinder, poured myself a glass of wine, and set about making dinner. While seasoning the spaghetti sauce, I thought about Nick. How were he and his team doing on finding the killer or killers? Should I call him and invite him over? He loved my spaghetti.

As if fate were listening in on my thoughts, the telephone rang. Nick was on the line.

I set the oregano aside and answered. "You've been busy. Want to come by for a bite? We can catch up."

"Wish I could. I'm taking my sister to an AA meeting."

I'd met Natalie a couple of times. She lived with Nick and worked at Safeway. She'd been sober for over a year. Taking care of her as dutifully as he did was one of the many reasons why I loved him.

"Anything new on the murder investigations?" I asked.

"Nothing I can share." Nick stifled a yawn. "Anything new with your note writer?"

"Gloria's scared. She feels she's being stalked." I told him about the gels and lights falling.

"Didn't you say the notes were written by someone who wants to protect her?"

"The light fiasco could have been aimed at her producer, I guess." I explained why and then gave him my take on Gloria's coworkers. Camille St. John was domineering. Beau was full of himself. Rick Tamblyn was meticulous to a fault. Vaughn Jamison was a passive-aggressive type, ready to erupt. And Tom Regent was an enigma.

"Sounds like you have a full roster of suspects, Sherlock."

"Don't make fun."

He chuckled half-heartedly. "Do any of them have motives for either murder?"

"I haven't figured that out yet. If I leave you the notes, will you take them seriously?"

"Yes."

• • •

In the morning, although I felt bleary-eyed and wrung out from nightmares peppered with falling lights and paper cuts, I ran my usual six miles with Cinder. A blistering hot shower helped recharge my brain. A brisk rub with aloe lotion revived the rest of me.

On the way to the kitchen, however, I caught a glimpse of myself in the antique mirror in the hallway. Dull eyes, limp hair. The brown Earth Day T-shirt I'd donned over my beige capris wasn't helping.

I quickly changed into a red shirt—wearing red always enhanced my mood—and then rapped on Candace's door. "You awake?"

In spite of her protestations about my needing to entertain her daily, I'd contacted Waverly's mom and set a date for today. My house; my rules. Waverly was on the mend. The girls would go shopping and then to a late lunch and an early movie.

I rapped again. I didn't hear any movement. "Candace?" I opened the door and saw her lying facedown on the guest bed, covers kicked off, feet hanging over the end. I rushed to her. "Sweetie, are you okay?"

"Huh?" Candace turned her head toward me. Her face was creased with wrinkles from her pillow cover but her color was good. She wasn't ill.

I breathed a sigh of relief. Would I ever get past the worry that she'd revert to her old habits of purging or starving herself? I said, "Time to rise and shine. Waverly and her mom will be here in an hour."

I fed Cinder and ate a protein bar while keeping an ear out for Candace. By the time she emerged a half hour later, she looked happy and clear-eyed and ready for a day of fun.

As I drove to work, I thought again about the link between Gloria and Dr. Fisher and Tony Vittorio. Why did the murderer think the victims would hurt Gloria? Would Heather know whether Gloria and Dr. Fisher had clashed?

I phoned Dr. Fisher's office. Heather answered. She sounded distracted, upset. I would be distressed, too, if I had to manage an office where not just a murder but the murder of my mother had occurred. Under the pretense of needing another doctor—Coke was a bust—I asked Heather for a new referral. She provided one.

I was about to ask her about Gloria, when she blurted, "Edward"—her voice caught—"Bogart."

"What about him?"

"Would you check on him? He's staying at the motel in Tahoe City. The American one."

"America's Best?"

"That's it. He came to town to meet with the sheriff and to handle the funeral."

My heart ached. "When will that take place?"

"In a couple of days. Mother wished to be cremated. No mourners. No fanfare. You understand."

I nodded. Many people wanted privacy on such occasions.

"Would you check on him?" she went on. "We don't have the best relationship, but I'm worried about him."

How could she have a good relationship with a man who'd basically disowned her?

"Please," she begged.

I agreed.

"Thank you. Bless you. If that's all."

"Before you hang up," I said, "may I ask you a question?"

"Yes, I'm taking care of my mother's dog. That nice detective said you were worried about him."

"I'm glad to hear that, but that wasn't my question. It involves a patient or a possible patient, so if telling me anything conflicts with your confidentiality agreement—"

"I didn't have one seeing as I was the boss's daughter. Mom was lax that way."

"Was Gloria Morning a patient?"

Heather gasped. "Is that who you're working for? Miss Morning?"

"Yes."

"She wasn't a patient. Not ever. She came in that one time to interview Mom, and then my mother went to the studio to do some *pick* things. What do you call them?"

"Pick-ups."

"Yes. She was very nice. Very professional. She came with a cameraperson."

"Tom Regent?"

"A young man. Very proper."

"Rick Tamblyn."

Heather giggled. "Yes, that's the one."

"Did your mother and Gloria argue or clash in any way?"

"Not that I know of. Like I said, it was all very professional."

After thanking her and ending the call, I couldn't help thinking about what she'd told me. Rick had met Dr. Fisher. Was that significant?

...

As I made the turn onto North Lake Boulevard, I got in touch with Edward Bogart using the cell phone number Heather had given me. No use dropping in unannounced. I explained who I was and asked if we could meet. He agreed.

The motel had looked the same for as long as I could remember: L-shaped, white with green trim, and clean. Though the doctor probably could have afforded a ritzier place, he might not have been able to secure one. From Memorial Day to Labor Day, Tahoe properties were booked.

As I locked my Jeep, I caught the savory scent of lunch preparations at the Mexican restaurant next door. My stomach rumbled in protest. A protein bar and cup of coffee were not enough to carry me through the day. I would fix that after the meeting.

Approaching Edward Bogart's room, my hunger pangs were replaced with apprehension. Was the man a killer? Was meeting him alone a mistake? Nick maintained that Bogart had a solid alibi. On the other hand, he was an adept surgeon who knew his way around scalpels. Could he have driven the distance from Reno to Lake Tahoe in the wee hours of the morning and killed his ex-wife while the child he'd operated on was in recovery?

For Gloria's sake, I pressed on. When he admitted me, I would leave the door ajar. No one, however clever, would kill me in broad daylight while people roamed the parking lot.

When Edward Bogart opened the door, I breathed a tad easier. He was the human equivalent of a mayonnaise sandwich on white bread: white hair, pasty skin, and bland expression.

I introduced myself.

"I have ten minutes." He gestured for me to enter and then moved further into the room and perched on the edge of the bed.

As planned, I left the door open and took one step inside. "Sir, as I stated on the telephone, Heather asked me to meet with you."

"Why?"

"She's worried about you."

"Why?"

Man, he was stony. "Because your ex-wife died."

"What do you do, Miss Adams?"

"I used to be a therapist."

"But you're a PI now, isn't that true?"

"Yes." Heather must have given him a heads-up.

"Are you investigating my ex-wife's murder? If so, I've already spoken with the sheriff's office. I was in surgery the night Kristin died. Heart transplant for a seven-year-old."

"I heard he lived. Congratulations."

"*She.*" He massaged his slender hands as if they were dough. My ex-husband had done the same before and after conducting his brilliant orchestra. His hands were his life. "You have questions, Miss Adams. Ask them, but remember I'm in a hurry."

Though my only promise to Heather was to make sure her ex-father was okay, his icicle-worthy demeanor made me want to dig deeper. Questions about motive scudded through my mind. "Sir, according to Heather, you're mentioned in your ex-wife's will."

Bogart stopped kneading. "Correct. I stand to inherit a portion of her estate. She was supposed to have changed her will years ago but didn't. She wasn't a fan of money. She was forgetful about it. I've arranged with the estate lawyer to give the whole lot back to Heather."

If so, that would be a noble gesture.

"I care for Heather, despite what she may think," he went on. "I left her mother because—"

"Heather said you expected too much of her. She couldn't rise to the occasion."

Bogart's mouth puckered as if he'd sucked lemon juice. "I can be quite stern, expecting perfection even from a girl as young as Heather was then. I was not an ideal father."

"You renounced the adoption."

He sighed. "Not my finest hour."

At least Bogart recognized his shortcoming.

"Heather could benefit from that admission," I said.

"We'll see."

"One question before I go. Do you know Gloria Morning?"

He stood up, arms loose by his sides but hands clenched. "I was mistaken earlier. You aren't investigating Kristin's murder, are you?"

If I expected him to be truthful, I ought to be, as well. "No, sir. If I misled you about my intent, I apologize. I represent Gloria Morning, a news anchor for KINC. She has received notes from someone we believe to be Dr. Fisher's killer."

"Don't know her. Don't watch the news. If there's nothing further." He moved to the door and stood with his hand on the knob.

The moment I stepped outside, Bogart closed the door and locked it. I bit back a laugh. Had he expected me to bust back in?

Once I was situated in the Jeep, I rang Heather and told her about the encounter. She was sincerely grateful that I'd reached out to him. I assured her that he was fine. He wasn't pining for her mother. I also assured her that he was innocent; he had a solid alibi. Lastly, I advised her that he was planning to cede his portion of her mother's estate to her. I suggested she reach out to the estate attorney to move that along.

Chapter 14

Later that morning, after setting a new doctor's appointment for the middle of next week—it was the earliest she could accommodate me—I drove to KINC. I found Gloria in her dressing room, pacing with nervous energy. "A detective from the sheriff's office came by. Hernandez."

Good. Nick had taken the situation seriously.

"He checked out the lights and gels and determined the cables were naturally frayed. Due to wear and tear. They weren't cut. It was an accident." She flitted from her bathroom to her dressing table to the clothes rack, where she checked the buttons and zippers of each of her jackets and blouses. "He suggested I might be overreacting to the letters. Because you have them, I couldn't show them to him."

"I'm going to deliver them to the sheriff's office later on. Let's see what they say after they view them."

Gloria whirled around. "Beau thinks I'm hallucinating about everything." She resumed chewing on her ragged thumb.

"You're not. I've seen the notes." I'd dealt with plenty of feverish patients at BARC. Repeatedly, their families explained reality to them, but Gloria wasn't making anything up. I reached over and pulled her finger from her mouth. "What's going on, Gloria?"

"Nothing. I—" She tittered. "I . . . I got another note." She lifted a piece of white, eight-by-eleven paper and opened it so I could read it.

Dear Miss Morning, You are so beautiful.

"That's it?"

Gloria screwed up her mouth.

"There's no signature," I said. "No threat. No promise of protection. It's another fan letter. Pure and simple."

"The paper is the same."

Sure, the weight of the paper felt similar—all computer paper did—but I didn't detect a hint of roses.

"Aspen, I feel like I'm going nuts. I—" Gloria held her finger to her lips and then jerked a thumb toward the dressing room door. I'd left it open an inch when I'd entered.

Something squeaked in the hallway. Was someone eavesdropping on our conversation?

Suddenly, the door to Gloria's dressing room swung open and Rick poked his head in. Collared shirt. Freshly shaven. "Ten minutes, Glo." He disappeared as quickly as he came.

Gloria let out a high-pitched giggle. "I'm ridiculous, aren't I, seeing spies around every corner?"

Spies, falling lights, and notes. Alarm signals blared in my mind.

The door swung open a second time, and Vaughn Jamison strutted inside. "Hey, hey, hey." He balked when he saw me. "Oh. Didn't know you had a visitor. I'll come back another time."

Gloria stiffened. Was she afraid of Vaughn? Dressed in a bright yellow Hawaiian shirt plastered with huge yellow parrots tucked into blue jeans, he looked tame. No flare-up on the horizon like yesterday. Was it possible he was bipolar and not passive-aggressive?

"How's your car?" Gloria asked Vaughn. To me, she said, "Two tires blew out on his SUV on the way to work."

"The body shop gave me an estimate," Vaughn said. "What do you think a paint job for a Chevy Suburban costs? Five k." He held up one hand, fingers spread.

"That's steep," I said. "What happened?"

"I skidded along a building and scraped off the paint. Barely held it together. Glad I didn't take out any tourists. Also glad they still stock the color Tahoe blue." He peered at me. "Who are you?"

"Forgive me. I'm a terrible hostess," Gloria said. "Vaughn Jamison, this is my friend Aspen Adams."

As we shook, I was struck by how devoid of energy he was, which made me wonder how he was able to drum up the oomph to perform on camera.

Gloria said, "Aspen is investigating the letters the murderer sent." To me, she said, "I let Vaughn read the one about Tony Vittorio."

"And touch it?"

"Of course not." She pouted, hurt that I'd even think that.

"It was innocuous," Vaughn said.

"Do you happen to get the same kind of fan mail, Mr. Jamison?"

"One promising to protect me from harm?" He snorted. "As if."

"Did you know Tony Vittorio?"

"Knew of him. Never visited the restaurant."

"Was your wife a patient or former patient of Dr. Fisher's?"

Vaughn offered a cockeyed grin. "What is this? The third degree?"

Gloria said, "Answer her questions."

Vaughn hooked his thumbs through the loops of his jeans. "My wife is a lawyer with barely enough time to breathe."

"She sees a gynecologist, I presume," I said. "According to the few articles I've read about you and your family, you have children. Two boys, if I'm not mistaken."

"Both delivered in Fresno, California," he snapped, his calm exterior cracking ever so slightly.

"Vaughn's wife is a saint," Gloria said. "How she puts up with him and his ego is beyond me."

His face tinged red. Was she goading him on purpose?

He stowed his anger and said, "You have aspirations, too, Gloria. Don't play coy. You're hoping for the *Today Show* or *Good Morning America*. Heck, we all want national exposure, don't we?" He held out a fist.

Gloria fist-bumped it, but her spirit wasn't in it.

"I have to go. I need to review tonight's news." He jutted his chin at the door. "It's been real, Miss Adams."

As contentious as Vaughn and Gloria's relationship seemed to be, I couldn't imagine him sending her love notes promising to protect her. Making lights crash down upon her was a likelier prospect, but I didn't have a moment to consider that notion because Tom Regent rapped on the doorframe.

"Gloria, got a sec?"

I wondered how she tolerated the open-door policy.

"Miss Adams," Tom said, "what a nice surprise."

"Can't talk, Tom," Gloria said. "I've got to prepare. You understand." She prodded my shoulder. "You, too, Aspen. I'll call you later. After the taping, I have to run right out. I have a Skype meeting with my agent in LA."

I exited with Tom. When Gloria locked the door, I chuckled. Apparently she did need privacy.

Tom stared at the door, a hurt expression in his eyes. "I know you're not a reporter, Aspen"—he ran a finger under the collar of his blue T-shirt—"so if you want to ask me more questions about Gloria and this note thing and the murders, go right ahead."

The *note thing* was obviously no longer a secret. Okay, I could work with that.

"Did you write the letters, Tom?"

"Ha! I like how direct you are. Nope. I'm not a writer."

"Where were you last Friday morning?" I asked, probing to find out if he had an alibi for Dr. Fisher's murder. I couldn't determine his motive, but if he were the killer, I'd figure it out eventually.

"Depends what time. I get up around five. I'm here by eight. In between I eat, read the paper, watch the national news, and go caving."

"I heard you were a spelunker."

"Yep."

"Did you go caving with anyone?"

"I'm a solo act."

So his alibi was iffy.

"What do you know about the note Gloria received pertaining to Dr. Fisher?"

"Ho-ho. Coming at me from all angles." Tom ran his hand along his jaw. "I don't know anything except it's written on white computer paper. I don't even know when she got it."

I'd forgotten to ask Gloria about the delivery of the first note and made a mental note to follow up. "How about the lights that fell yesterday, Tom? They almost struck Gloria. What do you think happened there?"

He yanked his hands from his pockets. "That was an accident."

"You left shortly afterward."

"For a dentist appointment. Man, having a tooth extracted sucks. Anything else you want to ask me?" He shifted feet. "If not, I've got to get back to work."

"That's all for now."

As I watched him go, I replayed the lights falling scenario. Camille had been on the set seconds before Gloria. Had she been the target and not Gloria? Had Tom set the incident in motion?

No, Hernandez determined it was an accident. Case closed.

Or was it? I flashed on Camille handing a fan letter to Gloria yesterday. She said the spiky-haired girl had delivered it—*the* not *a*. She'd recognized her, meaning the girl had delivered something before. Was it possible she had dropped off the first note regarding Dr. Fisher? Was she the killer's accomplice? Did the killer want Camille out of the way so she couldn't identify the delivery person?

• • •

On the way home, with the late afternoon sun blazing through the windshield, I dialed Gloria's cell phone. I wanted to find out how and when she'd received the first letter. She didn't answer. The call went to voice mail.

Next, I checked in with my aunt. She didn't have any tasks for me today and told me to have a nice evening with my niece.

Seeing as Candace wouldn't be home until after the movie, I swung by the sheriff's station. Zook informed me Nick was in the field with Hernandez and King. I handed the two notes Gloria had received to her. She promised she would personally carry them to Evidence to preserve the chain of custody.

Minutes later, as I was making the turn south on Highway 28, my cell phone rang. Candace was on the line. Hands-free, I answered.

"Aunt Aspen!" Candace cried. "Cinder is all right, but you have to come home right now."

Adrenaline shot through me. "What do you mean he's all right? What happened?" I stepped on the gas, bypassing slower drivers.

"Someone . . . Someone . . ." She slurped back tears. "Waverly's mother is here. She—" Candace moaned.

"Put Wendy on the phone," I ordered.

"Aspen," Wendy Winston said in a forced neutral tone, "everything is fine. Someone played a cruel trick on your dog. He's scared and shaking, but he's okay."

Driving like an Indy racer, I sped south toward Homewood. As I veered onto my street, a dark blue SUV barreled at me and forced me to the side. Dust kicked up. My tires screeched. I slammed on the horn, as if that would do any good. The SUV disappeared.

Regaining the road, I tore ahead and into my driveway. Wendy had parked her RAV4 near the cabin.

I sprang from the Jeep, heart hammering my chest, and yelled Candace's name.

"On the back porch!" more than one female shouted.

I tore around the side of the house and sprinted up the rear stairs. Candace, in denim shorts and crop top, was lying on her belly, hand extended beneath the bench to the left.

Wendy, who was as tall and curly-haired as her teenaged daughter, said, "Cinder's huddled under there and shivering with fear. He won't come to me. There's a dead squirrel—"

"And flies. It stinks," Waverly said.

"Cinder is tied to the bench," Candace hissed, not moving from her spot. "I think if he moves, he'll choke."

I crouched down and assessed my dog. His paws were curled beneath him, his eyes wide with fear. The squirrel was pinned in place by wire. *Poor Cinder*. No creature wanted to lie beside something dead.

"Hey, fella, it's okay." I kissed Candace on the head and said, "I've got this. Stand up."

She scrambled to her feet.

Using a gentle voice, I extended my hand to the dog so he could smell me. "I'm going to untie you, fella. But first I'm going to get this squirrel out of here, okay, buddy?" I peered at my niece. "Candace, get me a garbage bag and a pair of garden gloves and wire cutters."

She darted away and returned in seconds, letting the screen door slam behind her. She shoved the items at me. I slipped on the gloves and, doing my best not to inhale, cut the wires, and then removed the squirrel, shoved it into the garbage bag, and tied a knot. I flung the bag and gloves and wire cutters to the right to eliminate the stench from the area and reached under the bench again. I swatted at the lingering flies; they dispersed. Then I scratched Cinder's ears.

"Okay, boy, here we go." I untied the knots on the rope—not nautical or professional; just knots—but if he moved an inch, he would choke. The whole scenario was disgusting. Diabolical. "I need your paws, buddy." Worming my hands beneath him, I freed one paw and then the other. "Time to act like a marine, Cinder. Inch out on your belly. Let's go."

As he wriggled his way free, my blood boiled with anger. Who had tormented him? In the past few months, crime had crept into the neighborhood. Not violent crime. Petty stuff like painted street signs and toilet-papered trees. Attacking my dog was the last straw. I would patrol the roads and forests nightly, if necessary, to make the area safe again.

I sat up and patted my lap. Cinder climbed into it and let me stroke him. As I checked his body for bruises, the notion that the attack might have been personal scudded through me. Had someone hurt him to scare me because I was helping Gloria? Tom? Vaughn? Beau? I shook off the unsettling notion and nudged Cinder to a stand. "C'mon, boy, let's go inside and get you some water and a treat."

While he lapped water in the kitchen, I thanked Wendy and the girls profusely.

Candace said, "We were on our way to the movie, but I remembered I didn't bring a sweater, and you know the theater. It's so freaking cold. So we came home and . . ." She was prattling. I couldn't blame her.

The doorbell rang. I hurried to the foyer. Cinder trotted beside me.

Nick and Detective Hernandez were standing on the porch. Nick's Wrangler was parked at an odd angle in the driveway. "Candace called," he said, his tone tense. "Is Cinder okay? What happened?"

Words poured out of me. "The dog was tied up. With a rope that didn't belong to me. A rope that might have choked him if he moved. There was a dead squirrel, too. Cinder was beside himself. I'm wondering if this has something to do with Gloria and the notes and me investigating. Does the killer know where I live? Did he come here to torment the dog so he could get me to back off?"

"Phil," Nick said to Hernandez, "go around to the back porch. Check it out."

Candace popped from behind me. "I'll show you, Detective." The Winstons joined her.

As they disappeared, I led Nick into the kitchen. "Want some coffee?"

"I'll pass. I've been downing caffeine for hours." He bent to pet Cinder, who, by the expression on the dog's face, was experiencing the sixth level of Nirvana. He adored Nick. "He seems fine."

"He'll have nightmares."

Detective Hernandez tapped on the porch window and beckoned Nick.

"Anything?" Nick asked.

"No discernible footprints. No tire tracks."

Candace said, "It's like it was a ghost."

I shivered.

Nick caressed my shoulder and said, "We'll canvass the area. We'll find whoever did this." His promise sounded lackluster.

Before he exited, I said, "Wait. Did you get the notes I left at the station for you? The ones Gloria received."

He shook his head.

"I gave them to Zook. She took them to Evidence. Check them out and let me know what you think."

Chapter 15

Candace didn't go to the movie with Waverly. She didn't want to leave the dog's side. Dinner was a somber affair for the three of us. Throughout the meal of hastily thrown together grilled cheese and soup, Candace and I didn't talk much. Cinder rested his chin on the thigh of whichever of us spoke. At bedtime, Candace asked to sleep in my room. How could I say no?

When the alarm clock shrieked Thursday morning, Cinder lumbered to his feet. I was relieved when I didn't find any lingering bumps or bruises around his neck—the rope had been so tight—but I didn't think he needed to run. Neither of us did.

I showered to clear the cobwebs. As I was zipping my chino shorts, I heard a metallic crash. I dashed down the hall. Candace was in the kitchen on her knees in her nightgown dealing with scattered spoons, forks, and knives and an upside-down drawer.

"What's going on?" I asked.

"I'm a klutz." She laughed. "I'm nervous about graduation."

"Graduation," I cried. "It's tonight!"

"Yep."

"I can't wait." I helped her pick up the silverware.

When everything was back in place, she said, "Is it okay if Waverly and I go river rafting today?"

"Of course. But we have to be dressed and ready to go by five o'clock."

"Got it. Um . . ." She gazed at the floor.

"What's wrong?"

She lifted her gaze to meet mine. "I realize having me out of school is a burden."

"No, it's not, sweetheart." I hugged her and stroked her hair. How could I put into words what I was feeling? I loved having her in my life. I adored her energy and her wit. However, if I were to admit it, yes, I was overwhelmed by the responsibility of caring for a teen. Instant mom. There were no courses for that. I needed to make more time for her.

Cinder padded into the kitchen and nudged Candace.

"Hey, fella. You look good." She scratched his ears. "What about him?"

I gazed at the dog.

"If you're worried about him," she said, "he could go next door to Opal's while you're working. She adores him. Her mom's there, too." My neighbor was a gifted crafter who worked out of her home.

"Great idea."

"Can I go online until Waverly shows up?" She grabbed an apple from a bowl on the counter. "I thought I'd check out Paiute Indians."

"Why?"

"Tripp Ambrose got me interested. You know I like learning about the history of Lake Tahoe."

"Okay, but don't believe everything you read online."

"Gotcha."

"And you have to eat more than an apple."

"Promise." Candace stopped in the doorway and turned back, her face pinched with worry. "Whoever hurt Cinder won't do it again, will he?"

I shook my head. The gesture felt hollow.

...

I didn't leave the house until Cinder was safely situated at the neighbor's and Candace was in the car with Waverly and her mother. The drive to Incline, with the beautiful view of the lake on my right, eased my jangled nerves.

When I entered the detective agency, my aunt offered me a cup of coffee. I didn't want it. My stomach was sour. Not to mention the temperature outside was already eighty-five degrees. By midafternoon, the weatherman had promised a surge to one hundred. I was glad I'd donned a short-sleeved shirt and shorts.

Max set the coffee down and handed me a photograph and a memo with a name on it. "Today's job: serve this guy." Then she gave me a skinny folder.

"So much for 'Hi, how are you?'" Quickly, I recapped what had happened to Cinder.

"Why didn't you bring him here?" she asked.

"The cats."

"Bother. They'll adjust. I'm the boss. Next time . . ." She laid a hand on my shoulder. "Not that there will be a next time. How are you?"

"Shaken." I sighed. "Lake Tahoe isn't proving to be the relaxing environment I'd hoped for."

"You're not here on vacation."

"I know. I suppose it's like working at Disneyland. If you see what's behind the magic, then the magic is gone."

"Exactly." She directed my attention to the folder. "Back to work." She never let me have a pity party for longer than a few minutes. I appreciated that. Wallowing wasn't good for the soul.

I read the label on the folder: *Northwest Construction*, one of the firm's biggest clients. "What did the guy do?"

"He didn't do anything. He's an accountant for one of Northwest's competitors and has intel that the competitor's CEO was skimming. They go down, Northwest's stock goes up. Loyal to the company, he would like to bow out of a deposition. Deliver this subpoena by the end of the day. You can find him on Thursdays at this gym." She handed me another memo. "That's all I have." She swept past me, her lavender muumuu swishing as she moved. No idle chitchat, no discussion.

An hour later, after researching crime in Lake Tahoe to see if there were other dog-versus-squirrel incidents—there weren't—I stepped outside, prepared to do Max's bidding. To my dismay, a herd of reporters and camerapersons waylaid me by my Jeep. Each reporter shoved a microphone in my direction.

"Miss Adams, can you tell us about the letters Gloria Morning is receiving?" asked a blonde.

"Is it true that Gloria Morning hired you to investigate?" asked the woman next to her.

"How long have you been an investigator?" a third reporter asked.

An oversized man in work shirt, jeans, and boots hustled into the group and knocked me against the side of my car. I tumbled to my bare knees, scraping the right on the pavement. Shoot. So much for thinking I was smart to have worn cooler clothing. The man tore off before I could get a good look at him.

"Does anyone know who that was?" I asked.

No one did. The guy climbed into a navy SUV and ground it into gear. I couldn't make out the license plate. Was it the same guy who'd run me off the road last night? Had his attack been intentional?

I shook free of the paranoia—lots of people in Tahoe owned blue SUVs. Most likely the guy—an overly eager reporter—was embarrassed that he'd plowed into me. I threw up both hands, done with the onslaught. "No comment. Everyone, shoo!"

With blood trickling down my leg, I climbed into my Jeep and sped off. I'd administer first aid later.

• • •

While hanging outside the gym in Reno waiting for the accountant to emerge, worry coursed through me. Who had written the notes to Gloria? Who had scared my dog? Had the guy who'd shoved me into my Jeep done so as a warning? I touched base with my neighbor to check on Cinder. She told me he was merrily playing with her beagle.

The glass door to the gym swept open and I spotted my target, a world-weary man dressed in a cream-colored suit. He made a beeline for the parking lot.

I ran after him and yelled his name. He peeked over his shoulder, confirming he was who I believed him to be. Quickly, I thrust a document into his hand. "You've been served."

"You can't do this."

"Yes, sir, I can and I have."

He shook his fist and cursed me, but he pocketed the subpoena.

Job completed, I climbed into my Jeep, tended to my knee injury, and then drove back to the office. On the way, I thought of Nick. Had he reviewed the notes yet? If so, why hadn't he checked in with me?

I telephoned the station. He wasn't in. I tried his cell. The call went to voice mail. I hung up.

As I was passing Vittorio's Ristorante—the restaurant had yet to reopen—I noticed dozens of people swarming the area. Some were taking photos of the building. Some had spread out on blankets in the parking lot and were serving up picnics. The ghoulish scene made me shiver. I was ready to step on the gas when I caught sight of Enzo Vittorio smoking a cigarette while answering a KRNV newswoman's questions.

Curiosity getting the better of me, I pulled to a stop. After all, Finn Ambrose had recruited this guy for his casino's restaurant and yet Enzo hadn't mentioned it to the sheriff. Had Nick or his detectives questioned either man since I'd realized the connection?

After parking along the road, I climbed out of my Jeep and gazed at Enzo. His brother had died two nights ago, yet he didn't appear to be outraged. He seemed composed and in his element. I supposed time, even a few days, could dampen one's outrage.

Not far from the duo, a middle-aged cameraman was chatting with a redheaded reporter for KTVN. A cluster of people in swimsuits stood nearby, craning an ear, trying to glean whatever gossip they could. I drifted toward the throng.

The cameraman said, "I heard this place underwent all sorts of reconstruction due to the fire six months ago."

The redhead nodded. "Get this. Tony Vittorio had a fistfight with the owner of Tahoe Bistro across the street. He accused him of starting the fire."

I eyed the bistro. Like Vittorio's, it was only opened nights. Its parking lot was empty.

"Bistro Guy swore he didn't and countered that Tony was stealing customers," the redhead continued.

"Bet you didn't hear this," the cameraman said, lowering his voice. "Tony's widow was having an affair."

Was everyone on a first-name basis with Mr. Vittorio, or did murder make everyone feel they *knew* the deceased?

"With whom?" the redhead asked.

The cameraman whispered the answer.

"No way," the redhead said.

"*Way*. Tony wanted to destroy him."

"Stop these lies!" Enzo Vittorio shot his arms into the air and stomped toward the KTVN team.

Oho. So the man did have emotions. He wasn't an automaton.

"Have you no respect for the dead?" Enzo bellowed. The reporter he'd been chatting with followed him. "My brother was an honorable man, and his widow is a saint."

"Did you hear who Tony Vittorio wanted to destroy?" I asked a zaftig woman in a summer cover-up.

"That hotel mogul, Finn Ambrose," the woman said out of the side of her mouth. "He and Tony used to be partners in a restaurant. Didn't you see the news this morning? Ambrose was on channel eleven. He claimed he and Tony broke it off and opened their own restaurants, and then Tony tried to damage Ambrose's business by using a smear campaign, discounting the quality of the products he used and such."

Whoa. Did Finn Ambrose kill Tony Vittorio in retaliation? Maybe he hoped by getting ahead of the story he could establish his innocence.

"Couldn't have happened to a nicer guy," the woman added.

"You don't like Finn Ambrose?" I asked.

The woman sneered. "He's as pretty as a peacock and just as arrogant, if you ask me. And his casino is unfair to its gambling patrons." She thumped her chest. "I should know. I lost a fortune there last night."

Before I could ask her if she meant the casino's staff cheated, she called to a woman carrying a cooler and hurried toward the public beach.

Why hadn't Finn Ambrose given Gloria the scoop about Tony Vittorio's smear campaign? Was he worried she would nail him about having an affair with Vittorio's widow? If that rumor were true, perhaps Finn killed Tony so he could marry the widow.

Except, why would he have sent Gloria a note saying he was killing *for your glory* if he was in love with another woman?

Chapter 16

As I drove to Tahoe City, I reflected on the facts I'd gleaned so far. Finn Ambrose and the dead restaurateur had been rivals. A rumor was circulating that Finn was having an affair with the restaurateur's widow. Did he murder Tony Vittorio so he could marry the widow? If the same person committed Vittorio's and Fisher's murders, as the letters to Gloria indicated, was it possible Finn Ambrose had a connection to Dr. Fisher? Had his ex-wife been a patient? Did I dare ask Heather to reveal another confidence? She had access to the doctor's patient list.

Yes, I had to. I owed it to Gloria.

I contacted the office and asked Heather if I could drop by. She said of course.

When I strolled into the office, I nearly heaved from the intense odor of Lysol. Heather must have scrubbed every inch of the place. Her face was blotchy and puffy from crying. She removed a scarf from her hair. "I must look a wreck."

"Why didn't you hire a cleaning crew?" I asked.

"I wanted to do it. For my mom."

"Have you visited the therapist I mentioned?"

"I did. I really like her. She's says crying is normal. She wants me to join a grief group. I'm not a group-type person, so I told her I'd think about it. She did blood tests and put me on medication. She says I might be suffering from depression, which is normal after a shock." Heather held her hands out. "Aspen, I don't want to take medicine all my life."

"You won't have to. She wants to stabilize you. Take the full dose until you see her again, and then map out a plan, okay?"

She nodded. "Hey, what happened to your knee?"

It had swollen and was throbbing, but the bleeding had stopped. The couple of bandages I'd applied were holding. "It's fine. I fell."

"I'm so sorry."

"Listen, Heather"—I faltered; how bold could I be?—"the reason I came in today is I'd like to see a roster of patients."

Heather's face clouded. "I can't show it to you."

"I don't want to see their files or any of their diagnoses. Just their names. It might help my client, Gloria Morning." I told her about the notes Gloria had received.

"You think one of my mother's patients is the murderer?"

"Or someone related to a patient."

"The sheriff went through the list already."

"I'd like to have fresh eyes on it, if you'd let me. Just the names," I reiterated.

Heather slipped out of the room and returned with a printout six pages long, each page containing alphabetized names, last name first, in two columns. As Nick had warned, there were over three hundred patients.

I scanned it. None of the names of Gloria's coworkers—Jamison, St. John, Flacks, Regent, or Tamblyn—were on the list. Next, I searched for Vittorio. Zilch. Ambrose was also a bust. I sighed. What had I expected, a flashing neon sign? Okay, if I were truthful, I'd held out hope.

Reviewing the list a second time, I noticed what could have been a misprint. "Heather, this patient"—I stabbed the paper with my finger—"Camille John."

"Oops. That's a mistake." Heather placed a hand on her chest. "It should read Camille St. John. The program I used must have considered the *St.* a middle name. She should be listed in the *S*'s or removed entirely. She's no longer a patient. She found another doctor over a year ago."

"Camille suggested that Gloria Morning interview your mother."

"Yes, I believe she did."

"So there was no bad blood between them?"

"Bad blood?"

"Was Miss St. John healthy?" I asked.

"She's a vegetarian. She—" Heather blinked, her eyes widening in understanding. "Oh, I see. You want to know whether she would have blamed my mother if she had misdiagnosed something female-related pertaining to Miss St. John? Let me check." She withdrew a file from the shelves and flipped through it. She frowned. "Miss St. John is, um, unable to bear a child, but I doubt she would have blamed my mother for that. The file says she had known her situation for years."

I gave up on the connection to KINC employees and said, "Without revealing any names"—I didn't want Heather to get in legal trouble—"could you tell me whether any patient had a miscarriage or died in your mother's care?"

Heather searched her memory. "There was one accidental death because of anesthesia. The anesthesiologist is under investigation for that one, not my mother. There was one preemie death, but that couldn't be helped. Its heart hadn't formed." She tapped her jaw. "There were two miscarriages, but both of those women got pregnant afterward. No reason for them to hold a grudge against my mother. Miscarriages are common."

I reviewed the list of names one more time and, except for the fact that Camille St. John had been a patient, discovered nothing new. I thanked Heather and headed out.

The moment I reached my car, I recalled that Heather's last name didn't match her mother's. Hers was Bogart; her mother's was Fisher. How many on my suspect list had sisters with different surnames or wives who'd retained their maiden names or mothers who had remarried? The number grew exponentially.

I dialed Gloria. When she answered, after a brief hello I launched into my questions. "Was Tom ever married?"

"I'm not sure."

"Does he have a sister or mother or significant other who lives in the Tahoe area?"

"I don't know. Why?"

"I'm trying to find something to link the Vittorio murder to the Fisher murder and wondering if someone who had a beef with Tony Vittorio might have had a loved one who was a dissatisfied patient of Dr. Fisher's."

"Tom didn't have a beef with Tony Vittorio."

"Right." I pressed on. "What's Beau's sister's name?"

"Stacy. Simmons. They're twins. She lives in Arizona."

I jotted down the information. The surname didn't sound like one I'd seen on the doctor's list, but I didn't have a photographic memory.

"Beau didn't have a beef with Tony, either."

"Beau might have been jealous of him."

"Jealous? Don't be ridi—"

"Gloria, he's territorial. If he felt Mr. Vittorio was hitting on you—"

She sighed. "Beau is not a killer."

"Rick was your cameraman at Dr. Fisher's interview. Do you know if he—"

"Rick." Gloria snorted. "He couldn't hurt a fly. He saves spiders and releases them into the wild."

Was she going to rebut every theory I had? "Did you know Tony Vittorio and Finn Ambrose were rivals?"

She snorted again. "Get out of here."

"Ambrose gave an exclusive to channel eleven earlier and said Tony Vittorio used smear tactics to try to destroy the reputation of one of Ambrose's restaurants."

"Channel eleven?"

Was that her only takeaway from my news?

I told her I wanted to meet with her tomorrow and suggested that she review her datebook, her list of acquaintances, and her past relationships, searching for anyone who might harbor a deep passion or hatred for her. She agreed.

After setting the time, I ended the call and sat idling in the Jeep wondering why Gloria had mocked all my theories and why she hadn't known about Finn Ambrose's contentious relationship with Tony Vittorio. Hadn't she done her homework? She was nothing if not thorough.

Was there something else she was hiding?

Chapter 17

An hour later, I picked up Cinder at Opal's and walked him home. He was happy and content. So why did I feel like I was a bad pet mother? Because the sight of him trapped beneath the porch bench would haunt me for a long time.

When Cinder settled onto his pillow, I addressed the pain in my knee. After an ice pack and a couple of Advil dulled the pain, I sat down at the makeshift office in the dining room to review email and quickly realized the one thing Candace hadn't done this morning was turn off the computer—a requirement. Worse yet, she hadn't logged off the Internet. Typical teenager. While I prided myself on being open to technology, I valued an individual's right to privacy and worried about creeps that hacked into computers.

To be safe, I accessed Candace's account—one of our agreements—and reviewed her incoming emails, which included a few from museums as well as generic sites offering free ebooks. One email from *Rorycrazyman* caught my eye. So did the last entry, *TrippA*. Candace hadn't mentioned exchanging email addresses with Finn Ambrose's son. I opened the email and breathed a little easier. Tripp had shared a list of websites for Paiute Indians. Nothing more.

I logged off, stood up, and stretched.

Cinder, knowing my work was complete, scampered in circles, then sat and lifted his paw. I offered him a dog biscuit, which he wolfed down, and we headed out for a short walk without a leash.

Whenever I hiked in the fragrant woods, I breathed easier, imagining myself living in the time when my Washoe ancestors experienced Lake Tahoe free of tourists. For ten minutes, I relished the calm, until a squirrel leaped from a tree and Cinder took off after it, yapping as the rodent scrambled up the side of another tree. *So much for peace and quiet*, I mused, but I was happy that my dog, after his horrific experience, was not terrified of the critters.

On the way home, I noticed a carving at the base of a tree—an Indian with a spear standing over a female lying flat on the ground. A shiver ran down my back. Candace had told Tripp that we lived in Homewood. Had he shared that information with his father? Did Finn Ambrose, worried that I might figure out his connection to the murders, track down where I lived, taunt my dog, and leave the carving as a warning to back off on my investigation?

Ridiculous. How could he be certain that I'd pass that particular tree? I shook my head. Paranoia, as they say, lived in all of us.

Paranoia aside, however, when I returned to the cabin, I decided to take Mr. Ambrose up on his offer to get to know him better. I set an appointment to meet the next day.

•••

At half past four, Candace rushed in. "I'm home."

"You're cutting it close." I was already dressed in my aqua blue sheath. I ticked a to-do list off on my fingers. "Shower. Hair. Dress. In the car in thirty."

"What about Cinder?"

"He's going with us. The ceremony is outside. No one should have qualms about him accompanying us."

On the drive to school, Candace begged me to let her go with Waverly and her father to Virginia City tomorrow. They were going to take the Pony Express tour. Her excitement was infectious. How could I say no?

Graduation went off without a hitch. Candace had worn the yellow summer dress we'd bought last week. With her hair blown dry and a touch of lip gloss, she sparkled. In the procession, Waverley, because her surname was near the end of the alphabet, was situated as far from Candace as possible. She, too, had worn a summer frock. A week ago, the girls had chatted to make sure they didn't buy the same dress or, heaven forbid, a dress of the same color. Rory was not present. He had gone on a short vacation with his family and would return tomorrow. It was the only time his father could get away. Candace confided that a travel memory was more important to Rory's parents than an eighth-grade graduation ceremony.

Cinder was the perfect gentleman, sitting by my side without a yip or a bark. Nick slipped in just as the procession began and apologized that he couldn't stay long. He and Detective King had a lead on the Vittorio murder. Max attended along with Darcy and Yaz, who were a study in contrasts. Darcy, who had big eyes, prominent cheekbones, and a wide mouth, had dressed as if she were meeting a judge. Yaz, who, although he'd once served as a buttoned-down marine, was as flamboyant as his art deco shirts and had recently changed his orange hairstyle into a two-tone Mohawk. Everyone joined in the applause as Candace crossed the stage.

In less than forty-five minutes, the principal spoke, a student sang a rousing version of "The Star Spangled Banner," and all of the students received their diplomas. After the ceremony, the school provided a lovely reception with ice tea, lemonade, and treats.

All through our celebratory barbecue dinner Candace talked about how happy she was to be living with me and heading to high school in the fall. As I nestled into bed, I reviewed the evening, treasuring that Candace and I could share such a wonderful event in the midst of all the drama.

• • •

Friday morning, Candace hurried to the breakfast table and wolfed down eggs and toast. Before Waverly arrived, she dressed in cutoffs and a Lake Tahoe T-shirt and offered to take Cinder to the neighbor's house—Opal was willing to watch him again until I figured out a better daytime option.

When Waverly and her father arrived, Candace blew me a kiss and tore out of the house. Oh, to have that kind of energy.

I showered and dressed in a red shell and white capris—it was going to be another blisteringly hot day—and then I drove to South Lake Tahoe, taking Highway 28 past Emerald Bay. I arrived at Ambrose Alley by midmorning. The casino's sparkling silver-and-onyx trim made it look like a gigantic gift box. Massive potted palms guarded the entrance. Uniformed attendants hurried to assist patrons.

Inside, business was booming. I worried that the older casinos on the main drag would suffer. On the other hand, if what the zaftig woman outside Vittorio's Ristorante had said about Ambrose Alley was true, then Finn Ambrose might not win over South Lake Tahoe gamblers so easily. The new shiny toy might be more attractive at first, but shiny didn't last forever. Fairness mattered.

The lobby's bright lights screamed *Wake up* to all who entered. Rock music, heavy on the bass, thumped tirelessly. The crimson décor didn't appeal to me—it was over the top—but patrons seemed to find it invigorating.

At the reception desk, a young woman greeted me with a frenetic smile. I hitched my tote higher on my shoulder and gave her my name. I said I had an appointment with Mr. Ambrose. She held up a finger and asked me to wait. Seconds later, she apologized. Mr. Ambrose was busy. However, his head of security would be more than happy to meet with me. She acted like I should be as pleased as punch. I wasn't.

As I waited for the guy to appear, I glimpsed an oversized man in work shirt and jeans darting around the corner. He resembled the bruiser who'd plowed into me outside Vittorio's. Did he work at the casino?

Before I could pursue him, a formidable thirty-something with long blue-black hair dressed in black leather jacket, black jeans, and tooled black cowboy boots exited the elevator and strode in my direction. She had a slight limp but covered it with grace. Her intense gaze never wavered.

"Miss Adams, how nice to meet you. I'm Sorcha McRae, Mr. Ambrose's head of security."

A female. Interesting. Finn Ambrose was an equal opportunity employer.

"Miss McRae," I said, hand extended. Luckily my knee was feeling better and my limp undetectable. Otherwise, the woman might have thought I was making fun of her as I moved toward her. We shook hands.

"Please, call me Sorcha. May I call you Aspen?"

I nodded. "Sorcha is an unusual name."

"It's Gaelic. It means radiant. When I was born, I had a halo of blonde hair, if you can believe that." She smiled easily. "Mr. Ambrose—Finn—is truly sorry he couldn't meet with you. There's a huge Asian tourism convention coming soon. He's in a meeting with the coordinators." She motioned to a cluster of comfortable-looking gray couches. "Why don't we sit over there and chat?"

"How about you give me a tour of the casino instead?"

"Sure." She led me through the area that was equipped with one-armed bandits, blackjack tables, and bars.

As we strolled along a black-carpeted wing of the casino teeming with high-end shops, I said, "What did you do before your employment with Mr. Ambrose, Sorcha?"

"You can call him Finn. He's a casual guy. And what makes you think I haven't always worked for him?" She grinned, clearly toying with me. "Prior to this job, I was a cop in San Francisco. I had an accident and"—she paused—"I left the force." Tears brimmed in her eyes. Perhaps the reason for them would explain the limp. "Fortunately, Finn knew my father. When he learned of my situation, he offered me this job." She led me through another hallway, flanked by hotel offices. "You're a PI, aren't you?"

"I work in a PI firm. I have a ways to go before I'm official."

"You've got to start somewhere. When I left the force, I considered opening a private detective agency, but this opportunity came along first. So, what did you want to talk to Finn about?"

"You've heard about the Tony Vittorio murder, I assume?"

"Yes, two men from the Placer County Sheriff's Office came by yesterday, wishing to speak with Finn. Detective Sergeant Shaper and his associate, Detective Hernandez." She pressed a button and summoned an elevator. The door opened and we stepped inside. After she pressed a security code and the elevator started to ascend, she continued. "What a tragedy."

"I assume Nick Shaper questioned Mr. Ambrose . . . Finn . . . as to his whereabouts at the time of the murder?"

Sorcha hesitated. "Finn couldn't meet. He had a flurry of meetings."

Finn had to be cocky or stupid to put off Nick.

"Did you answer for him?" I asked. I didn't add, *as you're doing for him now.*

"Yes. We discussed the relationship between Finn and Tony as well as the hiring of Tony's brother."

"How about Finn's wife? Was she available for questioning?" I asked, searching for a deeper understanding of why Tripp Ambrose had been so vague about his mother.

"Finn's wife divorced him some time ago. She doesn't live in town."

"Does Tripp see her often?"

"I have no idea."

As the elevator doors opened, I said, "I heard that Tony Vittorio had a long-standing feud with Mr. Ambrose . . . with Finn."

Sorcha didn't move. "No, he didn't. That was a publicity stunt. They figured if people thought there was a feud, more customers would flock to both restaurants to see what the ruckus was about." The elevator doors began to close. She shot out her arm to hold them at bay. "Finn and Tony spoke often. They shared a good laugh about the hubbub they were stirring up. There's no such thing as bad publicity."

"I also heard that Finn had an affair with Vittorio's widow."

"Ha! Finn said you were a woman who gets to the point. Rumors are like fire, Aspen, easily dismissed if there's no smoke. He's not having an affair with the widow. He's engaged to be married to a wonderful woman." Sorcha stepped out of the elevator and motioned like a tour guide. "This is The Vista, Ambrose Alley's premier restaurant."

"The one Enzo Vittorio will oversee?"

"Yes. Soon."

I gazed at the leather banquettes, chrome-and-glass tables, and plate glass windows providing a two-hundred-and-seventy-degree view of the lake. "It's beautiful."

Sorcha crossed the lush carpet to a window with the view of the western side of Lake Tahoe. She drew in a deep breath and let it out. "It's not just beautiful; it's breathtaking."

"Why isn't it located on the top floor?"

"Finn reserved that site for his residence."

Pricey digs, I mused.

"Follow me," Sorcha said. "We'll get the chef to prepare a snack." She pressed through a swinging door and stopped cold.

Finn Ambrose stood at the chopping block in the middle of the room, wielding a meat clever. Surrounding him were a number of

Asian men and women all focused on the pile of beef lying on the wood block. Finn tossed the cleaver between his hands, and when it was once again in his left, he slammed it into the meat. The visitors *ooh*ed collectively, as if the slab had been vanquished.

When Finn caught sight of Sorcha and me, his gaze turned dark. He set the cleaver aside and, with a towel, dabbed at the meat juice that had spattered onto his black-themed floral shirt and taupe trousers. Why hadn't he donned an apron?

"Hello, Miss Adams." He wiped his hands and crossed the room to greet us.

"Finn," Sorcha sputtered, "I'm so sorry. I had no idea you were here."

"My guests wanted a demonstration." He winked at me. "I used to be quite a chef. Self-made. No official training." He made a magnanimous gesture. "Give us a minute, will you? I want to see my guests out."

As he led the group toward the kitchen's exit, my cell phone vibrated in the outside pocket of my tote.

I answered after one pulse.

"Aspen?" Gloria sounded breathy. Panicked. "There's been another murder."

Chapter 18

"Who was killed?" I said into the cell phone as I dashed out of the kitchen, registering the shock on Finn and Sorcha's faces.

"Miranda Tejeda, a schoolteacher."

"When?" I ran across the dining room to the elevator and punched the Down button.

"Late last night. She was stabbed. With scissors. Someone found her an hour ago."

Late last night—not minutes ago—which meant Finn Ambrose didn't necessarily have an alibi. Did he or anyone at KINC have a connection to the teacher?

"According to the report," Gloria went on, "she was working on a class project, pinning pictures of the Seven Wonders of the World on her wall."

"At night?"

"School's out. No students to bother her. Beau thought she might have preferred the quiet of the evening."

"You talked to Beau about it?"

"Camille told us. We're both at the studio."

"Gloria, did you interview Miss Tejeda?"

She hesitated. "No."

"You don't sound sure."

"It wasn't an interview, per se. Not a scheduled one, anyway. About a month ago, she was outside the studio. It was raining. She was holding a sign and—" Gloria sucked back a sob. "I received another note, Aspen! It says Miss Tejeda won't hurt me again."

"Did the author write *for your glory*?"

"Yes."

Three notes. Three murders. Gloria hadn't interviewed Miss Tejeda, but she had met her. Was meeting the person the connection? No, the killer felt these people had wronged Gloria.

I said, "How did you receive this note?"

"Camille gave me a stack of envelopes. It was mixed in with my other mail."

"How did you get the note that referred to Dr. Fisher?"

"A delivery girl brought it Saturday morning. Camille handed it to me. Why?"

Different delivery systems. One by messenger, one left on the doorstep, one by mail. Was that significant?

"Poor Miss Tejeda," Gloria went on. "Why kill her? She was nice. Kooky. She taught kids, for heaven sakes." She smacked something. A tabletop. "What do we do now?"

"I'm not sure. Where are you?"

"In my dressing room."

"I'm on my way to you. Don't go anywhere."

On the drive to KINC, I telephoned Nick at the station. Zook said he was out with Hernandez. They were investigating a new murder. Of a teacher.

"Tejeda," I said.

"Yes, how did you know?"

"Tell him I called," was all I said and hung up.

I tapped the steering wheel with the passion of a drummer. Something was bugging me. When it occurred to me that I hadn't followed up with Heather about Beau's sister, I reached out to her and asked if Stacy Simmons had been a patient of Dr. Fisher's. Heather said she had been, but after a few visits Mrs. Simmons found another doctor.

"That was over three years ago," Heather added.

"Do you know why she wanted another doctor?"

"I think she was moving to another state. She wasn't upset when she left, if that's what you're wondering. She and my mother hugged."

I couldn't see Beau resorting to murder if his sister was no longer Dr. Fisher's patient. However, with the coincidence of Camille and Stacy both having been the doctor's patients, I couldn't rule out that women in Tom or Rick or Vaughn's lives—not necessarily wives or sisters—might have ties to Dr. Fisher, too. Friends shared the names of doctors.

On the other hand, what connection did the KINC employees have with Tony Vittorio and Miranda Tejeda? The murderer hadn't picked them at random.

• • •

I found Gloria in her dressing room rubbing lotion on her hands. Her cheeks were pasty, her lower lip quivering.

"There it is." She pointed. Sitting on her bureau was a piece of white bond paper similar to the paper used for the previous notes. Gloria dabbed her nose with a Kleenex. The cuticle of her thumb was even more ragged than before.

"Is Camille on-site?" I asked.

"She's getting a facial. Disturbing her at the spa would be like waking Vesuvius. She should be back soon." Gloria clasped my hand. "Please, Aspen, you have to find out who's doing this to me."

"And to the victims."

"That's a given. You have to stop this."

I donned latex gloves and scanned the note. The paper was yet again nondescript. However, on this one, unlike the others, a string of smudged ink marks marred the left side. My printer would mess up in similar fashion when the toner was low.

> *Miss Morning, you are my sunshine. I'll protect you from those who try to diminish your light. Miss Tejeda will never harm anyone again. I did it for your glory. Keep your heart open for my love.*

Gloria chewed on her thumb. "It's such garbage."

"The killer wrote *anyone* not just *you*."

"I noticed that, too."

"Tell me about meeting Miss Tejeda."

"It was in May. Vaughn and I were outside reporting on the rainy weather. We were, you know, mingling, and she was waving at me. I remember because she had this funky wig on and she was carrying one of those religious signs, but the message was funny. It said, *Thomas Michael 2:4*. I know there's no book in the Bible with that name, so I asked her about it. She said those were names of two of her special education kids. She works . . . *worked*"—Gloria's voice cracked—"with all sorts of challenged children, many with ADHD or autism or speech issues."

Rubbing her face, trying to stimulate circulation, Gloria plopped into a chair and cried, "Aspen, what am I going to do? I can't sleep. The worry, the guilt. These people are dying and it's somehow my fault."

My heart ached for her. For them.

"Did Miss Tejeda do anything to harm you? Even something as silly as punching your arm or making you sound foolish?"

Gloria splayed her hands. "No. She was collecting books for her school. Easy readers and such."

"Did she make a snide remark?"

Gloria shook her head.

"Wait a sec. You said this was in May. Was that the day of the electrical storm?"

"Yes."

"Did Finn Ambrose come in that day?" His feud with Tony Vittorio gave him motive for at least one murder. Had he witnessed Gloria's exchange with the teacher?

"Yes. For a moment. He left after the snafu with our equipment happened."

"Was Beau there that day?"

"Of course he was." Gloria tilted her head, catching my point. "I promise you, Beau's harmless."

"Were Tom and Rick working, too?"

Gloria's gaze searched mine. "Is everyone a suspect?"

"C'mon, help me out. I'm trying to piece the puzzle together." I peered at the note once more, trying to read something, *anything*, between the lines. "Whoever wrote this note had to have seen you and Miss Tejeda talking."

"Tom was here. Camille, too. She was not happy about the exchange."

Camille. She had been Dr. Fisher's patient. Could she have written these letters? Could she have killed three people?

Gloria snatched the paper from me. "This guy says Miranda Tejeda hurt me. She didn't."

"What if you're his or her proxy?"

"Her?"

"A female could be doing this."

Gloria gagged.

"It's possible that Ms. Tejeda hurt the killer, intentionally or unintentionally," I went on, "and this is the killer's way of getting back at her." In fact, that could have been the circumstance in every murder. The author of the notes had been the victim.

Gloria covered her mouth. "Miranda Tejeda didn't deserve to die."

"No, she didn't." I slumped into a director's chair.

"A detective named King wants to talk to me. She's coming by later. She wants to see the third note. The first one was a fluke, right? And the second hints that there's something going on. But three?" She held up three fingers. "Why is the killer fixated on me?"

That was the big question.

Gloria rubbed her neck. "What a day. Beau breaks up with me and now this."

"You two broke up?"

"We have different dreams." Gloria battled tears. "He wants to move to Los Angeles or New York right away to further his career. My agent doesn't think I'm ready. I need more time in a small market before I can aspire to higher goals."

Why was Beau so eager to leave town? I said, "Where is he? I'd like to talk to him."

"In the control room editing clips for tomorrow's show." She fanned the air, pretending not to care, but I could tell she did. As I opened the door, Gloria said in a pitiable voice, "Help me, Aspen. Please."

"I will."

I strode to the studio. Through the glass door of the recording booth, I spied Camille in a skintight aqua dress, leaning an arm on Beau's shoulder. Her face was glowing from the recent facial. She raked her fingernails up the nape of Beau's neck, but he pushed her away and moved a shuttle knob on the control board with ease. Images of Lake Tahoe played forward and backward in rapid succession on the centermost TV monitor.

I tapped on the glass door and entered.

Like a kid caught snitching candy, Camille whisked her hand away from Beau. "Don't you knock?"

"I'm glad you're here," I said. "Could you tell me who delivered today's mail?"

"How would I know? It was pushed through the slot." She swept past me, the essence of roses hanging in the air after she was gone.

I eyed Beau. "Got a sec?"

He signaled for me to sit in the swivel chair next to his. "You look good in red."

A compliment from him was about as worthless as the fortune in a Chinese cookie.

Using his left hand, Beau twisted the fader knob. Then his hand flew across the control board, hitting one button after another. With his right, he jotted notes on a lined yellow pad. When a whirring sound began, he set down his pencil and swiveled in his chair. "Okay, I'm free. To what do I owe the honor?"

"Your sister Stacy was a patient of Dr. Fisher's, the gynecologist who was murdered."

"If you say so."

"It's a bit of a coincidence."

"What is? My sister knowing a doctor?"

"And Gloria getting messages from the murderer about the doctor as well as the other two victims."

Beau crossed his arms over his chest. "I think the notes are bogus."

"Three murders, three notes."

"Gloria could be sending them to herself."

"For publicity?"

"For whatever reason. She has some issues. You're her friend. You know that."

No love lost there.

Beau crossed to the water cooler in the corner of the booth. "Want some?" When I didn't respond, he filled a paper cup for himself and chugged it down. "Did Gloria tell you about Stacy?"

"I asked. She said you and your sister are twins. Do you look alike?"

"Yup. She's a five-foot-two strawberry blonde and weighs about a hundred pounds. We look a lot alike. *Not.*" I'd bet he'd laughed every time he said that. *Har-har.* He returned to his chair and typed in a message on the keyboard. The computer screen flickered, and the image from the television segment began to play, showing a clean beginning and fade to black at the end.

"Was there bad blood between your sister and Dr. Fisher?" Heather said there wasn't, but she might not know the whole story. A hug goodbye didn't necessarily mean the doctor and Stacy had been on good terms.

"Anyone has the right to change doctors and not be considered a murder suspect," Beau said. "End of discussion. Unless you're accusing me of murdering the doctor to avenge my sister. Are you?"

"Where were you Friday morning before eight o'clock?"

"Okay, sure, here we go." He folded his arms. "I was at the gym. I do an hour of cardio followed by a two-hour stretch class. I go every Friday. Lots of witnesses. Now, if you'll excuse me." Beau tapped his watch. "I've got a lot to do for the evening news."

I moved to the door and turned back. "Did you know the teacher who was murdered? Miranda Tejeda?"

"Nope. You're not going to blame me or my sister for that, too, are you?" He scratched his chin. "When did she die? Last night? That's a bowling night. I was with Rick."

I peered at the set of one-inch videotapes on the shelves behind him and recalled the DVDs Candace had borrowed from Camille. Was Gloria's meet up with Tejeda recorded on one of them? "Do you happen to have DVDs of segments filmed in front of the studio?" I asked.

"All I've got are professional grade tapes. Camille has DVDs in her cubicle. Check with her."

"Thanks for your time."

A few minutes later, I knocked on the partition to Camille's cubicle. When she didn't respond, I peeked around the corner. The area was as organized as an IRS office. Paper clips in one jar, pushpins in another, and separate containers for pencils and pens. Folders were stacked neatly in the upper right corner. Magazines and newspapers were piled in the upper left. A computer monitor sat squarely in the center of her desk. DVDs, each marked with a date, stood in jewel cases on the credenza behind the desk. The inbox was empty; the outbox, too.

Before I could think about the legal ramifications, I snatched a few DVDs recorded in April and May, hoping one might show me Gloria's interaction with Miss Tejeda, hid them in my tote, and bolted out of KINC.

Chapter 19

A short while later, I strode into the office, sank into one of the winged-back chairs, and closed my eyes. *A doctor, a teacher, a restaurateur.* Stringing the words together reminded me of a nursery rhyme. *Sick, Aspen. Really sick.*

The sofa creaked loudly. My eyes snapped open. Max stared at me, hands folded in her lap, the hem of her purple muumuu obscuring her ankles.

"Special education kids have unique needs," she said, as if she'd joined me in the middle of a conversation. "Some parents can't handle the pressure." One of her boys had a severe learning disability. At times, he would overload like a computer and shut down until his brain could reboot.

I sat up and blurted, "Tripp Ambrose."

"What about him?"

"When I met him, I noticed he had a slight speech impediment. What if he has other challenges? What if he went to school in the Mt. Rose district? What if Miss Tejeda was his teacher? If his father grew frustrated with the teacher's ability to fix his son—" Another idea struck me. What if Tripp were the killer? No. The only person I could see the poor kid killing was his bombastic father.

"Pin it down," Max said. "Go back to Finn Ambrose."

"And get answers and alibis."

"Also, if I might suggest, you should visit with relatives of the schoolteacher as well as the restaurateur."

"I'm sure Nick's staff will be conducting extensive interviews."

"That's all well and good"—my aunt's mouth turned up at the corners—"but you have a client to serve."

• • •

On the way to Ambrose Alley, I phoned Tony Vittorio's widow and made an appointment to meet with her the next day. Then I dialed Mt.

Rose Elementary. The principal agreed to see me on Saturday, too. She would be finishing up office work before she took her summer break.

When I arrived at the casino, I was pleased to learn Finn Ambrose would meet with me. My guess? He hoped to erase the memory of my having seen him wielding a meat cleaver.

I followed a guard into the exclusive penthouse-only elevator. The guard pressed four digits on the security panel, and we sped to the top floor.

Finn Ambrose met me at the door to his residence. "Miss Adams. Come in. Please." His manner was warm, his gaze direct. "You look lovely."

Red was obviously my color if two men were offering me a compliment.

"Thank you."

"Let's talk in my study. You want to discuss Gloria Morning?" he asked over his shoulder as he crossed the living room.

"Yes, sir."

"Dear sweet Gloria. She's a triple threat. Well educated and beautiful with high aspirations."

Brains, beauty, and goals didn't typically fit the definition of a triple threat, but I let it slide.

The sleek décor in the room was tasteful and quite different from the gaudy casino setting. The U-shaped white couch, white satin pillows, and white bearskin rug were eye-catching, but the view, as in The Vista one floor below, was the star. Artists would covet the perspective.

"Gloria is an astute reporter," he went on. "I like how she digs deep on each subject she tackles."

Finn ushered me into his pine-paneled office, which was more in keeping with the rustic look of most Lake Tahoe homes. A deer antler chandelier lit the room with a warm glow. A sizeable Mission-style desk and mocha-colored leather chairs complemented the log cabin theme. On the far wall hung a black-and-white pinto hide and some Indian artifacts, including an arrowhead collection that rivaled the one given to me by my grandfather. The only thing not in keeping with the theme was the HP printer sitting on the built-in file cabinet. The unit was spitting out copies.

Finn moved to the printer, placed a new document on the scanner, and pressed Copy. "Forgive me. I've got to complete this project. Every minute counts. The bank is demanding info. It's financial in nature or I'd have my executive assistant handle it. I hope Miss McRae gave you the full tour earlier." He smoothed his eyebrows with his left pinky, a practiced move.

"As you know, our meeting was cut short."

"Ah, yes, you left in a hurry. A teacher was murdered. That brings the tally to three, doesn't it? I hear the sheriff's office isn't sure it's the same killer."

"Miss McRae said you weren't available to talk to anyone from the sheriff's office."

"I tried my best, but I couldn't break free. Sorcha chatted with Detective Sergeant Shaper on my behalf and filled me in later." He seated himself behind his desk and gestured for me to sit in one of the high-backed leather chairs. A wadded-up shirt lay on one. I chose the other. "Tell me about your arrangement with Gloria," he went on. "She hired you to look into the notes she's been receiving, is that so?"

"Notes from the killer."

"How can you be sure they're legit?"

I eyed the HP printer. Would the toner leave a smudge of ink down the left side of a copy? "Because the killer claims he's doing so to protect and honor Gloria. The notes coincide with all three murders."

"So Gloria knew each of the victims?" The smug way Finn laced his fingers behind his head irked me.

"She interviewed two for her 'This Is Your Tahoe' segments. The third, Miranda Tejeda, was in the crowd outside the studio the day you were scheduled to do an interview. The day of the electrical storm."

"It was raining that day. We left when the interview was canceled."

Why didn't I trust the guy? Because I didn't trust anyone. And his answer was glib and quick. Too quick.

"Miss Tejeda and Gloria had a nice exchange," I said.

"You think the murderer witnessed this chat and believed the teacher threatened Gloria?"

"Possibly. Miss Tejeda was a special education teacher at Mt. Rose Elementary. It's a nearby school district." I hoped to see a reaction. I didn't. "Did she happen to teach Tripp?"

"We don't live in that district."

"Sometimes special education children are transferred to other districts."

"Aha. You picked up on his disability." Finn aimed a finger at me. "You're very perceptive." He took a sip of water from a glass on the desk. "If there had been some kind of intra-district transfer, my wife would have handled it. She dealt with all things that involved education."

Of course, the elusive wife.

"Sorcha says your ex doesn't live in Lake Tahoe. How can I contact her?"

The telephone on his desk rang. Finn reached for it but the ringing stopped.

Within seconds a mature platinum blonde in a flare-skirted dress, chunky jewelry, and stiletto heels waltzed into the room. She was holding a half-filled goblet of white wine. "Finn." Overly long bangs fell into her eyes. She swooped them off her face. "It's for you. Your portfolio manager. He sounds grumpy."

"Jules, sweetheart"—Finn grabbed the cordless phone receiver as he rose to his feet—"this is Aspen Adams. Get her something to drink, would you?" He gave her a peck on the cheek and patted her shapely rump. "You smell nice. New perfume?"

"Estée Lauder's Tuberose."

"I like it." He moved into the kitchen, speaking into the phone as the door closed. "How're you doing, man?"

"Want a drink?" Jules jiggled the one she held as if I didn't understand English and sign language might work.

"No, thanks." I rose, eager to inspect the pages Finn had printed.

"I don't normally go for it this early, but I've got bad cramps. They can lay me up for days at a time. My doctor can't figure it out."

"Mine recommends lots of water."

"What's your guy's name? Anybody would be better than the guy I go to." Jules drank a bit more.

"She's, um, deceased." The words caught in my throat. "She was the doctor who was murdered last Friday."

Jules blanched. "I'm so sorry. I—" She peered past me. "Hey, Tripp."

I swiveled.

Tripp stood just inside the doorway, bare-chested, his pajama bottoms dragging around his ankles, his eyes at half-mast and puffy. He was barefoot, which was why I hadn't heard him enter. In his right hand he held a copper lamp that was about two feet tall.

"Is that new?" Jules asked.

Tripp murmured, "Yes." A taller version of the lamp stood by one of the leather chairs, the lampshade punched with holes, letting light spill through.

Jules winked at me. "Tripp makes all sorts of artistic stuff. He has a real eye for beauty. He takes art classes at Lake Tahoe CC."

"So he said the other day."

"Oh, you've met?" Jules raised an eyebrow.

"At KINC, when Gloria Morning interviewed Finn."

Tripp yawned. "What t-time is it?"

"Late. If you don't get a move on, you'll miss your meeting."

"Got a smoke for me before I go?"

"Absolutely not. Nice try." Jules chuckled. "Get dressed."

"Need my shirt."

Jules grabbed the wadded-up shirt from the other leather chair and tossed it to Tripp.

He caught it with his free hand and turned to leave.

"Hey, wait, Tripp, come back." Jules tiptoed to the kitchen door and listened for a moment, and then stole back to the desk. Lowering her voice, she said, "I have to ask you something."

"What's up?" He shuffled toward her while eyeing the glass of wine and licking his lips. My sister, who had an addiction to everything other than work, would do the same thing.

Jules whispered, "I found an order for flowers in the bills. Do you know to whom they were sent? Was it to her? To Gloria Morning?"

"Maybe. Maybe not."

Jules glowered. "C'mon. Be honest. Did you make the order? Wasn't your father man enough to do it himself?"

Tripp glanced in my direction. Jules blanched.

Pretending to ignore the mini-soap opera, I inched to the printer and took a peek at the top page. No smudges or ink marks. Dang. I turned back, ready to make my exit, but Tripp blocked me.

"Sorcha told me you're investigating on behalf of Miss Morning. It might help you to know that Tony Vittorio's widow and her brother-in-law are having an affair." Without waiting for a response, Tripp slinked out of the room.

As he disappeared, I realized I was holding my breath. That news about Enzo Vittorio and his brother's widow was a bombshell I hadn't expected. Was Tripp throwing me a curveball to clear his dad's name?

I turned to Jules. "How long has Tripp been an alcoholic?"

"You could tell?"

"Mm-hm."

"Two years. He's been sober six months, but he craves it."

That explained why, when I'd first met him, he said he'd been ill.

"He goes to an AA meeting every night. His father's been adamant that he does. He even takes him to some of the meetings."

"Did he take him last night?"

"Yes. Thursday nights I go to my book club."

"Does Finn stay at the meetings with Tripp?"

Jules's gaze narrowed. Was she peeved at me for asking or wondering whether Finn left to have a tryst with another woman when he was supposed to be supporting his son? "Look at the time." She ran her fingers through tangled locks. "I'm late for an appointment. My hair gal will only see clients after five. Ridiculous." She headed toward the door.

Because I wanted more from her, I followed. "Jules, do you work?" I asked. How lame. I could do better at chitchat.

But apparently I didn't have to.

Jules pulled a business card from the pocket of her dress. "Jules Marsh. Private events hostess for Ambrose Alley. "I was a caterer in L.A. My sister was an actress. B movies, mostly. I worked out of a food truck and dished up meals for the actors. Finn met me at a gig and hired me to work for him. Then we . . ." She raised her wineglass in a toast. "Then we fell in love and he asked me to marry him. Engaged for two years and counting." She coughed out a bitter laugh, which explained the sadness in her eyes.

The kitchen door squeaked.

Seconds later, Finn tramped into the office. "Jules, I need to go out. We're having problems with a lender." He retrieved the papers that he'd printed and stuffed them into his briefcase. "Miss Adams, I'm sorry to cut our chat short."

What chat? He'd avoided me with ease. Max would not be pleased with my interrogation skills. Why should she be? I sure as heck wasn't. When dealing with my patients, *you steer the ship* had been one of my mantras. Finn Ambrose had applied my own tactic against me.

"I hope you'll come to The Vista as my guest," he went on. "Any time."

He left so fast that he wasn't in the hall when I exited.

Questions cycled through my mind as I waited for the elevator. Was Tripp capable of murder? Was Jules? Her perfume was rose-scented. Had she sent the notes to Gloria? No, that wouldn't make sense. Maybe her aroma had transferred to the paper Finn used. Was he connected to all the victims? Was Nick following up on that?

When the elevator doors opened, I was surprised to see the cab was empty. No guard. Perhaps he was only required to escort me up, not down. The doors closed and the elevator began to move.

Then suddenly, it plunged.

Chapter 20

Every muscle in my body tensed. I tumbled into the back wall. My left shoulder took the brunt. I braced myself with my palms as my life flashed before me. I'd never bear a child. Never save Candace from her mother. Never—

The elevator screeched to a stop. Had an emergency brake kicked into gear?

The lights flickered and went out. The walls vibrated, as if the whole unit was hanging by one cord and ready to plummet again. I didn't scream, worried that I might upset the delicate balance of air and metal.

After a long moment, the lights came on and something whirred and then cranked.

The car began to creep downward in short spurts. Each jolt made me catch my breath.

When the elevator came to a standstill and the door groaned opened, I realized I'd landed safely at the lobby level. I stumbled out and gulped in air. I scanned the area for a guard so I could report the faulty equipment but stopped when, out of the corner of my eye, I caught sight of a shorthaired woman in a skintight dress scurrying toward the exit.

Camille St. John. What the heck was she doing at the casino?

And then, out of nowhere, Enzo Vittorio darted across the foyer and left through the same door.

I gazed after them. Were they together? An item? Were the gossipers wrong about Enzo and the widow? Had Enzo and Camille rigged the elevator to kill me?

Get real, Aspen. My mind reeled with conspiracy theories. In order to time the crash, either Camille or Enzo would have needed to know when I'd left Finn Ambrose's penthouse suite, which meant that if someone had triggered the event, it would have to have been Finn or Jules.

"Hi, Aspen." Sorcha McRae, dressed in black silk blouse and

trousers, strode toward me, a smile on her face. "Nice to see—" She gripped my elbow. "Hey, are you okay? You're as pale as a ghost."

"The elevator. To the penthouse. Plummeted. With me inside."

"Oh, no. We had it serviced a week ago. I'm so sorry." She guided me to a chair and made me sit and then marched across the carpet to an attendant. She ordered him to place an *Out of Service* sign by the elevator door. The two exchanged words. She won.

When she returned to me, she said, "I'm afraid Ambrose Alley is such a new casino that glitches are the norm. How are you feeling? Do you need water? Ice? A doctor?"

"I'm fine." My shoulder was aching, but the rest of me was intact and my heart was beating normally again. I gazed at Sorcha, curious whether she might supply Finn Ambrose's alibis for all three murders, seeing as he'd blown me off. "Did you hear the news? A teacher was murdered. Odds are by the same killer."

"How horrible. You can't think Finn had anything to do with it."

"I don't know what to think. Do you know where he was last night? Was he taking his son to an AA meeting?"

Sorcha pursed her lips. "You know about Tripp's illness?"

"I figured it out."

"Then yes, he was. He does so nearly every night." Sorcha swept her hair over her shoulder. "Look, I don't have time to talk right now—there's a crisis in the ballroom—but if you ever want to grab a bite to eat, I'm up for it. I'd love to know more about the life of a PI."

"How about tonight?" No time like the present, and in a casual atmosphere she might divulge more about her boss. "The Tavern in Homewood."

"I've heard of it. Seven?"

"Perfect."

• • •

I swung by Waverly's house and picked up Candace who couldn't stop raving about her trip to Virginia City. The train ride. The tour guide. The history. As she carried on, a sheriff's vehicle passed me. Quickly, I made a U-turn. The sheriff's station was only a mile away.

Zook was sorting manila folders into the horizontal file drawers. She coughed and blew her nose with a tissue. When she saw Candace and me, she smiled. "Hi, Aspen. Nick's busy."

"Could you let him know we're here? It's important." I wanted to talk to him about Finn Ambrose and his son, and I wanted to know whether Nick or anyone on his team had tracked down Ambrose's ex-wife.

"Sure thing." Zook disappeared through the door leading to the jail and rooms at the rear of the building.

My stomach grumbled. To keep myself from thinking about how long it had been since I'd last eaten, I paced the narrow hall outside the reception/records office and read the posters pinned to the corkboard. I grinned when I read that the Truckee Junior College was offering summer night classes for administration of justice, jewelry making, and keeping Tahoe blue. Talk about a diverse program.

"*Psst*, Aunt Aspen." Candace beckoned me. She was peering through the reception window. "See the file at the top of the inbox?"

The file's cover was tilting toward us, propped up by the myriad other items in the inbox. "What about it?"

"Can you read the yellow Post-it notes that are attached to it?"

"No." My eyesight wasn't bad, but I couldn't make out writing at that distance.

"It's for Dr. Fisher's investigation. Mud was found in her office as well as bits of clay and metal and brown horsehair."

"Horsehair? Not dog hair?"

"That, too. Boy, the notes sure are *CSI* technical. The sticky note for dog hair mentions *with roots* and *without roots*. What does that mean, *without roots*?"

"My bet, you can test DNA on hair with roots but not on hair that is, say, cut off."

The burly jailer stepped out of the office to the left and veered toward us.

I grabbed Candace's elbow and steered her away from the window.

But Candace persisted. "I learned on *CSI* that police could figure out whether the killer owned a pet. Do you think that's why they're collecting all the hair evidence?"

"Absolutely," the jailer said as he stepped into the foyer, a set of car keys in hand. "A good techie can even determine which hairs come from which species." The guy must have had supersonic hearing.

Swell. I felt my neck and cheeks flush. Nick would be ticked to the max if he knew we'd been snooping.

"Good night, ladies." The jailer turned right and pushed through the door leading to superior court.

"I've been thinking," Candace went on, "that the notes the killer wrote to Gloria were childish."

"Are those posted on the file's cover, too?"

"Nah, some reporter read one on the radio today. Waverly's dad thought it was sick."

It *was* sick. Where had the reporter obtained it? Had Gloria or someone else at KINC made a copy and leaked it?

Just as Candace and I turned toward the reception window, Nick and Zook entered the room through the rear doorway. Zook pointed in our direction. Nick looked horrible. His eyes were lackluster. His skin was taut across his cheeks.

I offered a supportive smile.

He joined us in the foyer and kissed my cheek. "I'm sorry, Aspen, but I don't have time to talk."

"Gloria received a third note."

"I'm well aware."

"Also, I went to Ambrose Alley and asked Finn Ambrose whether his son, who's slightly challenged, might have required a special education teacher. He ducked my questions, and then, when I got into the elevator—"

"I'm sorry, sweetheart. I really can't talk. We have a suspect in custody. Not Ambrose. I'll call you later."

As he returned inside and crossed to the rear door, I spied Vaughn Jamison standing in profile in the hall. He was wearing a red Hawaiian shirt and jeans and his hands appeared to be cuffed behind his back. He looked panicked.

Chapter 21

On the drive home, Candace's cell phone rang. She answered and mouthed *Waverly* to me. A second later, she tapped and held the Mute button. "Some kids are going to the movies. Can I go, too? Waverly's mom will chaperone."

"I thought we'd have dinner with a new friend of mine."

"Please?" she mewled. "They're at the theater now."

I gave in, not because Candace begged—I was determined not to be a pushover—but without her at dinner, I might stand a better chance of prying information from Sorcha. "Grab two twenties from my wallet."

Moments later, as I pulled into the cinema parking lot, I tensed up. The area was jammed with teenagers. Where was Wendy Winston? Waverly materialized beside the passenger door.

"See you," Candace said to me and darted from the car. She wasn't interested in her friend. She was scouting the crowd.

I didn't spy an Adonis, which was how Candace had described Rory, but he had to be there. His family vacation was over. Refusing to allow Candace to be part of a huge group without supervision, I decided to park. I didn't think she had duped me. Waverly's mother must have had a conflict.

"Aspen." Wendy dashed up as I was attempting to turn the car around. "Sorry." She was out of breath. "I had to park a block away. After the movie, I'm taking the girls to the ice cream parlor. My treat. Okay?"

"Of course, but you and your husband are doing too much."

"We're happy to. Waverly needs the company and I adore Candace." She squeezed my forearm. "I'm so glad you took custody of her. She's terrific. You're doing a bang-up job."

I didn't feel like I was doing a *bang-up* job, especially given the extra hours I was putting in on Gloria's case, but I gratefully accepted the compliment.

A short while later, after stopping at home and changing into a sky blue sweater and skinny jeans, I strolled into the Tavern. The hostess seated me at a table on the patio. The temperature was perfect, not a hint of a breeze. The guitarist was playing a soft-toned melody. The evening crowd was subdued. An outboard boat with skier in a wetsuit sped by on the lake. I shivered, knowing how chilly the water was until August.

"Your date phoned," Gwen said as she set a basket of fresh-baked bread on the table. "She's minutes away."

"Whoa. What's this?" I clasped her hand and studied the sizeable diamond ring she was wearing. "You can't be engaged."

"I am. He's driving up as we speak." Her cheeks warmed. Her eyes sparkled. "You'll meet him. He's yummy."

"But you've only been dating two months," I argued, trying to sound like the voice of reason. *Not.* My ex and I had known each other a mere two months before careening into our failure of a marriage. Two months overflowing with lust followed by three years of emptiness. How I wished I could listen to classical music without being reminded of his betrayal.

"I know a good man when I meet one, and this one is terrific. We're getting married July Fourth." She cleared her throat. "Also, heads up, I'm going to sell the Tavern."

"What? No."

"It's time I traveled. Had fun. He wants to spoil me." Gwen ogled me. "Want to buy the place? You'd be a fabulous owner."

"I wouldn't have a clue what to do."

"My day bartender wants to manage it, and truthfully, that's what she'd do best. Three years of pouring drinks and she's still hopeless. But she's great with the staff and knows the books. Now Peggy is another story. She's pathetic at both but she has pluck." Gwen winked. "C'mon. I'll give you a lease-to-buy offer that you can't refuse, and I'll cosign any loan. Let's get you out of the PI business. No more danger. Nick would approve."

Peggy, looking frazzled, ran to Gwen and whispered in her ear.

Gwen said to me, "I've got a shipment to sign off on. Think about my offer." She pointed at my waitress, who was taking an order at a nearby table. "Darlin', bring this table two glasses of merlot on me."

If an 8.0 quake rocked the area, I couldn't have felt more shaken by Gwen's news. Questions people had asked me in the past two years popped into my mind: *What are you doing with your life? Are you satisfied? Are you happy as a PI?* Buy the Tavern? That was sheer lunacy.

Sorcha swept into her chair, yanking me from my battle with self-doubt. She was dressed in a simple black sweater, capris, and sandals. "This place is gorgeous."

"Did you have trouble finding it?"

Sorcha shook her head. "I often ski Homewood in the winter."

"You ski?"

She grinned. "I wrap my knee and chew on a bullet."

A woman who could handle pain. I admired her. My shoulder was still smarting from the ride in the elevator.

Sorcha rolled some kinks out of her neck and nabbed a slice of bread from the basket. "This is my first night off in a long time."

"Is Finn a taskmaster?"

"Hardly." She laughed easily. "No, it's my own doing. I'm an overachiever."

"Why is an overachiever working as a security guard? I mean, I know you had an accident, and if you don't want to talk about it—"

A waitress set two glasses of wine on the table and asked if we were ready to order. We weren't, so she moved on.

Sorcha took a sip of wine and set the glass down. "I was chasing a perp who had murdered his wife. He was dragging his son from the apartment. I had the guy in my sights, but I couldn't shoot because of the child. Instead, the guy shot me and I went down. That split second of indecision . . ." She shook her head. "Luckily, he's behind bars."

"And the boy?"

"He's been through two foster homes."

My past roared into focus, and I envisioned my last patient. A sensitive fourteen-year-old. A gifted sculptor. Abused by his father, abandoned by his mother. Shuttled between foster homes. Failed by the system. Failed by me. I'd arrived at the rehab clinic that morning and heard screaming down the hall. The boy was holding a doctor hostage. One of the nurses claimed the doctor had dissed the boy's mother. I rushed in and tried to get control of the situation. I urged the boy to release the doctor. He lashed out and connected with my jaw. The blood pouring out of me set him off. He howled as if *he* were the one in pain. I comforted him and assured him I was fine, but that night, he used his bedsheet to hang himself. I would always wonder whether, with more training, I would have sensed he'd turn his anger on himself.

"Hey, are you okay?" Sorcha touched my arm.

"Yes." But I wasn't. I hoped I would be, in time. "Do you like working for Finn?"

"Most of the problems at the casino involve obnoxious drunks."

"Do you trust him?"

Sorcha opened her menu. "Are you trying to get the lowdown on him because he's a charming, attractive man, or so you can pin a murder or two on him?"

Nailed. I took a sip of my wine and studied her over the rim of the glass. "Did he send flowers to Gloria Morning?"

"I have no idea. He did not send her notes."

"About the rivalry between him and Tony Vittorio—"

She closed the menu. "Like I said before, if Tony Vittorio had a problem with anybody, it was his brother, Enzo."

Tripp's parting words echoed in my head. Was it true that Enzo was having an affair with his sister-in-law?

"As for the third murder," Sorcha said, "Finn swears he didn't know Miranda Tejeda."

Interesting. He'd told me the same thing in his penthouse. Why had he felt the need to reiterate it to his head of security? So she would drive the point home with me?

"What about Dr. Fisher?" I asked. "Did he know her?"

Sorcha shifted in her chair. "The sheriff didn't question him about her, but I'm sure he didn't. Since he's divorced, he wouldn't have need for a gynecologist."

"Jules Marsh might," I said, though I recalled Jules referring to her doctor as a man.

Sorcha's gaze wavered. "Can we not talk business?"

I smiled. "I'm sorry. Hazard of the job."

Our waitress returned to take our orders, after which our conversation turned to more mundane topics. Good books and movies.

What we liked and disliked in a man. When our dinners arrived, we talked about how much both of us loved living in Lake Tahoe. I shared a few of my hiking adventures; she revealed that she enjoyed jet skiing and kayaking.

Later, as I was paying the check, I caught sight of the time. "Whoa. I'm late. I have to fetch my niece at the ice cream parlor."

"Rats. We never talked about your life as a PI."

"Because you asked me not to talk business."

"Touché."

"Hey, I know, come with me. I'll drive you back to your car afterward."

"Don't leave yet." Gwen glided toward us with a handsome man in tow. She was beaming. "Honey, this is Aspen Adams and Sorcha McRae. Ladies, meet Owen."

Dressed in a collared polo and pressed slacks, his silver hair outlining his rugged face, Owen reminded me of an aging pro golfer. He offered a warm smile and gazed at Gwen with adoring eyes.

Gwen squeezed my shoulder. "Next week plan to have dinner at my place and spend a little time with us, okay?"

"Gwen's a fabulous cook," Owen said.

I liked him instantly. Gwen could burn water.

Chapter 22

Sorcha followed me into the ice cream parlor. I was shocked by the size of the crowd. There were three lines, each at least ten people long. If this was June traffic, I couldn't imagine what the lines would look like by the middle of summer.

Through a narrow opening in the throng, I spotted Candace and Waverly sitting at a white bistro-style table.

I approached them and introduced Sorcha. "Where's your mom, Waverly?"

"Where do you think?" Waverly toyed with her curly hair. "Another emergency at the shop." Her mother did very well selling Lake Tahoe memorabilia at a boutique in town. "She said she'll be right back, but you know Mom. She packs three days into two."

"Where's your ice cream?"

Candace pointed toward the counter. "Rory's getting it. That's him, center line."

I tried to determine which one he was. Two young men in the middle line had reached the counter. One, with a golden tan and curly tresses cascading around his shoulders, was wearing shorts and a sleeveless yellow shirt featuring a Grateful Dead logo on the back. Definitely an Adonis. Warning bells rang in my head. His sidekick, who stood in profile, had short hair, a square jaw, and a lean body. He wore a tame blue T-shirt.

Hiding my concern, I said, "How was the movie?"

"Lots of dumb jokes. And lots of drinking. The boys thought it was a hoot."

After the last teen movie I'd seen, I vowed I would never go to another—bathroom humor wasn't my thing—although with Candace in my life, I might have to break my promise.

"I'm never going to drink," Candace added.

"Never?" Waverly said.

"Well, maybe wine. Even you said you'll drink that, and you're a real stiff."

"I'm not a stiff." Waverly adjusted her ramrod-straight back.

"Yes, you are. Nothing bad comes out of your mouth, and nothing bad goes into your skinny body."

"You should talk. You're skinnier than me."

Waverly stuck out her tongue and giggled. So did Candace. I couldn't believe how quickly the girls had become friends. Amidst a second fit of giggling, Adonis and his sidekick arrived toting four banana splits.

The girls quickly sobered.

"Rory," Candace said, her cheeks blooming pink. "This is my aunt Aspen Adams and her friend Sorcha McRae."

Adonis thrust his hand out. I braced for the handshake. If the guy were half as bold as he came across, I would have to ground Candace for life.

"Hi, I'm Billy," he said.

Quietly, I breathed a sigh of relief, and turned to Rory, the one I considered more worthy of my trust . . . until he opened his mouth.

"Nice to meet you." His voice alone would rev any young girl's engine. "May I get you two something?"

And he was polite to boot? Shoot. I'd met lots of good-on-the-surface kids who, over the years, had turned out to be rotten seeds. How I hoped Rory disproved my concern.

"We'll get it," I said. "Eat yours before they melt."

As Sorcha and I joined a line to purchase ice cream, Rory drew two extra chairs to the table.

When we returned to our seats with our single scoops, Candace said, "Miss McRae works at Ambrose Alley, a new casino in South Lake Tahoe."

"Rad." Rory was a guy of few words.

"Tripp sure is cool," Candace said to Sorcha.

Rory frowned. "Who's Tripp?"

"Mr. Ambrose's son."

"Candace and Tripp have been emailing," I said to Sorcha.

"Oh, yeah?" Rory worked his tongue inside his cheek.

Candace petted his hand. "He's a friend. That's all. His mom died and he wanted to talk—"

"His mother isn't dead," Sorcha cut in.

"She died a few years ago," Candace said. "That's when Tripp started drinking."

"No," Sorcha countered. "You're wrong. Tripp's mother walked out. She and Finn are divorced."

Candace shook her head. "Tripp said his mom was very sick."

My insides fluttered with tension. How had Candace gleaned so much about the boy? And how had Sorcha not known about the mother? She looked shaken. Was she wondering if she could trust Finn Ambrose? If he'd lied about that, then maybe he'd lied about other things, like his various alibis and not knowing Miranda Tejeda.

"Tripp thinks his dad's girlfriend is nice," Candace said in an effort to smooth things over.

"You sure know a lot about this guy." Rory's voice had an edge to it.

"Cool your jets, you dork." Candace offered a dismissive look. "Tripp has a girlfriend. She lives somewhere in Incline, I think. Near or on the water."

Waverly said, "She's older."

As they continued to discuss Tripp, I was drawn to movement outside the ice cream parlor. Heather Bogart was tying the leash of a raggedy sheepdog to a pole. Nearby stood her ex-father, Edward. He said something and Heather smiled tightly. Was this their first meeting since her mother died? Had he reached out to tell her he was ceding his inheritance to her? Had she contacted the estate attorney? She had taken great care in putting herself together. Her blouse was starched and her jeans pressed. She was wearing her hair in a neat bun. In a rare burst of emotion, she nuzzled the sheepdog and kissed his forehead. The dog licked her like she was raw steak.

My mouth went dry when I saw Heather plucking dog hair off her face. I thought of the Post-it notes Candace had seen at the sheriff's office: *hair with roots; hair without roots; dog hair; horsehair.* I flashed on the techie at the Vittorio murder site using tweezers and tape to lift hair off the victim and floor and recalled Gloria brushing hair off her dress at the studio after hugging Beau in his kitschy horsehair vest. Could the hair *without roots* have come from it?

"Aspen." Candace tugged on my sleeve. "You're, like, gawking. Stop."

But I couldn't. Was it possible everything in the string of murders could be tied together by one strand of hair?

Chapter 23

On the way to Sorcha's car, she didn't say much. I think the news that Tripp's mother might be dead and that Finn lied to her about it was weighing on her. As she climbed into her BMW, I yelled out the window that I'd call her. She muttered her thanks and tore off.

On the drive to the cabin, Candace talked nonstop about Rory. Wasn't he cute? And a gentleman? Wasn't blue the perfect color for him?

After we picked up Cinder from the neighbor's house, Candace sailed to bed, and I sent an email to Max relating the facts of my day.

Later, when the house was quiet, I fell into a funk about Nick brushing me off at the station, so I did the only rational thing I could think of. I grabbed a bag of M&Ms, retreated to a chair on the porch, and wallowed in a late-night pity party. Cinder joined me and nudged my arm. I scratched his ears and leaned my head back to search for shooting stars in the cloudless night sky.

A half hour later, I admitted that Nick's silence about the case wasn't the only thing bothering me. I wanted more from our relationship. We were boyfriend and girlfriend, but I loved him beyond words and I wanted to be engaged. Not like Jules Marsh, engaged for years on end. I wanted to be like Gwen, engaged with a set date to be married.

Around midnight, too revved up to sleep—downing half a bag of chocolate might not have been the best idea—I decided to watch a few of the DVDs from KINC. Each jewel case was marked with a date. On closer inspection, some included names, too. I found one for *Vittorio: April 24* and slid it into the DVD player.

I settled on the couch and pressed Play.

A slate appeared, giving a title to the interview: *Tony Vittorio*. Gloria's interview with Tony was much like her interview with Finn, each trying to out-charm the other.

"Did you research the Lake Tahoe area before opening your business?" Gloria asked.

"Did you research it before becoming a newscaster?" Tony countered. He came across as a bit of a flirt. He was a handsome man in his fifties with high cheekbones and what some might call soul-searching eyes.

"Your food is exquisite." Gloria rubbed her forearm in a sensual way.

"You are more so."

"All right already. Cut!" Fuming, Camille climbed onto the set and ended the interview. The screen went blank.

I fast-forwarded the DVD but couldn't find any more of the exchange. I ejected it and inserted another marked with an April date on which Gloria interviewed an attorney championing the Clean Water Act. Camille interrupted that interview twice, inserting a few of her own questions, a producer's right, I supposed, though it made her look like a control freak.

I hit pause and considered Camille. Had she intentionally cut into interviews to sabotage Gloria's work? Gloria worried that Camille would fire her if she received more bad press, but I'd bet the truth was that Camille was interested in Beau and wanted Gloria gone. What if Gloria's contract was ironclad? What if Camille wrote the notes to scare Gloria so she'd quit?

No, someone who wanted to protect Gloria had written the notes, and Camille clearly did not want to do that. On the other hand, that could be the way she could steer the sheriff's detectives in another direction. If I were to print something from Camille's computer, would there be a string of ink smudges down one side of the paper?

I sorted through the remaining DVDs I'd swiped plus those Camille had offered Candace and found one marked *Ambrose*. Expecting to see the interview from the other day, I pressed Play. Gloria and Finn sat on the same set as before, but both were wearing different clothing. In seconds, Camille leaped onto the set and announced they were having technical difficulties due to the electrical storm. Man, she could be abrupt.

With a little diligence, I located the DVD for Dr. Fisher's interview. Heather was featured in the opening shot, which took place in the doctor's office. Heather, clearly starstruck, gushed when the doctor introduced her to Gloria Morning. She left the consultation room, and the portion of the interview I'd viewed at the Tavern began. My eyes welled with tears as I watched Dr. Fisher advise Gloria. How I would miss her. All her patients would, too. And Heather, most of all.

"Hey." Candace perched on the sofa arm and stretched her arms while yawning. "What are you doing?"

"I'm watching DVDs of Gloria's interviews." I stopped the disk and ejected it. "I'm sorry if I woke you."

"I didn't go to sleep. Waverly wanted to talk my ear off." She plopped onto the couch and tucked her legs under her rump. "Why do girls like to talk so much?"

I laughed. "Because they treasure their friendships, and exchanging ideas helps them work out problems."

"I suppose."

I pecked her cheek. "It's time to go to sleep. Good night."

"Uh-uh. Not on a bet. Tomorrow's Saturday, and anyway, I don't have school and I'm on vacation. I want to watch some of these." Sassily, she snatched the controller from my hand. "Put in another one."

I found one marked *V and G with Crowd on the Street, May.* Was this the meet up with Miranda Tejeda that Gloria had alluded to? I pressed Play.

On the screen, a throng of people, some huddled under tarps, others under umbrellas, gathered around Gloria and Vaughn, both of whom were in slickers. Rain drizzled steadily.

"I hope you liked Rory," Candace said. "He's—"

"Hush for a sec. This might be the tape featuring the special education teacher."

Gloria and Vaughn stood in front of KINC shaking hands and chatting with the people. They asked general questions like "Where are you from?" and "What brings you to Lake Tahoe?"

A pair of teenaged twins held up a sign: *It's our birthday.* A dowdy couple flashed a colorful poster: *Just married.* Some guy blasted Vaughn with a squirt gun. Vaughn wiped his face and glowered at Gloria as if it were her fault. She stifled a laugh.

From the right, a woman in a multicolored wig with big pink eyeglasses and a needle-thin nose appeared on camera holding a sign that read *Thomas Michael 2:4.* Miranda Tejeda.

Gloria peeked at Vaughn, who was busy interacting with the squirt gun guy, and then approached the woman. "Excuse me, ma'am, but I don't remember that passage in the Bible." She held a microphone in Tejeda's direction.

"It's not in the Bible. These are two of my special education kids. I'm a teacher. Reading is everything." Deftly, Tejeda pulled a second sign from behind the first. It featured an address for the Mt. Rose School District. "Please send one easy reader book to this address. You'll be helping tons of hopeful children."

Gloria grimaced. I wasn't sure why. Donating books was a good cause. Perhaps Camille had ordered no on-air promos, and Gloria knew her boss would hold her responsible. Maybe, because of this exchange, the killer thought the teacher had harmed Gloria's career.

My landline telephone rang. I jolted. Only bad news came after midnight. Candace raced into the kitchen to answer. I followed her. A second after she said hello, the color drained from her face.

"Who is it?" I asked.

"Mom." Candace turned her back to me and said, "What do you mean?" As she listened, she curled a strand of hair around her index finger. "I don't know."

I tapped her on her shoulder. "What don't you know? Do you want me to talk to her?"

"She wants me to visit her." Candace handed me the phone and fled from the room.

"Hello, Rosie."

"Well, Tree Stump, how's it hanging?" Years ago, my sister gave me the nickname. She believed naming me after an aspen *tree* was ludicrous. She'd added the word *stump* as a joke because I was shorter than her by a good six inches.

It didn't faze me. I had thick skin. "What do you want?"

"I miss my little girl. I want to see her." Her words slurred together, meaning she was either drunk or high. Swell.

"We'll set a date, but right now, it's late. We're going to bed. Good night."

She cursed me. I hung up.

Chapter 24

Six a.m. arrived hours before I was ready. Even though my knee still smarted from the run-in with the bruiser and my shoulder ached from the elevator plunge, I ran with Cinder. I followed the run with a steaming hot shower and then dressed for my morning interviews in ecru linen trousers, jacket, and white silk blouse.

After breakfast, I reviewed emails. Before heading north, I informed Candace that Gwen was coming over. She protested, but I insisted. I told her it was for Cinder's sake. Opal was on an adventure with her father. When I reminded her that I was taking Waverly and her hiking later, she stopped grousing.

The drive to Tony Vittorio's home was one of the prettiest I could remember. White puffs of clouds decorated the blue sky. The sun, blazing from the east, cast a glittering golden ray across the lake. Just shy of Incline Village, I turned left and weaved into the hills until I reached Pinto Court.

The Vittorios' house was elegant from the street. Flower beds were packed with purple milkweed and lavender pansies. Stately pines bordered the driveway.

Mrs. Vittorio greeted me at the door. Despite the fact that her eyes were red and her tawny hair was unruly, she was a handsome middle-aged woman. Her tunic top, which she wore over leggings, was cockeyed because she had fastened the buttons wrong. With her left arm, she held a black Shih Tzu. In her right hand, she clutched a well-used tissue. "Please come in, Miss Adams."

"Thank you for seeing me." The scent of spaghetti sauce, heavy on the garlic, filled the house and stirred my taste buds. I handed her a business card. "As I said on the phone, I'm a private detective working for Gloria Morning."

"She interviewed Tony, you know. He was very pleased with the interview. He said it boosted—" Her voice caught. "Boosted the business."

Mrs. Vittorio led me across the parquet foyer to a living room adorned with overstuffed chintz chairs and a gold brocade sofa piled with pillows. I sat in a chair while Mrs. Vittorio fluttered around the room, fixing this, straightening that, like a butterfly searching for nectar. The dog didn't seem to mind her hyperactivity.

When her gaze returned to me, she shook her head. "Forgive my rudeness. Do you want something to drink?" She set the Shih Tzu on top of a satin pillow.

"No, ma'am, thank you."

"*Ma'am*. Please. I'm not old enough to be your mother. Call me Viola."

"Viola." I knitted my hands together, eager to continue. "Have you heard that Gloria Morning has been receiving notes from the murderer?"

"Yes, it's on all the news channels. How terribly gruesome. The killer is in love with her, they say." Mrs. Vittorio sat on the sofa and stroked the dog's back.

"One of the notes mentioned that the killer—or the author of the notes, at least—believed your husband might have hurt Miss Morning."

"Nonsense."

"Are you familiar with the other victims, Miranda Tejeda and Kristin Fisher?"

The woman stopped petting the dog and fiddled with the buttons on her blouse, as if suddenly realizing they were out of order. "Miss Tejeda. Yes. She taught special education. Enzo, my husband's brother, knew her. She taught his children in grade school." Viola clucked her tongue. "Such a shame."

The front door slammed, followed by the sound of heavy footsteps crossing the foyer.

"What's a shame?" Enzo Vittorio strode into the room, his eyes alert and his square jaw tense. In his black boots and black button-down shirt tucked into black trousers, he appeared ready for a showdown. All that was missing was a black hat. "Who are you?"

"This is Miss Adams. She's a private detective."

I rose and extended my hand. Enzo clutched it and kissed the back. Oily didn't come close to describing him.

"She's working for Gloria Morning," Viola went on, "to find out who is sending the notes to her."

"I heard about the notes," Enzo said. "Seems fishy. Gloria can be quite fanciful." Something flickered in his eyes. The Shih Tzu hopped from his pillow and rubbed against Enzo's ankle. He gave the dog an irritated shove.

I returned to my chair and patted my lap. The dog leaped onto it and nipped my hand with its razor-sharp teeth. "Ow!"

In a flash, Viola swooped up the dog, returned it to the pillow on the sofa, and sat beside it. "There, there."

There, there? The little mongrel had bitten me. I would swear the cur grinned at me.

Viola said, "We were talking about one of the victims when you came in, Enzo. Miss Tejeda. You remember her? She taught the children."

Enzo crossed to the sofa and sat beside his brother's widow. "She was a good teacher."

"Were you disappointed with her instruction?" I asked.

"Until they met her, the children struggled. She taught them to read. They read a lot now."

"Not enough," Viola cut in. "Teenagers should read more. What do they do all day? The Internet. The video games."

"The funeral's tomorrow," Enzo said, switching topics.

"For your brother?" I asked.

"For him as well as Miranda Tejeda. I cannot go to both."

Tears welled in Viola's eyes. She dabbed them with a tissue. Enzo patted her thigh, the gesture aboveboard yet intimate. I recalled Tripp's comment. With Tony Vittorio out of the way, could love blossom between these two?

I shifted in my chair. "Viola, you said on the telephone yesterday that you'd met with the sheriff's people. I'm sure they asked you the questions I'd like to ask, but can you think of anyone who might have killed your husband?"

"That no good Finn Ambrose." Enzo cursed.

"Enzo, we don't speak that way." Viola clasped Enzo's hand. "Thirty years ago, Mr. Ambrose and my husband were good friends.

They met in Reno, right after Tony and I came to America. Tony was a cook in Italy. He wanted more. He dreamed of owning a restaurant. He worked as a chef for Mr. Ambrose in Reno and, within a year, he opened his own restaurant. A bistro. Mr. Ambrose was his backer. It became a success, but Mr. Ambrose had bigger ideas for Tony."

"Bigger ideas." Enzo snorted.

Viola said, "Tony didn't want to expand, but he gave in. He agreed to sell the bistro and aim higher. It is the American Dream, no?" She tucked an errant hair behind her ear. "The next restaurant failed. Wrong location."

"Too big," Enzo muttered.

"Tony went broke."

"Thanks to his wife, Mr. Ambrose was wealthy enough to sustain the hit," Enzo said with a bite. I recalled Tripp saying his mother had come from money.

"Mr. Ambrose invested in his next big idea," Viola said, "and it became a huge success." She gazed at the ceiling. "Everything he touched, other than my Tony's restaurant, turned to gold." She motioned to Enzo to continue, but he remained silent. "My husband saved every penny. When he was finally ready to open a restaurant in Lake Tahoe, guess what happened? Mr. Ambrose moved here to show him up."

"That's when I came to America. To support Tony." Enzo thumped his chest.

"Yesterday, I spoke with a woman who knows Finn Ambrose well," I said. "She told me their feud was for show. She said, 'There's no such thing as bad publicity.' She stated they were friends and cooked up the rivalry."

"That's a lie," Enzo hissed.

Who was I to believe? Were Enzo and Viola casting doubt on Finn Ambrose to hide their own nefarious plan?

I focused on Enzo. "I hear you're going to work for Mr. Ambrose at his new restaurant."

Viola shot him a look.

"I was going to before . . ." He swallowed hard. "Before Tony died. No longer."

Maybe he hadn't gone to Ambrose Alley for an encounter with Camille. Perhaps he'd gone there to quit.

I said, "Viola, did your husband start a smear campaign against Mr. Ambrose?"

"Never."

Enzo scowled. "Tony never said anything bad about anyone."

"Who stands to inherit from your husband's death?" I asked the widow.

"I do."

"What about your children?"

"We had no children," she answered. Grief flickered in her eyes. "I am infertile."

That might explain why she hadn't been Dr. Fisher's patient. On the other hand, even infertile and post-menopausal women needed regular checkups to rule out ovarian cancer.

"Do you or your wife inherit as well, Mr. Vittorio?"

"My wife is deceased, and no, I do not inherit." His jaw ticked with tension. Was he hooking up with his sister-in-law to seize his share of the wealth?

"Sadly, there will not be much to inherit," Viola said. "The restaurant is in dire financial straits. Without Tony to run it, we will have to close. I'll be lucky if I can keep the house."

Enzo smacked his thighs and rose to his feet. "If that is all."

Viola rose with the dog and trailed him to the foyer.

I followed.

At the door, I paused as a thought occurred to me. "Sir, how well do you know Gloria Morning?" A moment ago, he had used her first name. That smacked of familiarity.

Enzo glanced at Viola and back at me. "I met her once. At the restaurant. She asked to meet the chef. My brother introduced us."

"You called her fanciful."

"I watch her on the news. She is, how do you say, pert. She has no gravitas."

I moved on. "One more question. Where were you Thursday night?"

Enzo arched an eyebrow. "Why?"

Viola's face pinched with worry. "That is when Miranda Tejeda was killed, is it not? Miss Adams is trying to establish your alibi. You are a suspect in Tony's murder. If the same person committed all the crimes . . . ." She splayed her hands and then cupped them in prayer. "Tell her, Enzo. You have an alibi. Don't be ashamed. Be proud."

Enzo squared his shoulders. "My son wants to become a priest. I do not, for the life of me, understand why. God let me down—let *us* down—when my wife, his mother, died."

"She died in childbirth," Viola added.

"As a result, I left the Catholic Church. My son?" He sighed. "He wishes, as I said, to become a priest. I am not happy about his decision," Enzo said, "but it is his to make. That night, we were at St. Francis of Assisi on Mt. Rose Highway from seven until eleven speaking with Father Horton." He opened the front door. "Goodbye, Miss Adams."

Chapter 25

In view of the family's sad history and Enzo's solid alibi on the night Miranda Tejeda died, I removed him from my suspect list. Even though he might be good for his brother's murder, I truly believed there was one, and only one, killer.

The principal of Mt. Rose Elementary School turned out to be a thin woman with a tight smile. She gazed at me from behind her tidy desk, hands folded. As I regarded her, my heart thundered in my chest and my chair felt as hard as the cement on the playground outside the window. Memories of the few hours I'd spent in detention as a girl zipped through my mind. Not good memories. In record time, I'd learned to follow the straight and narrow.

"What else can I tell you that I haven't already told the sheriff? Miranda Tejeda was notorious for keeping late hours," the principal said in answer to my question. "She was dutiful, kind, and funny, although she was a bit of a loner. Very few friends. She often said she didn't want to waste her love on anyone but her students." Tears pressed at the corners of her eyes. She plucked at a loose thread on the collar of her beige dress and refolded her hands. "Dedicated, that's what she was. Dedicated."

"Tell me about the day Miss Tejeda visited KINC."

The principal gave me a recap that matched Gloria's account—the chat in the rain, the sign with the request for books.

"Myriad books arrived in the ensuing weeks. Miranda was thrilled." She sighed. "Senseless. Her death is senseless."

"Yes," I murmured, wishing I could console her but knowing she would shy away from a hug. "Would it be possible to get a record of the students Miss Tejeda has taught over the years?"

"Detective King asked for the same thing. Why would anyone need it?"

"A disgruntled parent might be a suspect."

"No parents were ever unhappy. At least, none that I know of."

"I would view the list on-site, if that would help."

The principal said, "I'll have my assistant provide one and set an appointment with you, but as I told Detective King, you'll have to be patient. My assistant is on vacation for two weeks. We're bare bones during the summer."

Two weeks? How many more victims might there be by then? Didn't King demand a speedier resolution? Perhaps she and Nick already had a suspect in mind for this murder.

I pressed on. "Does Miss Tejeda have family nearby?"

"Sadly, no. Miranda was an orphan. Her parents died over twenty years ago."

"Who's arranging the funeral? It's tomorrow, isn't it?"

"That would be me. If that's all?"

The principal rose and returned to the filing cabinet she'd been reorganizing when I'd arrived, ending our interview.

• • •

When I returned to the office, I found my aunt in the yard weeding a bed of declining daffodils. Her fingers were filthy.

We moved inside and for the next few minutes as she made coffee I filled her in on my meetings, starting with the Mt. Rose Elementary principal.

"What's your takeaway?" Max poured coffee into two mugs and joined me at the table.

"Either the murderer killed Miranda Tejeda because of a personal connection or the killer believed Tejeda's request for books on camera jeopardized Gloria's career."

"Go on."

Next, I shared all I'd learned from Enzo and Viola Vittorio—the possible affair and the fact that the restaurant was in dire financial straits, taking monetary gain off the table as a motive for murdering Tony Vittorio. I mentioned the conflicting report about Finn Ambrose's relationship with Tony Vittorio. His head of security believed they'd been good friends, but the Vittorios said Tony held no love for Finn. I added that Enzo's wife had died in childbirth and that Viola Vittorio was infertile, thus making it more than likely neither had been Dr. Fisher's patient.

"Lastly," I said, "Enzo Vittorio has a pat alibi for the night Miranda Tejeda was killed."

My aunt grinned. "You are a bundle of information. I'll have Darcy track the money angle. If that proves true, I agree, you can mark Enzo Vittorio off your suspect list."

I gave her the details of my meeting at Finn Ambrose's penthouse—the flowers sent to Gloria, the upset fiancée—adding that when I was in his office, I checked a recent printout, hoping to match printer smudges to the notes Gloria had received.

"Zilch."

"Maybe he cleaned the printer," Max suggested.

"Possibly." I recapped my dinner with Sorcha McRae. "She was surprised to learn Finn's ex-wife was dead. She believed they were divorced and the ex had moved out of town. I'm not sure if Finn lied to her or she inferred something that wasn't true."

"You should check that out."

"I will."

"Anything else?"

I balked, realizing I hadn't told her about yesterday's elevator incident, so I did. Quickly. Making light of it. No harm, no foul. "I survived."

"Obviously. Did authorities investigate?"

"Sorcha showed up moments after I emerged. She told me the unit had been repaired a week ago and that it was probably a glitch."

"Did you believe her appearance was coincidental?"

I considered the possibility. "She looked as stunned as I was. I did suspect Jules or Finn, but if it was a glitch—"

"I'm going to have Yaz follow up on this."

"Here's an interesting thing." I held up a finger. "Do you want to talk about coincidence? I saw Camille St. John running from the building as I was exiting the elevator. What if she—"

"No, no, no. I do not see her sabotaging an elevator. It would take insider knowledge. Also, I do not see her writing notes to Gloria. First of all, your note writer wants to protect Gloria, which suggests a man with a noble cause. Secondly, stabbing with a scalpel or knife or scissors is not a woman's typical MO."

"Camille has a barbed wire tattoo around her wrist."

"Many women have tattoos nowadays, even one as edgy as barbed wire."

"But if Camille has done time, she might know someone she could hire to commit murder."

Max frowned.

"Gloria thinks Camille isn't happy with her." I told my aunt about the DVDs I'd viewed in which Camille had lit into Gloria.

"Lots of bosses are domineering. Take me, for instance." Max chortled and poured herself more coffee. She nabbed a muffin from the refrigerator and came back to the table. She set her mug down with a clack. "Finn Ambrose. There are a lot of unanswered questions about him. I have not met him and yet I do not like him. What does Nick think? Where is his investigation leading him?"

"We haven't been able to talk. I stopped by the North Lake Tahoe Station yesterday and saw him with Vaughn Jamison. I think Vaughn's hands were cuffed."

Max raised an eyebrow. "Ha! Can you see that man wishing to protect Gloria? I think he'd rather see her dead." Even though my aunt lived in idyllic Lake Tahoe, she watched the news with religious fervor. All the news. Every station. "Why does Vaughn Jamison even have the job? He can barely say a sentence without stumbling." She bit into her muffin.

"One more thing about Camille." I held up a finger. "She was Dr. Fisher's patient. I'm not sure for how long, but it is a connection."

"Have you asked her about that?"

"Not yet."

Max frowned. "When was the last time you wrote your case notes?"

"Two days ago."

"How are you keeping all of this in your head?"

"My mental bandwidth is clogged and my head is about to explode."

She aimed a finger at me. "Do the notes. It clears the mind."

"Speaking of which, I'm taking the rest of the day off and going hiking at Cascade Falls with Candace and her friend."

"Good idea, sugar. You've been going full speed." Max rose and bussed our dishes to the kitchen, then sauntered to her cats and nuzzled each under the chin. "While you chill, I'll dig into Camille St. John. Be prepared to receive a full dossier by tomorrow."

• • •

With Norah Jones's "Come Away With Me" playing in my head, I was feeling calmer as I strolled into the cabin.

Until Candace screamed.

Gwen and Cinder charged inside from the rear porch. "What's going on?" Gwen yelled at me.

"I'm not sure." I grabbed a frying pan and raced down the hall, ready to bash whoever might be hurting my niece. I shoved her bedroom door open and gaped. Candace was emitting bloodcurdling screams while pummeling her pillow.

"What's the matter?" I lowered the frying pan.

"Rory broke up with me. It's a sex thing. I know it is. I hate him."

"A sex—"

"I won't have sex with him."

Gwen, who was lurking over my shoulder, bit back a laugh.

I elbowed her and whispered, "Go and thanks."

She saluted and zipped out the front door.

Using the sleeve of her T-shirt, Candace wiped tears off her face. "He's all sweet and nice, and then *wham*, he's ghosting me."

Cinder slinked into the room and tucked his head under Candace's hand. Automatically, she ruffled his fur.

I said, "Let's forget about Rory for now and change into our hiking clothes. It's girls' day out. No thoughts of boys. We'll pack a lunch and pick up Waverly and have fun."

• • •

As I drove the winding road toward Emerald Bay, the girls couldn't stop talking about how clever and funny Tripp Ambrose was. The stories he wrote. The jokes he shared. The fact that they were exchanging emails with a boy they barely knew disturbed me. I breathed easier when Candace reminded Waverly that Tripp had a girlfriend. By the time we pulled into a trailhead parking lot next to Bayview Campground, Rory and Tripp were history and the sale at a mall in Reno was the hot topic.

I put a leash on Cinder and led the way along a hillside ridge that was fragrant with pine. When we arrived at Cascade Falls, the girls *ooh*ed their approval. Even Cinder barked with glee.

Soon after, we chose a spot that provided a beautiful vantage point of Emerald Bay. As I was laying out a blanket and the contents of the picnic basket, the girls shrieked. I darted to them and peered over the edge, fully expecting to see a dead body sprawled on the cliffs below.

"Is that Vikingsholm?" Waverly jumped up and down, her curly ponytail bouncing in rhythm with the hem of her fluted cropped T-shirt.

I laughed in spite of the stress the girls had put on my heart. Not everything was a matter of life or death, I reminded myself. "No, that's Fannette Island."

The only islet in Lake Tahoe stood in the center of Emerald Bay. When I was young, I'd created fantastic tales about pirates inhabiting the island's miniature castle.

"Vikingsholm is the house that stands on the shore," I said. "We can't see it from here."

"Was it built by Vikings?" Candace asked.

"No. It was built in 1929 by Lora Knight, who, along with her architect, went to Scandinavia for ideas."

"My aunt is the authority on everything in Lake Tahoe's history," Candace said. "Is she cool or what?"

I loved that Candace held me in high regard. I hoped the feeling would last.

Candace clutched Waverly's hand and herded her toward the hiking trail. "We're going to pick some wildflowers, Aspen, okay?"

"Watch out for thorns," I warned and returned with Cinder to the blanket to soak up the sun. As I lay there, eyes closed, I tried to think of something other than murder, like Nick, for instance, lying beside me and running his fingers through my hair.

Cinder nuzzled me. He wanted treats. I fed him and then, pushing thoughts both negative and positive aside, concentrated on my breathing. I would be useless to Gloria if I didn't regroup.

Unfortunately, my cell phone buzzed, yanking me from my momentary relaxation. I was tempted to ignore the intrusion, but the incessant hum was so unnerving that I answered.

"Where are you?" My aunt sounded out of breath.

"Cascade Falls. I told you—"

"Aha, I see you." She disconnected and a moment later emerged over the horizon, dressed in a work shirt and denim capris. I couldn't remember the last time I'd seen her in anything but a muumuu.

Cinder bounded to her. She gave him a hug.

"Max, you shouldn't be hiking with your bad knees."

"Once a hiker, always a hiker. A little pain is good for the soul." Perspiration dripped down her face.

"Please don't tell me you're here about work."

Max plopped onto the blanket, plucked a bottle of water from the cooler, and twisted off the cap. Cinder nestled beside her. "The last two hours produced a ton of juicy info about Camille. Even I was surprised how much people were willing to talk. It must be my charming personality."

"She did time, right?"

Max guzzled the entire contents of the water bottle in one long pull. "About a year ago, she had a disagreement with an undercover policeman in Reno."

"About?"

"A fee for sex."

"She was a prostitute?"

"No. It was a misunderstanding. She believed the guy was hitting on her, and being a little kinky, so she jokingly offered him a discount. The cop had no sense of humor and arrested her. She graced the state of Nevada's penal system with her presence for a single night." Max chuckled. "She went to a tattoo parlor the next day to commemorate the event."

"Which means she has no connection to anybody in jail."

"Correct, but wait. There's more." Max held up a finger. "I

checked out florists in the North Lake Tahoe area to locate the company that had delivered flowers on Finn Ambrose's behalf. That tidbit stimulated my gray cells, if I may borrow from Hercule Poirot." Max loved Agatha Christie mysteries. "And lo and behold, Floral Wizard delivered the roses from Finn Ambrose that landed on Camille St. John's desk."

"Jules Marsh was certain he'd sent flowers to Gloria."

"If I may continue." Max cleared her throat. "I also discovered that the same florist delivered roses to Gloria."

"How'd you learn that?"

"I took in a receipt you scrounged up on your latest garbological expedition. I waved it at the salesgirl and demanded an explanation for a misplaced delivery. She was more than happy to straighten out the mess. She listed all the deliveries made to KINC in the past month."

"So Finn Ambrose sent flowers to both women? His fiancée is going to have a conniption fit."

"No, my dear. You rush to conclusions." Max cackled, a clear signal that she had more gossip. "The salesgirl informed me that Gloria received flowers from none other than Miss Camille St. John."

I gasped.

"May I?" My aunt picked up a sandwich.

"Be my guest." I'd made enough for an army of teenage girls. "Maybe she wanted to reward Gloria for doing a good job."

Max shook her head. "You said that Camille was incensed with Gloria to the point of abusing her."

"Perhaps she sent them to make nice."

"With the words 'I love you' on the card?"

"No lie?"

Max grabbed a handful of trail mix, picked out a red M&M, and tossed it into her mouth. "I also talked to a disgruntled former female employee at the Golden Sun Spa."

"You are a locomotive."

"Aunt Max, what're you doing here?" Candace hustled toward us and stopped short of the blanket. Waverly trailed her. "Is it about the murders?"

"Candace," I warned.

She fixed me with a glower, the kind good old Rory wouldn't want to face. "C'mon, I want to know."

"This is between Max and me," I said. "Grab some sandwiches—"

"And go away?" Candace hissed through gritted teeth. "Fine."

That one word *fine* expressed all her teenage anger better than any other. After the girls foraged in the hamper, they trudged away.

"A curious mind is a good thing," Max said.

"Don't encourage her. Go on."

"Allegedly Camille hit on the former employee."

"Do you think Gloria rebuffed Camille and hurt her feelings?"

"If so, why not kill Gloria? Has she not mentioned the flowers or Camille's advances?"

I shook my head. Was Gloria embarrassed, or did she return Camille's affection? Was that the real reason Beau and she had broken up?

"Have you ruled out Gloria writing the notes to herself?" Max asked.

I considered the notion. Enzo Vittorio suggested that Gloria was fanciful and Beau intimated that Gloria had emotional problems. What if she did like Camille and fabricated the notes because she'd seen Camille hanging on Beau? The notion sounded absurd.

"No, the notes are specific to the murders. Gloria is not a killer. We're missing something."

Max chugged another bottle of water. "Sugar, I'll keep working the issue. As for you? Enjoy those girls. You don't have much time left before they're adults. The doubts will be here tomorrow." She handed me a tuna sandwich and struggled to her feet. "Eat. You'll need your energy. This killer will strike again. Count on it."

Chapter 26

An hour later, I phoned the station, eager to tell Nick what my aunt and I had discovered, but after learning that he'd gone home, I decided to pay him a neighborly visit. I dropped the girls at Waverly's house and drove on. Sensing my mood, Cinder poked his head over the edge of my seat. I petted his nose and cooed, "I'm fine, boy. Settle down." Loath to leave him at home, I'd taken him along for the ride.

The sun was setting, casting long dark shadows across the road. By the time I reached Nick's cabin, the sun had set. His cabin, similar in size and shape to mine, had a deck that circled the house. On it were cedar rockers and chairs that he'd made. He was quite an amateur craftsman.

I climbed the steps to the porch and knocked on the door.

Glass smashed inside, then a woman screamed, "You jerk."

Nick yelled, "Sit there. Don't move. I'll be right back."

Not prepared to be in the middle of whatever this was, I retreated toward the Jeep.

But Nick was quick. He whipped open the door and said, "Yeah, what?" When I spun to face him, he said, "Oh, geez, Aspen, sorry." He peeked over his shoulder and back at me. He tucked the tails of his striped shirt into his jeans and swept a hand through his hair.

"Natalie," he went on. "She got fired and fell off the wagon."

Natalie, who had the same bone structure and piercing eyes as Nick, appeared over his shoulder. I'd met her a couple of times. She'd always been in good shape. Today, however, her lipstick was smeared and mascara marred her cheeks. Even from the base of the steps, I caught the odor of whiskey. I was embarrassed to be a witness to her downfall. If I could have found a rock to crawl under, I would have.

Nick turned to his sister and nudged her with his hand. "Wait in the kitchen for me, okay, Nat? Drink some water." Then he walked onto the porch and shut the door. "What's up?" His voice was hoarse with exhaustion.

"I wanted to discuss the case. I have some ideas—"

"Save it. We arrested Vaughn Jamison for the murder of Tony Vittorio, Kristin Fisher, and Miranda Tejeda."

"Why?"

"When he was serving in Iraq—"

"He served?"

"Yep. And he had quite a scuffle with another soldier. It involved knives. The guy lived. Jamison was discharged. Plus he's left-handed."

"Why kill Tony Vittorio?"

"Vittorio pulled the plug on Jamison's interview with him and rescheduled it with Gloria Morning."

"Don't you think he would have been mad at Gloria, thinking she'd scooped him, rather than Tony Vittorio? Also, his wife wasn't a patient of Dr. Fisher's. She gave birth in Fresno, before they moved here."

"Wrong. Turns out his wife moved to Lake Tahoe before he did. In fact, that's why he took the job at KINC. Mrs. Jamison was a patient of Dr. Fisher's."

"I didn't see her name on Dr. Fisher's patient roster."

"Who gave you permission to check?" He arched an eyebrow.

I flinched at the challenge but kept mum.

"She goes by her maiden name," Nick said. "Seems she had a bad run with the doc and lost a baby girl. A preemie."

Was that the preemie Heather had mentioned?

"And there's one more piece to the puzzle," Nick went on. "Vaughn Jamison's name was on the visitors' log at the Truckee Hospital a few weeks ago. His daughter twisted her ankle. So he could have swiped the scalpel."

"What about his connection to Miranda Tejeda?"

"His daughter—the same one—goes to school at Mt. Rose Elementary."

If the principal at Mt. Rose had granted me more time, I might have discovered that tidbit on my own.

"Was the child Tejeda's student?" I asked. "Was she challenged? Did Tejeda bully her or hold her back?"

"Look, sweetheart, we have his hair at Vittorio's restaurant, too, and we have trace evidence from the restaurant in his car."

"What evidence do you have from the doctor's office or the school?"

"That's confidential."

"Doesn't he have an alibi for any of those times?"

Nick sighed. "He was running on Friday morning. No witnesses. He was driving to clear his head Monday afternoon. Again, no witnesses. And he was home alone on Thursday night. His family went to visit his mother-in-law."

"So the guy has bad luck."

"Or opportune timing."

My jaw ticked with tension. "I think Vaughn Jamison is the wrong guy. The notes the killer sent to Gloria claimed he wanted to protect her. Vaughn wouldn't do that. He and she have a contentious relationship."

"Truth?" Nick rubbed the back of his neck. "The DA doesn't think the notes have anything to do with the murders."

"You think the author of the notes is making lucky guesses?" I exhaled sharply. "C'mon, Nick, that's turning a blind eye. Gloria—"

He held up a hand. "We're not dismissing them entirely, but for now we believe we have the right guy."

"I want Gloria to be free of this insanity. Can you promise that arresting Vaughn Jamison will end this madness?"

He didn't respond.

I turned to leave and swiveled back. "By the way, I have information you don't have, but seeing as you won't return my messages, why should I share?"

"Don't get snippy, Aspen." Nick strode to within an inch of me. "Do you think I got where I am because I'm inept? I've been investigating since you were a teenager."

I steeled myself for more of his tirade, but he didn't continue. He turned heel and disappeared into the house. Before closing the door, he said, "I don't have time for this."

"Neither do I," I muttered.

Angry that he'd dismissed me, I raced to the Jeep and burned rubber out of the driveway. Cinder barked.

"Cool your jets, dog!" I shouted, sounding like my niece.

As I turned onto the main road, I screeched to a stop and pounded the steering wheel. "I hate men! I hate them!"

But I didn't really. Not all men. Not Nick.

• • •

Needing activity to keep me from turning to the emotional dark side, I swung by the Winstons' house and picked up the girls for a sleepover. The moment we arrived at the cabin, Candace and Waverly hurtled inside and scooted down the hall to do girl things: hair, makeup, and boy-talk. I knew that might include time on the Internet. I did my best not to worry. I was their age once.

"Dinner in a half hour," I yelled.

"Cool," Candace said and shut her door.

I set chicken brushed with olive oil on the barbecue grill, poured myself a glass of wine, and took up residence on the porch accompanied by a notepad, my laptop, and my cell phone. I would show Nick I knew what I was doing. Vaughn Jamison was the wrong guy.

For a long while, I jotted all the notes I had for my case file. Then I rang up courier after courier and asked whether any of the businesses had delivered a letter to KINC, specifically to Gloria Morning. None had.

The screen door squeaked. Candace stepped outside.

"What are you doing?" She drew near and skimmed my notes listing each courier's name.

I explained. "And what are you two up to?"

"Oh, Waverly's online with Tripp again. Geez. She has a thing for him." Candace cocked her hip and folded her arms across her chest, what I dubbed the know-it-all stance. "I keep telling her he has a girlfriend and he's old, but she's not listening." She reached past me and tapped my list. "You know, it'd be easy to fake being a delivery girl. I'd swipe the company's uniform and put it on and who'd question me? Just saying." She darted back to her bedroom.

Conceding she could be right, I abandoned my quest to find the delivery service and declared it was dinnertime. The chicken was a little overdone but the cornbread muffins slathered with butter made up for it.

During the meal, the girls and I discussed movies and music. Surprisingly, they didn't make fun of my opinions.

Later, while I was washing dishes, the doorbell rang. Cinder barked like a maniac and bolted toward the door. He scraped the already well-clawed wood.

Was it Nick, coming to apologize for his Neanderthal behavior? *Don't set yourself up for disappointment,* I warned. Even still, my heart rate spiked and my hands flew to my hair to smooth it as I rushed to the door.

I peeked through the sidelight and felt a prickle of apprehension. Tripp Ambrose stood there in a T-shirt, jeans, and tennis shoes. He hoisted an arty copper desk lamp that was different from the one he'd carried into his father's study. It featured clear tubes that encased the wiring, its shade merely shavings of metal welded together, which made the shade look like leaves gathering in a windstorm.

"Hi, Miss Adams. I brought this for Candace," Tripp yelled.

I gripped Cinder's collar so he wouldn't run out and opened the door. Cinder growled.

Tripp flinched. "H-h-hi, boy. Friend, not foe."

"I think it's the lamp," I said and gave Cinder a tug. "Sit. Sit," I repeated. The dog obeyed.

Tripp didn't make an attempt to pet Cinder. "Is your dog going to b-bite me?"

"No, he won't bite. What are you doing here, Tripp?"

"I'm heading to my girlfriend's."

"Candace said she lived in Incline. You sure took the long way to get there. Going north from South Lake Tahoe would have been quicker."

"Yeah, but I thought I'd take photographs on the way—I have a photography class at school—and this side of the lake is much prettier. The light was so cool at d-dusk, the way it hit the water on Rubicon Bay. Taking photographs at night is a fun challenge. I bought a quality tripod, and I learned how to work with different film speeds and shutter speeds to capture it best. I must've taken over one hundred pix." He twisted his right foot as he spoke. Nervous energy, I supposed. "Uh, I brought this for Candace." Tripp waggled the lamp. The clear tubing clicked against the metal rod. The glow from the porch light flickered through the lacy shade. "She emailed me that she didn't have a reading lamp."

"She has one." My favorite, actually, the one with the deer-etched lamp cover.

"Well, she knows I make these, so maybe . . ." Tripp peered past me down the hall. "Is she home?"

"Wait here a minute." I didn't ask Tripp inside. I wasn't happy with the late hour of the visit and was uncertain of his intentions. Instead, I left Cinder standing vigil by the door, with the admonition to stay, while I went in search of my niece.

When Candace opened her bedroom door, I laughed. Both girls had donned sky-blue facial masques. "You've got company."

Candace's face lit up with hope.

"No, not Rory," I said.

Candace's shoulders sagged with disappointment, her peeve with him over.

"It's Tripp. He brought something for you."

"A lamp?" Candace clapped her hands in anticipation. She turned to Waverly. "Remember I told you he was an artist?"

I glowered. "How did he know where we lived?"

Candace's eyes grew wary. "Um, email."

Way too much information was getting passed around. I would have to put my foot down but not now, not with Waverly over.

"Go get the lamp, say thank you, and tell Tripp it's too late to stay."

"What about this?" Candace pointed to the masque on her face.

"You look like you belong in the Blue Man Group."

"The what?"

"A performance art group. If Tripp gets grossed out, that's on him."

Candace giggled and hurried to the foyer with Waverly at her heels, which made me feel better about their intentions with Tripp. I doubted either girl would have risked face-masque humiliation if the visitor were Rory. I followed but hung back.

Tripp shrieked when he saw Candace and Waverly's blue faces. "Aliens."

"Cut it out. We're not aliens." Candace grabbed the lamp. "*Ooh*, it's so pretty."

Tripp blushed when Candace's fingers grazed his, and once again warning bells rang out in my mind. Candace was too young to have so many boys fawning over her.

"Candace, it's late," I said.

"Right." She sighed. "I'm sorry, Tripp. My aunt—"

"I heard her. It's okay. I've g-got plans."

"To see his girlfriend," I inserted.

"That's right." Tripp smiled shyly. "Um, Miss Adams, don't tell my dad about her, okay?"

Candace poked him. "Is he afraid you'll run off with her?"

"I'm supposed to be at an AA meeting."

Had Tripp skipped other AA meetings? Ones that might give his father an alibi?

"See you." Tripp turned to go.

"Tripp, wait," Candace cried. "Sign the lamp for me. Who knows? You might be famous one day." She raced into the kitchen and returned with a black permanent marker. She handed it to him.

Balancing the lamp with his right hand, he signed and handed the pen back. "Hey, if you want any more information on Indians, send me another email, okay?" He trotted down the stairs and climbed into a silver Cadillac sitting in the driveway—not a typical ride for a teenaged boy.

Candace gave me an accusing look. "You know, you didn't have to hover. It's not like anything would happen between Tripp and me or him and Waverly. His father has a choke chain on him."

I'd bet he did. In fact, I'd bet Finn Ambrose would check the mileage when the kid returned home and give him what-for.

"Ever since his mom died," Candace went on, "he said his father never leaves him alone except for when he goes to his AA meetings and school."

School. Shoot. I should've asked Tripp whether Miranda Tejeda had been his teacher. His father might not know, but he would.

"C'mon, Waverly." Candace gripped her pal's arm. "Let's check how this looks in the dark." They disappeared into Candace's room.

Despite Candace's assurances about Tripp, I stared out the front window for another few minutes, wondering about his father, a man so self-centered that he knew nothing about his son's love life or his son's passions. Tripp's concern that his father would find out about his girlfriend seemed valid. The other night at the ice cream parlor, Waverly said that the girlfriend was older. How much older? Where had Tripp met her? Junior college, most likely.

I headed for the kitchen but stopped when I remembered Candace, or was it Waverly, saying Tripp's girlfriend lived in Incline Village. Near or on the water. Was it Camille? Had Tripp been the one to send her flowers and not his father? No way. She was twenty years older.

Don't be a prude, Aspen.

That could have been the reason he'd acted sheepishly when Jules had questioned him about the order.

Chapter 27

I awoke Sunday morning feeling groggy and agitated. I didn't know who was sending Gloria notes, and I was still ticked at Nick. Rather than dwell on the negative, I dressed in all white to infuse myself with positive energy, poured myself a strong cup of coffee, and sat on the porch listening to the peal of church bells.

Candace shuffled through the kitchen door wearing a pair of flannel shorts, a tank top, and flip-flops. She shielded her eyes from the sun and plopped next to me on the bench. "He emailed." Telling by the radiant smile on her face, I deduced that Rory was the *he* in question. "He wants to take Cinder and me boating. He has a dog that he says Cinder will adore."

"I thought you hated Rory."

"I don't. Not really. I know I can make him understand about the . . . you know." She gripped my forearm and squeezed. "Please say yes. His older sister is going, too. She'll chaperone. And he said it's okay if Waverly comes, too. She already asked her mom."

"Did she?" I smirked. "Yes, you can go." Just because my life was off-kilter didn't mean my niece's had to be, too, and an older sister watchdog was better than none.

"Hurrah!" Candace leaped off the bench and tore inside, calling Waverly's name.

After breakfast, I decided work was the best way for me to stay on track.

• • •

On weekends, KINC was staffed with a skeleton crew. Even the receptionist was off duty. Rick Tamblyn was in the main studio giving orders to an older employee. While he spoke, Rick stroked a newly sprouted goatee and mustache. I smiled to myself. If he was trying to get rid of his choirboy image to appear more mature, he had a long way to go.

"Excuse me," I said, following him as he strode into the control room.

"Sorry. Can't talk. I'm in the middle of a project. Vaughn Jamison arrested. Who'd have expected that? I'm here four weeks and this is the biggest story we've had. I need pictures of his wife, his kids."

"Vaughn's the wrong guy," I said.

"Not according to the sheriff." He perched on the edge of a chair and pressed a shuttle knob on the control board. Images of Vaughn with children, without children, with wife, without wife, scudded across the center screen. "Boy, I love my job. Wait. That didn't sound nice. I like Vaughn, too, but if he's guilty . . ."

"Gotcha."

Rick hit a button. An image of Vaughn at his wedding materialized. He pressed another button. The image of Vaughn at his anchor desk appeared on the rightmost TV monitor.

"Rick, you went with Gloria to do the interview with Dr. Fisher, isn't that right?"

He whirled around, looking wary. "Yeah."

"What did you think of her?"

"Nice lady."

"Did she treat Gloria okay?"

He held up both hands. "Whoa. Slow down. Tom warned me about you. I did not kill the doctor."

"I didn't—"

"That's what you're implying. FYI, I know exactly where I was when she was killed. So do all the folks in my Bible study group. At Crag Lake watching the christening of one of our believers. I can give you names. Numbers."

I smiled. "Got it. Innocent." He really was a choirboy. "You've told the sheriff's staff?"

"I haven't been questioned, but I will now. Vaughn . . ." He twirled a finger. "He's the one who has to worry."

"I'm sorry if I—"

"Forget it. I know you're concerned for Gloria."

"Speaking of which, where is she?" I asked. "She's not answering her cell phone. I figured she'd be here prepping for the week."

"She's at the Golden Sun Spa taking a personal day. That's Miss St. John's former business, if you didn't know. Very chichi. Gloria gets a massage every Sunday."

Lucky her.

"How about Camille?" I asked. "Is she here?"

"Went home sick an hour ago. Bad cold."

Feeling sneaky, I said, "Mind if I use her office to make a telephone call? My cell ran out of juice."

Rick pressed the shuttle knob and sped through another section of film. "Be my guest."

I stole into Camille's cubicle. Her television was tuned to a morning talk show. The computer on her desk was in sleep mode. A silver-blue helix danced on the screen. I hit Enter on the keyboard and a request for password emerged. On a whim, I typed in *control freak*. Nothing happened, of course. I entered *KINC*. Again, nothing. I tried: *news*, *truth*, *trust*, and *scoop*. None of the obvious choices worked.

When I spied a business card for the Golden Sun Spa tucked into the edge of the desk blotter, I typed in *Golden Sun* and the monitor came to life. I opened the most recent document and pressed Print. The laser printer hummed to life. I waited with itchy fingers while the sheet cycled through. When a page emerged, I snatched it and goose bumps broke out on my arms. Down one edge there were inky smudges similar to the pattern on the third note Gloria had received. Had Camille sent the note to her, or had someone else who worked at KINC?

I pocketed the paper and continued my search.

The desk was not as neatly arranged as the other day. In fact, there were so many stacks of business documents on top of it—purchase orders, file folders for vendors, and assorted bills—I questioned whether the woman had anything to hide. Even at home, I locked up my bills and sensitive materials. Perhaps Camille believed no one would dare intrude in her affairs. Or maybe she had been so sick, she hadn't remembered to stow everything away before leaving for the day.

At the top of one stack lay a letter from Nielsen Ratings that said *KINC Evening News* was losing in its time slot. Right beneath the report was the most recent set of financials for the station. Though I wasn't a bookkeeper, I could see the station was in debt.

On another stack, I found a file folder with a draft of a letter giving Gloria two weeks' notice, dated three days from now. Words had been scratched out and others substituted, but the intent was the same. Camille intended to fire Gloria. Would she do so if she were in love with her? Had the note that accompanied the flowers been a mistake?

I flipped through other documents and found telephone records, credit card printouts, and invoices from local firms. The receipt from Floral Wizard, referencing a delivery a week ago, had been circled. Was that the day Camille had sent the flowers and note to Gloria?

An ad for Bulova watches popped onto the television, reminding me that I was taking too much time. I peeked around the partition. Rick was hunched over the editing board in the control room. The only other person in the area was a janitor who was emptying garbage cans. The white-haired man I'd seen earlier was gone.

I jiggled the top drawer of Camille's desk. Locked. I rummaged around for something to jimmy the catch. A nail file. A letter opener. Nothing. If only I'd thought to carry my toolkit; it was sitting in the glove compartment of the Jeep.

I spotted the end of a key chain jutting from a zipper pocket of Camille's datebook. A key might work. I tugged on the metal loop. The datebook flipped open and a set of keys slid out, making me think again how ill Camille must have been to have left the studio without attending to the items on her desk.

On the inside cover of the datebook, I caught a glimpse of her home address on Lakeshore Boulevard and whistled softly. It was an odd number, which meant the house faced the water. Pricey. Was KINC in debt because she had been funneling money into her personal account to afford such luxuries?

The morning news host returned to the television screen. Breaking news about a storm crawled in a text-based news blast at the bottom of the screen.

Tick-tock, tick-tock, Aspen. Time's a-wasting.

I tried each key in the center drawer lock, which would allow access to all of the drawers in the desk. The third key was the charm.

The drawer slid open. Although the top of Camille's desk usually screamed order, chaos reigned in the drawers. Loose credit cards, packs of cigarettes, and broken pencils filled the top left drawer. In the top right, I found a wad of business cards. The bottommost right contained half a dozen business-related files, one of which stored a one-page agreement of partnership. I breezed through it, noting that if either Tom or Camille died, the other would assume ownership of the entire operation. Simple and direct. No legalese.

The sound of the janitor pushing a broom near the office made me jerk upright. I slid the drawer shut, locked the desk, returned the key to the datebook, and peeked out the door. When the janitor was gone, I slipped out, hopeful that Gloria could fill in the blanks.

Chapter 28

When I entered the Golden Sun Spa, I became acutely aware of the pressure in my shoulders and neck. Could I ever use a massage. Soon, I promised myself.

Marble and brass fixtures abounded. White tile with an imprint of Grecian columns graced the entry. *Beethoven's 9th* resonated from speakers. I asked an attendant who was lighting a cluster of vanilla candles if she would page Gloria. The attendant hesitated, but when I explained that I had vital news for her, she responded with lightning speed.

Gloria appeared a minute later, hands shoved into the pockets of a white terry-cloth robe, a look of disgruntlement on her face. "I'm just about to get a massage."

"We need to talk."

She beckoned me to follow her down a softly lit hall. When we entered the massage room, she dropped her robe and slid naked under the sheet on the massage table. With her face mashed into the donut-shaped face cradle attached to the head of the table, Gloria said, "What's so important you had to find me now?"

"You received flowers."

"I get lots of them."

"From Camille."

Gloria turned her head sideways. "That witch wouldn't squeeze an extra nickel out of her budget for me."

"The florist confirmed the delivery. The note said: *'I love you.'*"

"That's a good one." Gloria rolled her face back into the donut hole. "You don't have anything new, so you decided to tease me. Ha-ha. Very funny. Go away."

"I'm not kidding. You never received them? They were sent a few days ago."

"Roses were delivered. No card at all. No 'I love you.' No 'To Gloria,' so we set them on the receptionist's desk."

"Didn't you question the florist?"

Gloria peeked at me, her face flushed with confusion. "Identifying the sender fell into the black hole of paperwork. They were flowers, for heaven's sake. Stop tapping your foot," she said, and then amusement replaced the confusion on her face. "Are you saying Camille sent me a token of love?"

I didn't know what to believe. Truthfully, Camille being in love with Gloria didn't make sense. It certainly didn't go with the postdated dismissal letter.

The door opened and a bronze-skinned woman wearing a white and gold running suit stepped inside. When she spotted me, she shrieked.

"Don't worry," Gloria said to the masseuse. "This is a friend of mine. You can start." She kicked a leg free of the sheet.

The masseuse tucked the sheet under Gloria's leg, but her jerky attempt at massage belied her calm.

Gloria said, "Can we talk about this later, Aspen, please? I've got so many knots I feel like a macramé project."

"Sure." The fumes from the vanilla candles were giving me a headache anyway.

"Camille in love with me." She snorted. "That's rich."

As I opened the door to leave, Gloria said, "Speaking of flowers, Finn Ambrose sent me roses with the note *Loved every minute.* That irritated Beau no end. Serves him right, though, since he's two-timing me with Camille."

So she did know.

• • •

A chorale of wind chimes greeted me as I sauntered up the path to Camille's exquisite lakeshore home. Countless pots of geraniums filled the corners of the porch. Clippings from plants, soiled gloves, and cutting shears lay nearby. A pair of gnomes guarded the door. Truth be told, I hadn't expected Camille to cultivate such a homey atmosphere.

The instant I rang the doorbell, a dog barked. A jet-black Labrador ran at the window and pressed its nose to the glass.

"Zorro, back away." Camille, clad in a blue chenille robe, opened the door and held the pooch at bay with her foot, but he broke free and charged me, tongue hanging out of his mouth.

I presented my palms and let him lick away. "Nice collar," I said. It was black and studded with quartz and other polished rocks.

"Bought it at one of those street fairs. It's supposed to be therapeutic for his hips. What do you want?" Camille's nose was chafed. Wads of tissue were spilling out of the pockets of her robe.

"The station said you were home with a cold."

"They gave you my address?"

"I was making a call from your office—my cell phone wasn't working," I said in explanation. "Sometimes I wonder why I even carry a cell phone. *Can you hear me now?*" I said, making light of the advertisement that used the slogan. "Anyway, your datebook was open. You'd penned your address inside. A PI takes every opportunity—"

"You have a lot of nerve."

"I have a job to do. I'd like to ask you a few questions about the notes Gloria has been receiving."

"Such nonsense."

I attempted an apologetic look. "It'll just take a few minutes. May I come in?"

Camille turned away but left the door open.

Enter at your own risk, I mused.

I stepped inside and admired the rough-wood beams, Berber carpet, and L-shaped sofa overflowing with throw pillows. A floor-to-ceiling picture window offered a grand view of the lake. Nothing matched the domineering woman I'd met at KINC, not even the sounds of Johnny Mathis singing "Twelfth of Never" on the stereo.

Camille clicked a button on the remote she was holding. The front door shut automatically.

"Who knew you could afford all this by starting your own news station?" I joked. "Want to start another? I'll manage it for you."

"When I sold the spa, I invested in the stock market and made a nice nest egg."

That confirmed what Tom had said.

"Unfortunately, KINC is running me into the ground, if you must know." So she admitted to having a financial problem.

"Why do it then?"

"I don't want to massage bodies for the rest of my life."

"Do I smell mint tea?" Enjoying a cup of tea might give me more time to ask questions.

"You want some?"

"That would be lovely."

Camille blew her nose and slogged through the living room, Zorro at her heels. I followed her into her sizable kitchen, which was stocked with top-of-the-line appliances and utensils. Cocoa granite counters and black Spanish tiles added warmth and class.

On a small couch in the adjoining room, Camille had constructed a nest of blankets. The TV was tuned to the news. Was she dedicated to her job, or was she trying to keep up with the latest on the murders and, thereby, stay ahead of the investigation?

The teapot let out a shrill whistle. Camille filled a mug with water, added a teabag, and handed the mug to me. "Let's get some sunshine."

I followed her to the porch.

The azure water moved in a steady pattern, north to south. Delicate whitecaps rolled across the top. On any given day, the view would relax me. Unfortunately, I was wound tightly. I wanted to solve this madness. For Gloria's sake.

I sat on a rattan chair and sipped the tea as Johnny Mathis started to croon "Misty," my mother's favorite song. I waited for Camille to speak. She didn't. Instead she set her mug on a mosaic table and plucked dead leaves from a geranium, reminding me of Viola Vittorio, too restless to sit, too edgy to provide direct eye contact. Years of counseling had taught me to remain mute until the patient opened the conversation.

After a long while, Camille caved. "Okay, ask."

"Let's start with the messenger who delivered the murder-related notes to Gloria at the studio."

Camille blew on her tea and took a sip. "A young woman showed up Saturday to deliver the first one. Gloria received the second at home on Monday. I think the third came with the regular mail Friday. I suppose it could have been dropped through the mail slot."

"Which delivery service did the girl work for?"

"Let me think. She wore a cowboy shirt, jeans, and a bandanna. It was a uniform."

Wearing Western garb was a cute gimmick. Customers wouldn't confuse the messenger with the UPS or FedEx guys. "Can you describe her in more detail?"

"She had spiky purple hair and a fit body."

"If I recall, you said a girl with purple hair delivered a regular piece of fan mail the first day I came to KINC."

"Yes, she's delivered to us before. The company she works for is"—Camille gazed at the lake—"Nevada or Bust. That's what it said on her shirt."

"Do they also deliver flowers?" I was fishing to see if Camille would confess to the bouquet she had sent Gloria.

"Don't have a clue."

"Does Gloria receive a lot of flowers?" I sipped my tea.

"Yes. She has a big fan base."

"May I ask why you aren't happy with her performance?"

"Who said that?" Camille pointed the shears at me. "Rick? He drives me nuts. The dope has been here a month and thinks he's God's gift to television."

"Not Rick."

"Who, then?"

I didn't respond. "Gloria said you think she's attracting bad publicity."

"She is now."

"Rumor has it that you're considering firing her."

Camille worked her tongue inside her cheek. Was she trying to figure out whether I'd seen that particular document on top of her desk? "I might threaten now and again. Being the boss is all about intimidation. I've got to keep the troops in line. But with the contract Gloria has—she had a top-notch agent work out her deal—she won't be leaving unless for cause."

"Could the fact that a murderer is sending her notes be cause for dismissal?"

"Not a chance. Our ratings are up. All sorts of people have tuned in because of the murders."

Based on the Nielsen report I saw, I'd wager that many had tuned out, too.

Camille tugged a marigold plant out of a pot and waggled the dirty mass in my direction. "I hate these. They constantly require deadheading. I've told my gardener not to plant them, but does he listen?" She peered at me. "What else do you want to know?"

"Are you jealous that Beau's in love with Gloria?"

Camille coughed out a laugh. "As if. I know you saw me toying with him, but that's our thing. There's no chemistry between us. I do it because it irks him."

And irks Gloria.

I said, "I heard Beau wants to move to a big city to advance his career."

"Beau's staying in Tahoe for the moment." Camille's eyes glinted with annoyance, but she stifled it and returned to her plants, snip-snip-snipping them into submission. "Tahoe isn't a sinkhole. It's a good market." She attacked another batch of dead flowers. "Beau needs to learn more before he'll get bigger offers."

For a moment I wondered if I was wading through some freakish production of *A Midsummer's Night Dream* where everyone was in love with someone else . . . who wasn't in love with him or her. Including Tripp.

"Finn Ambrose's son is cute," I said.

"He's sweet."

"Did you know he has a girlfriend who lives near here?"

"Goody for him."

I didn't detect an inkling of interest, which made me breathe easier.

Camille yanked a tissue from her pocket and blew her nose. "These questions have nothing to do with Gloria receiving notes. Get back to the point or leave."

I couldn't dance around the topic any longer. "I have reason to believe that you sent Gloria flowers a week ago."

"I did no such thing."

Zorro, picking up on his mistress's distress, sprinted to her side. He snarled at me. So much for Mr. Friendly.

I pressed on. "I was checking out another lead and—"

"I never sent flowers." Camille kicked a flowerpot. It flew in my direction and hit me squarely on the shin.

"Ow!"

"I'm sorry. I didn't mean to . . ." She disappeared into the house and returned with a bag of frozen peas. "Use this."

"Thanks." A bump was already developing beneath my white jeans. Dang. I was becoming one of the walking wounded with nothing to show for my trouble. I took the peas and applied them.

Camille said, "Look, Miss Adams—Aspen—I discovered a charge on my credit card. I did not make it, if that's what you're referring to. I called the credit card company to complain. I'm assuming your next question will be did I send her the notes? No. I have not sent her notes about any murders. I do not have feelings for Gloria. I do not swing both ways."

"Really? I heard you made a pass at a female employee at your spa."

Camille frowned. "She misread my intention. Please leave."

"One more thing. Dr. Kristin Fisher was your doctor, was she not?" I asked.

"At one time."

"You suggested Gloria interview her."

"True."

"Any ill will between you and the doctor?"

"Are you accusing me of—" Camille thrashed the shears at me. "That's it. I did not kill Kristin or anyone else for Gloria's *glory*. Get out. Now."

I sprang to my feet and made a beeline for the exit.

Camille pursued me. "The nerve." She beat me to the front door and held it open. Zorro stood like a sentry by her side. "You are not welcome at KINC again. Do you understand?"

Chapter 29

Next door to Nevada or Bust Delivery Service, which was located in Incline Village Shops, was Mom & Pop Café. I couldn't have been happier. My stomach ached with hunger. I purchased a small green salad with chicken and ate every bite before walking along the wooden boardwalk to search for the mystery delivery girl.

A chime signaled my entrance into the mock-western office. The front desk was unmanned. A blast of refrigerated air hit me as the door swung shut.

"Hello," I yelled, but nobody answered. I dinged the silver bell sitting on the rough-hewn counter with my palm.

A toilet flushed and a door to my right opened. A young woman with spiky purple hair—not a girl, but not older than twenty-one—exited the bathroom. "Hi, help you?" she asked in a high-pitched voice. She was clad in a bowling shirt, jeans shorts, and sandals. Her only western gear was a bandanna. She wiped her hands on a paper towel and tossed it into a bin behind the counter.

"Aspen Adams." I handed her a business card.

"Laila. Walton." She tucked my card in her pocket.

"Did you deliver a letter to KINC a week ago Saturday?"

"I deliver lots of stuff there, but . . ." She peeked over her shoulder. "Let's go outside." She scurried out the front door.

I followed.

"Look, I don't want my boss to know about the letter you're referring to," she said. "We're not supposed to, you know, take outside business, but this guy hired me and was willing to pay up front. Then I heard that Miss Morning got a sick-o note, and well . . ." She fiddled with the half dozen dangling earrings inserted in her right earlobe.

"Where were you when the guy hired you?"

"At the bowling alley. Incline Bowl."

"When?"

"Friday a week ago. I don't know who he was. I was sort of drunk."

A fake ID wouldn't have persuaded me to serve Laila alcohol. Perhaps the bartender at the bowling alley was myopic.

"It was dark," she went on. "I was sitting on one side of the slatted partition, and he was on the other. He was wearing a hat. I heard him, but I didn't, well, you know, see him. Because of the slats." Laila toyed with the fringed hem of her shorts and peeked over her shoulder.

Exactly how much trouble would she get into if her boss found out about her moonlighting activities?

"You didn't ask his name?"

"Uh-uh." Laila gave a nervous jerk to one of the loopy earrings, as if the action would stimulate her brain cells. "He was wearing a floral shirt."

I thought of Vaughn Jamison and his penchant for floral shirts. Maybe Nick did have the right suspect. "Big print, small print?"

"Not sure. It was sort of green. He smelled good. Musky, you know?"

"How'd he know you were a delivery person?"

She giggled. "I'd come straight from work." She pointed to her bowling shirt. "I just came on duty. I was about to change when you walked in. We wear a cowboy shirt with the company logo on it."

Camille had been right about the uniform.

"How tall was he?"

"He was sitting, so I can't be sure. He could have been five six or five eight or taller if he was hunching down." Laila used her hands to tell the tale. "I'm five-foot-four."

"Broad or thin face?"

"Didn't see it." Laila twisted the silver unicorn ring on her pinky. "It was dark."

"What did he say?" His voice or choice of words might identify him.

"He said he had fan mail for a special lady, but he was too shy to deliver it. I thought that was sort of cute. In retrospect . . ." Laila tittered.

I smiled reassuringly. "Do you bowl often?"

"I'm in a league every Tuesday. Same group of people that goes caving on Sundays."

"Do you know Tom Regent? He likes to spelunk," I said, adding Tom to the mix of possible suspects who had hired Laila even though I still couldn't come up with a reason for him to have murdered anyone.

She shook her head. "This morning when we went," she said, changing the subject, "it was so cool. The sun was directly overhead. Perfect for exposing niches. We went above Cave Rock." Her face glowed with eagerness. "Did you know there are dozens of caves there? Formed from volcanoes millions of years ago."

"Aren't there some eco-groups up in arms about you spoiling the area?" I happened to know the Washoe tribe wasn't keen on anyone scrambling over what they considered a sacred site. A century ago, Indian religious ceremonies had taken place inside the largest of the caves.

"They don't mind us. We don't use any tools. And if we climb, we only use toeholds and fingerholds. That's the natural way. You've got to see the caverns. Some of the stalactites are incredible." Laila mimed the tapered structures with her hands. "There are red and yellow ones—those are the ones with iron. The white ones are made up of calcium carbonate stuff. I go sometimes by myself, you know, before work. It's like a spiritual awakening."

If allowed, I'd bet Laila would talk for hours about her adventures, but I had more urgent business. "Do you think if you saw the guy who gave you the note again, you'd recognize him?"

She tugged on her earrings again. "You know, it could've been a woman who hired me."

"Why would you say that?"

Laila tapped her head. "The voice. It was husky and sounded forced like he was putting on an English accent."

The hinges on the wooden door squeaked and Laila jumped. "Hey, boss." She stood at attention.

A Dolly Parton look-alike, dressed in western garb and what I hoped were fake pistols in the holster hanging around her hips, stepped outside and stared at Laila with open hostility.

Laila sputtered. "I was just saying goodbye."

Chapter 30

I left Laila and her boss to hash it out and drove to Incline Bowl. In the parking lot, I squeezed between a forest green Navigator and midnight blue TrailBlazer, both big enough to carry a slew of kids. The bumper sticker on the Navigator read *Cavemen do it better.* On the TrailBlazer: *Stop abortion or else.* Seeing them made me recall the SUV that had almost run me off the road the other night. At the time, I'd considered the near miss an accident. Had it been on purpose? Vaughn Jamison drove a Tahoe blue SUV. Gloria might have let slip where I lived. Had he been lying in wait for me because I was helping her? Had he taunted my dog? If he'd hired Laila, that could add one more checkmark to what Nick already considered a closed case.

I strode into the bowling alley and took a moment to orient myself. The throbbing clatter of balls rolling and pins falling reminded me of times as a kid when I'd bowled with my dad. We would drink soda, eat popcorn, and laugh a ton. My mother wouldn't go along because she hated the noise, but when we got home, she begged for a play-by-play account. How I missed them.

Half of the twenty lanes were in use. In the farthest lane, a man with the zeal of a convert bowled by himself. *Zoom*—the balls sped down the polished wood. *Smash*—the pins fell. In a room to my right, bells clanged as kids played old-fashioned pinball machines and stereophonic video games. A dozen grammar school–aged children wearing party hats sat at a long narrow table. No doubt about it. The bowling alley was a cash cow.

As I moved toward the bar area, I spotted an odd twosome on the center lane. Beau was cheering on Tom, who had just rolled a last-frame strike. For two guys reluctant to acknowledge each other's existence at work, they seemed quite buddy-buddy on a Sunday. After finishing his set, Tom let his bowling ball return into the turnaround and staggered up the stairs in my direction while fetching his wallet from his left rear pocket.

I stole into the bar, slid onto a stool, pulled a bowl of peanuts toward me, and studied an appetizer menu. I didn't plan to eat anything, but I didn't want Tom to know I'd seen him.

Out of the corner of my eye, I kept tabs on him. He moved to the counter, slightly off-balance, and thumped his fist on it.

"Barkeep." Judging by Tom's bear-like size, I had trouble believing that he could have been the person who had given Laila the note. Even hunched in a booth, he wouldn't look five-foot-six. But Laila had admitted to having too much to drink. Everything she'd said about the person who'd hired her could be off the mark.

The bartender wiped his hands on a stained towel. "I should cut you off, Tom."

"But you won't."

The bartender, who by the look of his red-veined face was a regular imbiber himself, said, "The usual?"

Tom nodded.

"You and Beau are going to float out of here." The bartender filled a pair of plastic cups with Budweiser from the tap and set them on the counter. "Nine bucks."

"Keep the change." Tom tossed a ten-dollar bill at him. As he gathered his drinks, he spotted me. "Hey, there, Miss Private Eye."

I turned and acted surprised to see him. "Hi, Tom. Funny seeing you here."

"We're playing some frames. Care to join?" Tom tucked his *Cavers Rock* T-shirt into his jeans and ran his fingers through his chaotic mass of salt-and-pepper hair. "I'm trying to break my high of one ninety."

"Is that Beau with you?" I asked, looking toward the alleys.

"Yeah, him and me, we play once a week to blow off steam. C'mon, roll a few with us."

"Uh, I don't bowl," I lied, fearing that if I beat them I might hurt their egos. My father had been a good teacher.

"Are you doing PI stuff?" Tom took a sip of his beer.

"As a matter of fact, I am. I want to find out if anyone saw a guy ask a young woman to make a delivery to Gloria."

Tom didn't blink. In fact, his face filled with concern. "This thing with Gloria, is it serious?"

"This thing?"

Tom sighed, his fondness for Gloria unmistakable. "The notes. Does the sheriff really think the killer is writing them? Gloria is freaked out."

"I'm taking them seriously."

"The sheriff isn't?"

"It's debatable."

"I heard they hauled in Vaughn Jamison. Wrong guy, if you ask me." He leaned closer to impart a secret. "Beau wants to marry her."

"I heard they broke up," I said. "He might be seeing Camille."

"Uh-uh. That woman would eat him alive. He's not crazy." He took another sip of his beer. "Maybe you've seen Camille making eyes at him, but there's no reciprocation. Trust me. I'd know."

Okay, I was confused. Was Tom in love with Gloria or Camille? Or both?

"Does Camille have something going on with Finn Ambrose?" I asked.

"Heck no. That lily-livered—" He stopped short. "Him and his silk shirts and his oily voice."

"What about between Gloria and him?" I prepared myself for what could be an explosive response.

"No way." Tom moved closer, towering over me, the left side of his face twitching.

"So I found out this delivery person"—I hoped to rein in the conversation—"worked for a company here in Incline."

Tom ran a finger along the rim of his glass. "I don't understand why this note-writing dude would pay a messenger."

"Anonymity."

From the lanes, Beau yelled, "Hey, Tom, let's get this game going. I've got a schedule to keep." He didn't acknowledge me. I noticed that his speech was more slurred than Tom's.

"Gotta go, Aspen. I'll catch up to you later."

"Wait, Tom. Um, where were you last Thursday night?" The night Miranda Tejeda died.

"Guarding a cave, why?"

"Guarding?"

"Yeah, bats need privacy if they're going to survive, and there are a lot of gung-ho amateur cavers who don't understand that. I took the six-to-ten shift."

"You were there alone?"

"Yeah. A buddy I cave with took the ten-to-two. I gotta go." Tom hooked his thumb, grabbed Beau's beer, and moseyed back to the alley.

The bartender drew near and set a napkin in front of me. "What'll it be?"

Sure, now he was interested in my order. "Soda with lime." I offered my most winning smile. "You know Tom and Beau?"

"Without them, my little girl wouldn't have braces." He laughed.

I did, too, eager to bond with him. "So what schedule does Beau have to keep?"

"He's got a second job. At the Black Hawk Saloon Mondays and Tuesdays."

"Not tonight."

"Nah. He's just giving Tom a hard time."

I laid a twenty-dollar bill on the bar. "Why does Beau need another job?"

"To help his sister with her kid."

"He's a saint."

"Yeah, he is. Her flaky boyfriend ran out on her." The bartender spritzed some soda into a glass filled with ice, tossed a wedge of lime on top, slid the drink toward me, and then made change for my twenty. "He doesn't earn enough at the studio. Tells me he's real ticked at the ice princess for that."

"His producer, Camille St. John?"

"Yep. If Beau gets another gig that doesn't task his brain, can you blame him? He makes three or four hundred per night. He's a single guy, so he can do it. My wife wants me working days."

"Does Beau come in here a lot?" My mouth ached from smiling.

"Him and Tom, the dynamic duo. Sometimes I have to kick them out. They can get a little rowdy."

A disgusting notion hit me. Was their feud at work an act? Could Beau and Tom be committing murder together? Was driving Gloria insane their aim?

Honestly, Aspen. Get real.

"Do you know a girl named Laila Walton?" I asked.

The bartender winked. "She's a fun time."

"You dated her?"

"Nah! I don't step out on the missus." He held his palms up in defense. "I just mean Laila's always laughing, a real prankster. Why're you asking about her?"

"I'm a friend of her parents," I lied. "They want to know who she dates, what kind of trouble she gets into, that sort of thing."

"She's of age." He wiped down the bar, avoiding eye contact.

"No, she's not."

"Then she's got a fake ID."

I pointed over my shoulder. "She was in here a week ago Friday. Sitting in one of those booths by a divider. She said some guy in a Hawaiian shirt offered her a courier job. Nothing illegal. Know who it might've been?"

The bartender shook his head, stymied. "We're real busy on Fridays. Lots of guys are here. Could've been Tom or Beau or any of those guys from KINC. They all wear Hawaiian shirts on occasion."

"Do all of them bowl?"

"Yeah, Vaughn, Rick."

That confirmed that Vaughn frequented the bowling alley and might have been the person who'd hired Laila.

"Heck, even Gloria comes in to bowl occasionally," the bartender went on. "I don't think she bowls very well, though. I think she's afraid of breaking a nail."

My cell phone rang. It was Nick. "I've got to take this."

The bartender gave me a nod and moved away.

Nick said, "We need to talk. Your cabin in an hour." He hung up. No debate.

My shoulders slumped. He didn't sound even close to an apology.

Chapter 31

As I drove through Tahoe City, a sea of dark clouds gathered above the crest of mountains on the Nevada side. My insides felt as gloomy. My cell phone rang. Camille was on the phone. I answered hands-free.

Before I could say hello, she railed at me, "You went to Nevada or Bust."

"Yes."

"Why did you do that? I told you everything."

"Because I wanted to meet the delivery girl and find out who hired her."

"Her boss is ticked off. She gave me an earful. So I'm giving you one. Back off. Gloria does not need your help."

"When Gloria tells me that herself, I'll stop my investigation. And not before." I ended the call.

My cell phone rang again. I scanned the readout. Not Camille. Sorcha McRae was calling.

I answered.

"Sorry I left in a huff the other night. You didn't deserve that." Her words came out staccato, awkward, as if she'd never uttered an apology. "I talked to Finn and he admitted that his wife was dead. He asked why I'd thought she was alive, and I said he'd implied that she was, by talking about her in the present. That surprised him. He said he's always been candid about it. His ex-wife had an illness. An infection. Tripp was torn up about it. So I guess that explains it."

Not really, but I didn't press. Instead, I pursued another thread. "Did you know Finn sent flowers to Camille St. John as well as Gloria Morning?" I told her how Jules had been upset, wondering to whom he'd sent flowers. Even accusing Tripp of doing so on his behalf.

"He's a magnanimous guy. He loves to spoil women. What can I say?" She chuckled. "The life of a PI. It's definitely more exciting than being a security guard at a casino. Listen, back to the other night—"

"Forget about it. Water under the bridge." I turned into my driveway. "I've got to go."

"Keep in touch."

As I pulled to a stop, I spotted Nick standing to one side of the cabin, staring up at the sky, hands jammed into his pockets. I hopped out of the Jeep, shoulders back, chin held high, ready for whatever he was going to hurl at me.

He pivoted and strode toward me, hand extended. "Truce."

To say I was surprised was an understatement. "Why do we need a truce?" I asked, caution leading the way.

"Because we do."

"Is that what was so urgent?"

"Yes."

I shook his hand, appreciating its warmth. "Truce."

We stood silent for a long moment, gazing into each other's eyes. A shrieking bird broke the spell.

"Got a beer for a humble public servant?" Nick asked.

I couldn't fetch a Heineken fast enough and hurried inside. "Want a snack?" I asked while pouring a glass of chardonnay for myself.

"Sure. Where is everybody?" Standing in the kitchen doorway, he peeked down the hall.

"Candace and Cinder are on a date with Candace's boyfriend and the boy's older sister and Waverly."

"Safety in numbers."

"Exactly."

I put together a plate of cheese, grapes, and seasoned crackers, and ushered Nick to the porch. For a moment, neither of us said anything. I enjoyed the skittering of the squirrels and the breeze thrumming the trees. The knots in my shoulders loosened a bit. My jaw relaxed, too.

"Looks like rain tonight." Nick took a swig of his beer.

"Sure does."

As if on cue, lightning lit up the sky. Seconds later, thunder cracked.

"Want to go back inside?" I asked.

"Not yet. Rain is a ways off. Fill me in on everything you've learned to date."

"Why? You've arrested Vaughn Jamison. You've got your man."

"C'mon. You've done your due diligence. You deserve to be heard. Bring me up to speed. Just in case I'm wrong."

I took a sip of wine and briefed him about Tom and Beau and their rivalry at work, their feelings for Gloria, and my shock at seeing them bowling together.

"Guys are different from women," Nick said. "They can fight about the stupidest things, call each other vile names, and remain friends. Next?"

I filled him in on the delivery person, Laila Walton.

"Do you want to know my gut reaction?" Nick said. "Tom is your note writer, and Laila is your best bet in proving it."

"She said the guy was shorter than Tom."

"You said it yourself. He could have hunched down, and he's obviously in love with Gloria."

I set my wineglass on the table. "As for Camille St. John, she could have tucked her hair beneath a cap and lowered her voice. Laila said the English accent sounded put on." I told him about her tattoo and her anger at me for asking her about her relationship with Dr. Fisher. When I mentioned the flowers and the love note that she might have sent to Gloria, Nick cut in.

"The florist could have made a mistake or the receptionist could have gotten the recipient wrong."

"I'll cede the point. How about this little tidbit?" I tapped the table. "Tripp Ambrose, Finn's son, claims to have an older girlfriend living in Incline. What if it's Camille?"

"What difference would it make if he were having a fling with her? That doesn't throw a spotlight on his father."

"Tripp visited us last night."

"Here?" Nick stiffened. "How'd he get your address?"

"The girls were online with him. One of them must have let it slip."

Nick rolled his eyes. "I'll bet he was lying about the older girlfriend so Candace and Waverly would feel comfortable. My bet, he likes one of them." He sandwiched together a bite of cracker and cheese and polished it off.

I told him about the intriguing lamp Tripp had lugged with him. "It makes me sad how his father ignores him. The kid has talent."

Rain leaked from the sky. I grabbed the snacks and my wine and ducked into the kitchen. Nick followed me. I set the food on the counter as rain began to drum the rooftop. Hard. Harder. I considered calling Candace but knew she was smart enough to get in the car and head home.

Loving the nearness of Nick, I didn't move. I launched into my meeting with Finn in his penthouse suite. I replayed the interaction between Jules and Tripp.

"Sounds more like a soap opera than a day in the life of Lake Tahoe." Nick plucked a grape from the cluster on the platter. "You should submit it to *Sob Digest*."

"Ha-ha." I recounted my dinner with Sorcha and the alibis she offered on behalf of Finn. "If he drove Tripp to his AA meetings, he easily could have driven away, committed murder, and returned."

"Fair point."

"Sorcha also told me that the feud between Ambrose and Vittorio was a publicity stunt, but his brother and widow deny that."

Nick laughed. "Captains of industry plot to dupe their own families. Film at eleven."

"Speaking of Enzo Vittorio, I don't suspect him any longer." I recapped Enzo's alibi for the night Miranda Tejeda was murdered. "Of course, if a different killer committed each of the murders—"

"We don't think that's the case."

"Because of the crime scene evidence?"

He nodded.

"What's going on with Vaughn?" I asked.

"He's lawyered up."

"Is he out on bail?"

"Nope. Give us time and we'll find out if he's the one who's been sending the notes to Gloria, okay?" Nick lifted my chin and kissed me gently. "I'm sorry we've been at odds. My fault. I've been a boor. My sister . . ." He grimaced, unwilling to say more.

"Dealing with an addict is a challenge."

"When this is all over—"

The sound of a car screeching cut through the air. Then the front door slammed. Nick released me.

"Dang it!" Candace screamed.

I charged into the foyer. Nick trailed me. Cinder almost knocked me down to get to his water bowl. Candace stood fixed in one spot, fuming, her hair and beach cover-up dripping wet.

"Dang it, dang it, dang it!" She threw her purse and backpack on the floor and kicked the backpack.

"What happened?"

"Rory."

I gulped. "What did he do?"

"Nothing."

Nick stood so close I could feel his heat.

Unable to think clearly with him near, I clasped Candace by the arm and led her to the living room couch. "Let's talk. Want some cocoa?" Hot chocolate could fix almost any problem, especially in the middle of summer rainstorm.

"I'm not a little girl."

No, she wasn't. She was a beautiful flower ready to blossom.

"Dang it!" Candace repeated and kicked the base of the couch.

"Don't hurt yourself," I cautioned. "What *nothing* did Rory do?"

Candace glowered at Nick like he was an invader and folded her arms. I would have done the same at her age.

Quick on the uptake, he retreated to the kitchen.

"We were having a great day but then . . . but then . . ." Candace hiccupped. "Then after we dropped his sister and Waverly at home, he pawed me. My mother would've said go for it, but . . . but . . ." She sputtered. "I'm not ready. He knew that."

"Good thing Cinder was with you."

"Are you kidding?" Candace glared at me as if I was the stupidest woman to grace the earth. "That dog would do anything for Rory." Tears trickled down her flushed cheeks. She brushed them off with the hem of her cover-up and threw her hands in the air. "I'm so mad."

"Okay, you said no. What happened next?"

"Rory has ears. He's not dumb. But he never wants to see me again." Candace whimpered. "He's already had sex, you know."

Nick had to have heard that. He got Brownie points for not barging in and offering to neuter the boy.

"How old is he again?" I asked.

"Sixteen." Candace tugged at the strands of wet hair sticking to her cheek. After a long moment, she jumped to her feet. "I'm going to go online if that's okay."

"To talk to Waverly?"

"To Tripp. He'll know what I should say to Rory."

"Candace, I don't think you should—"

"I need some smart-aleck remark that will really hurt a guy's ego." She slogged down the hall. Over her shoulder, she said, "Why is Nick here? Has there been another break in the case?"

"We were discussing flowers."

She snorted. "As if."

Stymied, I slipped into the kitchen wondering what I'd been thinking, taking custody of a teenager. I didn't have mothering skills. Neither did my sister. Which of us was better for Candace in the long run? No question, me. I'd dealt with teens for a living. Just not my *own*.

Nick was talking on his cell phone. He said a quick, "Yeah, okay, thanks," and ended the call. He offered me a supportive smile. "Is she going to be okay?"

"I think so."

After a long moment, he wrapped his arms around me and tucked a loose hair behind my ear. "Let's see. Where were we?"

"You said, 'When this is all over.'"

"Right." He kissed me passionately and murmured, "When this is all over, we need to take a vacation. Just the two of us. Okay?"

Chapter 32

That night, as rain pounded the roof, I tossed in bed, my mind working frantically to sort through my life—Candace and her health, my relationship with Nick, my unsuccessful investigation. Lying on my side, I watched the red numbers on the digital clock change: *1:02, 1:03, 1:04.*

At *1:05,* I sat up. If I wasn't going to sleep, I could organize my thoughts the way I used to when I was working with a patient. Sometimes, when I put things in black and white, I could see answers that I couldn't reason out in my mind.

I switched on a light, grabbed a notepad from the nightstand, and dedicated a page to each of my suspects.

Camille St. John. Denied sending the flowers. Patient of Dr. Fisher's. Critical of Gloria's work. Nielsen ratings falling. Upset when Tejeda tricked Gloria into sharing the promotional sign. Seething at Gloria's interview with Tony Vittorio. Must get her alibis.

Finn Ambrose. Misled Sorcha about his ex-wife. Significant? Was wearing Hawaiian-style shirt when I visited his restaurant. Was the feud between Tony Vittorio and him real or not? Viola and Enzo Vittorio said there was no love lost between them. Sent flowers to Camille. Also to Gloria. Did he hire Laila?

I jotted a side note to consider whether Tom had sent flowers using Camille's credit card and then returned to Finn. His son might have been Tejeda's student at one time. Was he angry about the way the teacher had treated Tripp?

Tripp Ambrose.

I hesitated making notes about the boy. Did being his father's son make him a suspect? Did he have an obsession for Gloria or Camille? Was Camille his girlfriend or did he admire her from afar? He'd acted like a puppy around her at KINC. Did he, not his father, send her the flowers? Did he also send flowers to Gloria? Was he Tejeda's student? As far as I could tell, he had no connection to Dr. Fisher, unless his mother had been her patient, but neither Ambrose nor Vogel was on the patient roster.

Tom Regent. Weak alibi for Dr. Fisher's murder. No motive, though. Weak alibi for Tony Vittorio's murder, too. What motive did he have for that one? Was he jealous of Tony Vittorio? Adores Gloria but can't win her love. One flirty dinner didn't seem enough reason to kill the guy. If he wasn't the killer, was he simply trying to get Gloria's attention with the notes? Did he hire Laila? Does he own the SUV with the *Cavemen do it better* bumper sticker? Did he try to run me off the road?

Beau Flacks.

Like I had for Tripp, I hesitated. I didn't know enough about Beau. I hadn't had a chance to fully interview him. His sister had been a patient of Dr. Fisher's. Was that significant? He adored Gloria, and she vouched for him one hundred percent. Were her instincts on the mark? Had he been jealous of Tony Vittorio, as I'd presumed for Tom? What connection might he have had to Tejeda? If the notes Candace and I had seen at the sheriff's office were correct, horsehair had been found at the scene of at least one crime. Beau owned a horsehair vest.

My cell phone rang.

At the same time, lightning pierced the sky. Its flare flashed through the break in the drapes. Cinder yowled. A new wave of storms was coming through.

Shaken, I snatched the phone and stabbed Send. "Who is this?"

"Aspen?" a woman rasped. "Help me." A dog barked in the background. Cinder growled, obviously sensing the other dog's distress. "Zorro, *shh*," the woman said.

"Camille?"

Candace paused in the archway of my bedroom door, her nightgown twisted around her slim body. She rubbed her eyes. "What's wrong?"

"Someone's in my house," Camille rasped. Her cell phone crackled like it was having trouble finding its signal.

"Call 911," I said.

"They put me on hold."

Something on the other end of the line went thud. Zorro yelped. Cinder did the same.

"Camille—"

The connection died.

Candace raced to Cinder and wrapped her arms around his neck to calm him. "Was that Camille St. John? Her dog sounded frightened. Do you know where she lives?"

"Yes."

"Then go to her."

"No. I'm calling 911."

She flailed a hand at me. "They've got to be swamped with outages because of the storm. Aunt Aspen, she reached out to *you*. Go. She needs you."

"Why me?"

"Because you're like Switzerland. You're neutral."

Or mine was the last number she'd dialed and the easiest to redial.

"I'll go with you," Candace said.

"No way." I clambered out of bed and threw on jeans, a long-sleeved T-shirt, and tennis shoes. "Want to be helpful? Call Nick and tell him Camille St. John contacted me. She thinks someone is in her house. Then go to Opal's with Cinder."

"It's late."

"No arguments. Her mother said anytime, anywhere."

I kissed my niece's forehead, grabbed my tote, and dashed into the summer storm.

Speeding in the rain wasn't safe, but I sped anyway and pulled in front of Camille's house in half the time it would have taken normally, all the while wondering whether I was being tricked. After all, Camille had made it clear that I was persona non grata. On the other hand, she had sounded in distress.

Everything seemed fine from the street. Lights were on inside the house and out. No windows appeared to be broken. No strangers lurked in cars. After retrieving my flashlight and the hammer I kept in the glove compartment for emergencies—in case I got trapped in my Jeep and had to break a window from the inside out—I dodged puddles up the path. I paused when I realized the front door was ajar. I pushed it open and stepped inside, hammer raised.

"Camille?"

Silence. Zorro didn't bound to me. I checked behind the door and in the hall closet. No one leaped out at me. Even so, my shoulders tensed up and my breathing came in shallow spurts. With my free hand, I whisked raindrops off my face and scanned the living room. The overhead canned lights were dim. A reading lamp was switched on. No movement.

I listened intently as I tiptoed forward. The stereo hummed, as if it had reached the end of a recording and was ready to reboot. A whirr of something mechanical emanated from my right. And then I heard a dog whimper.

Zorro.

I sprinted to the kitchen and found him lying beside the island, his collar gone. Was he hurt? Just beyond him I spotted a foot. With painted toenails.

Camille, faceup, throat slashed, chenille robe open.

A metallic taste filled my mouth, as if I had been chewing rusty nails. I fought the urge to heave and scrambled to her side. Gritty dirt jabbed the palms of my hands. I gripped Camille's wrist. No pulse. Blood oozed from her neck and pooled on the floor beneath her head.

Suddenly the lights switched off. Everywhere. Power outage?

No, I heard soft footsteps.

Zorro whimpered but didn't budge.

I leaped to my feet, hammer raised. Darkness blinded me. I oscillated back and forth, listening for the intruder.

At the same time, I felt air whisk the back of my neck. I turned toward the movement and swung the hammer. Something hard cracked into my right ear. My head snapped to the left. Soft musty debris dusted my face and clothing. I went temporarily blind. A flurry of triangles and stars whizzed behind my eyelids. I stumbled over Camille's body and toppled to the floor.

As I crawled to get off of her, footsteps slapped the tile. The killer was getting away.

Chapter 33

With the room spinning around me, I lay on Camille's kitchen floor and stabbed numbers on my cell phone while cursing the lack of reception and furious that I'd been caught unaware. Camille had been right. A killer had been in her house. I hadn't stopped him. I hadn't saved her.

"Aspen!" a man yelled. Nick.

"In the kitchen." I prepared myself for his diatribe about entering the house without backup.

But he didn't curse me. He didn't chastise me. He set his flashlight beside me and said, "You're hurt." The concern in his voice was palpable.

De Silva trailed him.

"Camille." My mouth was drier than toast. "Over there."

"De Silva," Nick said and hitched his head. The fresh-faced detective hurried to Camille.

A two-way radio attached to Nick's belt crackled. A man said, "Nick, all clear?"

Nick flipped a button on the radio and said, "Get an ambulance."

"Camille's dead," I said. "An ambulance won't do her any good."

"For you."

"I'm fine. Help the dog."

"What dog?"

I pointed to Zorro. "He's in shock."

Nick scrambled to the dog and said into the radio, "Send a vet, too." He returned to me; De Silva tended to Zorro. "Can you sit?"

"No." The room was whirling. I'd suffered vertigo before. This was worse.

"What happened?"

"Killer. Hit. Me." In the glow of Nick's flashlight, I caught sight of the object the killer had used. A potted plant. A puny potted plant. I felt as stupid as a rock. But then I remembered the dirt by Camille. "Gritty stuff on the floor. By Camille. Evidence."

"It's not important right now."

"Yes, it is," but I couldn't remember why. And then I did. "The Post-its at the station. Your case notes. Mud."

"What are you talking about?"

Sheepishly, I admitted that Candace and I had caught sight of a series of Post-it notes on a file folder pertaining to Dr. Fisher's case at the station and had seen the words *mud, metal,* and more on them. "Don't be mad."

Nick brushed dirt and stray hairs off my face. "You're bleeding but it doesn't look bad. Good thing you have a hard head."

I wished I could appreciate his humor, but Camille was lying dead not ten feet away, and the killer had seen me. "Nick"—I gripped his arm—"Candace and Cinder could be in danger. I sent them to the neighbors."

"I'll have someone check on them."

"Gwen. Call Gwen."

Suddenly, the lights went on everywhere. The glare was harsh. I blinked to fight off nausea.

A moment later, Detectives Hernandez and King, their shoes covered by sterile booties, stepped into the area. A couple of technicians followed. Nick joined Hernandez and King.

I couldn't make out the discussion. I tried to sit, but I felt like clamps were compressing my head, so I lay back down. King nodded and left the room. Hernandez moved out of my line of sight.

Nick squatted beside me. "How are you doing?"

"Queasy. I guess this time it's okay for me to see the crime scene?"

"Lady, you *are* the crime scene." He didn't smile. His tone was grim.

I fingered the hammer resting by my side. "A lot of good this did me."

"Be thankful the guy didn't take your life."

Sobering words. I swallowed hard. "Why didn't he kill me?"

"He tried."

"No, he didn't. Not with a flowerpot." An irritating detail gnawed at me. "He didn't kill me because I haven't hurt Gloria. Did she receive a note?"

"In this short of a time? I doubt it."

"Nick," Hernandez cried, "you gotta see this."

I looked in his direction.

Hernandez plucked a piece of white paper from the laser printer in the kitchen nook—Camille's home office—and read it aloud: "*'Don't worry, my love. She won't steal your limelight. For your . . .'* It ends there."

"*Glory,*" I said, filling in the rest. "*For your glory.*" I shuddered. "Nick, I heard a clicking sound when I stole inside. I thought it was the stereo. I must have interrupted the killer when he was typing the message." I gazed at him. "This time the killer had it correctly. Camille *was* going to hurt Gloria. She was going to fire her."

"How would the killer know that?"

"There was a letter in Camille's office. In a file on top of her desk. With her open-door policy, anyone who worked at KINC could have known about her plan."

"So you think the killer is someone who works at the station?"

"It has to be." I licked my lips. "Is Vaughn Jamison still in jail?"

"Yes."

"Then that rules him out."

"If what you're saying is true, that rules out Finn Ambrose, too."

"Wait. No. Not necessarily." I raised a hand. "The day Finn did his interview, he went into Camille's office to make a private phone call. What if the file folder with the letter of intent was lying open on her desk at the time?"

Cycling through the suspect list I'd written earlier, I realized Tom had the most to gain by Camille's death. I told Nick so. If he became full owner of KINC, he would have the ability to promote Gloria as he saw fit. What baffled me was, with Camille dead and Vaughn innocent, all links between KINC and Dr. Fisher dissolved.

No, that wasn't true. Beau's sister. She had been a patient. However, she'd left amicably and moved to Arizona. Could the doctor's murder be a separate, isolated incident?

The lights in the room grew dark. Darker.

"Aspen, sweetheart, are you with me?"

I felt a warm hand on my cheek.

"Open your eyes," Nick ordered.

I didn't realize I'd closed them. I snapped to attention. "I'm okay. Really." I forced a smile. "Did you find the murder weapon? I didn't see anything around Camille."

"Yes. He used a louver off a klieg light."

"A louver?"

"One of the metal flaps. Looks like a blinder."

The murderer had yet again wielded a weapon specific to the victim. Using a klieg light suggested somebody from the studio had killed Camille, but that could be the murderer's way of implicating someone other than himself. Even so, the thematic weapon implied that one person was committing all the murders. Scalpel for the doctor, chef's knife for the restaurateur, scissors for the teacher, and a klieg light for Camille. It was not a game of Clue, but it was as puzzling.

I struggled to sit. Nick braced my back. I brushed Zorro's dog hair off my shirt and wiped dirt from my face and hair. "Water, please." My mouth felt as grainy as sandpaper.

Nick rose, poured a glass for me at the sink, and returned. He helped me take small sips.

Detective King strode into the kitchen. "Nick, a neighbor said she saw a black SUV in the neighborhood earlier."

"Was she sure it was black?" I asked. "Blue could look black. So could dark green."

"Did you see it?" Nick touched my shoulder.

"No, but Vaughn Jamison drives a blue SUV."

"He's locked up."

"Right. You said that. I think Tom Regent drives an SUV. A green Navigator."

"Nick." Hernandez signaled from across the room.

Nick took the glass from me and set it in the sink. While he talked with Hernandez, I saw a tech retrieve the glass and dust for prints. I shivered.

When Nick came back, I said, "Am I a suspect?"

"I think I can rule you out." He offered a crooked smile. "The cut to Camille's throat appears to be right to left, indicating a left-handed assailant, and—" He rolled his eyes up, averting my gaze.

"Are you weighing whether you should tell me what else you discovered?"

He peered at me. "You know me too well."

"Not well enough. Spill."

"The restaurant at Ambrose Alley delivers. They use dark blue Suburbans, and I just learned that a dark-colored SUV was seen in the vicinity of Vittorio's Ristorante on the afternoon of that murder."

"Go. Question Finn Ambrose."

"I'm sending Hernandez. Right now, I want to get you to the hospital. You might have a concussion."

"Not from a stupid potted plant. I didn't pass out." I rose to my feet but teetered. "I need to speak to Candace."

Nick clasped my arm. "Gwen is already with her. Candace and the dog are fine."

I could only imagine what Candace must be going through. Did she feel guilty for urging me to help Camille? Would she remind me that she'd wanted to accompany me? I anticipated a flood of reprimands when I saw her and sighed. Just what I needed—a fourteen-year-old bodyguard.

A pair of emergency medical technicians hurried into the kitchen. The taller one checked out Camille. The shorter knelt beside me and ran through the requisite questions and concluded that I had to go to the hospital.

Nick kissed my forehead and said he was following me. "Everything's under control here."

I didn't argue. A jackhammer had taken up residence inside my head. As the EMTs lifted me onto a stretcher, I said, "How's the dog, Nick? How's Zorro?"

"The vet is attending to him."

"If no one steps up, I'll adopt him." Owning one dog or two dogs, did it matter?

"We'll deal with that later."

Chapter 34

Around three a.m., Nick left me in the care of a frosty doctor at Truckee Hospital and went to convene with his team. Finn Ambrose and Tom Regent were on his main list of suspects. He added Beau Flacks because of the connection between Beau's sister and Kristin Fisher.

The doctor, while clucking his tongue, inserted a dozen stitches. I presumed he was disapproving of how I'd suffered the injury. If he only knew that my ego was more bruised than my partially shaved head.

At nine, a nurse wheeled me, bed and all, into a recovery room. "The doctor says you're fit to go home, and you can drive."

"Not without my car."

"It's in the lot. Someone from the sheriff's office delivered it. Your key is with your possessions. By the way, a few friends are here to see you. When you're through talking with them, I'll get a wheelchair and take you out, okay? Hospital protocol. Oh . . ." She offered a wry smile. "I almost forgot. The doctor said to apply ice to that hard noggin of yours every hour or so."

As the woman departed, Gwen, Owen, and Candace entered the recovery room. Gwen was pale. Owen looked honored to be included in the visit.

Candace, her face pinched with worry, skirted past both of them and clasped my hand, stroking me as if I were an injured kitten. "It's my fault." She sniffed back tears. "I don't know what I would've done if something happened—"

"It's not your fault." I knew exactly whose fault it was. Mine. "Where's Cinder?"

"Outside in Gwen's car. He's got water and the windows are open. It's cool enough for now."

Gwen wedged in beside Candace and glowered at me. Then to Owen she said, "Darlin', I warned you about my pal Aspen, didn't I? She's Miss Save the World. Geez, but she drives me to drink. Thank heaven I own a bar and get the liquor for free. Well, not for free, but I can charge my liquor to overhead."

Owen chuckled.

"Give me some room," I said and threw back the sheet. I dangled my legs over the side of the bed and sat up, feeling no dizziness, which was a good sign.

"Where do you think you're going?" Gwen demanded.

"They've released me. I've got work to do."

"Are they nuts?" Gwen snatched my chart and scanned it. She clamped the chart back in place. "Aspen, you are so darned impulsive and bullheaded. And now bald."

I gave her a sour look. "I'm not bald. I've got a bald patch."

"This is your third visit to the hospital in three months. What does it take to get through to you?"

I'd had a couple of minor emergencies, all work-related events, including cutting myself in a garbological expedition, twisting my ankle as I ran from an angry subpoena recipient, and receiving my first black eye, compliments of a client's ex-wife. But they were minor. As a therapist, I'd been slapped, choked, and pinned to the floor. *Wounds of life*, I'd christened the events.

"I'm fine."

"No, you most certainly are not. You're coming home with me. I'll feed you and fend off creditors."

I wasn't up to arguing, but I wasn't going to be easy prey. "Read my lips. I'm fine." I scuttled off the bed and grabbed my jeans and long-sleeved T-shirt.

"Idiot." Gwen shook her finger at me. Her curls bounced with fervor.

"Mother hen."

"As stubborn as a mule."

"Mules live long lives," I countered.

"Brainless."

I couldn't come up with another retort, so I stuck my tongue out. Real adult. Candace giggled and covered her mouth, which pleased me. Gwen's and my ridiculous exchange was defusing her stress. Mission accomplished. I glanced at the clothes in my arms and at Owen.

Getting the message, he said, "I'll be outside."

As he left, Sorcha McRae eased into the room while tapping on the door. She was dressed in black camp shorts, black T-shirt, and black Timberland boots. "Aspen, you're awake?"

"And brimming with company."

She quickly introduced herself to Gwen and hurried to me. "I can't believe it. First the elevator plummeting and now this."

"What elevator?" Gwen and Candace asked in unison.

I ignored the question. A conversation for another time. "How did you learn I was here, Sorcha?"

"Candace wrote Tripp, who told Jules."

I gazed at Candace, who worked her lip between her teeth, and returned my gaze to Sorcha. "Why aren't you at Ambrose Alley?"

"It's my day off. My brother—I told you I had a brother, didn't I?—he lives in Truckee. We'd planned to go hiking, but when I heard you were here—"

"You should know that the sheriff is questioning Finn as we speak."

"They don't think he killed Camille St. John and assaulted you, do they?"

"What's his alibi for this morning around one a.m., taking Tripp to another AA meeting?"

Sorcha shifted feet.

"That's what I thought." I waved a hand. "He's got an attorney. Let the two of them hash it out with the sheriff's people. Go. Be with your brother."

Sorcha petted my shoulder. "Take care." She turned to Candace. "You're a lucky girl to have her in your life."

"I know."

As she left, Heather Bogart breezed into the room. "Oh, Aspen, are you all right?"

I gawked. "How did *you* know I was here?" Surely Candace hadn't emailed her, too.

"I'm on a field trip." She struggled to free her tank top straps from beneath the bands of her backpack, which caused her to drop the notepad she'd been holding. She swooped it off the floor and hurried to me. "I started taking architecture classes, like you suggested. We're here to study building requirements for earthquake safety. When my teacher was signing us in, I saw your name on the white board. What happened to you? Your head . . ." She grimaced.

While Candace explained to Gwen who Heather was, I told Heather about the attack at Camille's.

Pain filled her eyes. She blinked back tears. "I can't believe a serial killer murdered my mother."

"The sheriff isn't sure of that."

A female about Heather's age poked her head inside. "Girl, c'mon." She tapped her watch. "We're moving."

"I hope you feel better soon," Heather said. "Call me." She scribbled her cell phone number on a piece of notepaper, tore it off, and handed it to me. "Let's have lunch." Like a breath of fresh air, she was gone.

An hour later, after making a promise to Gwen to take things easy—a promise I hoped I could keep—the hospital released me, and I drove toward North Lake Tahoe. Candace, refusing to leave me, was asleep in the passenger seat with Cinder curled at her feet.

I adjusted the ice pack I was holding to my temple to ward off the excruciating headache and reviewed last night's events. What if Finn Ambrose could account for his whereabouts at the time Camille was killed? What if somebody who knew that Ambrose Alley used dark-colored Suburbans as delivery vehicles was trying to frame Finn Ambrose by using a similarly colored vehicle?

I flashed on Tom Regent. He had the most to gain from Camille's death. Where was he?

I reached the office, parked, woke Candace, and we strode into the bungalow. The cats were sunbathing in the anteroom. One hissed at Cinder. Smart dog, he found a spot near the door to lie down.

"Max?" I yelled.

My aunt emerged from the kitchen and glowered at me. "Nick warned me that you were determined to get back to work. He's not happy. Neither am I. Nice hairdo."

My hand reflexively flew to my head. The injury throbbed but I would survive.

Max drew closer and assessed the dressing. "Looks decent. You need to eat."

"Stop. Please. Gwen and Candace have doled out all the mothering I can take for one day."

"I could eat," Candace said.

Max fetched two glasses of milk and two blueberry muffins. She handed them to Candace. "Make her eat one of these."

"You make her," Candace teased.

I grinned. How I enjoyed her spunk. I took a seat at the computer and logged on to the Internet.

Candace set the food to my right and pulled a chair close. She nibbled on her muffin. "It's delicious."

To appease my aunt, I took a swallow of milk and a bite of the muffin. Both tasted wonderful, but I would never admit it.

"By the way, Aspen," Max said, "Yaz went to Ambrose Alley. He's not sure he got the straight scoop. The technician can't pin down why the elevator plummeted that day, but he assures Yaz the elevator has been repaired."

"Good to know. And Darcy? Did she find anything about the Vittorio financials?"

"Not yet. She's doing a deep dive."

I clicked the search bar on the computer screen. "Max, how many SUVs do you figure look similar to a Suburban?"

"Go to Google and type in: *Images of SUVs*."

I did and an array of choices materialized. SUVs from small to large. A couple of luxury SUVs resembled a Suburban, including the Lincoln Navigator, which made me think of Tom. I'd bet anything the Navigator I saw at the bowling alley was his. Tom would have had access to Camille's office. Did he order flowers for Gloria using Camille's credit card? Was that why she'd circled the charge on the invoice? Maybe she rang Tom after my visit and lit into him, and Tom, having had enough of Camille's tongue-lashing for a lifetime, drove to her house and slit her throat. The gritty dirt on Camille's kitchen floor could have come from caves Tom explored. Was Nick checking that angle?

Leaving Cinder with my aunt and taking Candace with me—she wouldn't let me out of her sight—I climbed into the Jeep and sped toward KINC. Camille's caveat that I never set foot in the studio again was no longer valid.

Chapter 35

The circus of television trucks and crews camped outside KINC didn't shock me. Camille's death was big news. I pushed through the crowd with Candace.

Inside the foyer stood half a dozen reporters, each with a microphone thrust forward, each shouting questions about the SUV seen in the area.

"Mr. Flacks will not meet with any of you, nor will Miss Morning." Marie, the receptionist, aimed a pen at them. The remainder of her lunch, a quarter of a Big Mac and French fries, sat on the desk.

A matronly reporter tapped her clipboard with a pen. "Where's Tom? We're old friends. He'll speak to me."

"If you know him so well, you know where to find him." Marie rubbed under her nose.

"Get Gloria Morning out here," a big-nosed reporter yelled.

Marie shoved a French fry into her mouth.

"Her boss is dead," the guy continued. "She needs to make a comment. Camille St. John was one of our own."

Marie withdrew a nail file from a drawer and smoothed her burgundy nails. "No comment."

I'd bet she had been waiting all morning to say that line. During the onslaught of invectives that followed, I glanced at the door that led to the studio. The reporters, although intent on getting their stories, weren't trying to sneak in. Perhaps their reluctance had something to do with integrity. I, on the other hand, had no compunctions. I held a finger to my lips to Candace and steered her toward the door. Locked. Dang.

At the same time, Rick Tamblyn pushed through. His pants were perfectly creased, his white shirt starched. No tears stained his face. "What's going on out here?" He glared at me as if I was causing the ruckus.

"Reporters," I murmured. "They want to see Gloria. Let me see her first."

He held the door open and signaled Marie. "Take a break."

She didn't hesitate. She tore into the bathroom.

Rick yelled at the mob, "Everybody, gather around. I'm ready to make a statement on KINC's behalf."

A salvo of *who are you?* followed, giving Candace and me enough time to squeeze through the door unnoticed.

We sped to Gloria's dressing room. The door was ajar. I nudged it open.

Gloria sat hunched in the chair in front of her makeup mirror dabbing tear-swollen eyes with a tissue. When she spotted us, she shrieked. "Oh, heavens. Aspen, what happened to your head?"

"I'm fine." I filled her in.

"You are so brave to have gone there. You could have been killed. Poor Camille. The sheriff said—" Gloria shuddered with convulsive sobs. Tears dripped onto her blue silk dress as she ripped the tissue into shreds. "The sheriff said it was horrible."

"They've been here?"

She nodded meekly. "Detective Hernandez. He questioned everyone. Me, Beau, Rick. And he scoured Camille's office."

Someone burst through the door, grabbed my shoulder, and growled, "No reporters." He yanked me away from Gloria.

"Beau, you dope, it's Aspen," Gloria said. "Let her go. She's hurt."

Candace moved toward Beau.

I blocked her path with one arm. "Sit." She did.

Beau let go of me, but the damage was done. My arm began to smart something fierce, which sent shooting pains into my cerebral cortex. And then my knee and shin throbbed.

"Sorry," Beau muttered. "What happened to you?"

"Camille called Aspen for help," Gloria said. "The killer hit her and escaped."

"Why'd she call you?" Beau asked.

"Because she's like Switzerland," Candace said, repeating her earlier claim to me, "neutral."

"Camille didn't know who she could trust," I said.

Gloria sniffed. "Meaning me."

"Any of you." I shot a look at Beau.

Beau threw up both hands. "I didn't do it."

Gloria sucked back a sob. "Oh, Aspen, I'm scared. And sad. And worried. This monster . . . killed again."

Beau crossed to her. "Babe, don't think about this any more today. You should go home and rest. We'll cancel tonight's show. Your fans will understand."

"I can do the show."

"Not when you're this vulnerable." Beau caressed her shoulder. "You're in no shape to go under a barrage of hot lights."

Gloria was relishing his attention. Why shouldn't she? With Camille out of the picture, she could have Beau all to herself. I forced the nasty thought from my mind. Gloria did not kill Camille and slam me upside the head. Beau, on the other hand . . .

"Did you receive a note, Gloria?" I didn't mention the partial note found at Camille's. Nick or his people would want that information kept under wraps.

"No." Her eyes widened. "Does this mean it's a separate incident? Camille didn't want to hurt me."

"Of course she didn't." Beau brushed a single strand of hair off Gloria's face.

Rick burst into the room. "Reporters are carnivores." His shirttail was pulled free; his shirtsleeves were grimy. "Every last one of them." He pointed at Gloria. "Except you, of course."

"It's their job," she said.

"I gave them the basic response—the sheriff's office is investigating—and told them to leave, but they want more." He tucked his shirt into his trousers.

Beau pecked Gloria on the cheek and stood up. "You're beat. Let's get you home." He turned to Rick. "Tell Marie to unlock the rear door and escort Gloria there. I'm going to pull my car around." He marched out of the room, not open to objections.

Rick picked up the telephone receiver and punched in a number. "Marie, meet me and Gloria at the rear entrance. She's going home. She's under the weather. And lock the front on your way so none of those reporters sneak back here." He offered his hand to Gloria. She didn't take hold. "Help me, Aspen."

Too stubborn to admit I was in pain, I said, "C'mon, Gloria.

Candace, follow us." Together, we traipsed through the air-conditioned studio to the rear entrance.

Marie was already there. She draped a light jacket over Gloria's shoulders, even though the temperature outside was nearly a hundred degrees. "Hope you feel better."

A horn honked. Marie opened the sliding metal door and peeked out. "All clear."

Rick and I slipped outside with Gloria leaning heavily on me for balance. I jolted when I spied Beau in a midnight blue TrailBlazer. It was the one I'd seen at the bowling alley with the bumper sticker *Stop abortion or else*. Could his have been the SUV seen in Camille's neighborhood? And in mine?

Before I could find my voice, Beau ushered Gloria into the passenger seat and sped off.

I tried to assure myself that Beau wouldn't hurt her. If he was the guy sending her the notes, he'd vowed to protect her.

"Let's go," Rick said, holding the door open for Candace and me to return inside. "That way to reception." He pointed.

"Oh, gee. I left my car keys in Gloria's dressing room." I hoped he wouldn't notice the bulge in my pocket.

"And I need the bathroom," Candace said.

I wasn't sure if she was picking up on my need to scour for clues. At this point, I didn't care.

"Don't be long," Rick said and hurried in the direction of the studio. "Marie, see them out."

Marie closed the rear door and locked it. "By the way, what happened to your head?"

"Brain surgery," Candace quipped as she disappeared into the ladies' room.

Marie gasped.

"She's kidding. Small accident." I didn't feel the need to tell her I'd been attacked at Camille's. "I could use some ice."

"Sure."

"Before you go, tell me about the bumper sticker on Beau's car."

"His sister had a bad go of it. Some doctor in Tahoe City messed up."

I jolted. "Messed up how?"

"When Stacy was pregnant, the doctor didn't realize until, like, week twelve that the fetus was growing in the tube. It's called ec-something."

"Ectopic pregnancy," I said, knowing the dire nature of the term because a friend at BARC had suffered the same thing. The fetus wouldn't survive in the tube, and if allowed to grow, it could threaten the mother's life.

Marie said, "But then she did realize it and fixed it. Stacy had an abortion."

"And Stacy blamed the doctor?"

"I don't think so. She adopted a little girl and is thrilled. Beau's happy for her."

"You sure know a lot about him," I said.

"He's my kids' godfather."

I gawped. Beau had helped the bartender at Incline Bowl with his kid's braces and now this? Had I misjudged him? Was he a Good Samaritan?

"You have a child?" I said. Marie was barely past needing a babysitter herself.

"She's two. I'm a lot older than I look. I—"

"Marie!"

Three of KINC's staff crowded the receptionist and began shouting rapid-fire questions at her: *When could they get back to business? Were the vultures gone? Where was Tom?*

Seizing the distraction, I stole toward the cubicles hoping I could locate a home address for Tom. I tiptoed past the editing booth where Rick was reviewing some tapes. He didn't glance up.

Yellow sheriff's tape crisscrossed the opening to Camille's cubicle, prohibiting entry. I assumed Detective Hernandez had found everything I'd previously uncovered, including the agreement between Camille and Tom—unless Tom had squirreled it out.

The adjoining cubicle belonged to Beau. Either he had taste or he'd hired a designer. Intriguing black-and-white photos covered the walls. The lamp and desk accessories were made of black tortoiseshell. Even a black shag rug complemented the ebony furniture.

I heard somebody whistling—a man, not Candace. I presumed she'd returned to Gloria's dressing room to wait for me. The whistling grew stronger. Pulse racing, I scurried into the office beyond Beau's and crouched down. When the whistling faded, I stood up and realized I'd landed in Tom's cubicle. Perfect.

Like Beau's space, a television and DVD recorder sat on a bureau against the far wall. Unlike Beau's office, this one was a mess. Piles of books, old magazines, and used foam cups were everywhere. An old-fashioned Rolodex and stacks of paper and business cards cluttered the desk. I spotted a landline phone buried beneath a pile of papers and dreamed up a cover story about my cell phone having no connectivity and needing to contact my office.

As I pulled on the telephone to clear it, its cord whipped up and scattered the business cards. Cursing softly, I began to gather them but paused when I noticed one for Floral Wizard, the outfit that had delivered flowers to Gloria and Camille. Having a business card didn't prove any wrongdoing on Tom's part, of course. I would bet he and Camille had shared all sorts of contacts.

I twisted the knob on the Rolodex, prepared to file the card under *F*, when it dawned on me that Tom might notice. To my surprise, when I'd paused, I'd landed on the card for Beau Flacks. On it was a number for a relative, in case of emergencies: *Stacy*.

Chapter 36

I peeked around the cubicle wall and, seeing no one, lifted the telephone and dialed Stacy's number.

"Hello?" a woman answered.

"Can I speak with Stacy?"

"I'm Stacy. Who's this?"

"Um, my name is Audrey," I said hastily. Why lie? Because Beau might have talked to her about me. "I'm a reporter for the *Tahoe Tribune*."

"Yes?" Stacy sounded like a woman with a lot of time on her hands, the kind who responded to all telephone surveys.

"You were a patient of Dr. Kristin Fisher, a woman who was killed in Lake Tahoe, and I'd like to ask you a few questions."

"I was her patient for a nanosecond."

"I'm working on the angle that a pro-life advocate might have killed the doctor. I was wondering—"

"You want to talk about my abortion?" Stacy groaned. "Boy, I tell one personal interest story to a newspaper and everybody wants to glom on. What did you do, run an Internet check and come up with all the names of women in the U.S. who confessed to having an abortion?"

"I—"

"Look, I agreed to do that article for the *Phoenix Times* because women needed an insider's perspective on how it felt to have her body invaded. There's no shame in having an abortion when it's necessary to survival, you know? But there's pain and loss, and women need to know that."

"Of course, they—"

"Women need to band together. We need to take care of ourselves. Men won't do it for us."

I could picture Stacy on a stage with a microphone in hand.

"Look, I heard about Dr. Fisher's murder. It never occurred to me that her willingness to do an abortion would factor into it."

"We're not sure it does."

"Look, I was going to die. I chose to live. And my resulting infertility wasn't Dr. Fisher's fault."

Aha. So that was why she had adopted.

"I had a mess of a uterus. Everyone I knew, even the pro-lifers, suggested I abort. I did a lot of soul searching, and I guarantee that any woman who goes into a doctor's office for that kind of operation has taken the time to think about it. She has discussed it with her loved ones. Neither she nor anyone she loves is going on some doctor-killing rampage afterward." She paused and clicked her tongue. "Who did you say you were again?"

"I'm with the *Tribune*," I said, not repeating my phony name.

"Look, if you want more, read the article I gave the *Phoenix Times*. It's all in there."

When Stacy ended the call, I took a moment to reflect on Beau. If his sister was at peace with her decision, then perhaps he was, too, and I needn't worry about him escorting Gloria home.

I reconsidered Tom. Where was he? Did he have an alibi for the time Camille was killed?

I rotated the Rolodex to search for his home address.

"There you are!" Candace raced in and thrust a DVD at me. "Look at this."

"Where have you been?"

"I knew you had your keys. I could see they were in your pocket. So I decided to snoop, like you." She tapped the DVD. "You've got to see this. Remember the segment we watched with Gloria and Miss Tejeda? Beau's name was listed as the director."

"Doesn't he direct them all?"

"This one's different. It has Rick Tamblyn's name on it. So I watched it. Is it okay to play it here?"

"Yes." Her excitement was infectious. I was all in. If we got caught, we got caught.

She slipped the DVD into the machine, grabbed the TV remote, and queued it up.

What came into view on the screen was the Tejeda segment, but it was being shot from a different angle, paralleling the other DVD we'd viewed. Gloria and Vaughn were attaching their microphones to their raincoats while discussing the nasty weather. As in the other DVD, a viewer targeted Vaughn with the squirt gun, after which they exchanged terse words. Following that, Gloria approached Miranda Tejeda, who was holding her clever sign regarding literacy.

"Look." Candace pointed at the screen, savoring her role as spy.

"What?" I felt the stitches tugging at my scalp. "I don't see anything different."

Amid countless umbrellas were people holding rain-drenched signs broadcasting their home states.

"There." Candace tapped the screen. "See them? Tripp and his dad."

"Where?" I peered harder. I didn't see anyone that bore a resemblance.

"In the hooded jackets. By the red umbrella. You missed them. I'm going to rewind." She did and pressed Play. "There." She paused the DVD.

I gasped. Finn Ambrose and his son, huddling beneath black rain ponchos, looked like a pair of Grim Reapers. Finn told me he'd left KINC the moment his stint was canceled. In addition, he'd said he didn't know Miranda Tejeda.

He'd lied.

Chapter 37

Nick answered his cell phone with a hushed, "What's up?"

"Where are you?" I asked as I steered Candace toward KINC's reception area.

"Ambrose Alley. I can't talk—" He coughed.

"Stay there. I'm on my way."

"Where are we going?" Candace asked.

"I'm taking you back to the office then I'm going to meet Nick in South Lake Tahoe."

"I'm going with you."

"You can't."

"Why? Isn't it safe?" Her voice rose with heart-wrenching anxiety.

"Of course it's safe," I said. I didn't want her to worry, although my getting clobbered by a potted plant hadn't helped on that front.

"You're hurt. I need to stay with you."

"Candace—" I pushed through the door to the lobby.

"There you are." Marie rose from her desk to offer me an ice pack.

I took it and eyed the reporters standing outside the front door. "Could you let us out?" I asked.

Marie moved to the door, unlocked it, and with the authority of a bouncer bellowed, "Stand back."

Candace and I squeezed through and hurried to the Jeep. A skinny male reporter trailed us shouting questions. Neither of us responded.

Once we were inside the vehicle, Candace said, "You think I'm too young to understand, don't you?" She buckled her seat belt. "Well, you're wrong."

I ditched the bag of ice on the car floor and drew in a deep breath. "Finn Ambrose might get mad about what you and I discovered."

"Tripp won't be. I'll hang out with him."

"No. This discussion is at an end."

Candace crossed her arms and huffed. I remembered doing the same thing whenever my parents shut me out of an argument. I'd survived. So would she.

While driving, I phoned my aunt and explained the situation. Like Candace, Max wasn't fond of my plan, but I convinced her that I was feeling fine. All I was going to do was deliver evidence to Nick, and then I'd return to the office.

Candace and I arrived in record time. Without saying a word, she clambered out of the car and trudged up the path.

When I arrived at Ambrose Alley, I left the Jeep with valet parking and stepped inside the casino. Ignoring the stares of patrons studying my weird hairdo, I sneaked past the elevator guard, who was busy giving a guest directions, and stole into the penthouse-only elevator. Quickly, I entered the four digits I'd seen the guard use on the keypad, and the lift moved upward.

Although the trip to the top floor seemed endless, I was thankful that the elevator didn't plunge. When the doors opened, I charged down the hall toward Finn Ambrose's residence. The front door was open.

I stepped inside and came to a stop when I realized there was a full house. Finn Ambrose was perched on the sofa. Beside him sat a somber man with silver hair and a hawk's beak for a nose. In his dark suit and Hermes tie, he reeked of power and money. Behind the sofa stood Jules, allying herself with Finn, her back erect and fists clenched. Just how much did she know? Would she ditch him if he was guilty?

Sorcha McRae stood beside Jules. So much for visiting her brother. She was dressed again in her typical black shirt, black pants. Her gaze shot in my direction. What part was she playing in the drama?

Nick's face was ashen. The collar of his starched white shirt was drenched with perspiration. He spied me and said to the group, "Excuse me a moment." He strode to me and clutched my elbow. "You should be in bed."

I knew he was right. I was sweating more than he was, but I didn't budge. "You're the one who looks ill," I countered.

"Touch of flu. Came on suddenly. Maybe food poisoning."

"You're overworked. Go home. Let Hernandez handle this."

"Can't. We're stretched thin. Why are you here?"

"Finn Ambrose lied. He knew Miranda Tejeda." I held out the DVD and explained what I'd seen on it. "The only victim you can't connect Finn Ambrose to is Dr. Fisher. If you look harder, maybe—"

"It's no use," Nick said. "Ambrose's lawyer is stonewalling everything. He won't let us look at any of the casino's vehicles without a search warrant." He pulled a handkerchief from his pocket and dabbed his forehead. "We're working on getting a telephonic one." The telephonic search warrant was a means of obtaining a warrant when a judge wasn't in chambers. Judges were on call in the evening, on weekends, or holidays. Not all warrants were guaranteed, however.

"Detective Sergeant Shaper," Hawk Nose said.

I pivoted. Nick stepped away from me.

"If there's nothing further, you should leave the premises," the lawyer said. "We have a meeting with investors in ten minutes."

Finn stared at Nick with a gaze as placid as Lake Tahoe at sunrise. A smile graced his lips. I wanted to throttle him.

Nick said, "I'll go, but I'll be back. With the warrant. And if I were you, Mr. Ambrose, I wouldn't have your hotel's delivery vehicles detailed quite yet. You wouldn't want to be accused of interfering with our investigation, would you?"

Finn remained unfazed.

I accompanied Nick to the lobby and out of the casino. He paused next to a column near the valet stand, unbuttoned the top button of his shirt, and checked his cell phone for messages. I did the same and noticed I had missed two calls. One from an anonymous number and the other from Gloria.

I moved to one side so I could listen to Gloria's message first. She was home and doing much better. Beau was being the perfect nurse. She said if she sounded a little loopy, it was because she'd taken a sleep aid. She was going down for a long nap.

The next call was from the delivery girl, Laila, left at six thirty a.m., hours before Gloria's message. "Miss Adams, it's Monday morning. I'm out caving because, well, I am, and anyway"—she sounded out of breath—"I saw the guy again. The one I told you about. This time I can describe him. Call me on my cell phone." She rattled off the number.

I raced to Nick, who was also on the phone. "I just got a message—"

Nick held up his hand, warning me to be quiet. "Are you kidding me? On my way." He ended the call.

"What's wrong?"

Nick flashed his badge at the valet and handed him a ticket stub. "Get my car. Pronto." He turned to me. "You remember the delivery girl you told me about? Laila Walton?"

The tension in his tone made my heart leap into my throat.

"I sent King to interview her, but the girl didn't show up for work. Her boss said Laila never missed a day and that the girl often went caving before her shift began."

"Yes, she's caving. I got a message." I held up my cell phone. "She—"

"Laila's no-show had her boss worried, so she dialed 911," Nick continued. "Laila's dead. Murdered. In a remote cave."

"Oh, no." Tears sprang to my eyes. She was so young.

"King is there now," he went on. "What do you bet Ambrose has an alibi for this one, too?"

"Do you want to go back and ask him?"

"And get stonewalled? No."

"If only I'd seen Laila's message earlier." A thought occurred to me. "Tom," I blurted. "Regent."

"What about him?"

"He's a spelunker and I think he owns a Navigator. It's as big as a Suburban. Plus, he's left-handed. What if he killed Laila and Camille and—"

"C'mon, Aspen," Nick rasped. "First, you think it's Ambrose. Now, you think it's Regent?"

I didn't bridle; I understood why he was angry. "You said he was on your radar, too."

"Only because of the notes to Gloria and his business deal with Camille."

The valet drove up in Nick's Wrangler. Nick marched to it, opened the door, and grabbed a bottle of water from the cup holder. He drank the contents in one long pull and slipped behind the wheel.

I stopped him from closing the door. "Tom Regent didn't come to work this morning. He was at Incline Bowl when I was asking about Laila."

"I've got to go." Nick's eyes were glassy, unfocused.

I clutched his arm. "You're in no shape to drive and certainly in no shape to venture into a cave by yourself. I'll drive." I wouldn't take no for an answer.

Chapter 38

The cave's opening was barely visible to a passerby. Detective King, dressed in uniform, met us at the entrance and handed us the same kind of cloth booties that encased her shoes. Once we put them on, she led us through the narrow passageway. Fluted stalactites hung from the cave's ceilings. Mounds of white dripstones covered the floor.

"I've notified Douglas County Sheriff's Department," she said. The cave was on the Nevada side of Lake Tahoe. "They're willing to work with us."

The cavern was filled with gold formations that resembled a flapper's fringe skirt. Fifty feet inside, the air grew heavier and the stench of mold was rife.

King paid no attention to the spiderwebs that brushed against her face. I shuddered—I hated spiders. Once or twice, the detective eyed the bandage on my head, but she didn't say a word. No doubt she'd seen worse.

Toward the end of a path, we ducked under an arch and King held up a hand. Two techs were already in the location. Laila, her blue denim shirt and jeans splattered with blood, lay on the ground faceup. A stream of sunlight cascaded through a vent that opened to the sky and highlighted the girl's tanned face. A backpack was open to her right.

The muffin I'd eaten at the office threatened to resurface. I braced myself against the clammy wall and drew in deep gulps until the nausea passed.

"Do you have an idea when she died?" Nick whispered, as if being in the cave demanded reverence.

"Three to four hours ago," one tech said. "It's so cold in here, though, it could be longer."

I said, "She left me a message at six thirty."

"How'd you stumble on this place, Kendra?" Nick asked.

"Her boss, who's quite a character by the way, said the girl talked about three caving areas nonstop."

"Is Vaughn Jamison still in jail?" Nick asked.

"Yes. It's taking time to process his release."

"That rules him out."

I said, "You should take a sample of the dirt, in case it matches what was in Camille St. John's house."

"Already done that," King said.

Nick knelt beside the body. "What do you think the weapon was?"

"I thought an ice axe at first," King said. "You know, the kind that climbers use in the winter. Long and narrow and wider at the end." She crouched beside him and pointed. "But see the depression? It's a conical plunge. I'm thinking a piton. Shorter and narrower than an ice axe."

"Is all her equipment accounted for?" Nick glanced up at her.

"A coil of rope, canteen, gloves. No pitons."

Nick rose to his feet and brushed off his knees. "Have forensics test the canteen for saliva."

"Will do."

"Have you found out whether Gloria received a note?" I asked.

"Funny you should ask. We found a note on-site"—Detective King pulled a baggie from her pocket and handed it to Nick—"but it's not addressed to Gloria Morning."

I peered over Nick's shoulder as he perused the note. It read:

> *You should pick your friends better.*
> *To her glory, I give my life.*

"He used the word *glory*," I said, "but you're right. It's not the same. *For your glory* is the term. Could a copycat have done this? Or is the killer getting sloppy?"

Nick flicked the paper. "Pick your friends is a pretty disgusting play on words."

King grimaced. "Tell me about it."

"Tom Regent might own a pickaxe," I suggested.

"Already thought of that," King said, "but Regent isn't the perp. He's in emergency at Northstar Clinic. Has been since one a.m. Seems he drove into a telephone pole. Hernandez informed me while you were on the switchback."

If Tom was incapacitated at the time of Laila's death, then he couldn't have killed her. Who else had the opportunity? I pictured the shadow box filled with Indian artifacts in Finn Ambrose's office and said, "Nick, do you think the weapon could have been an arrowhead?"

• • •

Because Detective King would inform Laila's next of kin of her death and Detective Hernandez and Nick were preoccupied with obtaining the vital search warrants, I took it upon myself to break the news to Laila's employer. She might know the names of Laila's hiking buddies. Laila said she'd seen the guy. When? This morning? Had a group of cavers met up for coffee before going their separate ways?

On the drive, I phoned Gloria. Although there was an unfinished note in the cave that I was certain was meant for her, that didn't preclude the killer from having sent a separate one. She didn't answer. I knew she'd taken a sleep aid, so I left a voice mail asking her to check in with me.

As I entered Nevada or Bust, I threw my arms around myself for warmth. Like before, icy air spilled from the air-conditioning vents, and also, like before, the desk was unmanned. I heard a woman humming and moved toward the sound. The bathroom door was open an inch. I saw a pair of tennis shoes and bare calves and then a denim-covered rear end. The woman was on her knees scrubbing the white tile floor.

"Hello?" I tapped on the doorframe.

"C'mon in," she said, her voice raspy.

I pushed the door open further and caught a whiff of Clorox. The noxious fumes made me wince.

The woman—Laila's boss—reminded me, yet again, of Dolly Parton, even with a red bandanna wrapped around her bleached-blonde hair. "These kids. What slobs. I would hire adults, but adults expect more than minimum wage. It's not in my budget. Now, what can I do for—" She took a second glance at me and gaped. "What in the heck happened to you?"

"I had an accident. It's nothing." I swallowed hard. "I'm here about Laila."

"That girl." The woman sat back on her haunches. "Did they find her? What did she do this time, put herself in the hospital? I'm not a fan of her caving and climbing. Too dangerous. I've told her—"

"Ma'am, Laila's dead."

The woman's face turned the color of the tiles. "Oh, no."

"She was stabbed," I said, prepared for an outpouring of emotion.

Tears pooled in the woman's eyes but none fell.

A second later, a squat, sunburned girl about Laila's age poked her head into the room. "Hey, boss, I'm back from—" The girl paused. "Why are you crying?"

Laila's boss swung her gaze from the girl to me and back to the girl. She stood up, dropped the sponge into a sink filled with other cleaning utensils, and gripped the girl by the shoulders. "Laila's dead. She was murdered."

The girl gasped. "When? How?"

The boss removed her Playtex gloves and stuffed them into the sunburned girl's hands. "I'll tell you later. Right now, I've got to talk to this nice gal. You clean the bathroom." She urged me into the hallway and pulled the door closed. "Best thing for the kid is work. No dwelling, I always say. Now, what's your name?"

"Aspen Adams."

"Eileen."

After explaining the situation to her, as best I knew it, I asked if she would mind providing a list of Laila's friends so I could personally inform them of her death. Eileen said Laila only had one true friend, the girl who was scrubbing the bathroom. She led me to her postage stamp–sized office.

"Laila was such a sweetie. We had our squabbles, but I really enjoyed her. She had a head for business, but would she use it? No, she would not. Too busy being young. Came to work during her junior year of high school. She was a bitty thing then. Her hair was dark and long, not that ugly purple hairdo she wears." Eileen swallowed hard. *"Wore.* Memories. They're all I'll have left of her, aren't they?" She sighed. "I was forever asking Laila not to take personal calls. The others, too, but do they listen? Social butterflies, that's what kids are. No focus. I'm not complaining. I'm not, it's—" Tears slipped down Eileen's cheeks. "She could've taken over this business someday."

"Ma'am, do you happen to know any of her caving group?"

Eileen's mouth dropped open. "No idea at all. I'll give it some thought. I'll—" Suddenly, tears spilled down her cheeks. She fanned her face trying to stem the flow and waved for me to leave.

I returned to the reception area and heard a thwacking sound coming from the bathroom. I pushed the bathroom door open. The sunburned girl sat on the toilet seat, hunched over, beating her thighs with the Playtex gloves.

I knelt beside her and quieted her hands. "You were Laila's friend."

"Mm-hm." The girl wiped her nose with the back of her sleeve. "We went to high school together. We were planning on going to college. In Reno. When we saved enough money."

"What were you going to study?"

"Business. Laila and me, we could do anything. I can't believe she's—" She pressed her lips together, refusing to say the word *gone*. She donned the rubber gloves, grabbed a container of powdered Comet, and splattered the floor. Then she wet a toothbrush and began to scour the edges of the room with it.

"Are you a caver or climber?"

"Neither. I'm into waterskiing." She peered at me, her lips quivering. "Are you with the sheriff's department?"

"Sort of." It wasn't a complete lie. "Did you know any of her caving friends?"

"No. She had a long line of boyfriends, though"—by the scrunch of her nose, I could tell she didn't approve of Laila's choices—"so if you're searching for suspects, you could start there."

"Any of them hurt her before?"

"Nah. She was little but she was tough. There was a boat painter at the marina." The girl tossed the toothbrush in the sink and ticked off a couple other men Laila had dated—a bartender at a casino, a fellow spelunker, and one handsome older guy. "What was his name?" She snapped her fingers.

"Was it Finn Ambrose or Tom Regent?"

"Neither of those ring a bell. He worked at a restaurant."

My pulse skyrocketed. "Enzo Vittorio?" Had I crossed him off my list too soon? Hoping to strike gold, I said, "He's a chef at Vittorio's Ristorante."

"No. This guy worked at a steak restaurant. He was a waiter. Joe something."

I didn't strike gold; I struck out.

Chapter 39

Rather than disturb Nick with what might be wild ideas, I drove to the office.

Darcy and Yaz were tossing the remains of their burgers into the garbage as I entered.

"Still working on the financials for you," Darcy said and exited the bungalow.

"Thanks."

Yaz said, "I'm going back to the casino tomorrow to question a few more people about that elevator." He threw on his New York skyline dress shirt over his T-shirt. "Got to keep the mustard off the duds."

"Smart."

"How's the head?" He nodded in my direction.

"Achy but functional."

"Ice."

I nodded. "Where's Rowena?"

"Ha! She graced us with two hours of her sweet smile today."

"Two? That might be a record," I joked. "Did she bring something packed with sugar?"

"Mini Oreos. She is a master briber. She told your aunt she had to run an errand and never returned."

"And where is my aunt?"

"With Candace and the dog. She left you a note. Gotta run. See ya!" He flew out the front door and let it slam shut.

I read the note. Max, my niece, and my dog had gone to pick up Max's granddaughter. She had been itching to take the five-year-old boating. Afterward, they were going to buy a pizza for dinner. I could fetch Candace and the dog at my aunt's house later.

Knowing my niece was occupied and safe, I dialed Gloria, and again she didn't answer. I was a little concerned about how doped up she'd sounded earlier. How long could she sleep? Was she all right? Worried that Beau might have figured out I'd talked to his sister and, out of spite, taken Gloria's cell phone so I couldn't get in touch with her, I called KINC and asked for him. Marie said he was on his way to his second job.

By dusk, the office turned as quiet as a ghost town, the silence disturbed only by the steady drone of the refrigerator and the white-noise hum of the computers. Even the cats went into hiding. I popped two Advil to help the stiffness in my neck, a result of keeping my head steady so it wouldn't throb, and then I emailed Nick the list of nameless men Laila's associate believed she'd dated.

I eyed the cold pot of coffee, the cinnamon scent whetting my appetite, but I avoided the temptation. My already sour stomach didn't need another acid thrown into the mix. I scrounged through the refrigerator and opted for a carton of boysenberry Greek yogurt and a handful of almonds.

After downing my makeshift meal, I set a poster board on an easel and affixed Post-it notes to it, one at a time. On five of them, I jotted the victims' names: *Tony Vittorio*, *Kristin Fisher*, *Miranda Tejeda*, *Camille St. John*, and *Laila Walton*. Tears pressed at the corners of my eyes. I willed them away.

On other Post-its I wrote my suspect's names: *Finn Ambrose*, *Tom Regent*, and *Beau Flacks*. Was he innocent, as Gloria believed? I added *Vaughn Jamison*, even though he had been in jail when Camille and Laila were killed. He could have had an accomplice.

On another set of Post-its, I entered the weapons: scalpel, knife, scissors, a metal louver from a klieg light, and a climbing or caving tool, possibly an arrowhead.

On yet another set, I noted the evidence Candace and I had seen on Post-its attached to the file at the sheriff's office: *dirt*, *mud*, *metal* and *clay*, as well as *dog hair and horsehair*. Mud, dirt, and dog hair would have been found at Camille's. Mud and dirt were definitely evident in the cave.

I attached lines of string from one Post-it to another.

From Gloria to Tom and from Tom to Laila. From Laila to the dirt found at Camille's. And on it went, Gloria to Finn Ambrose to Tony Vittorio and their feud. From Finn Ambrose to Laila, in case the killer had used an arrowhead.

An hour later, I stood back from my handiwork and grimaced.

What a mess. The dreamcatcher hanging over my bed didn't look as complicated.

I removed all the string, tossed it into a garbage can, and started over, this time without any string. I concentrated on the first victim. Dr. Kristin Fisher. Who had wanted her dead? She had been caring and attentive to patients. Why kill her?

Other than Vaughn Jamison, who else did Nick consider a suspect? I berated myself for not expanding my suspect list accordingly, but I had been so fixated on Gloria's plight and the people who knew her that I'd forgotten what had made me impassioned about my investigation in the first place—the death of my doctor.

Out of nowhere, I wondered whether the insubstantial suspect list was the reason the police had botched my parents' murder investigation. The notion made my breath snag. *Stop, Aspen.* I could not think about my parents now. The case would never be solved. But this one could be. It was my job to help Gloria find closure.

With great effort, I refocused.

Dr. Fisher. What had driven the killer to choose her first? Nick believed Dr. Fisher's killer was left-handed. So was the one who had murdered Tony Vittorio, according to the tech at the crime scene. Nick had mentioned the same thing at Camille's.

Convinced there was one and only one murderer, I pressed on. Gloria was the connection to all the victims whether Nick believed that or not.

The Post-it with Beau's name drew my attention. Was he innocent? In the control room I'd seen him moving a shuttle knob with his left hand while jotting notes with his right. Was he right-handed or ambidextrous?

Finn Ambrose was a lefty. In the kitchen at the casino, he had wielded the meat cleaver with his left hand.

I eyed the Post-its and another thought came to me. Brown horsehair was found at Dr. Fisher's crime scene. Was horsehair found at other crime scenes? Was the killer an equestrian?

At the computer I opened Google and typed in a string of terms. A page of websites relating to DNA and hair evidence materialized. There were over five thousand. I clicked on a site that claimed even dummies could understand the information. I read the first page, which broke hair evidence down to length, color, thickness, and texture.

Reading on, I gleaned that each species of animal possessed hair with characteristic length, color, shape, and root appearance. Also, there were microscopic features that could distinguish one animal from another. The article talked about outer hairs—or guard hairs—as well as finer fur hairs, and tactile hairs, such as whiskers. Last but not least, it mattered whether the animal was alive or dead. That prompted me to scroll down further. During the anagen phase, hair was growing. During the telogen phase, the hair was resting. Specifically, these hairs were mostly due to shedding.

On my way to becoming a therapist, I'd taken a ton of science classes, so I was understanding the material in general terms—namely, that the horsehair found at the crime scenes could have originated from a pelt or, as I'd suspected, even from a vest like the one Beau had worn the day I met him. However, I refused to convict Beau based on that because at least one out of ten people in Tahoe had an animal hide someplace in their house.

Including Finn Ambrose.

Chapter 40

To rule out Beau, I drove to the Black Hawk Saloon. I paused inside the front door. The country music blasting through the speakers made my head ache.

The bar was beyond the dance floor, where line dancers were toe heeling in rhythm to a lively song. Beau paced behind the bar looking comfortable in his element. He tossed a bottle of Jack Daniel's in the air, caught it by the neck, and poured a shot of whiskey into a tumbler. A customer slid him a bill. In rhythm to the music, Beau spun around, rang up the charge, and returned to the patron with change and a smile.

I sauntered to the counter and waited until I caught his attention.

"What'll it be?" Beau moseyed over and, recognizing me, said, "How's your head? Need some ice?"

"I'm cool. Nothing a little aspirin can't solve." *Liar.* "How about a club soda with lime?"

Beau fixed my drink, slid a napkin in front of me, and set the drink on top.

"How's Gloria doing?" I asked as I laid a ten-dollar bill on the bar.

"She's not answering her cell phone."

"She took an Ambien. That knocks her out."

"For how long?"

"She was sleeping like a log when I left her. I'd give her until the morning to respond." He pushed the money back to me. "But that's not why you're here, is it? What brings you in?"

"I'd like to ask you a couple of questions. The answers might help me track down the guy who is taunting Gloria."

Beau scanned his customers, all of whom appeared content, and returned his attention to me. "Fire away."

"Do you know a young woman named Laila Walton?"

"Never heard of her."

"She frequents Incline Bowl."

He frowned. "Nope."

"She's the person who delivered one of the notes to Gloria."

"Still not registering. Camille might know. She—" He had the decency to falter. "Poor Camille. Hard to believe she's gone. May she rest in peace."

"She's the one who helped me locate the delivery girl. Laila said a man wearing a disguise hired her to deliver the note about Dr. Fisher."

"It wasn't me. I'll prove it. Have the sheriff put me in a lineup."

"Too late for that. Laila is dead. Murdered."

Beau's mouth fell open. "When?"

"Earlier today."

"You saw me. I was at the studio and left with Gloria."

"Earlier than that. Around dawn."

Beau grabbed a towel and wiped the bar with gusto. "Not me. I am not a murderer."

"Laila left me a message this morning before she was killed," I went on, "claiming she could identify who'd hired her."

"One more time, it wasn't me."

"The forensic specialists have determined that animal hair was found at all of the crime scenes," I said, the lie tasting somewhat bitter.

"I don't own a dog or cat. Guess that lets me off the hook."

I kept quiet.

His jaw ticked with tension. "Give me a break. Anybody could've tracked hair into the crime scenes. Practically everyone in Lake Tahoe owns a cat or dog."

"It could be horsehair."

"I don't own a horse, either." He stabbed the counter with his index finger. "In case you hadn't noticed, I'm a little strapped for cash. That's why I'm holding down two jobs." Beau whipped the towel at a fly. He didn't nail it because it buzzed past my ear. Even so, he pretended to pick up the fly and fling it into the sink.

Quietly I said, "You wear a horsehair vest."

His mouth dropped open. After a long moment, he closed it. "It doesn't shed, as far as I know."

"Are you sure?"

Beau braced both palms on the bar. "Look, babe, should I get a lawyer?" He blanched. "Sorry. Didn't mean to call you *babe*. It's just—"

He scrubbed his neck. "This whole interrogation thing has me wrapped around the axle. So, should I? Get a lawyer?"

Coolly, I took a sip of the club soda.

"C'mon. I'm willing to help any way I can. I did not do this." Beau splayed his hands. "No way, no how."

"Hey, bartender, another round," a customer yelled from the far end.

"Back in a sec." Beau thumped the counter as if it were a set of bongo drums, filled the order, and returned. "Let me tell you my alibis. For every murder. How about that? Let's start with the Fisher murder. When did that take place?" He held up a hand, fingers separated.

"A week ago Friday. Early in the morning."

"As I told you the other day, I was at the gym. I do an hour of cardio followed by a two-hour stretch class. I go every Friday." He bent his index finger. "Plenty of witnesses. Lots of regulars." He leaned toward me, his face inches from mine. "Tell me, why would I have killed her?"

"Your sister Stacy had an abortion."

Beau's eyes flashed with fury. "Aha, you're the one that called her."

"You don't believe in abortion. You have an anti-abortion sticker on your car."

"I'm pro-life. Sue me." He pointed a finger at me. "Look, I understood why my sister needed it. She would've died otherwise. I didn't blame the doctor. And honestly?" He grinned maliciously. "If I were going to kill someone, it would've been the chump who got my sister knocked up in the first place. Next." Beau drummed the bar again, this time like he was playing high stakes poker and winning. Just because he was cocky didn't mean he was guilty.

I said, "Tony Vittorio was killed around two p.m. last Monday."

"At that hour, I'm at the studio going over footage and outtakes. Not as many witnesses as stretch class, but enough." He held up his hand again and bent down two fingers. "Two down."

"The teacher, Miranda Tejeda, was killed Thursday night around ten."

"I was bowling with Rick Tamblyn. You can ask him. Rick never lies. It's against his religion. There were—"

"Plenty of witnesses."

He aimed a finger and mimed pulling an imaginary trigger. "Right."

"Camille died early this morning, some time after midnight. You weren't here; you weren't at KINC, and you weren't bowling, though I saw you at the bowling alley earlier."

"Yeah, but bowling came into play. See, I was walking off a major headache. For some reason, the sound really got to me. Couldn't sleep. I must've hiked for two straight hours. A car or two passed, but who knows if the driver could ID me. It's a weak alibi, but it's all I got." Beau smacked the bar. "FYI, I wouldn't have knifed Camille. Her skin was too taut. I'd have beaten her with a baseball bat."

"She wasn't killed with a knife. She was——" I hesitated.

Had Hernandez kept that information from Beau when he'd questioned him, or was Beau hoping to deflect suspicion by pretending not to know the weapon?

A buff waiter slammed a tray down and yelled, "Two chocolate martinis, a Manhattan, and two chardonnays."

Beau seemed relieved by the interruption. He filled the order and returned, the tension in his forehead erased. "What else do you want to know?"

"Were you having an affair with Camille?"

"No way."

"I saw you two flirting."

"Yeah, we flirted. I'm a flirt. Heck, I've even flirted with Marie, despite the nose rings. It's in my nature." He propped an elbow on the bar. "Look, I want to get out of this town. I want to move to LA or New York and give my lackluster career a boost. I flirted with Camille hoping she might make some phone calls on my behalf. Now, she'll never be able to. But I swear, we never had a roll in the hay. Ever." He filled the sink with soapy water, gathered a couple of empty glasses off the bar, and tossed them into the liquid. "Why would I kill all these people? What's my motive? I get where you're going with the doctor thing, but the rest? I'm not going around killing people and sending Gloria ridiculous notes to scare her. I love her."

"You broke up. You said she had some *issues*."

"I was . . ." He fanned the air. "It doesn't matter. We're back together. I told her before she went to sleep that I won't relocate until she's ready. She's my soul mate and I'm hers." Beau buffed the bar as if it were scarred with an indelible stain. "Whoever's doing this is a lunatic. Speaking of lunatics, if you want to round up a good suspect, check out Tom. He owns a horsehair rug. Plus, I heard him and Camille arguing the other day." He hurled the towel at a laundry bin and grabbed a fresh one. "And between you and me, he's frustrated because he's never going to get to first base with Gloria. She likes a guy with brains."

"Like you?"

"I went to Berkeley. Graduated top of my class."

That caught me off guard. If Beau was smart enough to go to Berkeley, why was he bartending?

Aspen, honestly? My bias drew me up short. Over the past year and a half, many people had asked me why I, with a Stanford degree, was now working for a private investigation firm, as if all Stanford graduates should become doctors, lawyers, or nanotech geeks and being a PI was the bottom rung of the career ladder, second only to garbage collector.

I slid off my stool. "You know, Beau, as a sign of good will, you might want to give your horsehair vest to the sheriff."

"I can't. After Gloria made fun of it, I donated it to the Salvation Army."

Chapter 41

I returned to the office and, unable to tolerate having a bandage on my head any longer, removed it and treated the wound using items in our well-stocked medicine cabinet. I washed my face, brushed my teeth, and felt generally healthier in a matter of minutes.

Next, I checked in on Nick to see if he'd received my email about Laila and the men she'd dated. He sounded even sicker than before and had gone home. His sister was fixing him chicken soup. Hernandez was in charge of obtaining the warrant. Unfortunately, the judge had demanded more probable cause. Seeing a nonspecific van in the area of a murder wasn't enough.

Nick asked me if I'd learned anything else I wanted to share. I told him about Beau Flacks and his brown-and-white horsehair vest.

"Did you get that tip from the Post-its?" he asked.

"Yes. Candace has good eyesight. Anyway, Beau got rid of it because Gloria hated it. At least that's his story." I went on to add that after interviewing Beau, I believed him to be innocent. He had some pretty solid alibis.

Nick said he'd send someone to verify them. I added that Finn Ambrose had a white bearskin rug and black-and-white pinto hide in his penthouse and asked if a warrant would let Nick search for one with brown hair. He said yes. The warrant was to include Ambrose's entire premises as well as the casino.

I asked him if Detective King had interrogated Tom Regent yet. Nick said she'd gone to Northstar Clinic, but she couldn't rouse Tom because he'd been sedated. However, she confirmed that the clinic admitted him around one in the morning and that his accident had occurred about a mile from the clinic. He promised to keep me apprised of his next step and wished me good night.

As I was hanging up, my aunt texted me. Her granddaughter was out for the count, but Candace, Cinder, and she were binge-watching *Friends*. I didn't need to rush to pick them up.

Given the extra time, I decided to visit Tom Regent. Maybe he was no longer sedated.

• • •

With a little cajoling, the admissions clerk at Northstar Clinic divulged that Tom was alert. She sent an aide to find out if he was open to seeing a visitor.

Pacing the foyer, I wondered about Tom's ever-so-convenient time of arrival. If he'd killed Camille, he would've had to race over the hill in record time to sustain the accident. Doable, yes. Likely? No. Also, if he really had been admitted around one a.m., he couldn't have killed Laila.

"Miss Adams?" A nurse the size of a refrigerator strode into the foyer. She stared at my injury and said, "Come this way."

As I followed, I heard her mutter, "Shoddy work." Apparently she didn't think the stitches on my head were done well. I didn't care. My head wasn't aching and the hair would grow back. She led me to Tom's hospital room and left.

One glance at Tom made me queasy. His skin matched the pasty white walls. Deep purple bruises marred his face. His left arm was in a sling, and his right leg, its knee bandaged, was resting in a continuous passive motion machine. Glucose trickled into his right arm via a tube. A second bag for pain medicine, which was empty at the moment, was secured to his other arm.

"Hi, Aspen." Tom licked his parched lips. "How do I look?"

"Pretty bad." I wasn't going to lie.

He raised his cast. "Arm's wrenched bad, knee's shattered." His speech was slow and slurred. He lifted a plastic cup from the over-bed swivel table, used a straw to drink, and set the cup back down. "I downed one too many whiskeys. Stupid. Never going to touch booze again."

I would bet he'd made that promise before. On the other hand, a serious car crash could do wonders for changing bad behavior problems. A couple of my patients at BARC had stopped doing drugs after setting themselves on fire.

"Why are you here?" he asked.

To determine whether he was making beautiful, peaceful Lake Tahoe a killing ground, but I couldn't say that.

"Everyone at KINC is concerned about you."

"That's nice to hear." He jutted his chin in my direction. "How did you bang your head?"

"Gardening."

"Ouch," he said. I didn't detect guilt in his eyes. He was innocent. He had to be.

Even so, I wanted to ask a few more questions so I could totally exonerate him. "Tom, someone died today. I thought you might know her. She was a caver and climber, like you. Laila Walton."

Tom's face clouded over. "Name doesn't ring a bell, but like I said, with the drugs . . ." He ran his tongue across his lips again. "How did she die? Did she fall? Too many people without the right kind of training are getting into the game, if you ask me. They're free-styling and not using the proper equipment."

I assumed free-styling meant climbing without benefit of pitons and ropes—Laila's preferred way to climb.

"She didn't have an accident," I said. "She was murdered."

"Oh, man." He ran his fingers through his hair. "Did Gloria receive another note?"

"Sort of."

"What does that mean?"

"There was a note at the crime scene. It wasn't complete. Could be a copycat. Are you sure you didn't know Laila? She was a delivery girl. I was wondering if you'd hired her in the past."

"To do what?"

"Make a delivery."

Tom's eyes narrowed. "Are you hinting that I hired this Laila person to deliver one of the notes to Gloria?" Apparently lingering drugs weren't making him as dopey as he'd implied. "You're grilling me just like Camille does. You and she would make great prosecutors." He was speaking in present tense. Either he didn't know about Camille's death or he was a heck of an actor.

"When did you and Camille discuss this?"

"Yesterday morning. We went at it."

Confirming Beau's account that they'd fought.

"She asked if I was the one hounding Gloria. She said she knew I was in love with her."

"Are you?"

"I am, but I'm a realist. I know I don't stand a chance. I swore to Camille I would grow up and move on." Perspiration beaded on his forehead and above his lip. "She doesn't believe me, of course. She never does." Again he spoke in the present tense.

"Tom, I hate to be the one to break it to you, but Camille is dead, too."

"What? No!" He coughed and grabbed the plastic cup. After a few sips of water, he set the cup aside. "What happened? She was the epitome of health. She couldn't have had a heart attack."

"She was . . . murdered."

"No-o," he keened. "No. No. No. Where?"

"In her house."

"So that's why the detective stopped by earlier. To question me about her. Not about this." He hoisted the arm in the sling.

"You met with Detective King?"

"No, my nurse told me I'd had a visitor. I was out of it. Man—" He coughed again and reached for the plastic cup. He knocked it over.

In an instant, the enormous nurse marched into the room. She glared at me but didn't say a word. She patted Tom on the back, grabbed the plastic cup, and made him drink slowly, calmly. When he was steady, she checked his vitals, left the room for a second, and returned to replace the bags attached to the drips.

"Tom," I went on, "my understanding is that with Camille dead, you will assume ownership of KINC."

"Big deal." He grunted. "It's worthless. We're in debt up to our eyeballs. Oh, man, what will I do without her?" He choked back a sob.

"When did she die?"

"Late last night."

"After I hit the tree?"

"Right before."

"Before? You can't think . . ." He licked his lips. "Uh-uh. No way. I'd never kill her. She was my bellwether. My rock. We were a team." He rubbed his chin hard. "Has anyone reached out to her family? Who's going to take Zorro? I suppose I'll be in charge of her funeral."

"I suppose."

Tears leaked down Tom's cheeks. He wiped them with his fingertips.

"You need to leave," the nurse said to me.

"Yes, ma'am." I started toward the door and turned back as I recalled something Beau had said. "Tom, one more question."

"Fire away."

The nurse glowered at me.

"Beau told me you own a horsehair rug."

Tom snorted. "That ugly thing? Camille made me get rid of it a couple of years ago. Made her itch. Guess it's been a while since I had Beau over to dinner." He coughed and then coughed again. Harder.

"Miss," the nurse said.

Unwilling to incite her to full-throated anger, I headed out.

At the door, I turned to wish Tom a speedy recovery but held my tongue, stunned by what he was doing. While the nurse jotted notes in his chart, Tom removed the medicated drip tube from his arm and dumped the contents into the open end of his cast.

Chapter 42

Headlights strafed the windshield as I drove to my aunt's house. Doing my best to focus on the road and not the glare, I tried to figure out why Tom would pour medication down his cast. I wasn't a doctor, but I was certain it wasn't supposed to be applied topically. Was he too drugged out to notice, or was he trying to dump the stuff so he could remain clear-headed enough to fool an interrogator? Had he incurred the accident in order to establish an alibi for the time Camille was murdered? Purposely breaking his arm and injuring his knee seemed drastic. And what about Laila? He could not have killed her. However, if I believed Vaughn could have a co-conspirator, then Tom could, too.

Candace was bubbling with extra energy when I fetched Cinder and her. She'd had so much fun with Max's granddaughter that she wanted to become a kindergarten teacher. And *Friends* was her new favorite television show. Cinder, the poor guy, was a blob. The granddaughter had worn him out.

Minutes after we arrived home, I checked messages. Gloria had left a voice mail. She was fine but sad about Camille and crying way too much. She signed off saying she'd ring me in the morning.

Desperate for sleep myself, I crashed into bed.

• • •

Tuesday morning, I took Cinder for a long run. When I returned, Candace was in the kitchen, the landline telephone pressed to her ear, its cord coiled around her hand. Tears pooled in her eyes.

Who is it? I mouthed, praying someone else hadn't died.

Candace mouthed, *Mom.*

What does she want? My sister rarely woke before noon.

Candace covered the mouthpiece. "She's mad that you hung up on her. She says if I don't go see her, she's coming here to see me. I don't want her to. She'll take me back with her."

I held out my hand. With a heavy sigh, Candace released the

telephone cord. It uncurled like a maniacal snake. After giving me the phone, she tore down the hall sobbing.

Mustering a firm tone, I said, "Hey, Rosie, what's up?"

"I want to see Candy." Rosie thought naming her daughter the slang version of her habit had been funny. "I'm coming up tomorrow." She sounded clear. Not strung out.

"How about next week? I'm working a case."

"Then she's free to hang out with me."

"Actually, she has plans with friends."

Rosie snuffled. "What's the deal? Why are you giving me the runaround? Am I not good enough for you?"

"C'mon, don't go there. She really does have plans. Lots of them. She's got a life. What about you? Have you found a job?"

"I did. On a pot farm."

Perfect, I thought snidely. Just what she *didn't* need to do, hang around drugs, legal or not. On the other hand, a job was a job. If she could stay straight . . .

"Let's discuss this next Sunday," I said. By then, she would have forgotten she'd called.

"Sunday," she said and ended the call.

I stared at the telephone for a long moment wondering how the two of us had grown up in the same household. I followed rules; she broke them. I liked order; she preferred chaos.

I hurried down the hall to Candace. She was slumped on the bed, hands in her lap, chin lowered, hair hanging like a curtain around her face.

"I don't want her to get custody of me." She sniffed.

I sat beside her and stroked her hair. "She won't. She has some hoops to jump through before she could ever regain custody. However"—I lifted her chin with my fingertip—"if she found out that I ran off in the middle of the night to save Camille and left you home alone, she could wield it over me."

"But I wasn't alone. I was with Opal."

"Even so."

"You want me to keep your secret."

"For now."

She crisscrossed her heart and offered her pinky. I looped mine around hers.

• • •

I was halfway dressed, eager to meet the second doctor Heather had referred, when the telephone rang again.

Candace shouted, "Got it."

When I was tucking my plaid shirt into my chinos, I poked my head into Candace's room and asked who'd called. Candace said Waverly's mother wanted to take the girls to the Summit, a mall in Reno. They'd be gone all day. I said yes, but felt guilty about it, concerned by how difficult it was to keep a teen that didn't want to go to day camp occupied during the summer. I had to make a better plan. For now, I was more than happy to have her join Waverly again. I would buy Waverly's mother a huge present of thanks. Opal, too. And Gwen. And Max. My extended family.

A half hour later, after dropping Cinder at the neighbor's, I stood by the front door, peeking through the sidelight. Candace hovered beside me, looking adorable in cut-off jeans, a hot pink tank top, and pink-striped cross-body purse. She'd attached the friendship cat charm Waverly had given her as a graduation present to one of the purse's O-rings.

"You're sure Waverly's mom said she was minutes away?" I asked. I did not want to miss the appointment. I needed answers.

Candace said, "Go."

"If she doesn't show up for any reason—"

"I'll call you. Leave." She pushed me toward the door.

"Do you have enough money?"

"I've been saving my allowance." She kissed my cheek.

Reluctantly, I left the house.

When I arrived at the doctor's office, I noticed a text from Candace: *All is well. In the car.* I breathed easier.

An hour later, after a positive appointment with the new doctor, I had answers. Good answers. Answers Gwen would like to hear.

While soldiering through tourist traffic to Gwen's house—phoning her to deliver my momentous news was something she would never forgive—I called Candace to check in. My message went to voice mail. I asked her to text me when she arrived at the mall.

Next, I touched base with Nick. He sounded better. He said he must have had the twenty-four-hour flu. Quickly, he brought me up to speed on his investigation. King was following leads regarding Laila, and Hernandez had obtained the search warrant. Nick was meeting him at Ambrose Alley in less than an hour. I told him my news. He was thrilled for me. We ended the call with a kiss.

Gwen's house, like mine, was a cabin at the end of a lane. No view of the lake, but she didn't mind. She had a view of it at work.

She answered the door, no makeup, her unruly hair secured by a clasp. Even though the temperature was in the eighties, she was wearing jeans and a long-sleeved shirt. "Come in." She clutched my elbow and tugged me inside. "I heard about the murder of that girl in the cave. Is it related to the others?"

"Seems so. I'd interviewed her. She was sweet."

Gwen growled. "What is going on around here lately?"

"Bad karma."

"Bad people with bad karma."

I gestured to her getup. "Why the warm clothing?"

"Owen and I are going ballooning."

A year ago, Gwen and I made bucket lists of things we wanted to do in our lifetimes. On mine, I'd written parachuting out of a plane, bungee jumping off a cliff in South America, and sailing around the world in a sailboat. Gwen's had included hot-air ballooning, eating on the banks of the Seine River, and climbing Mount Everest. Today, she was crossing off one, and I would bet her honeymoon trip would land her in Paris. I was jealous.

"After the balloon ride, which only lasts forty-five minutes, we're getting our blood tests and hitting up all my doctors and dentists for files. I haven't had a physical in years. I'll bet my reports are stowed off-site gathering cobwebs." She glowed with excitement. "Then I'm closing out all my bank accounts and we'll be—"

"Off to the wedding planner." Owen, in jeans and long-sleeved shirt, emerged around the corner and handed Gwen a down jacket. "Better get a move on, my love, or we might get rained out."

"No way."

"Way."

The ring of mountains that surrounded Lake Tahoe could keep a summer storm at bay only so long.

Gwen eyed me. "Why are you here?"

"I've got some good news." I told her about the positive results of my ultrasound. "No cancer. No need for surgery."

"Oh, darlin', yay! Why didn't you lead with that? You and Nick need to celebrate. With a vacation. A big-time vacation."

"After these murders are solved."

"You are a righteous mess. A dedicated righteous mess." Gwen grabbed me in a hug. "But I adore you and your devotion to a cause."

• • •

I drove to the detective agency haunted by memories of good vacations, all of which had taken place before my divorce. None since. I tried to convince myself that living in Lake Tahoe was like having a full-time vacation, but my battered body told me otherwise. Lake Tahoe was beautiful, but it was not always serene. I pondered what I'd done for fun lately other than taking Candace and Waverly hiking and came up with nothing.

Candace. Why hadn't she checked in with me by now? It was nearly noon. I texted: *What's up?*

And then I remembered Gloria. She'd said she was going to ring me in the morning.

I tried her cell phone. The call went to voice mail. I hung up and called KINC. The receptionist said Gloria had phoned in sick. She asked if I wanted to talk to Beau. I said no and shook off the worrisome feelings. Gloria had a right to privacy. Gwen was right. I was a mess. I—

Gwen. Something she'd said niggled at the back of my mind.

Near the Brockway Theater, her words came to me, not about needing a vacation but about her medical records. She'd joked that it had been so long since her last physical that her files were likely stowed off-site and gathering cobwebs.

Were Dr. Fisher's office files incomplete? Could information that linked Tom Regent or Finn Ambrose to Dr. Fisher be housed somewhere other than the Tahoe City office?

Chapter 43

I scrambled through my purse, found the scrap of paper Heather had handed me when she'd visited me at the hospital, and dialed her cell phone. On the third ring she answered, sounding quite chipper. I explained my reason for calling.

On her end, a siren wailed and then a dog began to bark. Hysterically.

Heather said, "Just a sec." She yelled something away from the phone and a man hollered back. Seconds later, a door slammed.

"Heather, are you still there?" I asked.

"Um, yes, sorry. My boyfriend is taking my dog—my mother's dog—to the park. She gets very excited when a fire truck zooms past. You were asking about old files. Let's see. All the records for Tahoe City patients are in the Tahoe City office, I'm certain of that, but my mom's practice was in Reno before she moved here two years ago, and she stowed those files in a warehouse."

She had practiced in Reno? The Vittorios and Ambroses had lived and worked in Reno before moving to Tahoe. Tom and Camille had worked at a ritzy spa there.

I said, "Did you mention this to the detectives?"

"They didn't ask."

"Would you know the name of the facility?"

"Let me get Mom's address book from my bedroom."

The receiver clunked on something hard. I heard Heather clip-clopping through the house. She picked up the telephone. "Reno Store and Lock. Guess I could've figured that out without the address book, huh? It's on California Street. If you want it, I found a key on her key chain with that name on it."

Of course I wanted it.

• • •

Reno Store and Lock, an imposing string of gray buildings with metal pull-down doors, occupied a full city block. Sun gleamed on the window of the facility's office. Unlike Nevada or Bust, the place didn't have air-conditioning. It was sweltering inside. To add insult to injury, the rank odor of cigarette butts permeated the air.

A dumpy manager with a weary gait approached the service desk. "Hiya, honey." He rubbed his globular nose. An unlit cigarette waggled from his mouth. "What can I do for you?"

"Can you guide me to unit 176?" I showed him my key. "I've forgotten the way, it's been so long."

The guy led me around the back of the building and jerked his thumb to the right. "Hope there's nothing not kosher in there, get my drift?"

Although that sounded like the guy's standard line, I shivered. Five deaths in a little over a week was making me jumpy. Was there a body stored inside? I hoped not.

I strode to the unit, unlocked the padlock, and pushed up the grooved metal door. An overhead fluorescent light went on automatically. The space was about the size of a walk-in closet and filled with file cabinets. Each drawer had been labeled by year, dating back twenty years—the commencement of Dr. Fisher's practice.

I surveyed the topmost drawer of the first cabinet on the left. The date of a patient's initial visit was marked on the folder. Subsequent visits were noted on a chart stapled to the inside left cover. An adjustable bracket on the right secured detailed handwritten notes, with the most recent on top. Many of the patients had lived in Reno and nearby towns. I would wager that most hadn't wanted to travel to Tahoe City when Dr. Fisher relocated.

Minutes turned into hours. My fingers ached from rummaging through more than a thousand files. I didn't find any for Beau's sister or persons related to Tom Regent or the Vittorios, and there wasn't a file for Ambrose, either.

Ready to pack it in, I paused when I discovered a folder in the U–Z cabinet with the name Lana Vogel on it. I paused. When we'd first met, Tripp had made a comment about his mother being one of the Virginia City Vogels. Was it possible Lana Vogel was Tripp's mother?

I flipped open the file and read the left-hand data sheet. Eighteen years ago, Lana Vogel had been a patient of Dr. Fisher's. Attached were a picture of her holding a brown-haired baby and a thank-you note from *Lana, Finn, and Tripp.* Lana looked familiar. I studied the photo until the realization hit me. She was nearly the spitting image of Gloria—brunette hair, Cupid's bow mouth, and big doe eyes. No wonder Finn Ambrose had been attracted to her.

The last page of Lana's history, dated a little over two years ago, was blotchy and puckered. Had Dr. Fisher been crying when filling out the page? I scanned it quickly and gagged.

> *Patient, divorced, entered office 7:00 a.m., unaccompanied.*
> *Pregnant 28 weeks.*
> *Inseminated; no father.*
> *Patient was suffering acute contractions.*
> *Tenderness to palpation in the region.*
> *Patient claimed stomach pains, possible flu.*
> *Patient admitted to heavy dose of OTC pain medication.*
> *Patient maintained she stumbled. Bruises found on back and hipbones support theory of fall. Patient denied additional abuse.*
> *Massive hemorrhaging occurred 7:07 a.m.*
> *Lana Vogel died with complications, 7:15 a.m.*
> *Infant, male, stillborn, extracted at 7:16 a.m.*

A note scrawled down the margin said:

> *Ambrose doesn't seem the type. Don't jump to conclusions.*

Chapter 44

With the file resting on the passenger seat, I dodged semis and RVs that hogged the road and mentally prepared a case against Finn Ambrose. His wife got pregnant by insemination. Finn found out. He hit her, which resulted in her death and the death of the child, but the doctor couldn't prove it. Even so, he worried that she might find a way to prove his guilt, so he killed her.

I paused. Why not kill her then? Why wait two years? Because the doctor had moved. Except surely her office would have provided a forwarding address.

Then it dawned on me what had triggered it. Finn met Gloria in May and became obsessed with her because she reminded him of his wife. Faithfully, he watched her show. When he saw her interview the doctor, all the history, all the betrayal, came rushing back to him. The doctor had to be executed. The next morning, he went to her office.

Why kill Tony Vittorio? I tapped the steering wheel. Maybe killing Dr. Fisher lit a fire under Finn. He felt the need to exact more vengeance, so he murdered Tony because of their rivalry. He dedicated the murder to Gloria because his love for her was blossoming.

As for Tejeda, Finn slayed her because, now in full-on obsession mode for Gloria, he worried about her career. Tejeda's hijinks outside the studio had jeopardized that.

Why bump off Camille? Perhaps, when he'd gone into her office at KINC, he'd seen the memo that Camille was getting ready to end Gloria's career. Or maybe Camille, who had figured out that Finn, after accessing her office on the day of his interview, had not only used her credit card to order flowers but had also used her printer paper to write one of the notes to Gloria, blackmailed him. KINC was in dire financial straits. She could use the money. I imagined the scenario. She summoned Finn to her house on Sunday night, but Finn opted not to pay.

The motive for Laila Walton's murder was the easiest to explain. Laila knew the identity of the person who'd asked her to deliver the note. She must have seen Finn that morning on her way to the caves. Driving by? In a grocery store? It didn't matter where. He followed her to the cave and ended her life.

• • •

I sped to Ambrose Alley and parked in the general parking lot. I was pleased to see Nick's Wrangler and a host of other official vehicles crowding the casino's valet parking.

Racing through the entrance with Lana Vogel's file in hand, I cut through the banks of one-armed bandits, past the jackpots packed with customers, and sprinted to the penthouse-only elevator. A young man who looked as stoic as a Buckingham Palace guard was standing beside it.

I slipped around the corner and scanned the crowds at the one-armed bandits. Standing next to an avid middle-aged gambler was an attractive teary-eyed young woman. I approached her and, after a hasty bit of chitchat, learned that she had blown her daily allowance. I offered her twenty bucks if she would ask the elevator guard to guide her to the gift shops. The layout of the casino was a maze; getting lost wasn't out of the question. The woman assessed me warily, but I could tell she was hungry to have another go at the slots.

With money in her pocket, she approached the guard and toyed with her hair. She said something to him. The guard blushed and soon after guided her away from the bank of elevators.

I slipped into the penthouse elevator and pressed the appropriate security code. The ride upward was interminable.

As I reached for the doorknob to Finn Ambrose's suite, the door opened and a group of Placer County Sheriff's Office technicians marched out, the female with rust-red hair in the lead. None seemed happy.

I stepped into the penthouse foyer and spied Jules standing in profile in the kitchen, the door wedged open. Her makeup was minimal, her hair barely combed. She was pouring a drink. Her lower lip was quivering. I inched toward the living room where Nick faced Finn Ambrose's lawyer—Hawk Nose. Hernandez mirrored Nick's defiant stance. The Placer County district attorney, a dapper guy with a pencil-thin mustache, stood on Nick's left. Finn, sitting on the couch, poked at his teeth with a toothpick. Sorcha McRae was nowhere in sight. Did she know what was going down? Had she quit her job?

"You have nothing, Detective." Hawk Nose glowered with unbridled resentment. "No evidence whatsoever. You're done here. Please leave."

The DA conferred with Nick. After a long moment, he said, "I'm sorry to have put you out, Mr. Ambrose."

Finn Ambrose grinned like he had won a Get Out of Jail Free card.

I itched to blurt what I'd learned, but I owed it to Nick to follow decorum. I waited, tapping my fingers on my thigh. Nick registered my presence but kept his attention focused on the attorney.

"This was an invasion," Hawk Nose said. "A social injustice, which caused damage to my client's character and to his business."

"Don't blow this out of proportion," the DA warned.

Hawk Nose snapped his briefcase shut. "As for you, Detective Sergeant Shaper, may our paths never cross again."

When he swept past me, I got a whiff of Aqua Velva. Cheap stuff for a seven-figure guy.

The DA followed him into the hallway, but I remained rooted to my spot.

Nick, who looked better than when I'd seen him last, drew near.

"What went down?" I whispered.

"The arrowhead collection is intact. There is no brown horsehair rug, therefore, no fibers matching those at the crime scene. All of the service vehicles have been scoured for trace evidence. Zip. We struck out. We've gathered more trace evidence at the cave site," Nick went on, "but nothing conclusive until the lab reports are completed. No DNA other than Laila's in the canteen. Why are you here?"

"I've got proof Ambrose's ex-wife, Lana Vogel, died two years ago, possibly from abuse. She was twenty-eight weeks pregnant by insemination. Dr. Fisher was her doctor when she was based in Reno." I held up the file.

Nick took it and opened it. I directed him to the doctor's notations. He read them. His eyes widened. "Why would Ambrose lash out now?"

"Gloria looks a lot like Lana Vogel. I think he became fixated on her. When Gloria featured Dr. Fisher on her show, Ambrose caught the segment and something snapped. Maybe he felt the need to protect Gloria from the doctor because he blamed the doctor, not himself, for his wife's death. After the first kill, the rampage started. He—"

I stopped short. Pivoted. "No. I'm wrong."

"What?"

"Tripp."

On the day of his father's interview, Camille had sent Tripp to fetch her stopwatch from her office. He could have taken the piece of smudged paper used to write the third note. He could have borrowed Camille's credit card information and ordered flowers. Tripp told Candace he had an older girlfriend. What if Tripp was the one who had become fixated on Gloria because she reminded him of his mother?

Had Tripp learned his mother was pregnant with another baby? Had her pregnancy made him feel insufficient? Did he abuse her and cause her death? He'd turned to alcohol two years ago. Did he hope by killing Dr. Fisher he could expunge himself of his wickedness?

Tripp was on the set when Gloria had interviewed his father. He learned from Candace that I was a private investigator. Soon after, Cinder was hurt. Candace had let slip that we lived near Homewood. Had she given him the exact address? Had Tripp hurt the dog to scare me so I wouldn't dig deeper? The night he dropped by the cabin to deliver the lamp, Cinder had snarled at him.

When I'd come to the penthouse to meet with Finn, I recalled Tripp slipping in. He'd heard me talking to Jules about the flowers. Had he sent them to Gloria? Did he think I'd figured out he was the killer? Minutes later, the elevator plummeted.

If Camille realized that Tripp had used her credit card to order flowers, she might have asked him to come to her house to discuss it.

As for Laila, it was possible Tripp was a member of a caving group. He'd joked about looking like an albino bat. Maybe Tripp and a group of other cavers ran into Laila that morning. Seeing him triggered her memory—he was the one who had hired her—so she left me a message. Unfortunately, he overheard her.

"Mr. Ambrose," I said. "Where's your son?"

Finn Ambrose folded his arms across his chest. "No comment."

"I'm not a reporter, sir." I exited the penthouse suite and scanned the hallway. There was one other unit on the floor. Did Tripp live there? He had been wearing pajama bottoms when he'd interrupted Jules and me.

Ignoring Nick and Finn's shouts, I charged ahead, speeding past the DA and the attorney, who were queued up waiting for the elevator. I pounded on the door to the unit. No one answered. "Does Tripp live here?" I yelled.

Nick hurried to me. "What's going on?"

"Tripp is left-handed." When Candace had asked him to autograph the lamp he'd brought her, he'd used his left hand. I turned the knob. The door swung open.

Let's hear it for the rich and neglectful.

"Don't enter that apartment, young lady," the lawyer ordered.

I didn't, but I peeked inside and hooted. In plain view, a brown-and-white pinto rug lay on the entry floor. Then I saw something on a side table to the right that made my insides snag—a pink-striped cross-body purse. I pointed. "Nick. That's Candace's purse."

He gazed past me. "Are you sure?"

"See the cat charm on the loop? Positive. Candace, are you here? Candace!"

Silence.

I noticed other items next to the purse and my heart wrenched: Zorro's dog collar; Laila's bandanna; Dr. Fisher's diamond necklace. Tripp had kept mementos of his kills.

"Candace!" I shouted and clasped Nick's arm in panic.

"Where is she, Mr. Ambrose?" he asked.

"Who?" Finn's jaw was set.

"Candace Adams. Aspen's niece."

"I don't have a clue."

Nick said to the lawyer, "A missing girl is probable cause for me to enter."

"And the horsehair rug," I stated. "It's in plain view."

The attorney's face flushed with indignation. "You have no right."

"We have a warrant."

"For Mr. Ambrose's premises."

"For the entire building. Read the warrant again."

Nick forged ahead, searching left and right while calling Candace's name.

I pulled my cell phone from my pocket and speed-dialed Candace. A phone jangled. In the purse. Meaning Candace didn't have it on her.

"She's not here," Nick said, returning to the foyer. He stormed into the hall. "Where is she, Ambrose?"

"You knew your son was a murderer," I said. "That's why you covered for him with those ridiculous Alcoholic Anonymous alibis."

"Don't be absurd," Finn shouted.

"Your son owns a brown horsehair rug, sir," Nick said. "Horsehair evidence has been found at the scenes of the crimes. I repeat, where is he?"

"For heaven's sake." Jules burst into the hall, a glass of wine in hand. "Tripp is at school. Lake Tahoe Community College."

"That's enough!" Finn took a menacing step toward her. She cowered. Finn turned to Nick. "Detective, my son is innocent. He attends classes and works for me at the casino. He has zero time to get into trouble."

Nick put Hernandez in charge of the warrant proceedings and then addressed the lawyer. "We will find Tripp Ambrose and sort this out. Neither you nor your client nor anyone in his employ is allowed to warn the boy. Have I made myself clear?"

Chapter 45

A handful of cars were blocking Nick's Wrangler at the entryway to the casino.

"Follow me," I yelled. "I'm in the self-park lot."

We raced to my Jeep and scrambled inside. Nick secured his seat belt and, using his cell phone, dialed Kendra King. He gave her the rundown and asked her to bring backup to the community college.

Driving south on Highway 50 with traffic moving at a nice clip, I said, "Remember how I told you Tripp brought a lamp to the house? He used medical tubes to encase the wiring for the lamp."

Nick frowned. "I'm not following."

"I saw Heather Bogart at Truckee Hospital, and she said her architecture teacher had signed her in. Tripp is taking architecture at the junior college. There might be no record of him visiting Truckee Hospital if, say, his class went on a field trip there. He could have slipped in and stolen a scalpel."

"That would only link the kid to Dr. Fisher's murder." Nick rubbed his neck. "Why kill Tony Vittorio?"

"To avenge his father. He killed Tejeda because he believed her exchange with Gloria would get Gloria in trouble. Remember I told you he and his father were outside the studio that day. As for Camille, he killed her because he saw the letter in her office that she was going to fire Gloria. Either that, or Camille realized he'd used her credit card and she called him on it. As for Laila, he'd hired her to deliver a note to Gloria; he murdered her because she recognized him."

My cell phone rang. Anonymous caller. I answered anyway.

"Aunt Aspen," Candace cried. "I'm so sorry. I lied to you. I didn't go shopping with Waverly."

"Where are you?" I could barely breathe.

"At the Summit."

Where she was supposed to be.

"My mom called back while you were putting on makeup. She said she was coming to Tahoe City today no matter what. I . . . I didn't want to see her, so I made up the story about Waverly." She

258

whimpered. "When you left, I phoned Tripp. He told me he'd be my wheels whenever I asked."

I moaned. Boy, had I botched things. "Are you with Tripp now?"

"No. He dropped me off here, and I didn't realize until just now that I left my purse in his car, and my cell phone—"

"Is in your purse."

"Uh-huh. So I went to the security office and they let me call you."

The steel bands holding my lungs in check released. She was safe. "Stay there. Don't budge. I'll have Max come get you."

"I'm really sorry."

"We'll discuss this when I get home."

"Where are you?"

"I'm with Nick. We're looking for Tripp."

"About him." Her voice cracked. "Um, remember how he said he had an older girlfriend? I think it might be Gloria Morning. He couldn't stop talking about her all the way here. He said he was going to do something really fun with her after he left me. I didn't like the way he said *fun*."

I thanked Candace, told her to stay put, stabbed End, and turned to Nick. His jaw was ticking.

"Gloria called in sick this morning. What if Tripp kidnapped her?"

"I'm on it." While he contacted Detective King, I rang my aunt and told her about Candace's situation.

• • •

Before the Y, I turned left toward Lake Tahoe Community College. The school was set on wooded grounds. We parked and made a beeline for the Admissions Building.

A curly-haired seventy-something receptionist sitting behind a desk lowered her romance novel and studied us over bifocals. "Yes?"

"We're trying to locate a student," I said. "Tripp Ambrose."

"Tripp. Such a sweet boy." The woman dog-eared her book. "Very industrious. Works two days a week in the file room to make money so he can buy art supplies."

"Is he here now?" Nick asked.

"Yes."

I squeezed Nick's arm. We had him.

"He brought that pretty girl with him," she added. "The reporter."

To the receptionist, I supposed Gloria might seem like a girl.

"She was quite pale, like she was under the weather, poor thing."

Gloria had taken an Ambien last night. Had Tripp dosed her with another one so he could manipulate her?

"Where will we find him?" Nick asked. He had yet to show his badge.

"Where he always is when he's not filing. In the art department. I heard him tell his date he's working on a ceramics project today."

We turned to leave.

The woman cleared her throat. "Excuse me. Hold it right there."

Nick and I pivoted.

She tapped a large tome on her desk and held up a ballpoint pen. "All visitors need to sign in and wear one of these." She pointed to a basket filled with LTCC buttons. "Helps avoid crime."

After we signed the roster and donned a button, she gave us directions to the art classroom, which was located in the *S* Building.

We raced to it. I peered into classroom windows and stopped at one. "Nick, I think this is it."

Bags of red clay sat on the counters. Statues, both elegant and crude, stood on display tables around the room. Half a dozen kilns lined the far wall. A youngish man about Tripp's build and coloring was washing his hands at a sink, his back to us. I didn't see Gloria.

Nick opened the door, and the young man turned. It wasn't Tripp. Nick released the door and hurried ahead.

I grabbed the handle before the door closed and said to the young man, "Have you seen Tripp Ambrose?"

"Yeah, a few minutes ago. He went to the machine shop."

"Where's that?"

"If you came from Admissions, it's back the same way and down the inner hall to the left. S-119." The guy pointed. "However, there's a shortcut if you go that way." He flung his other arm in the opposite direction, reminding me of the Scarecrow in the *Wizard of Oz* when giving Dorothy directions.

I thanked him and searched for Nick, but he'd disappeared. Reluctant to lose a second of time, I made a U-turn and took the shortcut. I located a classroom marked *Machine Shop, S-119*. The door was solid with no windows. I heard something inside the room rumbling like a drier filled with rocks. I twisted the knob. The door stuck, but the handle wasn't locked, so I tried again.

The heavy door whipped open and bits of tin billowed in front of me. As I shaded my eyes and covered my nose and mouth, I flashed on the evening when Tripp had come to our house with the lamp. His tennis shoes had been dirty. Did they have bits of metal stuck in the soles? Metal like the evidence tracked into Camille's house or other crime scenes?

I yelled, "Nick! Over here. 119." I stepped inside.

Boxes marked *Metal Scraps* sat on shelves. Sculpting tools were laid out uniformly on trays on the counters. On the opposite side of the room, more than a dozen blades, which could be fitted into any of the cutting machines, hung on hooks affixed to a perforated board. Beneath that was a counter filled with more tools. Art samples were displayed inside glass cases.

"Nick!" I yelled again.

Someone moaned. I turned to my right and spied Gloria behind the door, tied to a chair, her mouth gagged. Her eyes were closed; her head lolled to the side.

I made a move toward her but someone from behind shoved me deeper into the room, and the door slammed with a clank.

Chapter 46

"You!" Tripp hissed at me. His gaze was wild. Steely.

Years of counseling advice replayed in my head: Keep the patient invested in the conversation. Never lose eye contact.

Tripp reminded me of many of the teens I'd counseled at BARC: wary, primitive, and troubled. What had he suffered in his young life? In his left hand, he wielded a self-made weapon, its handle like the grip of a bicycle, its blade the shape of an elongated arrowhead. Had he used it on Laila?

"Hi, Tripp," I said as calmly as I could, although my heart was jackhammering my rib cage and I was breathing high in my chest. Too high. If I weren't careful, I'd pass out.

"A little off the b-beaten path, aren't you?"

"Why did you bring Gloria here?" I asked. "Do you intend to kill her?"

"No. I'm going to take her home and take care of her. I brought her here to show her what I do. I want her to be proud of her boy."

I moaned inwardly. Did Gloria represent his mother now? Was he suffering a classic case of transference? "She looks tired," I said calmly, though my heart was hammering my chest. "We should find somewhere for her to lie down."

"She's fine."

"I'm here with Detective Sergeant Shaper, Tripp. Did you meet him?" I positioned my arms in front of me. It wasn't an overtly defensive stance—I didn't want to threaten him—but I was ready to strike if he attacked. "He wants to ask you questions about the murders. In regard to your father. Would that be okay?"

"You're a b-bad liar." Tripp pulled a cell phone from his pocket and flashed the screen at me. The screensaver picture was Lake Tahoe during a storm. "My father isn't a suspect. His ex-lawyer texted me."

Smart man, Finn. Sack Hawk Nose so he could legally defy Nick's order and warn his son.

"He said I'm wanted for m-murder." Tripp smiled, but his eyes were as icy as the lake in January. "What t-tipped you off?"

"Your mother's medical file."

His eyes widened. "You know about my m-mother?"

"She had the nerve to leave you and then get pregnant. Did that make you feel unimportant? Did you think she was replacing you?"

He blinked rapidly.

"It wasn't your fault, Tripp. She didn't leave you. She left your father."

"No."

"They fought, didn't they?"

More blinking. I was on the right track.

"They didn't fight about you. Your mother loved you."

"Liar!" Tripp lunged at me.

I tried to defend myself, but before I could connect with his forearm, he gripped my wrist with his other hand. He shoved and released me. I stumbled backward and slammed into a counter. I couldn't glance at the tools on the counter without taking my gaze off Tripp. Blindly, I groped for something hefty. The first thing I touched was the size of a ballpoint pen. Worthless.

"Brown horsehair fibers were found at each of the murder sites," I said. "There's a rug with those fibers in the foyer of your apartment."

"Not anymore."

His father had destroyed evidence? What wasn't he afraid to do for his son?

"The grit from this workshop was at Camille St. John's house," I said, not allowing my face to reveal my concern. "It'll be lodged in the soles of your shoes."

"I've got an alibi for her murder."

"AA meetings aren't held that late."

"Some are."

"I'll bet you missed it that night. The leader of the group will testify that you weren't there."

"I've been g-going to different locations. There're a lot of drunks in Tahoe. Even if someone doesn't r-remember me being at one, they'll think I was at another. I was a star pupil, no relapses." Tripp repositioned the weapon in his hand. "And with you dead—"

"You didn't kill me at Camille's. Do you know why, Tripp?" I asked, my gaze fixed on his. "Because you wanted me to figure out it was you. You wanted me to stop the insanity."

"Uh-uh. No shrink stuff. I've had enough psycho-babble." Tripp moved toward me, raising and lowering the tool like an automaton. "Candace says you do that. Always analyzing."

"Do you have alibis for the times when Miranda Tejeda and Tony Vittorio were killed, Tripp?"

He hesitated, giving me a chance to glance at the door. Where was Nick? He had to be near. Even if he searched full circle, he would return to the ceramics room. The student would tell him about the machine shop. Unless the student had left. He had been washing up.

"Why did you kill Laila?" I asked. "She was an innocent. All she did was deliver a note for you."

"She figured it out. She—"

Gloria mumbled something. I glanced at her. Her eyes were open. Wide. Scared. Whatever Tripp had given her was wearing off.

"Quiet!" Tripp yelled at her.

She whimpered.

Tripp grinned at me. "You know, if I didn't already have Gloria as my girlfriend, I'd p-pick Candace."

Over my dead body. I traced my fingers along another tool. Not sharp enough.

"Did you love your mother the same way you love Gloria?" I asked, changing tactics. "Is she a replacement for your mother? She looks just like her. A younger version of her."

"Leave my m-mother out of this." He slashed at me.

I raised my right arm to defend myself. The arrowhead nicked me under the arm, above the elbow. Blood oozed out. I couldn't staunch the flow and attack him at the same time. Ignoring the pain, I clasped the handle of the next tool I touched and thrust it at him. It was only a skinny serrated saw, but he backed up a step, granting me a momentary reprieve.

"Camille contested the charge for the flowers you sent Gloria, didn't she?" I flailed the saw again. It arced with the force. "You also sent Gloria flowers using your father's credit card, didn't you? The day I visited him at his penthouse, you and Jules argued about the gift. You glanced at me. You worried that I'd find out about the special order, so you rigged the elevator. You're good with electrical things."

"Ha! You see? I *was* trying to get rid of you."

"You didn't count on the emergency brake taking control."

"Stupid." Tripp swung the weapon at my chest.

At the same time the door opened and Finn Ambrose and his ex-lawyer burst in.

"Tripp, no!" Finn yelled.

Tripp glared at them. "Leave!"

"You killed your mother, didn't you, Tripp?" I said. "You beat her and she convulsed. You were the *Ambrose* the doctor noted in the file, not your father."

Finn moaned.

"There were bruises on your mother's back," I went on, "but your mother told the doctor that she'd fallen. She didn't rat you out. The doctor couldn't see the deeper bruises you'd inflicted in her abdomen. That's why she didn't turn you in to authorities. She couldn't prove that you were a monster."

Finn Ambrose said to his lawyer, "Do something."

"You tracked down your mother and hurt her because you wanted to kill the life inside her. After she and the baby died, you punished yourself. You drank yourself into oblivion. But everything changed when you met Gloria."

Tripp's eyes brimmed with tears.

"Two years was a long time to suffer, wasn't it?" I held my hand out, imploring him to relinquish the tool. "You thought you could redeem yourself if you could persuade Gloria to love you. That is until you saw Dr. Fisher on Gloria's show. Seeing her triggered the killing spree. You were angry that the doctor was alive. You were furious that she didn't turn you in after you abused your mother. She was supposed to put you out of your misery and sentence you to death."

"Yes." He sucked back a sob.

"You should've been punished."

"Yes." Veins bulged in the boy's neck.

"You entered a dark, scary place after killing your mother, didn't you?" The addicts I'd treated talked about the black holes of self-loathing and doubt that they lived in. "But then you got clean and sober, and the real world was even more frightening, wasn't it?"

"It was my fault. And that doctor—"

"When you met Gloria you felt an instant connection. You convinced yourself that if you could win her heart, then your brutal acts would be banished to the past. After you killed the doctor, you told yourself that you had done it for Gloria. For *her* glory. But that wasn't entirely true. You were doing it to salvage the beautiful memory of your mother."

He glanced at Gloria. "She's not her."

"No, she's not your mother, Tripp. Your mother is gone."

"She left me." Tripp's voice cracked with sorrow.

"She didn't leave *you*, Tripp." I pointed at his father. "Like I told you, she left because *he* drove her away. Killing Tony Vittorio was your way of lashing out at your father, wasn't it? You thought the sheriff's detectives would throw your father in jail for his murder. When they didn't, you kept going. Do you know why?"

"No more talking!" Tripp growled and lunged at me.

I threw up both arms to ward off the blow.

At the same time, Finn cried, "Stop, son. Don't hurt her."

Tripp froze. He glanced at his father and back at me, as if wondering which of us to kill first.

Nick raced into the room, gun drawn. "Tripp, drop the weapon or I'll shoot."

"No, Nick, don't," I begged. "Everyone, hush. Tripp"—my voice quavered; I couldn't hide the fear—"your mother would be disappointed if you hurt me. I'm not the enemy. I'm the person who can shine a light on your pain."

Tripp's body grew still. Very very still.

Until Finn said, "Son, I'm sorry."

And then everything happened fast.

Tripp plunged the weapon into his father's chest. Finn stumbled.

I kicked Tripp's feet out from under him. He toppled.

Nick charged him and cuffed him.

The lawyer squatted beside Finn.

I hurried to Gloria, removed the gag from her mouth, and untied her from the chair. Steadying her with both hands, I said, "You're going to be fine."

Tears streamed down her face.

After Nick called for backup and was assured an ambulance was on the way, he joined Gloria and me. "Are you okay, Aspen?"

No, I wasn't. I had just attempted to talk down the devil and lost.

Chapter 47

Max had beaten me to the cabin. Candace stood beyond her in the living room, arms crossed and hands tucked under her armpits. Cinder sat beside her, as vigilant as a sentry. Max drew me to one side and asked if Tripp was on his way to jail. I said he was and his father, who had been whisked to the hospital, was being charged with aiding and abetting. She kissed me, told me how proud she was, added that we would have a debriefing in a few days, and left.

Candace whispered, "I'm sorry. I . . . wasn't thinking. I won't ever do something like this again. Ever."

Tears pressed my eyes as I hugged her. "How can I trust you?"

"You have to. Please?" Her voice cracked.

"You scared me. I'd thought—" I'd thought the horrible incident we'd experienced in January was repeating itself: Candace kidnapped, injured, and possibly dead. "You are part of my life now. I need to protect you." On the drive home I'd questioned whether I had to rethink my career. I couldn't continue to put me, and therefore her, in danger. "If I lost you . . ."

"Tripp never would have hurt me."

"I couldn't imagine he would hurt Gloria, either, but he took her, drugged her, and bound her to a chair. If we hadn't shown up, I'm not sure what he was capable of. You can't be so trusting."

"I had a gut instinct."

Her words—words I often uttered—punched me in the solar plexus. I opened my mouth to respond and then closed it.

She pressed apart. "How about if you get me self-defense classes so I'll be prepared for . . . you know . . . whatever . . . in case."

"How about I lock you in your room and throw away the key until you're twenty-one?"

"I'm not Cinderella, and just for your information, I think I could find a mouse or two to help me escape."

"I bet you could."

• • •

Rosie didn't show up. Two days later, she called and claimed she'd gotten sidetracked. I didn't ask by what. I knew. We chatted for a minute about her new job, one of the most civil conversations we'd had in a long time. Before ending the call, she said she still wanted to see Candace. I told her I'd work something out soon, knowing I wouldn't. Not yet.

A week later, I sat on the porch and nursed a cup of coffee, the morning paper opened on my laptop. Something pop-cracked in the forest and I dropped the mug. Porcelain shards and teaming liquid splattered at my feet. "Dang it." My nerves were shot from the ordeal with Tripp. My dreams were plagued with lunatic automatons, knives, scalpels, and serrated saws. I'd visited a therapist who had told me exactly what I would have told my patients—*recovery takes time.*

The screen door squeaked. Candace popped outside carrying a kitchen towel. "Did I hear something break?" She let the door slam shut and tossed the towel at me. "Let the party begin." She was enjoying the not-so-perfect me. My frequent mishaps were making her feel like less of a klutz.

I mopped up the mess.

"Wish I had some sparklers to celebrate." Candace sank into a patio chair.

"Very funny."

Camille's dog, Zorro, wearing a protective cone around his neck to prevent him from scratching off the bandage on his head, loped to her and put a paw in her lap. I'd thrown away the collar Tripp had swiped. Bad voodoo, as Gwen would say, and bought Zorro a new one. Over the course of the last seven days, whenever Candace cooed sweet nothings to the pooch, Cinder scurried up and vied for her attention, too. He adored his new pal, but he did have a slight jealous streak.

Candace eyed the laptop and tapped the newspaper's banner. "It's sad, don't you think?"

The story was about the Vittorios'. It wouldn't have made the headlines if Tony Vittorio hadn't been murdered. Darcy had discovered that Tony Vittorio had burdened his restaurant with so much debt that his wife and brother were forced to declare bankruptcy. They were selling everything and moving from Lake Tahoe to start over. Darcy had given the scoop to the reporter.

Candace toyed with her hair. "I was watching KINC with that anchor who replaced Gloria Morning, the one with the toothy smile."

Rumors were circulating that Tom and the new anchor were already an item. In the past three weeks, Tom had tried all sorts of innovative programming at the woman's suggestion and viewership had risen. When I'd dared to ask Tom about the drugs he had poured down his cast, he'd blushed and said he had been clean and sober for six hours and hadn't wanted anything to interfere with his recovery. He was sorry he'd given me any reason to doubt him.

"Anyway," Candace continued, "she said that Mr. Ambrose put his casino up for sale and the money's going toward Tripp's mental treatment and murder defense." She fiddled with the hem of her tube top. "Poor Tripp." Ever since his capture, she had chastised herself for being stupid enough to trust him. I'd assured her that very few could have identified his mental illness. Even I, a trained professional, had missed the signs. "The anchor went on to say that Gloria is moving to Los Angeles to do the evening news on some small cable channel. Did you know that?"

"I'd heard."

Candace crossed her arms. "Why didn't you tell me?"

"I forgot."

She huffed. Being kept out of the loop clearly didn't sit well with my niece. I would have to do better.

I said, "Gloria didn't think she could get a gig in New York having only worked in Lake Tahoe, and since Beau got an offer to direct a reality program in Hollywood, they're moving together." My friend was starting over and in love, and I was happy for her. I glanced at my watch. "Oh, no. We've got to run. Lock up the dogs and get dressed."

"Does Rory need a tie?" Candace asked. Rory had returned to demigod status because he had agreed to her no-sex decree.

Was I ever glad I didn't have to relive my teenage years.

"No tie, but a long-sleeved shirt would be nice."

"Got it." She scooted into the house.

I followed her and set my laptop on the counter, tossed the broken shards of my mug into the garbage, and hurled the wet towel into the sink. Then I tore down the hallway to my bedroom. I slipped into the yellow spaghetti-strapped dress I'd laid on the bed. Gwen was getting married in two hours and I had promised to arrive early enough to help with her unruly hair.

Less than a half hour later, the doorbell rang. I opened it and smiled. Nick, looking hip and sexy in his camel linen jacket, slacks, and white shirt, no tie, kissed my cheek.

"Your chariot awaits." He whispered in my ear, "What's on the agenda for later?"

"After the bit about Gwen saying 'I do,' I'm all yours."

About the Author

Daryl Wood Gerber is the Agatha Award–winning, nationally bestselling author of the Cookbook Nook Mysteries, featuring an admitted foodie and owner of a cookbook store in Crystal Cove, California, as well as the French Bistro Mysteries, featuring a bistro owner in Napa Valley. Under the pen name Avery Aames, Daryl writes the Cheese Shop Mysteries, featuring a cheese shop owner in Providence, Ohio.

As a girl, Daryl considered becoming a writer, but she was dissuaded by a seventh-grade teacher. It wasn't until she was in her twenties that she had the temerity to try her hand at writing again . . . for TV and screen. Why? Because she was an actress in Hollywood. A fun tidbit for mystery buffs: Daryl co-starred on *Murder, She Wrote* as well as on other TV shows. As a writer, she created the format for the popular sitcom *Out of This World*. When she moved across the country with her husband, she returned to writing what she loved to read: mysteries and thrillers.

Daryl is originally from the Bay Area and graduated from Stanford University. She loves to cook, read, golf, swim, and garden. She also likes adventure and has been known to jump out of a perfectly good airplane. Here are a few of Daryl's lifelong mottos: perseverance will out; believe you can; never give up. She hopes they will become yours, as well.

To learn more about Daryl and her books, visit her website at DarylWoodGerber.com.

CPSIA information can be obtained
at www.ICGtesting.com
Printed in the USA
BVHW071208110720
583502BV00001B/218